THE
Governess
AND THE
DUKE

THE Governess AND THE DUKE

LYDIA DRAKE

Entangled Publishing, LLC
644 Shrewsbury Commons Ave., STE 181
Shrewsbury, PA 17361
Visit our website at www.entangledpublishing.com.

Amara is an imprint of Entangled Publishing, LLC.

Edited by Jen Bouvier
Cover design by Bree Archer
Photography by Shirley Green
Cover art by Pinkystock/Shutterstock
Interior design by Britt Marczak

Print ISBN 978-1-64937-498-1
ebook ISBN 978-1-64937-448-6

Manufactured in the United States of America

First Edition January 2024

AMARA

ALSO BY LYDIA DRAKE

RENEGADE DUKES

Cinderella and The Duke
The Governess and The Duke

DEBUTANTES OF LONDON

The Duchess and The Wolf

At Entangled, we want our readers to be well-informed. If you would like to know if this book contains any elements that might be of concern for you, please check the back of the book for details.

For Nora, the newest and sweetest addition to our family. Please don't read this until you're thirty-five or I'm dead.

PROLOGUE

It is the rare woman who falls in love twice in the same day, but such was Miss Viola Winslow's fate on the morning of April 18, 1807.

The twenty-year-old had just made the exhaustive trek from Northumberland all the way south to Somerset to take a posting at Lynton Park, the Duke of Ashworth's seat. She was two miles from the house and trudging along a muddy road that the spring rain had inconveniently left in her path. The stagecoach had broken an axle half a mile back, and she couldn't wait for it to be fixed.

She was expected, and as far as Viola saw it, being expected to do something meant it was already good as done.

Her arms ached as she carried two worn satchels at her sides containing everything she owned in this life. Two gray dresses, one plain, one with a bit of lace at the collar; a pair of good boots; primers of French and geography; a book of poetry she hoped her new little charge would enjoy; and a rag poppet that her sister's child had gifted her Auntie Viola for company before the journey to the county of "sunset."

She was a long way from home down here. Then again, she'd been a long way from home since she was eight years old. Viola didn't have a home. She had work. That seemed to be her fate, and she had accepted it with a cheerful if staid resignation.

She looked to the side as something white flashed in the air. It was an egret, common for this area.

Viola smiled. As a lifelong student of the natural world, she loved few things better than to observe the comings and goings of birds. If she hadn't somewhere to be, she might have rested for an hour and tried to identify the different variations of avian song that trilled overhead. Viola whistled an easy tune, lending her own music to the natural symphony. Miss Adams, the proprietress of her last school, would have been mortified.

A governess does not whistle, my girl! How is she to educate the daughters of good society if she has no better manners than a ruffian herself?

But Miss Adams was not here, and in her own quiet way Viola had always liked to flout convention. Better to bend the rules a bit than to break yourself under their rigid application. So long as you were careful about which ones you bent, of course.

Viola's whistling stopped when she heard the thud of hoofbeats coming up the road behind her. To give the rider room to pass, she stepped to the side and waited. Soon, a chestnut horse of astonishing beauty cantered into view. Viola expected it to go by, but the rider pulled on the reins and stopped.

"Hello there! May I be of any assistance, Miss?"

The speaker swung down from the saddle and led his stallion to where Viola waited. As he approached, she felt herself unable to speak. Or even to think.

For one thing, he was the tallest man she'd ever seen, well over six feet. As she barely scraped five foot and three inches, she had to crane her neck to look up at him.

He was also the most handsome creature she had ever espied. She'd never seen such fine golden hair, blue eyes of such vivid warmth, such a distinguished aquiline profile, such chiseled perfection of cheek-bones and jaw. His lips, especially, she could not help but wonder at. He'd a mouth simultaneously masculine and kissable; she'd never imagined a man could possess such beautiful lips.

Reeling, Viola recalled tales of Greek myth. Zeus, king of the gods, would come to earth in varied forms to woo and bed young maidens. He'd pretend to be a cow, a swan, even the husband of an intended conquest. If Zeus had chosen this man's form, no woman would ever have resisted him.

"Miss? Are you all right?" the god asked.

"Thank you. Yes. That is, I'm walking to Lynton Park. I'm to take a position there. Thank you. Um. How are you?" Viola preferred to listen and observe rather than speak, and this blundering conversation was proof as to why. If asked to give her name at this moment, she might not recall it. She might just say "Sally" or "Fred" and then faint.

"Lynton Park? That's my destination as well. Please, allow me to give you a ride." The handsome young man patted his horse's neck. "Hector may look a brute, but I assure you he's gentle as a kitten."

"Oh!" Viola dropped into a mortified curtsy. "Your Grace, the Duke of Ashworth?"

If Viola had fallen desperately in love with her employer, this was going to be misery itself.

"No, I'm not Ashworth. I'm, well, James Montagu, Miss. And your name?"

Mr. Montagu. Well, that was far less of a social chasm between them. He was clearly wealthier and better born than she, but at least he didn't seem titled. Or even worse, a duke.

"Viola Winslow, sir."

"So, Miss Winslow. Shall we?"

There were instant warning bells in her head, and Viola stiffened.

This Mr. Montagu could be a rogue who believed stopping to aid a girl of little means meant he was entitled to do as he pleased with her. But despite her intuitive wariness, Viola could not make herself afraid of this young man. Perhaps her soul had recognized his as essentially kind. Or perhaps he was so good-looking, she didn't care if he murdered her. Either way, she was willing to take the risk.

Viola allowed Mr. Montagu to help her onto his horse's saddle. He put one satchel in her lap and carried the other himself. Such chivalry! Or perhaps he was trying to rob her! Either way, what fun!

As they walked along, Viola tried to keep her seat. She grabbed a fistful of the horse's mane, praying she didn't tumble off. She'd never been good with horses.

Mr. Montagu walked at her side, holding the reins while they made pleasant conversation. "So, you're to take a position at the Park?"

"Yes. The duke has hired me to act as a governess." Her cheeks flamed. "I mean, governess to his ward. The duke himself doesn't need a governess."

"When you meet him, you might change your mind." Mr. Montagu laughed, a delightful baritone. Viola prayed she would not start sweating.

"You know the duke well, sir?"

"We were at Oxford together. And where do you hail from, Miss Winslow?"

"I was teaching in East Yorkshire until recently, though I'm from Northumberland originally."

"Really?" He seemed astonished. "You haven't any accent that I can detect."

"I thought a more refined dialect would help me

with potential employers."

"I quite understand, though I find the northern cadence to be beautiful. My own family hails from Northumberland, you know! The most glorious country in England."

"I quite agree." Viola would never have left if leaving hadn't been essential to her safety. But she didn't want to think of unpleasant topics now.

She could scarce believe that such a refined gentleman could also be so gallant and so kind. He was as chivalrous as he was handsome. All of Viola's most passionate and deluded girlhood dreams had appeared before her in this one man. If possible, she'd have let Mr. Montagu lead her around on horseback the rest of their lives, or at least until it started to rain.

The miles sped by too quickly for Viola's liking and, as they walked, she listened as Mr. Montagu spoke of the beauty of Lynton Park, of the Duke of Ashworth's good humor, of how adorable little Felicity, Viola's new charge, was.

As he spoke, Viola imagined how she might answer him if she were a woman of wealth and beauty. But if she should be too friendly or, heaven forbid, flirtatious, he might think she was setting her cap at him. Mr. Montagu might warn the duke that Viola was ill-equipped for a position at Lynton Park. So Viola barely spoke two words together, though in her mind she answered his questions as she wished she might.

"Are you fond of reading, Miss Winslow? I assume you must be, given your job."

I'm mad for poetry, sir. Mr. William Blake's language in particular has such a simple yet devastating power. Have you read "The Songs of Innocence and

Experience?" I've often thought poetry could change the world. Poets are the ones who see reality most clearly for what it is and can be. What are your thoughts?

"Yes, sir. I enjoy reading poetry," was her actual reply.

"Is this your first time in Somerset?"

Yes, and I adore it. I'd love to see Bath, though not for the society parties. I've longed to wander the ancient structures of the Roman ruins. I fancy that I might spy the ghost of a lost legionary if I stroll about at sunset.

"Yes sir," was all she said.

All too soon they left the forest behind and approached the imposing façade of Lynton Park itself. To Viola, it looked like a palace of the Greek gods themselves, with stately marble pillars upholding carved, triangular friezes depicting the Ashworth coat of arms. How astonishing to think she'd call such a grand place her home. At the front of the house, Mr. Montagu lifted Viola from the saddle and set her upon the ground. She held her breath, drunk on his gentlest touch.

"I hope you will take to your new position, Miss Winslow." He tipped his hat to her.

"Thank you, sir."

"Oh! Your Grace!" A middle-aged woman hurried out the building's entrance and descended the steps. A ring of keys jangled at her side, indicating her as the housekeeper. "Forgive us, we were not expecting you!"

Your Grace? Viola's gut twisted. So, this *was* Ashworth? Why on earth would he lie to her about such a thing?

"Ah. Hello, Mrs. Sheffield." The duke nodded to

the older woman. "I found your governess wandering in the forest and escorted her home."

"Forgive me, Your Grace. I didn't realize," Viola murmured.

"No, the fault's mine. I should have been more forthcoming." He gave a poised and shallow bow of his head. "James Montagu, Duke of Huntington. At your service, Miss Winslow."

At once, she felt better and worse.

He hadn't lied to her; he wasn't Ashworth. But he *was* a duke! And it was worse than that, even. The Duke of Huntington's ancestral seat, Moorcliff Castle, was mere miles away from her own family home.

Their backgrounds could not be more incongruous. This wasn't a divide between them; it was an ocean of difference. One they could never cross. Whatever meager scraps of hope she'd clung to during the journey evaporated.

Viola numbly stood to the side as the housekeeper, Mrs. Sheffield, spoke with His Grace. He asked if Ashworth was home and was told the duke was traveling. Mrs. Sheffield invited him to stay if he liked, but His Grace announced he must retire to his own estate not five miles from here.

Viola, meanwhile, suffocated in silence under the weight of her own infatuation and newfound misery.

She should have known not to be swept away by her feelings. That was for wealthy women, titled women. And the duke would be only five miles away! He and the Duke of Ashworth were friends! Viola could not bear the thought of seeing him regularly, of yearning for him without hope. Perhaps she ought to beg Mrs. Sheffield's forgiveness and walk back along the road to the nearby village. It was only fifteen miles or so. Hopefully it wouldn't rain. Again. But she must leave, because Viola knew there could be nothing at Lynton Park that was worth the pain of such deep and impossible love.

And then someone else appeared at the top of the steps. It was a very small someone, a little girl no more than three or four years of age.

She had brilliant black curls, a jam-smeared face, and wore the most insolent expression Viola had ever seen on one so young. The child had draped strands of pearls around her neck (where she'd gotten those Viola could not imagine), and wore a tasseled, tricorn hat that drooped heavily over one eye. She carried a wooden spoon and was missing one of her shoes. With great solemnity the child marched down the steps and stood before the Duke of Huntington.

"Well. Hallo, Felicity." His Grace beamed at the girl.

"Not Felicity!" The small girl pointed her spoon in a threatening manner at the duke's kneecap. "I'm the Piwate Queen Black Bob."

"Oh dear." Mrs. Sheffield gave a weary sigh. "This again."

"Now, Felicity." The Duke of Huntington struggled not to laugh as he lifted the hat from the girl's curly head. "I mean, Black Bob. I hope we can be friends."

"Piwates don't have fwiends! Raaaaar!" The little hellion began to whack at the duke's booted calf with her fearsome spoon. She charged and feinted and dodged around the man, caterwauling and combating his ankles with the surly mien of a true pirate. Viola had never seen such a willful, wild girl in all her life.

For the second time that day, she fell in love. She couldn't resist laughing as the Duke of Huntington heroically allowed the assault to continue.

"Miss Felicity! You must stop this at once!" The poor housekeeper appeared exhausted by the child. "Young ladies are not pirates!"

Viola stepped in and knelt before the pirate queen.

"You know, there *have* been famous pirates who were women," Viola said gently. "Some of the greatest to ever sail the seven seas, in fact."

"Weally?" Felicity stopped her snarling and arring as she came face-to-face with Viola. She pointed the wooden spoon. "How you know that?"

"I've read of Grace O'Malley, of Mary Read, and Anne Bonney. Bonney in particular was a menace. She left a wealthy family behind for a life of infamy. She commanded her own ship and escaped imprisonment and execution. She was one of the most terrifying women who ever lived."

Felicity's green eyes were wide as plates now. She appeared delighted.

"Mowe! I wanna know mowe!" She whacked Viola's shoulder with the spoon, but she easily disarmed the girl.

"I can teach you all about the great pirate queens. But you must behave like a young lady, or I shan't speak a word. Have we a deal, Black Bob?"

Felicity deliberated as only a four-year-old may. She screwed up her cherubic little mouth, narrowed her eyes, and nodded. "We gonna sail now? I must find my buwied gold."

"What?" Mrs. Sheffield groaned. "You buried the snuff boxes *again*? How?"

"We shall dig it up together." Viola took the

child's hand, and Felicity did not fuss or fight. Apparently this was a great achievement if the astonished looks from Mrs. Sheffield and the duke were anything to go by.

"Oh, I think His Grace made a fine selection in you, Miss." The housekeeper looked ready to collapse with gratitude. "I may sleep through the night again."

"I should leave you ladies to become acquainted." The Duke of Huntington laughed as he made them a bow. "I believe you shall do very well here, Miss Winslow."

Her heart pounded once again, and her throat tightened. Viola felt that black shroud of misery descend over her. Part of her wanted to leave right now, to ensure she would never see the Duke of Huntington again. But Felicity swung her hand about in Viola's, and the governess knew she could not go anywhere.

"Thank you, Your Grace." She curtsied and watched the duke mount his horse and canter away. She watched the sunlight flash on his golden hair, watched the powerful set of his shoulders as he rode off. She watched him with a sinking heart until he'd vanished into the trees.

"Come on! Time to dig!" Felicity dragged Viola away.

That was how Viola came to know life at Lynton Park.

Truthfully, it was not long before she was as happy as she'd ever been. Her spirited charge was a delight as much as she was a challenge, Mrs. Sheffield and the servants were kindness itself, and Viola eventually came to know her employer as a decent, if rather overly adventurous sort of man. For a woman of her birth and background, fate had been unusually generous.

But as the years passed, Viola knew one thing for certain. She knew it whenever the Duke of Huntington came for a visit, to give Felicity presents from his travels or to play billiards with Ashworth. She knew it whenever Huntington rode away, and she stood at a window and watched him until he disappeared. She knew it whenever the duke greeted her with a smile and a nod and then forgot her as Viola did her best to blend in with the wallpaper, hiding lest he pay too much attention and notice her feelings.

Viola knew that no matter how long she lived, she would always love James Montagu, Duke of Huntington, as she had from the moment they met: fully and hopelessly.

CHAPTER ONE

Strictly speaking, Viola had no objection to drawings of catapults.

Indeed, a skilled artist could craft a most memorable image from such a subject. The only issue arose when someone was supposed to draw a castle and, instead, drew the aforementioned catapult. And when that someone also created armies of men flanking said catapult, ready to lay siege to a castle that had not made an appearance.

"Felicity, you're supposed to be sketching Moorcliff," Viola said.

Her darling charge, Felicity Berridge, all of fourteen and wilder with every year that passed, tossed her black curls with glee and continued sketching with what can only be described as a hacking sort of motion. "I must add the right air of menace, Miss Winslow! How else am I to create a mood? You said an artist should always strive to evoke mood in her pictures."

"Perhaps that aim might be achieved through careful application of shading and texture, rather than in the creation of weapons that currently do not exist."

"Oh, but wouldn't the sketch be so much *better* with a catapult? Everything is! Birthdays, weddings, funerals…"

"I fail to see how a catapult is useful at a funeral."

"They must get the coffin in the ground

somehow, mustn't they?" Felicity was the most per-
verse child in the world, and Viola adored her for it,
even as she despaired of the girl ever being what the
ton considered a lady.

Throughout the last decade, Viola had done her
best to help Felicity take to the feminine arts: pianoforte, sketching and watercolors, poetry, French,
needlework, and literature. Felicity was an able student when she wished to be, but the girl refused to
retain any of the polish her governess struggled to
apply.

Felicity's taste in literature ran more to the tales
of sensational horror published in the lowest sorts of
pamphlets than to Chaucer; her French, while well-
accented and grammatically correct, was most
frequently employed in service of creative vulgari-
ties; and as for the pianoforte, she'd once tried to
turn the instrument at Lynton Park into a bomb.
She'd told Viola that she wanted to see if detonation
could be achieved through the vibration of different
chords.

Viola had suggested they work on Felicity's sing-
ing instead, an idea the Duke and Duchess of
Ashworth had heartily endorsed.

"I must be the worst governess on earth," Viola
had once muttered.

"Nonsense," Ashworth had said. "You're the reason no one's died yet."

Since Felicity showed at least a touch of interest
in sketching and painting, Viola had suggested an
autumn tour through the north of England. There
was such varied and wild landscape to capture, and
Felicity grew bored easily. Time away from the mo-
notony of life at Lynton Park would do wonders for
her.

Viola hadn't intended to bring them to within shouting distance of Moorcliff Castle. Yet here they were on an afternoon in mid-October, easels set up to draw the Duke of Huntington's family seat.

Felicity had surprised Viola as they'd been leaving North Yorkshire, wanting to head all the way to the Scottish border in Northumberland, rather than continue into Cumbria as they'd planned. The thought of being so near Moorcliff had caused Viola to feel uneasy, and she'd tried to dissuade the girl.

But Felicity Berridge was the epitome of willfulness, and for whatever reason, she'd elected to be doubly willful about this. So now here they were, the Duke of Huntington's seat straight ahead.

The two ladies stood about a half mile from the castle, trying to capture the quality of light and shadow as the sun began to set.

Viola had spent time defining the crenellations of the castle wall, as well as the turrets that dotted its length. The main residence was a beautiful combination of the medieval with the more recent. The eastern section was all Gothic windows and heavy stone battlements, while to the west an ancestor from one or two hundred years past had built a handsome abode with columns in the classical style.

The Duke of Huntington was rumored to be in residence now.

He'd not been seen in London since the summer before last, when his proposal of marriage had been rejected. Viola knew the lady in question, then Susannah Fletcher, now Winters, to be a good person who had regretted causing the duke heartache.

The day Viola had learned that Huntington would not marry Susannah, she'd felt as though a death sentence had been commuted at the last minute. Even if Viola knew there was no hope of him ever loving her, she liked to have at least the possibility of his affection. Once Huntington was married, that dream would end forever.

Viola had waited for Huntington to return to town, as had the Ashworths and the rest of their peers in the *ton*. But it had been fifteen months or more, and the duke had not left Northumberland. She gazed wistfully at the castle's imposing structure, wondering where inside its walls Huntington concealed himself.

"Why can't we just stay at Moorcliff, anyway?" Felicity, bored again, dropped her pencil and turned a cartwheel. Her skirts flew upside down, a most unladylike display.

"Because we have not been invited. Felicity, young ladies do not show off their undergarments to the world!"

"But the duke's His Grace's friend, isn't he? I'm sure he'd be happy to see us."

"If you were with the Duke of Ashworth or the duchess, that would be one thing. As a governess, however, it would be improper for me to call upon the Duke of Huntington, even if we are acquainted."

Felicity made an affronted noise. "That's ridiculous! We fought a bloody Revolution over that sort of thing, didn't we?"

"Are you referring to the French or American Revolution?" Viola asked, trying not to weep. How many hours had she labored to instruct Felicity in history?

"The one where they cut people's heads off."

"I feared as much. That was the one in France, dear, as we have been over before."

"Well, if you can't call on the Duke of

Huntington just because you're a governess, then maybe we ought to chop a few people's heads off until everyone sees sense."

"Sometimes, Felicity, I don't know whether you're joking or not." Viola shivered as an autumnal breeze knifed past. She closed the sketch pad so that the papers wouldn't fly about and began to take down her easel. "We can continue tomorrow. Right now, I think we should return to the inn. The sun will be down soon."

"But I wanted to go nearer the castle! I'm sure there are other places to sketch."

Felicity continued to prove baffling. Normally she could not wait to be freed from work. Now she wished to spend more time at her craft?

"We won't be able to sketch when the sun is down. Come along."

"But it's lovely here! We've been standing still in one place or another the entire day. I want some exercise!" So saying, Felicity snatched Viola's sketch pad out of the governess's hands and began bounding away across the field. They were situated upon a hill overlooking Moorcliff, and Viola cried out in fond exasperation as she started taking down Felicity's easel as well.

"Felicity Alice Berridge! You come back here this instant," she called. Of course, Viola didn't have it in her to be hard on the girl. No matter how wild Felicity grew, everyone adored her. Felicity had the gift of natural charisma, which Viola often wished she could possess in even some small amount.

"No! You'll have to catch me first!" With a squeal of joy, Felicity started running along the hill's incline, waving her arms to keep her balance. Viola finished tying up the easels. She put away the pencils and various art supplies in a bag, then slung it over her shoulder.

"I'm not carrying your easel all the way back to the inn! Do you hear me?"

"No, can't hear you! Better chase me," Felicity shouted. She got tired of being so far away, and thus trotted toward Viola until the governess began to come after her. Shrieking with gleeful abandon, Felicity tossed the sketch pad aside and raced along the hill again, the grass waving about her ankles. Viola took up her sketch pad with a sigh.

Ignoring Felicity would put a damper on her high spirits much faster than chasing her would. While Viola waited for the maniacal girl to run out of energy, she looked at Moorcliff again and felt her gut twist.

Perhaps Felicity had a point.

Why did they have to live in a world where a woman like Viola couldn't call upon a duke? Why couldn't a woman in her position hope to love and be loved by him as well?

You'll never have anything, Vi. No man, no family, just your books. Hope they keep you company in your old age.

More than ten years had passed since she'd heard those words, and they still froze Viola in her place. Her heart beat faster, and her palms began to itch. Breathing deeply, Viola reminded herself that he was not here. That he was miles away. That she didn't have to ever see him again, not even for her sister's sake.

Viola put down one of the easels and massaged the base of her throat. She could feel it, like a line of heat, after so many years. Viola never wore a lower neckline for fear someone would see and ask about…it.

My name is Viola Winslow, and I'm perfectly safe.
She always thought those same words when she
needed to ground herself. It worked, mercifully. She
reminded herself she was an invaluable employee to
the Ashworths, that her future would not be the
grim, poverty-stricken ditch her father had prophe-
sied all those years ago.

Indeed, she felt much better now. Ready to con-
front the world.

"Miss Winsloooow! Why won't you bloody chase
me?" Felicity turned back and raced toward Viola,
looking the epitome of amused annoyance.

"How many times must we tell you, Felicity, not
to use language like that? 'Bloody' is not a word for
young ladies."

"I refuse to let men have all the good words,"
Felicity said, giggling as she hurried over to Viola.

And then in a moment both instantaneous and
never-ending, Felicity's shoe slipped on the damp
ground.

With a shrill cry, the girl took a tumble down the
rather steep incline, going head over heels until she
arrived at the bottom in a muddied heap. When she
didn't immediately spring to her feet, Viola knew
something was wrong. The girl clutched at her left
leg and moaned in a horrible fashion.

"Felicity!"

Viola dropped the supplies and raced down the
hill.

CHAPTER TWO

Hunt opened his eyes and found that he had not made it to his bed last night.

His back and shoulders were stiffer than wood as he pushed himself off his desk, across which he'd lain dead asleep until morning. Worse, the sun was far too low and the shadows too long in the wrong direction for it to be anything other than late afternoon.

"Let me think. What was I doing last night?" He slid his fingers through hair that had grown increasingly disheveled over the past fortnight or two. "I sat down to go over the accounts..." He laid a hand to the ledger by his side. "I finished up my work. Afterward, I thought I'd indulge myself in some reading for pleasure." He'd recently procured the six volumes of Mr. Giffords's history of the Roman Republic. To Hunt, the past proved an inexhaustible source of delight. "But before I got round to it, I started to do something else." He blinked and squinted. "What was it?"

A large black raven flapped onto his desk from out of bloody nowhere, fixed its beady bird eyes upon Hunt, and croaked, "Whiskey."

"Ah." Of course, that would explain the empty bottle to his left. "Thank you, Cornelius. As always, you cut straight to the heart of the matter. I admire that in a bird."

"Knickers," quoth the pet raven.

"I wish I knew who taught you such vocabulary." With a bleary sigh, Hunt rose to his feet and stumbled immediately, collapsing onto the foot of his bed with a juicy curse. Cornelius repeated the obscene word back to him, which Hunt knew the dowager would not love. "Well. I've contributed to it myself, I suppose."

James Montagu, the twelfth Duke of Huntington, gazed out his bedroom window upon the rolling countryside and wondered if a person could die from a hangover.

Unlike his friend, the Duke of Ashworth, who'd been a carouser and libertine until marrying his duchess, Hunt had only ever been a passable rake. He'd bedded women, but not in obscene numbers. He'd drunk and gambled with the best of them, but usually in moderation. He'd always been preoccupied with the great task of his life, maintaining the Huntington estate and, in due time, siring an heir who would take up where his father left off.

Last year, Hunt had been prepared to marry the right woman and grow that next branch on the Huntington tree.

Unfortunately, and unexpectedly, the right woman had turned him down on the basis that he was not, well, right for her. Hunt had respected her wishes and bore her no ill will.

Soon after Miss Fletcher's engagement to a Mr. Rafe Winters had been announced, the *ton*'s astonished and incessant gossiping had prompted Hunt to leave London and return to Moorcliff Castle. He'd hoped his absence would calm speculation about the young couple, and in truth he was a bit disgusted by all the well-bred vultures of good society. They had flattered the duke with smiles and honeyed words, but the moment he suffered any kind of public embarrassment, they'd been only too happy to feast upon the corpse of his reputation.

Hunt had always planned to find a wife and then leave London. He preferred the quiet of a country life and the responsibilities of managing the family estate. Well, marriage hadn't worked out, so why should he not move on to the second half of his plan? After all, Moorcliff Castle had everything required for his happiness: work, whiskey, the love of his family, a foul-mouthed raven, absolutely everything.

Cornelius cocked his head sideways and stared at Hunt.

"Who let you in here, anyway?" the duke asked.

"Knickers."

"Please leave."

The raven obeyed, swooping out the half-open bedroom door.

The duke's chambers faced the south lawn, where during the spring and summer months whole banks of cultivated red and yellow tulips bloomed. In autumn, however, all he saw was a hilly stretch of overgrown grass and a few increasingly leafless trees.

And, also, two small figures.

Squinting, Hunt moved back to the window and gazed at what appeared to be two ladies sketching. Probably tourists staying in the village, enjoying the crumbling grandeur of Moorcliff Castle.

A knock sounded upon the door. He thought it might be his valet, but it turned out to be his elder sister.

"So, he arises at last." Agatha chuckled as she went over to Hunt and brushed his hair from his face. Ever since they were children, she'd always taken him in hand, whether he liked it or not. "How are you, Jamie?"

She was also the only person alive who could get away with calling him Jamie.

"Splendid. Delightful. Entirely sober." A headache pounded against his temples like a most impolite battering ram. "Why do you ask?"

"I saw Cornelius flapping down the hall. When I asked where you were, he issued a most foul word followed by 'whiskey' and then departed. I assumed you could do with some help."

"Ring for Smollett, then. A duke does not require being babied by his sister." Hunt attempted to sound as imperious as possible, so it was a bit irritating when Agatha patted his cheek. She had to reach up to do it, too. He was bloody six foot five.

"When a duke broods alone in his tower room all night drinking whiskey, his sister must check in on him."

"It was not all night. I must have passed out around four." Hunt realized that was not the cutting retort he'd wanted it to be. "And I was not brooding, Agatha. I was ruminating; there's a clear difference. Now I really must ring for my valet, if only to have him shave me. For heaven's sake, stop rubbing my face!"

"Apologies, brother dear. You know I find stubble fascinating in a tactile way."

Lady Agatha Montagu was forty years old and the only one of the three Montagu siblings to take after their mother. Unlike Hunt and Isabelle, Agatha was short, with a rather pointed, narrow jaw, kindly brown eyes, and hair of a bright gingery shade. A few streaks of silver were becoming evident in her corkscrew curls, but she retained as ever a youthful exuberance. She was the merriest spinster Hunt had ever encountered.

Hunt tugged at the bell pull before seating himself forcefully upon the bed. Agatha stood before him, tilting her head this way and that in appraisal.

"I've decided to voice an opinion," she said.

"Lady Agatha with an opinion? What an unusual occurrence." Agatha took up a cushion and lovingly struck him upon the head with it. "Such violence."

"It is my opinion that you've shut yourself away from the world for quite long enough. What happened last year was dreadful, but you must put it in the past. Isabelle and Granny and I love having you in residence, but we'd prefer it if you were happy!"

"Who says I'm not happy? I'm ecstatic."

"You drank half a bottle of whiskey alone in your bedroom."

"But I did it happily." His head felt like it was stuffed with gravel. *Happy* gravel. "It's not as if I'm up here every night carousing, you know. Difficult to carouse by yourself, anyway."

"That's precisely the issue! You should be carousing with others. One other in particular."

"Please don't say anything ever, ever again." Hunt did not want his elder sister to prod him toward libertinism or matrimony. He'd be sick either way.

"I can't worry over both my younger siblings. I've got my hands full with Isabelle mooning about the place and composing all that endless poetry." Agatha shuddered, and Hunt understood. Lady Isabelle Montagu's poetry was as incomprehensible in quality as it was voluminous in quantity.

"I know you don't understand my feelings. You've never known shame and disappointment," Hunt muttered.

"There's much you don't know about me." His

sister sat beside him. "But I know everything about you, Jamie. If you'd only allow yourself back into the world, you'd be surprised how quickly happiness would find you. Why shouldn't it? You're a handsome, youngish man with land and wealth and a title as old as England itself. The world was made to be a paradise for people like you! Yet you've holed up with us these last fifteen months and refused to meet it halfway."

"I'm not holed up. I'm overseeing my estate and my family's affairs. I'm doing my duty."

"Part of that duty entails fathering an heir." She looked meaningfully at him.

"I like to think myself conscientious, Agatha, but I can't marry a woman simply to have a child. Better Cousin Stephen should inherit Moorcliff and the dukedom than I should raise a family with an incompatible spouse. I've seen those marriages and what they've produced. If it hadn't been for Julia, Ashworth would be dead or in prison by now." The pounding headache had grown worse; he really needed some coffee, even more than a shave. "You're wasting time on me. Go look after Isabelle and I'll see you at dinner."

Agatha clucked her tongue in disapproval and left as Smollett, the valet, entered. Hunt had the tall, gangly man leave the shaving behind for a moment and bring him some coffee. While the valet hastened to obey the order, Hunt turned back to the window and gazed out at the two small figures of the ladies.

They were taking down their easels now, retiring for the afternoon. A good idea. The dark came on quickly in Northumberland at this time of year.

Hunt smiled as one of the figures started cavorting around, while the smaller woman went about the task of tidying everything up. He found himself gazing at that little figure, wondering who it could be. What she looked like, what her name was.

Since the disaster with Miss Fletcher, Hunt hadn't felt much desire to seek out the company of women, but there was something appealing about the quiet diligence of that faraway woman.

Then the taller lady took quite a fall, tumbling down the hill in a series of alarming positions. The other woman flung aside the easels and chased after her friend.

Though Hunt had been something of a rake in his university days, he maintained an ironclad belief in chivalry when it came to the fairer sex. He believed that all women, from duchess to scullery maid, deserved decent treatment and protection. The instant he saw the girl fall, he pushed back from the window prepared to act. The wind had begun to pick up and sweep across the hills while dark, swollen clouds rolled in from the east. The women would be caught in a freezing autumn storm before too long, and Hunt couldn't allow that.

He left his chamber and passed Smollett in the hall. The poor valet turned quickly, the silver coffeepot jangling on its tray as he hurried after his master.

"There are two ladies in need of assistance on the south lawn. Tell them to saddle my horse and prepare a cart as well."

"Certainly, Your Grace. Would you like a coat? And perhaps a shave?"

True, Hunt was in only his shirt and an unbuttoned vest, and his stubble remained. His blond hair was a haphazard mess. He looked less like a duke and more like a raving madman from one of

Isabelle's ostentatious Gothic epics. *Ah, well.* He couldn't have two ladies wait out in the rain while he finished his toilette.

"Thank you, Smollett. Yes to the coat, no to everything else. And forget the coffee, have tea prepared for the women."

"Certainly, Your Grace."

Hunt's rather incessant headache alleviated a bit as he slid on his coat and mounted his horse. He'd always been a man who preferred to do things, writing tasks down on a list and crossing them out one by one. There was pleasure in order, in looking after tenants and maintaining the estate. Perhaps that was one reason he'd been so disoriented the past year. When Susannah had rejected him, for the first time in Hunt's life, a plan had fallen apart. Rather disastrously so.

At least riding to aid two ladies would give some purpose to his otherwise amorphous day.

The men followed in the cart as Hunt cantered ahead, coming nearer to the two women. The smaller one was bent over the other's left leg, feeling at the stockinged ankle. The younger woman's slipper was off, and Hunt looked away quickly to avoid impropriety. A man shouldn't stare at a woman's ankles without being first acquainted, after all.

Though as he drew closer, Hunt realized he *was* acquainted with the ladies.

"I say!" He stopped his horse and gazed down in astonishment upon Felicity Berridge and her governess, Miss Winslow. Good lord, what were the two ladies doing this far north? And where the devil was Ashworth?

The governess looked up at him, and the forceful intent of her gaze nearly knocked Hunt backward.

He'd known Miss Winslow for more than ten years, but in all that time he could remember exchanging perhaps thirty words with her. She was an intelligent lady, but the epitome of a wallflower, the type to fade away whenever someone entered a room. Right now, however, there was nothing demure or wilting about her. The woman rushed to his horse.

"Please, the girl seems to have hurt her ankle! I can't tell if it's broken or not." The woman looked panicked but spoke with great firmness. Felicity, meanwhile, rubbed her foot and whimpered in pain. "Take us to the castle. We're acquainted with His Grace and I'm sure he will help us."

Hunt blinked in astonishment.

"He certainly will. I can speak for him," the duke said, dismounting his horse. "At your service, Miss Winslow."

Normally, the governess would lower her eyes and hunch her shoulders and mutter whenever Huntington was around. To his ever-increasing surprise, the lady's mouth dropped open in stark, naked wonder.

"Your Grace?" She sounded shocked.

"Ah. Yes." Hunt cleared his throat, realizing that, between the stubble, the longer hair, the flyaway clothes and, probably, the disheveled appearance that a whiskey hangover naturally produced, he must appear utterly changed to the woman. "There's no need to worry. I saw Miss Berridge take a tumble and ordered you both brought to Moorcliff. I didn't realize it was you at the time, though, which makes this surprise only more delightful."

Delightful might not be the proper word, as Miss Winslow continued to take him in with a vague expression of ever-growing horror. Hunt began to wonder if he'd allowed his relaxed appearance to go perhaps a bit too far. He almost wished he'd waited to let the bloody valet shave him after all.

"Thank you. Truly. I was afraid I'd have to go racing to the castle myself to demand help. You would have thought me horribly rude."

"Not at all." Truly, his first thought would have been how strangely beautiful she appeared. Miss Winslow was not a displeasing lady, but she always seemed so quiet and pale. Time in the country air had brought a pink flush to her cheeks and fire to her hazel eyes.

Hunt had never noticed the color of her eyes before, and he wasn't certain why he should be so attentive to that detail now. He turned his focus to helping the men load Felicity onto the cart. Already, the girl had stopped whimpering and seemed only too delighted to be the center of such fuss.

"Oh dear, I do hope the bone is not too broken! I should hate to have the foot amputated," the girl said.

"We would better believe that, dear, if you didn't smile with such enthusiasm." Miss Winslow sighed with evident, if weary, fondness as she began to climb into the wagon alongside her charge.

Hunt felt moved to approach her. "You might ride back with me, if you like."

Now why the devil had he said that? Both Miss Winslow and Felicity appeared surprised.

"There's room in the cart, Your Grace. I don't wish to inconvenience you."

Of course, she's right. Why would you even offer? Perhaps because, for the first time in fifteen months, Hunt had thought it would be nice to be close to a woman. Placing Miss Winslow before him on the saddle and riding back to Moorcliff with her pressed to his chest, his one arm slung about her waist for security, seemed most tempting.

Perhaps he'd spent too much time alone. What an impractical offer.

"Ah. Of course." He searched for a viable excuse. "Perhaps this reminds me of first meeting you on the road to Lynton Park years ago."

Miss Winslow reverted to the quiet, demure creature he'd always known. Casting down her eyes, she bobbed in a quick curtsy. "Of course, Your Grace. How kind of you to recall."

Hunt helped her into the cart and trotted back to Moorcliff alongside the women. The wind was picking up, rushing through the grass and mussing his hair even more. The air smelled faintly of nickel, the sign a thunderstorm was soon to begin.

"It was good fortune I spotted you both when Miss Berridge took a fall," Hunt said to Miss Winslow.

"Indeed, Your Grace. We'd have been lost without you."

The governess gave him another of her shy yet pleasing smiles and turned her attention to nursing her charge. As they returned to the castle, Hunt couldn't help remembering the fire he'd glimpsed in her, moments before. The bold way she'd approached and spoken to him before she recognized him.

Miss Viola Winslow, it seemed, had hidden depths, and he found that he desired to explore them further.

CHAPTER THREE

As a child, Viola had frequently wished for the power to become invisible, particularly when her father was in one of his moods.

She'd often thought how interesting it would be to stand around unnoticed, able to observe the tiniest goings on. To see people as they naturally were without any need to put on a show.

Right now, Viola wished she were invisible because she was so mortified. The Duke of Huntington had ridden up to their rescue on his horse, a prince from a faerie story, and she hadn't recognized him. Recalling that forceful way she'd spoken to him made her want to bury her face in a pillow and never look at another human being again. She hadn't been rude, but she'd been bloody ordering him about! Speaking as though she and Huntington were well acquainted, telling him that she *knew* the duke would help them. He had to think her the most conceited, arrogant woman in the world.

Though if she were being truly honest with herself, the duke's appearance had shocked her. No wonder she hadn't recognized him. He was still brutally handsome, but in an almost animal way. The Duke of Huntington she knew had always been the epitome of order, with the most perfectly clean-shaven face, the smoothest hair, the neatest and most fashionable clothing. Wherever he went, the duke seemed to be the man in control.

Now he looked, well, halfway wild.

She'd never seen him with hair that unkempt and

untrimmed before, or with any stubble on his face at all. She also had to admit the sight of him in such a disheveled, almost barbaric state quickened her blood. He looked less like a god in that moment and more like a man. A sinfully handsome, powerful man.

There's no way I can be around him for more than an hour or so. I'll get Felicity seen to and, if it's only a sprained ankle, I'll beg the duke to return us to the inn in his carriage. No, that's too forceful; I'll leave Felicity in his keeping and then return to the inn myself. No, that's abominably rude. I know! I shall hide in a closet all evening. There, the perfect solution.

"Why do you look so ill?" Felicity asked as the cart trundled through an arched gate into the castle's sprawling courtyard.

"I'm worried for your ankle, dearest."

"That's all right. I don't think it's broken." The girl sounded almost disappointed. Then Felicity brightened. "Oh! Do you think I might have a wheeled chair of some kind in which to push myself about? I should love to see how fast I could go, and I'm certain Moorcliff has halls of sufficient length for an experiment in velocity."

"My hope is that you shall recover swiftly, and that the doctor suggests we tie you to the bed so you can't move until then."

Felicity thought a moment, then grinned. "That was a joke, wasn't it?"

"Forgive me, my dear. You know humor isn't my strongest suit."

Felicity chuckled, already having the jolliest time in the world. Only a spirit such as Felicity's could turn catastrophe into adventure. Viola rather adored the girl, even when she despaired of her.

The cart deposited them before the castle's front entrance.

Two servants gently lifted Felicity and carried her into the building.

As Viola began to get out, the sky brightened with a bolt of severest lightning. Mere seconds later, thunder broke overhead, and rain began to patter down. Autumn rains were the worst, chilling to the bone in seconds.

"Miss Winslow. Allow me." The Duke of Huntington took her hand and helped her down from the cart.

Viola could not feel the touch of his skin through her glove, but the mere contact stole her breath all the same. In the years she'd known him, she had never once taken the duke's hand. Huntington was the embodiment of strength, and with his body so close to her own, Viola luxuriated in the warmth of his presence.

He had obviously drunk some whiskey, but his sharp and masculine scent was mouth-watering—clean linen and cloves, spice and soap. Viola could have stood here the rest of her life, sheltered by his body and warmed by him. It would have been heaven.

"What are you thinking, Miss Winslow?" the duke asked.

Oh, damn. If her naked appreciation of him had become too apparent, she was going to set her "hiding in a closet" plan into motion.

"That you've been kind to assist us, Your Grace."

Viola would have loved nothing more than to meet his eyes, but it would have been much too forward. Besides, she'd always believed people could read her thoughts in her eyes; she'd been told they were frighteningly expressive. If Huntington looked at her too closely, he would see the truth of her tender feelings.

Though with him this near and this unkempt, it was more than tenderness she felt. Indeed, she'd never had such vivid, potent fantasies about his physicality. She wanted to feel his lips against hers. She wished for his hands to caress her body. She yearned to see him unclothed in all his power and virility.

She must now be blotchy with embarrassment. Of all the times to become lewd, this was among the worst.

The duke hurried her into the castle and began to speak with a woman, probably the housekeeper, about preparing rooms for the two guests. Viola wanted to interject and say it was no trouble, they'd be on their way soon enough, but Moorcliff Castle's receiving hall stunned her into silence.

The arched and coffered ceiling rose thirty feet and was painted white with gold accents. The floor was pale marble, and ahead of them a grand, carpeted staircase led to the next level of the house. Marble balustrades provided further ornamentation, as did the gilded leaf and flower moldings on the ceiling.

On the wood-paneled walls of the lower level, imperious oil paintings of ancestors all seemed to have their gazes fixed upon Viola. She could imagine these men and women in ruff collars and powdered wigs whispering, asking what a mere governess was doing entering through the front door in the manner of a guest. Over the last ten years, Viola's self-confidence had developed. The Duke of Ashworth had given her a home as well as a job, and she felt certain she loved Felicity as a mother would. The shy, cringing girl who'd entered Lynton Park all those years ago had developed into a more poised woman, but Viola could never forget who she was and especially not where she came from. Her station as a governess was elegance itself compared to the wretchedness she'd left behind. No one, not even the Duke and Duchess of Ashworth, knew the full extent of Viola's lowly past. Women like her didn't enter places like Moorcliff Castle as a guest.

"Miss Winslow?" the duke said. It sounded as if he'd been trying to get her attention for some time.

"Forgive me, Your Grace! My mind, er, wandered. This is quite"—she wanted to say "splendid" or "palatial" but felt that would be too familiar—"quite large. Yes. It is very big."

A truly original observation, Viola. Indeed, you have articulated something no one else has ever considered before.

The duke smiled, and she was sure he was only being polite.

"Mrs. Moore will show you to your room. When you've seen Felicity settled in, please join me in the library. We'll discuss what's to be done."

"Your Grace, this is all too generous." Viola started reeling.

A room would mean spending the night. That would mean sleeping under Huntington's roof, speaking to him, seeing him in the morning. She imagined all the little interactions they would have, and this time there would be no Duke or Duchess of Ashworth to hide behind, no Susannah to play the pianoforte while Viola hugged the wall and maintained a pleasant silence. She was going to have to *converse* with him.

"Please, it's the least I can do," he said.

"I'm certain her injury isn't that dreadful." Viola prayed her voice wouldn't start shaking; that was really all she'd need to make this pathetic picture complete. "If you would only be gracious enough to have a carriage return us to the inn, I could manage everything from there."

As if to punctuate the absurdity of her statement, another enormous thunderclap sounded directly over the castle. Lightning flashed in perfect time with the thunder, and rain assaulted the roof. Even behind these stone walls, the howl of the wind outside sounded so bloody close.

Only a madwoman would dare such a journey.

"Miss Winslow, that is quite impossible," the duke said, appearing rather puzzled. "You must both stay the night at least. In the morning, once the storm has passed, we can discuss returning you to the inn."

He was right, and if she argued further, he'd think her the most ridiculous woman in England.

"Then we thank you for your hospitality, Your Grace."

Mrs. Moore took Viola up the staircase and down a few winding, carpeted hallways.

The housekeeper was a pleasant lady and spoke with warmth about the many distinguished ancestors whom Viola saw captured in the portraits that lined the walls. She was told Moorcliff also held rarer treasures such as tapestries from the time of the Norman conquests, and even some rather pagan carvings and weaponry from the ancient Celts. The history of England and the history of the Huntington line went neatly hand in hand.

Meanwhile, Viola was the first person in her

family who had learned to read. There was quite a difference.

At least Felicity seemed to be making herself comfortable. She was lying on an enormous four-poster bed when Viola entered, relishing all the fuss servants were making about her. One maid was pouring a basin of hot water to wash the girl's rather dirty face and hands, while another worked on elevating her injured leg properly with a cushion.

"I told you we ought to have stayed here! It's so much nicer than that drafty old inn." Felicity reclined against a mountain of pillows and sighed. "If only I were a few years older, I could marry the duke and live here forever."

"Felicity, it's shocking to say such things."

"I suppose if he's still unmarried in five or six years, I could try." Felicity wrinkled her nose. "Though he's rather old."

"The duke is thirty-six. I believe," Viola hastened to add, in case her immediate knowledge of that fact seemed a bit unusual.

"See? Practically ancient." Felicity was serious. Well, to anyone under the age of sixteen, anything over twenty appeared old as the hills.

"I must go down to the library and speak with His Grace. Can I trust you to rest in bed while I do so? No trying to limp about, no breaking windows, no mayhem."

"You talk as though I were some sort of a wild beast." Felicity beamed. "I do love you for that."

"Well, I know you too well." Viola attempted to be stern, but it was a half-hearted attempt.

"But you're going to change. Surely." Felicity sat up, looking quite engaged in critiquing her governess's appearance.

"I beg your pardon, young lady?" Viola was stunned. "I believe I am perfectly well-dressed and not unkempt in the least." The duke, on the other hand, was the embodiment of unkempt. The thought made Viola positively normal.

"Yes, but we're in a duke's house now! We must all look our best, don't you agree?"

Considering Felicity flouted convention at every turn, this sudden enthusiasm for propriety was rather disconcerting.

"Felicity, even if I wished to change I haven't any other gown than this one. All our things are back at the inn."

"I just think we need to do the Duke of Ashworth proud, that's all," the child grumbled. This was becoming more surprising by the minute. Felicity adored the Ashworths, but most of her energy was usually spent keeping them on their toes.

"His Grace and the Duke of Huntington are best friends. I think his honor is safe regardless of our appearance."

"Very well. But you might wear a bit of ribbon!"

"What?"

"Here." Felicity had worn red silk ribbons in her hair today. She did like to make herself look flashy. She undid one of the bows and handed it over. "At least tie it to your collar or something. It would be a splash of color against all the gray."

"You are making me feel rather uneasy about my appearance, young lady. That is not something a girl of good breeding should ever do."

"You always look lovely, Miss Winslow." The girl kept holding out the ribbon. "I just think you deserve to look even lovelier."

Viola sighed, fixing her charge with the

"governess eye." It worked, for Felicity lay back upon the cushions, the red ribbon trailing from her hand like a flag of defeat.

"I appreciate your good intentions. Truly. But I've no reason to look my best. There's no one here who would notice, anyway."

Felicity grumbled something Viola could not catch.

"What did you say?"

"I said that I shall sit here and be quite good if you would fetch my book from your bag."

Excellent. The girl was settling down for the evening. Viola opened the art supply satchel she was still carrying and found...

"Felicity." She shut her eyes. "What happened to *Patience and Grace*?" It was the title of a very appropriate novel for young girls that dealt with life lessons and the importance of virtue.

"Oh, I threw that in the rubbish back in Derbyshire. Sorry."

Viola pulled out a pamphlet by a Mr. C.D. Winthrop, another of those dreadful Gothics Felicity inhaled.

"*The Bloody Skull of Urlich Castle* by the author of *The Screaming Vampire of Whitewood Abbey*." Viola brandished the pamphlet. "I need one reason why I shouldn't throw this out the window."

"If you give it to me, I promise to sit in bed and read and take nothing apart." Felicity spoke with great primness. "If you toss it, I may resort to all sorts of devilry."

Viola gave the booklet to the girl, who opened it to where she'd left off while wearing a beatific smile.

The housekeeper led Viola back downstairs in a mild state of perplexity.

"She seems a most energetic child," Mrs. Moore said. It sounded like energetic was a polite replacement for another word.

All the annoyed good humor Viola had felt with Felicity vanished as the housekeeper showed her to the library. Viola stood outside the tall door a moment with her hand pressed over her palpitating heart. She had to calm down.

Another great flash of lightning and peal of thunder snaked and bellowed overhead, which did not help the situation.

Viola entered an enormous chamber with a blazing hearth directly ahead on the far side of the room, and shelves filled with books lining every inch of available wall. There was even a second level to the library, which could be accessed by a rickety spiral staircase. Viola had always found her greatest solace in books and entered with her fear forgotten for the moment. The curtains were open, allowing sight of the pelting rain outside. Another burst of lightning illuminated the room, gifting Viola a glimpse of Huntington standing beside the hearth.

There was another person in the room with them. The lightning flashed upon her enormous necklace of jewels, the diamond rings glinting upon her fingers, the precious stones of her earbobs. For a brief instant, the lady looked studded in blinding ice.

"Miss Winslow," the duke said. "Come over by the fire, please. Warm yourself."

Heart still pounding, Viola approached and curtsied to Huntington and the lady at his side. She was quite elderly, with wrinkled, crepey skin and an immaculate hairdo of brilliant white. The woman held herself with the regal bearing of a queen as she studied Viola.

"You must be the governess," the woman said, as if she were diagnosing a terminal illness.

"Yes, my lady."

"Your Grace." The old woman lifted her chin an inch higher. "The Dowager Duchess of Huntington, if you please."

"This is my grandmother," the duke said. "A most informal woman, as you can see."

Viola bit back a laugh; she didn't think the dowager would appreciate laughter.

"Is Miss Berridge comfortable?" The duke seemed genuinely concerned, which Viola appreciated.

"She is, Your Grace. We can't thank you enough for your hospitality. With the storm outside, I don't suppose there's much hope of getting a doctor tonight?"

"Unfortunately, no. In this weather, I wouldn't put anyone on the road to town in the dark unless there was a dire emergency. My sister, Lady Agatha, is headed for Miss Berridge's chamber. She's obviously not a doctor, but she enjoys the study of anatomy and medicine. Dr. Kenneth says she's quite brilliant. She should at least be able to discern if there's been a break."

"That's too generous, Your Grace." Viola prayed neither of her hosts noticed her hands were shaking. She laid them stiffly at her sides. "Members of your family shouldn't be waiting on us."

"Nonsense, the girl is the Duke of Ashworth's ward, is she not?" The dowager duchess gazed along the length of an especially hawkish nose to regard Viola with something akin to disdainful pity. "That makes her quite worthy of our attention."

"I see." Viola felt a rare ember of annoyance. It

made her hands stop shaking. "Of course, Your Grace. How foolish of me. Had Miss Berridge been any ordinary young miss from the village, Lady Agatha's attentions would be misapplied."

"Indeed." The dowager seemed unaware Viola was ever so slightly having her on. "Charity is a virtue, but there's no need to behave as though distinctions of rank don't exist."

Normally, Viola would be silent and that would be the end of it all.

But she thought of her sister, Betsy, and the children only a few miles from here. She thought of how she herself had lived until the age of eight, how hunger had always been a possibility, how she could not lie abed with a cold because there was too much work to be done.

Tonight, there were children sick or injured whom the dowager duchess would not think worthy of being tended to by a member of her own family, simply because they lived in a crofter's cottage instead of a castle. So even though Viola preferred to say nothing if she could help it, she spoke out now.

"A duke's daughter should only ever tend members of royalty or others of her own rank. Her delicate breeding will permit nothing else. Would you agree, Your Grace?"

"Well, I might not go *that* far, but it would seem more appropriate." The duchess appeared quite serious.

"Indeed. Daughters of marquesses, perhaps, are also too gently bred to move outside of the landed gentry. I gather an earl's children might soothe the fevers of a tradesperson, but only those of a certain rank, merchants and doctors and the like. Then the viscounts and barons might split the rest of the commoners between themselves."

The duke made a small noise, and Viola realized with some horror and some delight he was attempting to govern a smile. Though she had not intended to amuse him, she'd done so.

"That is a very fanciful notion, Miss Winslow." The dowager's pale blue eyes were half-lidded, the wrinkles about her mouth deepening as she pursed her lips. "I was not aware that governesses were allowed to be fanciful."

"Only when we are not in the schoolroom, Your Grace. In my free hours, I greatly enjoy fancifulness and painting with watercolors."

Where had all this cheekiness come from?

The pounding of Viola's heart no longer felt like the beat of fear but of excitement. Perhaps the dowager's withering contempt had fanned that ember of annoyance into anger, or perhaps because Viola could feel the Duke of Huntington's approving gaze upon her face. Had he ever truly looked at her before? Viola doubted it, because the most wonderful tingling sensation was rushing up and down her whole body. It was a new experience.

The conversation was cut short as the library door opened and a woman entered at a quick pace. From her smart manner of dressing and the way that her mouth reminded Viola of the duke's, this must be his sister, Lady Agatha. Viola curtsied.

"I've seen to the girl." To Viola's surprise, the lady spoke to her with a smile. "No need to fear. There's nothing broken, though the ankle seems rather sprained. I'm having a compress taken up to ease the swelling."

"Should we send for Dr. Kenneth?" the duke asked.

"If it gets worse, but I very much doubt that it will. A few days of rest and she should be fine."

"Thank you, my lady." Viola could not remember the last time she'd been alone in a room with so many high-ranking people staring at her.

More than ever, she wished she had the Duchess of Ashworth to hide behind. Julia possessed a bold spirit and a sharp wit, making her the darling of society. Meanwhile, Viola felt certain she'd pass out soon. The woman who'd spoken with courage earlier had vanished. She knew she'd wince to recall that moment even years from now. Viola's remembered failings tended to pop out and surprise her at the most inopportune moments.

"*Bonsoir,* Granny." Lady Agatha delivered a dutiful kiss to the old woman's wrinkled cheek. "You seem merry as ever. I hope you haven't been telling too many ribald jokes and scandalizing our guest." Lady Agatha and her brother exchanged a gleeful, almost mischievous glance.

"You young people display such shocking ease with your elders." The dowager's chin lifted even higher; she would be staring right at the ceiling by dinner if this kept up.

While Lady Agatha and the duchess further conversed, the duke beckoned to Viola. He was drawing her into a corner by the window. He wanted to speak with her. *Privately.*

Viola followed, though she felt ice forming in the pit of her stomach.

"You'll have to forgive my grandmother her little eccentricities," the duke said. "She was badly rattled by the French Revolution. Any perceived upset in the social order and she hears guillotines being sharpened."

"Not at all, Your Grace. I should not have spoken so informally." Viola clutched her left wrist and gave a firm squeeze, an old habit she'd developed to calm her when she felt liable to scream or run away.

"On the contrary, I wish you'd be more informal. A little levity's useful, especially in a place like Moorcliff during the darker months."

Lightning and thunder announced themselves in perfect synchronicity. The rain outside turned into a deluge. At this rate, Viola would not be shocked to find an ark floating past the castle.

"Well. I'll attempt to remain useful, Your Grace."

The duke frowned. "Am I that hideous, then? It's been ages since I examined myself in a mirror."

"Your Grace?" What on earth was he talking about?

"Why do you not look at me, Miss Winslow?" His voice caressed her name as sweetly as a hand might caress a body.

"Oh? Ah, I don't like to take such liberties, Your Grace."

"These are not the days of the Saxons. I won't have you horsewhipped for meeting my eyes." He sounded kind, if a bit bemused. Viola would make this only worse if she didn't look up, so she gazed upon the duke's face.

Viola's knowledge of Huntington's face was a bit haphazard, odd considering how long she'd known him. She mostly looked upon him when he was not looking at her. She did not know, then, how meeting the piercing blue of his eyes would stop her very breath. He had always been the handsomest man she'd ever known, but his beauty had been for other people, his attention directed elsewhere. Now, his attention and looks were all for her.

The structure of his face had sharpened in the decade she'd known him. The boyish smoothness had been lost, and a severe, almost brutally masculine rigor dominated. Yet his lips were still full and kissable, and his blue eyes warm. The stubble on his jaw seemed almost begging to be touched. The duke still had not put on a cravat, and the strong line of his throat made her mouth water.

To her shock, Viola felt a sweet leadenness in her limbs, a pulsating warmth between her legs she had never known before.

"There now," Huntington said, his voice low and delicious. "Nothing terrible has occurred."

"No, Your Grace." Viola needed to say something; she could not stand here helpless before his potent beauty. "Your library is exceptional. Even His Grace the Duke of Ashworth doesn't own so many volumes."

"I can't take credit for all of it," Huntington said. Viola looked about the tall shelves and felt the prickle of his gaze still on her face. "This room boasts the curatorial efforts of a thousand years of Huntingtons. I believe we've a Gutenberg Bible in a glass case somewhere."

Imagine not knowing where your Gutenberg Bible was. Viola almost laughed at the absurdity.

"I've added to its reserves myself, of course. Books on science and philosophy…and poetry." The duke canted his head to the left, appraising her in a way that brought a flush to Viola's cheeks. "If I recall correctly, you're fond of poetry, Miss Winslow. Or at least, you were when we first met."

Viola felt the throb of her pulse. Her voice came out almost weak with happiness.

"Oh. Did I say that?" She cleared her throat.

"How kind of you to remember, Your Grace."

The corner of Huntington's mouth hiked up in a rather rakish smile. "It seems I've a much clearer recollection of our first meeting than you do. I must not have made much of an impression. How sad."

Was he testing her? And if he was, why did that fill her with so much pleasure? If she simply lied and agreed with him, it would be an insult. But if she protested too enthusiastically, she'd betray herself.

"I believe I was too nervous about starting my position at Lynton Park to pay much attention to my own words. But I remember your kindness, Your Grace. There aren't many dukes who would permit a governess to ride their horse while they walked."

It was like a cloud passing over the sun. The merriment in his eyes diminished, and anger flashed across his face with the same mercurial charge as lightning. "You're undoubtedly right, Miss Winslow. That thought gives me little pleasure."

"I'm sorry. I don't mean to diminish your pleasure, Your Grace."

Her heartbeat was so loud, she'd be shocked if the entire room couldn't hear.

"You don't diminish pleasure, Miss Winslow. Indeed, your visit has only increased it."

There was an ache in the core of Viola's body, a thrumming across every inch of her skin. She wanted to feel his arms around her. She wanted his lips in her hair, on her eyelids, on her mouth. She wanted his velvet whispers in her ear, telling her how much pleasure she gave him. Viola wanted to feel the press of his body against hers. She could have swooned with the sudden, devastating power of that desire, and all because he had smiled at her. He had said she gave him pleasure.

It was probably for the best they would never touch or kiss. She might explode if that happened.

"What sorts of poetry have you added to the collection?" she asked, trying to control herself. Poetry seemed like a safer topic than pleasure.

"The usual. Coleridge, some of Shelley's less controversial work."

"Mr. William Blake?" Viola asked.

To her slight shock, the duke made a dismissive gesture. "Mr. Blake is a talented painter, but his poetry has the simplicity of nursery songs. Nice, I suppose, but not exactly a challenge."

"Just because something is simple doesn't mean it holds no challenge." Viola would never have spoken this way if the duke hadn't been insulting the work of a man she revered. "Indeed, sometimes the simplest things offer the most complex mysteries."

"That's a very forward opinion, Miss Winslow." Huntington frowned.

Viola should have lowered her head and apologized for her forwardness. Perhaps she was simply drunk on the thrill of looking upon his face so directly. Perhaps the storm was wreaking havoc upon her mind. Either way, she plunged ever onward.

"Mr. Blake conveys so much energy and opinion in so few words. He challenges every single convention we English take for granted as fact. I like him because he doesn't feel the need to make himself appear cleverer than he is by cluttering his poems with needless flourishes. Anyone can understand him, and that means anyone can talk about his ideas. He isn't writing for a learned elite, those who feel a sense of superiority for merely being able to decipher what he's saying. His work is for everyone."

"I see." The duke smiled and sounded almost

admiring. "That's quite a radical statement, Miss Winslow."

"Radical?" The dowager turned with the ferocity of a bloodhound on the scent. "What did you say, Hunt?"

"Granny has a horror of anything radical," Lady Agatha said with a laugh. "You'd better take care, Miss Winslow."

Viola silently cursed herself. What had she been thinking? She'd scolded him! Oh, she needed an escape. She needed to go upstairs and hide with Felicity the rest of the night; she'd even let the girl read that bloody skull book aloud, if only it would take Viola's thoughts from the spectacle she'd just made of herself.

"Beg pardon, Your Graces. I really must see to my charge." Viola gave a curtsy and kept her head down as she started for the door.

"Well, be quick about it," Lady Agatha said. "Dinner should be served presently."

Viola stopped, her lips clamped together to keep from screaming. They weren't going to send up a tray for both Felicity and her governess? The family couldn't want to dine with the help, could they? Viola had to put a stop to this.

"Oh, I can't thank you enough, my lady, but I'm certain it's improper for a governess to dine at the same table as your family."

"Quite right," the dowager snapped.

"Nonsense," Huntington said. "Miss Winslow. I expect your presence at dinner."

"But Miss Berridge—"

"Will be comfortable, fed, and looked after. You are my guest, not merely a governess. I trust I will see you at my table tonight." The Duke of Huntington regarded her with an almost hungry intensity.

Normally, he was the picture of courtesy and deference, but tonight there was something forceful about him. Something dominant that she'd never seen before. Or at least that she'd never seen directed at her. He was the sort of man whose orders were obeyed.

So even though she wished to protest, Viola whispered, "Very well, Your Grace. Thank you."

She left the library and had to place her hand against the wall when no one could see her. Viola almost slumped over, taking one deep, shaking breath after the other.

She'd spoken as an equal to the duke!

And now she had to eat a meal at his table, surrounded by his family, a common sparrow among birds of prey.

If only she'd been the one to sprain her ankle.

CHAPTER FOUR

Hunt gazed at the library door long after Miss Winslow had closed it.

He had not felt this much heated delight in such a long time.

When the governess had spoken of her love for Blake's poetry, there'd been an animation in her face he'd never suspected could exist. One needed only to poke the ashes of her soul to uncover a shower of embers. Perhaps a bit more prodding and the full flame of her personality would be unleashed. What a pleasure *that* would be.

Especially as Miss Winslow had such a rosebud mouth. He'd never noticed that before, had he? She had the kind of lips that begged to be kissed. Combined with the heat of her hazel eyes, the warm flush upon her normally pale cheeks, Hunt realized how hungry he was for a woman's touch. He had not wanted a woman in so bloody long. Now that he'd glimpsed the passion Miss Winslow kept hidden beneath a passive façade, he wanted more. He wanted to touch her. What must she feel like, quivering under his hands?

"Agatha, leave us." His grandmother's acidic tone pulled Hunt out of his delectable reveries. When the dowager duchess spoke in such a manner, someone was going to receive an earful and more.

"Best of luck," Agatha whispered as she left the library.

Hunt was not in the mood to be scolded. "Is something wrong?"

"I might ask you that same question."

"Grandmother, I'm not in the mood for games. I haven't eaten anything all day and my headache's a regular bastard."

"Such language in front of a lady." The dowager huffed. Her bejeweled hand gripped the armrest with surprising strength. "This is why you should have spent the Season in London. Your manners need polishing badly."

"Is that what this is about?"

"Your state of perpetual bachelorhood is what everything is about! You're thirty-six years old, and I have not yet been made a great-grandmother. I'm not long for this world, you know."

"My dear grandmother, Death will never carry you off. I'm certain the Grim Reaper is frightened of you."

"Well, then he has more sense than you," the duchess said tartly. "As has already been amply demonstrated tonight, your lack of propriety and common sense is appalling."

"What do you mean?"

"Why on earth did you invite Miss Winslow to dine with us?"

"Because she's our guest. She is *my* guest in fact, as Moorcliff Castle is my home, and everything and everyone within these walls is mine to oversee. She's Ashworth's governess, whom he practically sees as family, and she's as good as a mother to young Felicity. I've known the woman over ten years. Do you have any idea how rude it would be to send her up to her room with a tray?"

"Are good manners the sole reason you invited her to dine with us? Or have you some other motivation?"

"What the devil do you mean?"

"Don't take that tone with me, young man!" The old lady composed herself with the air of a martyr. "Goodness, you're as impossible as ever. If you are starting to hunger for female company, that thrills me only too much. But if so, you must choose a woman of your own station, not fraternize with a governess!"

"What are you suggesting?" Hunt tended toward good humor in his dealings with people, his family especially. But something in the dowager's words stoked his anger. Was it because she'd dismissed Miss Winslow as a mere servant?

Or because she was correct about his interest?

"Perhaps I've misunderstood your intentions as to the woman."

"You have," he said, "if you imagine anything other than friendly feeling and respect on my part."

"All right." She held up a hand. "Peace, then. I wish only to remind you of the promise you made to your father. That is all."

"Must we trot out his dying words every time an unmarried woman enters this place?" But Hunt recalled the scene clearly.

His father had suffered a stroke, and the doctors had told Hunt, then the Marquess of Roark, to hasten home in time to say farewell. That had been eleven years ago, and after a weeping Agatha and Isabelle gave them the room, the old duke had bidden Hunt kneel beside the bed, hold his hand, and allow the man to whisper into his son's ear.

"Only ever take a true lady," his father had said, "as Moorcliff's mistress. Like your mother. Promise me."

Hunt had given his promise, kissed his father's

forehead, and seven minutes later the old duke was gone. As his father had been the finest gentleman Hunt had ever known, he would die before dishonoring his final request.

Even if he wanted Miss Winslow, he could never have her, not in the honorable way of making her his wife. As she was only a governess, taking liberties with her would be the epitome of callous rakishness.

Then, of course, she was Ashworth's employee and an important member of his household. If Hunt tried anything with the woman, desperate to alleviate the sudden itch of desire, he'd be insulting her and his dear friend.

No, he needed to put Viola Winslow out of his head entirely. He told himself that the moment of desire had been just that, a moment. Nothing more. He hadn't seen a woman to whom he was not related for bloody months on end.

"I see my words have had some effect." His grandmother sounded pleased with herself. She loved nothing more than to be self-congratulatory. That and gardening were the major points of pleasure in her life.

"You're wrong as to my intentions toward Miss Winslow. Anyway, you should welcome the chance to have her at the dinner table. It will make a fine change from my brooding and Isabelle's performances."

The duchess shuddered. "Can't you simply forbid poetry being read aloud at the table?"

"It's the only thing that seems to bring her back to reality these days. I had no idea fifteen-year-old girls were this maudlin! If I'd known, I might have sent her to finishing school until she was eighteen. Or thirty."

"I only hope she's finished that epic about the ghost

stuck down in the well. She claims it's a metaphor for something, but I think it's mere self-indulgence."

Currently, Lady Isabelle's poem "Giselle, the Tragic Ghost" ran to ninety-two stanzas and approximately eighty-seven pages. In it, she had rhymed "Giselle" and "well" too frequently to count and had added the questionable poetic device of repeating sounds to simulate the effect of a voice echoing at the bottom of said well.

"Boo hoo hoo, hoooo hooooo hooo, ooooooooo" had repeated for several pages with no respite. She had insisted on reading every single line.

"Perhaps Miss Winslow can engage her in a discussion. She's very fond of poetry."

"Oh, that's only what we need." The dowager sighed. "An overeducated spinster indulging a moody adolescent."

"Don't call her that," Hunt said.

"I love Isabelle, but she is certainly moody and definitely adolescent!"

"Not Isabelle. Miss Winslow. Don't be dismissive of her like that."

Why should he care so much for what his grandmother said of the governess?

She *was* a spinster, after all; it was a simple fact. She must be twenty-nine or thirty now, and unmarried. Unable to stop himself, Hunt felt desire quicken his blood once again. No man had ever touched Viola—Miss Winslow. He had to call her Miss Winslow and not allow himself any familiarity, not even inside his own mind.

But the formality did nothing to stop his sudden and delicious fantasy of being the first man to ever kiss her neck, to kiss her lips, to slip one hand between her thighs and caress the pearl between her legs. He imagined her voice, weak with ecstasy, as she whispered his name over and over.

Hunt was in danger of growing, er, rigid before his grandmother, and forced himself to calm down.

"You've always been too much of a gentleman for your own good." The dowager tutted. She was quite good at tutting. "There's no need to defend the honor or delicacy of a governess, for heaven's sake."

"I'm of the radical opinion that governesses have feelings the same as wealthy ladies." Hunt really did not like this aspect of his grandmother, even as he loved her. "Careful, Gran. Attitudes like yours are what led to *la révolution* in the first place."

The dowager gave a muffled yelp and put a hand to her heart. "Must you say such appalling things? Really!"

Rattling the dowager was one of the few pleasures Hunt still enjoyed. Grinning, he kissed her cheek and headed for the door. He really must shave and comb his hair into something presentable before dinner.

"Wait!" the duchess said. "There's something more I want to discuss with you."

And he'd been so close to freedom, his hand resting upon the door handle. Hunt gave a beleaguered sigh.

"If this is about Miss Winslow or Giselle, the tragic ghost, might it wait until after dinner?"

"This is about the future of the Huntington line. I assume it's of sufficient importance for a two-minute chat!"

Weary and wary, Hunt looked at his grandmother. She sat in her chair with a militarily straight spine, wearing her jewels as a decorated general might display medals won in armed conflict.

"What is it?" he asked.

"Two days ago, I received a letter from the Viscountess Crawford detailing her eldest daughter's recent triumphs in London. You remember Catherine Crawford, naturally. She's apparently enjoyed quite the successful Season. Three proposals of marriage, one from an earl! She turned them down, of course. After all, there's no reason she shouldn't marry a marquess or higher. She's one of the leading beauties of the *ton* and her bloodlines are impeccable. The Crawford family is almost as old as our own and exactly our sort."

"Grandmother." Hunt's voice was icy with warning.

"I believe she would be very receptive to a marriage proposal from a duke. In addition, she's precisely what we're looking for. She has beauty, breeding, and she's only twenty-two. If you'd spent the Season in London, I doubt you could have found a more perfect bride."

"Why the bloody hell should Lady Crawford be writing to you about all this?"

"Such language! The girl's mother and I agree that it's time for the pair of you to be settled, so why not settle together?"

"Because I have met the young lady on perhaps three occasions and can't remember a single conversation we've shared! I'm not certain spending a lifetime with her will do much good for either of us."

"This isn't about your good, Hunt." The dowager frowned. "Men like you are not only men; you are keepers of a great legacy. Now don't look at me like that. I'm not a monster. Of course I want you to be happy in your marriage."

Yes, like his parents had been. The old Duke and

Duchess of Huntington had been one of the most celebrated love matches of the *ton*.

Hunt had been fortunate not to grow up like Ashworth, the discarded son of two neglectful parents. He'd known a true family, one filled with love and laughter, and he wanted the same for his children. He'd been born into a charmed life, after all, a handsome and healthy man with a title, wealth, and everything he desired.

He wanted perfection. He expected it.

But he also grudgingly knew that the dowager had a point. He had a responsibility to others, not just to himself.

"If you want me to be happy, then stop arranging matches behind my back," he said.

"Oh for pity's sake, I haven't promised you to the girl or the other way around! But really, I see no reason why you should object! We all of us need to move on from that disaster with Miss Fletcher. Once you're married to an appropriate lady, no one will recall that you made such an ass of yourself."

"Thank you, Gran. Tactful as ever."

"Life has dropped a perfect solution into your lap, and you're too stubborn to see it. Remember what you owe to your ancestors! Remember what you promised your father."

Everything his grandmother said was true.

While he wanted happiness for himself, he cared for his family's legacy more. Miss Crawford would likely suit him as well as any other appropriate young lady. If he took her, he'd have companionship and would have fulfilled the promise to his father. His humiliation before the *ton* would be at an end.

But when Hunt pictured this Miss Crawford, he could not help the way her features morphed into

those of Viola Winslow. The idea of seeing the governess at dinner filled him with selfish pleasure.
Despite all the warnings of common sense, he wanted that small, delicately curving woman.

And the knowledge he could never have her was
starting to burn him alive.

"I won't be pushed into anything," he said at last.

"Of course not," the duchess replied. "But do be
sensible, Hunt. That's all I ask."

Sensible. He'd been that way his whole life, the
good-natured and sensible son. The dutiful son. The
man who made sure he wanted only what was appropriate for him to want.

And look where that had bloody got him.

"I can promise to consider Miss Crawford. But I
can't promise to be sensible about anything."

Without waiting for the woman to speak another
word, Hunt walked out the door and let it slam behind him with some force. He stalked the halls as
lightning once again lit up the darkness all around
him. His temper was something foul now, and he still
could not get Viola Winslow out of his damned head.

CHAPTER FIVE

Viola really should have asked Mrs. Moore to wait and show her back downstairs.

After checking on Felicity, she'd neatened herself and redone her hair, not wanting to look a mess at the duke's table.

Thinking of Huntington, she had also allowed Felicity to talk her round to wearing the scarlet ribbon; it made a neat little bow in the middle of her collar, and Felicity claimed it brought out the coloring in Viola's cheeks. For her own part, the governess worried it looked like a splat of tomato.

Now she was clean and beribboned but had also become lost in the winding labyrinth of the hallways. She padded down the main staircase and made a left at the first floor, startled a bit when lightning rippled across the sky and thunder announced itself soon after. She'd forgotten how stormy the north could be.

"Oh!" Viola jumped backward as a face appeared alongside her in that burst of lightning. It was a man's face, with eyes that seemed to question what she was doing here.

Of course, it was a painting. An ancestor from the early part of the last century, she believed.

"How do you do?" she whispered, still feeling light-headed. "Terribly sorry to be skulking about." She shook her head. She did nothing but apologize, even to men made of oil paint and canvas.

Viola had behaved that way around the Duke of Huntington for over ten years, and he'd never looked twice at her. Then tonight, she'd scolded him about William Blake just once and he'd looked thrilled.

Perhaps Viola liked herself better when she could be a bit more forthright. When she didn't need to hold down her head with shame.

"Well. Fine. I'm not sorry, then," she told the painting. It offered her no hint of disapproval, or of any movement whatsoever. It was, after all, a painting. Hands on hips, Viola gave a curt nod. "There. In fact, I find you rather judgmental and unfriendly. How about that?"

In response, the portrait swore with surprising vehemence and vocabulary.

Or rather, the man now storming down the hall toward Viola did.

The Duke of Huntington came striding along the corridor in the grips of an apparently foul mood. In all the years she'd known him, never once had he been anything other than good-tempered, kindly, and polite.

In contrast to that gentleman duke, this one growled something obscene and looked the very devil. It shocked her, but it also made her heart beat faster. She thought again of that earthy, sensual man she'd seen on the hillside earlier today. The duke as she'd known him, or perhaps as she'd imagined him all these years, had been perfect and godlike. This duke was the sort of man she could imagine doing achingly human things, from stubbing a toe to breaking a dish by accident.

Or kissing her. She could scarcely have imagined Huntington really kissing her before, but now...

But now he was almost upon her.

"Your Grace!" she said.

Huntington stopped dead.

"Miss Winslow?" Surprised, he let slip one more

foul word. "God, please forgive my manners. I'm not exactly myself."

"It's quite all right. This is your home. You should not have to perform for me or anyone else."

"That's rather the trick of it, eh?" He gave a short, bitter laugh. "Sometimes I think it's all a bloody performance. Sometimes I can't tell where the real me ends and the damned false one begins!"

Viola knew this was not the thing he wanted to say in front of her. Later he'd resent her for having seen him at such a low point. The best idea would be to apologize for startling him, curtsy, and make a swift exit. But…

Viola had a way of taking others' emotions onto herself. When she was surrounded by happiness, she felt light and almost giddy. Likewise, sadness could sink her spirits for the rest of the day. Right now, her gut felt all twisted up by the duke's presence. She could sense the frustration that boiled under his normally composed exterior.

You shouldn't involve yourself in his affairs. It can't lead to anything good.

She often thought sensible things, but sometimes Viola deplored being sensible.

"What's wrong, Your Grace?"

"Nothing." The answer was short and brusque, and the duke shut his eyes. "Forgive me, Miss Winslow. I've been a beast the entire day."

"You must have something on your mind, then."

Any moment now he'd realize she was being much too forward with him and order her out of his sight. To her surprise, and a rather happy one at that, this wasn't the case.

"Family can be so damned meddlesome, don't you find?"

Oh, meddlesome is a rather light word in my experience.

"Of course, Your Grace."

"Forgive me. My grandmother is an intelligent woman, with the most strident opinions imaginable." The duke leaned his back against the wall right next to his ancestor's portrait. He still had not shaved, and his clothes were no neater than before. He looked so casual now, so relaxed in her presence. It only made her heart race, and that sweet, aching desire built in her body yet again.

"What are her opinions, Your Grace?" *You're playing with fire now, Viola. A handsome fire, to be certain, but you're overstepping the mark.*

"As is the case with all her opinions these days, it's to do with marriage."

A weight crushed her chest. *Of course.* His grief over Miss Fletcher could last only so long. He'd be expected to choose a new bride soon, for the sake of his family and the estate.

"I love the woman, I do. But sometimes it feels like all she sees when she looks at me is that damned title!" The duke rubbed his eyes. "Forgive me, Miss Winslow. You shouldn't be privy to this."

He was exactly right. Even though she ached to know every detail of this supposed argument with the dowager, it was hardly her place to pry.

"I'm sorry for disturbing you, Your Grace."

"I believe I'm the one who disturbed you, not the other way around. Why are you down here, anyway?"

"I, er, got lost on my way to the dining room."

Huntington laughed. Instantly, the foul temper lifted. "We ought to equip our guests with maps."

"Unfortunately, that wouldn't do much good. I have no sense of direction at all." She smiled.

"Felicity loves to tease me about that. You could blindfold her and tell her to point north, and she'd figure it out within seconds. Meanwhile, I couldn't find my own way out of a bag."

The duke laughed warmly. The brooding, furious man had totally vanished by now. "Come. I'll show you the way. I'm afraid Moorcliff's slightly more difficult to navigate than a bag."

They walked in the opposite direction, then took the stairs up to the second floor and headed down another carpeted hallway. There was at least better light up here, which made finding the way much simpler.

"I'm afraid I'll look like a disaster this evening at dinner. My apologies in advance," the duke said.

"Oh no, Your Grace. You…" She stopped just short of saying "You are strikingly handsome in any state." "You should be relaxed in your own home."

"And if we were in *your* home, would you go around not shaving and muttering foul words in front of the guests?"

"I'm fortunate that shaving isn't a pressing concern of mine." She was delighted when he chuckled at that. "But I think if I were in the midst of a personal problem, I'd like to let others know so they could help me."

Viola! You as good as volunteered to aid him!

"Would it be impolite to make an observation as to your character, Miss Winslow?" the duke asked.

All the blood rushed to her head. She'd made a mortifying display of herself.

"Certainly not, Your Grace," she whispered, bracing herself for the blow.

"If you were in the midst of a personal problem, I don't believe you'd ever let another soul know it." He did not sound reproachful. If anything, he sounded like he admired her, which caused her face to heat with pleasure. "I believe you have a good deal of self-control and strength."

To her shock, Viola realized the more she revealed of her true thoughts and feelings to him, the more he seemed to like her. Honestly, she seemed to like herself more as well.

"Well. It's not so much strength, Your Grace, as practicality. Governesses aren't paid to foist their problems onto everyone else."

"I think you'd find being a duke is rather the same in that respect." They both laughed at that.

"Then it seems we're quite similar."

"You know, there are times I've envied your employer. Ashworth has always embraced his own life with the most maddening sense of freedom."

"I remember before he married the duchess," Viola said. "That sense of freedom nearly got him shot on a number of occasions."

"Indeed. Perhaps he's not a perfect example of what I mean, but he's always seemed to know who he is and what he wants." The duke shook his head. "There's nothing in this world so terrifying as to wake up at thirty-six and realize you have no bloody idea what you want."

Viola could not picture that. She'd always been certain of the things she wanted. Freedom from her father, an education, the duke's love. She could have at least some of what she craved.

"Do you…?" Viola shut up at once. "Sorry, Your Grace, I was about to ask something foolish."

"I demand to know it. I enjoy foolishness."

"Oh, no. I shouldn't."

But he stopped Viola in her tracks. He was an imposing and impossibly handsome wall, and she tilted up her chin to meet his eyes. Every time he looked at her, she felt drunk with giddiness.

"I'm afraid we shan't go to dinner until you ask your question, Miss Winslow."

She wrestled a smile. "Isn't it better to starve than to lose one's dignity?"

"When the food is as good as ours, dignity can go hang."

Viola put a hand to her mouth as she laughed. He was teasing her, sporting with her. She felt like one of those debutantes she saw parading in and out of Carter House during the London Season, a rich young miss who flirted with the most handsome, titled men of the *ton*.

"Well. Do you think perhaps you *do* know what you want, only you're denying it to yourself?"

The duke's eyebrows lifted in surprise. "I must confess, that's not what I thought you'd ask."

Oh, damn. Had she perhaps grown too bold? "I'm sorry. What did you think the question would be, Your Grace?"

"There's no need to be sorry. It was a thoughtful question and deserves a thoughtful answer."

"No, I've been talking out of turn ever since you found us on the hill. Please forgive me." Viola had been too forward, too confident, but now the old, fearful version of herself came creeping back. When you displeased people, especially men, they had a way of taking it out in cruel ways. She felt that line across the bottom of her throat start to burn and resisted putting a hand there.

"Miss Winslow, I'm not angry. What I am, now, is curious. I didn't think the Duke or Duchess of Ashworth treated you with disrespect."

"Oh, they don't!" Julia and her husband were two

of the best people Viola knew.

"If you don't stand on ceremony around them, why should you do so with me? Do you think I'm so very different from them, that I'd belittle a governess for voicing a question?"

"Not at all, Your Grace."

This was turning into a nightmare. Viola's most cherished dreams had a way of doing just that.

"Then why can't you meet my gaze or speak easily with me? Have I offended you in some way?"

"Of course not!" She wished a bolt of lightning would burst through the roof and strike her dead. It was fast becoming the only acceptable way out of this conversation.

"I liked the way you spoke to me in the library earlier when you defended Mr. Blake's poetry, much as I like the way you've been speaking to me just now. I feel I've seen an undiscovered side of you. Did you realize that in all the years we've known each other, we've scarcely had a conversation?"

This was much too dangerous. The longer he poked and prodded her, the easier it would be for Viola to let something awful slip, like the way she felt for him. Viola needed to tread carefully.

"It has nothing to do with you, Your Grace. I simply know my position, and I know what's expected of me."

"Strange," the duke said. "You don't seem the sort of woman who loves convention."

"There's a difference between loving something and accepting it," she replied. She hoped someone would walk along and find them here, then point them toward the dining room.

The Duke of Huntington was being more than politely attentive to his guest. He had taken an active interest in her, and it was at once too beautiful to be real and too tragic to be allowed. Hope like this wasn't for women like her.

"For my entire life, I thought the same. It didn't matter how much I wanted to be a duke or how much I wanted anything else. This was my life; it chose me. It was my duty to make the most of it."

"Yes." Her chest ached. He'd summed up the entirety of her experiences.

"Would you agree, then, that I should simply get on with my duty and stop brooding about the castle? Marry a member of the *ton* and sire the next heir to Moorcliff?"

No, I don't agree. I hate that idea. "It's not my place to voice an opinion on that subject, Your Grace."

Viola was startled when for the first time she saw a flash of anger in the duke's visage. *Oh, damn.* She should have kept her bloody mouth shut.

"I wish I could find whoever made you believe that and shake some damn sense into him," Huntington growled.

Oh. His anger had been on her behalf, not directed at her.

"There's no one person to blame, sir. I've known the truth my whole life. A duke is a duke, a governess a governess, and both have their roles to play."

"Yes." The amiable warmth had vanished; he had returned to brooding. He was better at brooding than anyone Viola had ever met. "Much as I loathe it, I don't suppose there's much I could do to change anything, anyway."

"Well. Don't be too sure of that, Your Grace. Mr. Blake would disagree." Viola smiled as he laughed.

"Then I suppose there's no arguing it. Come. The dining room awaits."

She walked alongside Huntington, drinking in every second of his undivided attention. If only she could have put the whole episode into a locket and worn it always around her neck. Her happiness made her bold.

"You mentioned marriage, Your Grace. Have you found the right woman for your duchess?" Her heart banged against her ribs. *Please say no.*

"The dowager duchess thinks she's selected the right one." The duke sighed. "I suppose one young woman will do as well as another."

"Ah." Viola wondered if she could feign a sudden headache and disappear for the rest of the night.

"That was the great mistake I made last year." The duke shrugged, even that powerful motion poetry to watch. "I thought I'd marry for love after waiting for the perfect girl all those damned years." He scoffed. "I should have realized sooner. Love's a matter of choice and habit, not actual feeling."

"No, that's not true at all." Viola stopped, horrified. "Love is quite real. It can hurt as terribly as it can cause joy." She thought of how Huntington still pined for Susannah after all this time, and she felt ever more exhausted. "I understand, though, how you must be feeling, Your Grace. It's painful when you love a person who doesn't return your affection."

Huntington stopped beneath the portrait of his grandfather. Viola saw how remarkably similar they appeared, both strong-jawed, both with similar mouths resting in similar smiles. The duke must have seen mirrored reflections of his own face along these halls for decades. No wonder he felt trapped in a life pre-chosen for him.

"You've made me realize something, Miss Winslow. When Miss Fletcher rejected my proposal, it hurt bitterly. But my sadness at losing her lasted only a short while; my real pain came from embarrassment. I'd looked a fool before society."

"Yes, Your Grace?" Viola felt swift relief upon hearing that his feelings had altered. Still, she wasn't positive what he was driving at.

"If I'd truly loved her, could I have gotten past the pain of her absence so quickly? Perhaps love, even passionate love, can last only a short time."

"No. Forgive me, sir. I meant only to say that love is very real, and it endures. If it's true, it endures anything."

"Do you speak from experience, Miss Winslow?"

Thank God they were in a darkened hall; if he'd seen her blushing, he'd have known what was in her heart right away.

"No, Your Grace. I know someone else who, er, loved another someone else who couldn't love them back." Viola prayed she would not break out in a cold sweat. Lying disagreed with her.

"I see." Huntington sounded thoughtful. Then he extended his arm. "Shall we?"

"Your Grace?"

"It's customary for a man to escort a lady to dinner. So. Shall we, Miss Winslow?"

She should have refused, but Viola was enjoying the attention he was paying her far too much. Oh, why not? When the storm cleared tomorrow, the world would go back to normal. Tonight, she could allow herself a few moments of bliss.

"Thank you, Your Grace." She laid her arm through his and practically floated to the dining room.

CHAPTER SIX

Hunt wished that Viola was not a governess; he wished that his family was not seated around the table with them, behaving in the strangest manner possible; he especially wished that Cornelius would stop flapping about the room only to perch on the back of Agatha's chair and croak for a piece of meat.

Hunt didn't want any distractions from Miss Winslow just now. Every time he spoke with her, he wished for the conversation to lengthen.

He snuck as many glances as possible toward her from the head of the table.

Why the devil hadn't he noticed her beauty before tonight? Her heart-shaped face with its large, upturned hazel eyes proved an endless delight to consider. He didn't know when she'd tied that bit of red silk ribbon to her collar, but it only accented the healthy blush now stealing across her cheeks.

She sat with as much quiet dignity as a queen, and her hands were small and delicately made. She'd a gorgeous figure; even her prim governess's clothes could not disguise entirely the lissome curves of her body, the swell of her bosom especially. He wondered how that dark brown hair would look taken out of its severe style. He wanted that hair to spill along his hands; he wanted to grab fistfuls of it while he pressed his mouth to hers, one ravishing kiss after the next.

She was so demure, so sly in her own way. She dodged and feinted questions with a practiced ease.

Yet she could also grow flustered, particularly when talk turned to love.

"Knickers," said Cornelius, which broke Hunt's sublime fantasies straightaway.

"Honestly! Must that bird sit with us during dinner?" His grandmother frowned at the raven as Agatha fed him a bite of lamb. "Don't, Agatha! He's worse than a dog."

"Yes. Dogs sometimes fly and swoop toward the table," Isabelle said, only half-listening to the conversation as usual. She'd pushed her plate out of the way and was writing. They allowed her to keep paper and ink beside her during mealtimes. Hunt's little sister needed to be always prepared for a burst of inspiration.

"What on earth do you mean 'sometimes,' Isabelle? Dogs never fly!" The dowager was losing her patience, a not uncommon sight.

"Just because we've never seen one fly doesn't mean it's impossible." Isabelle gasped, lost in a sudden thought. "Oh! That's just what my poem needs." She began writing again, muttering the words as she went along. "I thought that I should never spy/a puppy that had learned to fly/but now he's barking in the air/and barking, barking everywhere."

Lady Isabelle Montagu often sat in silence, scribbling away until she was prepared to recite her newest masterwork to her captive audience. Unlike most girls her age, Isabelle refused to put up her hair. She liked weaving it in a messy, golden braid, or else left it in a tangle about her shoulders. She believed in living for her art completely and devoted her whole energy to it.

Agatha had once found Isabelle in the bath with flowers in her damp hair and petals strewn along the top of the water. When asked what the devil she thought she was doing, Isabelle had replied that she was writing a poem about *Hamlet*'s Ophelia and thought pretending to drown beautifully would lend a greater realism to her project. The final version had been called "Ophelia's Bathtub" and was about how much happier everyone in *Hamlet* would have been if they could have enjoyed a nice hot bath.

Hunt really needed to find another governess for his sister. The last one had quit after Isabelle's attempted séance had gone so badly wrong. They were never going to get the water stains out of the ceiling.

Normally, everyone would politely ignore Isabelle, but to Hunt's surprise Miss Winslow took an interest.

"I didn't realize His Grace had a poetess in the family," the governess said.

"Oh, I do prefer to be called a poet, if you don't mind." Isabelle sighed dreamily. "I believe that poetry is the food of the soul, and there is no difference between a man's soul and a woman's."

"I quite agree," Miss Winslow said. Hunt smiled. He did, as well.

The dowager snorted. "Another radical notion, I take it?" She chewed a bite of potato with an air of restrained menace. Hard to do that with a potato.

"Oh, leave Miss Winslow be, Granny." Agatha smiled across the table at the governess. "She's entitled to an opinion, as we all are."

"In *my* day, you weren't allowed an opinion until you owned land." The duchess sniffed. "That was when we had sense."

"Vive la révolution," Agatha called through

cupped hands.

The dowager dropped her fork and put a hand over her bejeweled chest, a standard reaction to that little bit of French. Isabelle giggled raucously, as did Agatha.

"Oh, I do love it when she does that," the girl said.

Hunt's grandmother took a large gulp of wine to restore herself while a footman hurriedly provided her with a new fork.

"As you can see, Miss Winslow," Hunt said as the raven landed atop his chair, "we're all quite mad here."

"Knickers," added Cornelius.

Miss Winslow had been covering up her laughter with a napkin the last two minutes. Mirth brightened her eyes, making them somehow more beautiful.

"May I ask about the raven?" she said when everyone had calmed down. "He's a rather unusual family pet."

"Yes, Cornelius is an odd one," Agatha said. "He's nearly as old as I am, and almost as eccentric."

"My goodness." Miss Winslow seemed surprised.

"Ravens can live over fifty years in captivity," Hunt said. "Though in Cornelius's case, I believe it's the other way around. He is holding *us* captive."

The raven flapped his wings, ruffled his neck feathers, and spoke.

"There once was a duchess of Kent
Whose income was less than she spent
To make her ends meet
She took to the street
And now she's a duchess for Rent."

Oh God, no. Agatha and Isabelle laughed in horror while their grandmother looked ready to faint.

Miss Winslow, however, seemed only too delighted.

"Who taught him that?" she asked.

"We think it was our grandfather," Agatha said. "He was fond of poetry. It seems talent runs in the family, Isabelle."

"Limericks are not true poetry!" Isabelle tossed her head in indignation.

"Must we endure bawdy rhymes at the dinner table?" the dowager asked in a beleaguered fashion.

Hunt took her point and asked a footman to escort the family raven from the room. The poor lad did so, staring at Cornelius in wonder as he fed the bird morsels of lamb.

"Where do you come from, Miss Winslow?" Agatha asked.

"Somerset nowadays, Yorkshire before that, for my education." Viola cleared her throat; she seemed a bit uncomfortable. "But the first eight years of my life were spent in Northumberland."

She'd told him that when they first met on the road to Lynton Park. It seemed the longer he spoke to Viola Winslow, the more memories he recovered from their initial meeting. Why hadn't he noticed then how sublime she was?

"Oh?" the duchess said drily. "I'd no idea you came from the area. I don't recall meeting any local Winslows."

"We wouldn't have moved in the same circles, Your Grace. My father was a solicitor in Hexham. After his death, I was sent away to school." The governess turned all her attention to her plate. Undoubtedly, the memory of the man's death still hurt. Hunt could certainly relate.

"Yes. I daresay the law is a gentlemanly occupation." The dowager cut delicately at her meat. "If one *must* have an occupation."

"Of course Miss Winslow's father was a gentleman," Hunt said to his grandmother, trying not to be short. "His daughter is evidence of that fact." He felt the way Miss Winslow appraised him, the shy interest that she took. That was the great tragedy of governesses, after all.

They were gentlewomen of good breeding who, without husbands or dowries, were forced to fend for themselves and instruct the more fortunate daughters of society in the art of being a lady. In truth, Miss Winslow's intelligence and manners were so remarkable, Hunt struggled to accept she wasn't the impoverished daughter of some landed, titled gentleman.

"There. Done." Isabelle put down her pen and neatened a stack of ten to fifteen pages. Oh dear. They might be stuck here until the sun came up over the horizon. Isabelle liked to take her time when reciting poetry. She claimed the words were never perfect until she knew they sounded good on the tongue. "Now, who would care to hear the culminating action of 'Giselle, the Tragic Ghost?'"

The three other Montagus swapped quick glances, each trying to urge the other to come up with a solution. To Hunt's surprise, but not his amazement, Miss Winslow spoke.

"Oh dear," the governess said. "And I've not heard the opening of the poem. I shan't be able to understand it at all." *There's no chance of you understanding it ever,* Hunt thought. *You could listen to it five times over and be more confused after every recitation.* "You did say it was a poem, yes?"

"Indeed. I hope to one day become England's first lady poet laureate."

"Lord, save us all," the dowager muttered into her wineglass.

"What a grand ambition!" Miss Winslow said. "I shall certainly be on the lookout for your publications. I'm immensely fond of poetry myself."

"Oh!" Isabelle clapped both hands to her mouth. "Would you like to read 'Giselle, the Tragic Ghost' in its entirety? I should love for someone with taste to judge my work."

"Don't bother the woman, Isabelle," the dowager said. "She has her own charge to attend to. She cannot make time for your poems."

"Yes. Little girls are a handful." Isabelle sounded disappointed.

"Not so little at all. My charge is just about your own age, my lady," Viola said.

"Oh? Really?" Isabelle clutched a page to her chest. "Is she as enthusiastic for the written word as I?"

"Felicity is, er, a voracious reader," Miss Winslow said carefully. "I left her upstairs with a book."

"Miss Berridge is the young lady who injured her ankle today," Hunt said. To his baffled delight, his younger sister grew more excited by the minute. It was so hard to get Isabelle to pay attention to the world around her these days.

"Oh, may I meet her? I never meet anyone my own age up at Moorcliff. Ever since Miss Simpson, my last governess, left, I've been ever so starved for company."

"I'm certain you can meet her tomorrow before we take our leave," Miss Winslow said.

Hunt knew it was right that she should leave.

It would be improper, not to mention lightly dangerous, for Viola Winslow to remain in this place while he wrestled with his ever-growing attraction to her. But he could have shouted his glee when Agatha frowned and spoke up.

"Why must you run off tomorrow?"

"Felicity and I are touring the north on a sketching expedition of sorts. We've spent the past three weeks traveling. We began in Derbyshire, then on into Cheshire. We've sketched the wildest country we could find in Yorkshire, and we've reached the pinnacle of our journey here in Northumberland."

"But is there any reason you must leave us so soon?" Agatha was a persistent and bothersome elder sister. Hunt usually endured such qualities, but right now he was grateful for them. "There's no reason to rush off if the girl's ankle needs to heal. I doubt the child should be moved for several days, or even a week."

A week. An entire week with Viola, that is, with Miss Winslow kept close to him would be paradise itself.

Hunt liked to applaud himself for being very self-controlling, but all that control could go hang now. He'd never known an appetite like this before, not even at the height of his infatuation with Susannah. The more time he spent listening to Viola, enjoying her conversation and beauty, the harder it was to imagine ever wanting anyone else.

He was greedy for her presence. He wanted to keep her in his castle like a monster from a faerie story. He wouldn't touch her, he swore to himself he would not, but if she left now it would drive him mad. And madness was less than a drive away and more a short walk these days.

"I don't think we should impose on Your Grace's hospitality like that," Viola said, appearing alarmed.

Was she afraid of him? Why should she be so

ready to leave? They seemed to get on well together, didn't they? Unless she was afraid of them getting on together rather too well.

"Why not?" Hunt asked. "I'd be only too happy to have you and Miss Berridge stay on until she's fully recovered."

"But we shouldn't impose," Miss Winslow said, already sounding overpowered. He was a monster for this, but Hunt wanted to overpower her. He wanted to feel the hot blood rushing in his veins as he took her in his arms, felt the delighted quivering of her body, the ecstasy in her kiss.

He imagined running his hands along her legs, parting her silken thighs, and then…and then Ashworth would appear out of nowhere and shoot him through the heart, as he would have every right to do.

"It's no imposition," Hunt said. "It's not as though we haven't enough room."

"Really, Hunt. You shouldn't keep poor Miss Winslow here against her will." His grandmother pursed her lips. She wanted the young woman gone so that Hunt could resign himself to Miss Crawford and a lifetime of duty.

He should send Viola away, but he already knew he'd fight to keep her here. At long last, he was giving himself what he wanted. Even if his bliss lasted a few short days, he wanted her with him.

"Are you a prisoner, Miss Winslow?" he asked.

"No, Your Grace." She was an intelligent woman, and he could already see the dawning realization in her eyes that there was no polite way out of this. "But… Well, that is…"

"Yes?"

"I'm certain Felicity could recover at the inn. It really is a cozy place."

"Oh nonsense," Agatha said, barreling on as was her usual way. Hunt could have kissed her in gratitude. "It's far cozier here, believe me. And if sketching's what you want, it would be easy to find any number of picturesque spots about Moorcliff and its grounds. It would be no trouble at all to take the girl anywhere she pleased and allow her to sketch away. If you stay at the inn, she'll be holed up in one room the entire week drawing pictures of the ceiling. A boring idea, that."

"Yes." Viola sighed. "And Felicity hates to be bored. But…all our things are back at the inn!"

"Easily managed," Agatha said with a shrug. "Tomorrow when the roads are clear we'll send a servant to pack your things and bring them to Moorcliff. It's no trouble at all."

"Oh, do stay!" Isabelle clasped her hands in pleading. "I want to meet this Miss Berridge, and I should love to have an admirer of poetry read my work. None of my governesses ever believed in my potential."

"Why, how very wrong!" Miss Winslow frowned; her indignation was authentic. "Young artists always require encouragement."

"Oh, I should love it if you would stay. Please?" Isabelle adopted that whimpering puppy look Hunt and Agatha could not seem to resist. It was hard to deny their youngest sibling anything.

"Your Grace, this wouldn't be too much trouble?" Viola asked.

"I assure you, Miss Winslow. Nothing could give me greater pleasure."

"Well, what an occurrence. What an occurrence," the dowager muttered, now sawing away at her lamb in a state of obvious irritation.

"Then thank you, Your Grace. We would be

delighted to accept." A shy smile ornamented her face and brightened her eyes.

Hunt barely recalled another word anyone spoke to him at the table that night. He scarcely touched another bite of food or sip of wine; the pleasure of Miss Winslow's presence was all that was needed to satisfy him.

• • •

Viola shouldn't have allowed this.

Not just staying on, but also allowing the duke to escort her back to her room. He'd offered on the pretense that she might get lost in the labyrinth of Moorcliff again. The duchess had said rather tartly that a servant could show Miss Winslow the way, but Huntington had replied it was no bother at all.

She couldn't believe how natural it felt to talk with him.

Her thoughts swam about almost drunkenly as she picked over her memories of the last two hours. Until this afternoon, her picture of the Duke of Huntington had been unchanged for over a decade. He was the most handsome man alive, as perfect and unchanging as the statue of a god. But that image had begun to shift ever so slightly.

His rather rough appearance had kindled an almost bestial hunger in her; Viola still quivered to imagine his lips upon hers, his hands caressing her body. Such thoughts stirred keen, almost wanton, desires she'd never experienced before.

Then there was the pleasure of his company. His Grace's manners were all ease and charm. Well, almost all. He could be so human, she realized, in his spectrum of emotions. He swore, he'd a temper, but then he became pleasant and attentive. Above everything else, Viola felt she'd finally gotten a true glimpse into the duke as he was.

He was more than a god; he was a man. A beautiful, brilliant man.

As he led her along the winding halls of Moorcliff, chatting about Isabelle's poetry and the antiques they passed in recessed alcoves, Viola felt the ache in her chest reach a new pinnacle of blissful pain.

She'd been in love with a phantom for years. Now that she was filling in the details of him, she was beginning to like him. Truly like him, which was even more frightening than love in its own strange way.

"You seem pensive," the duke said with a frown. "Are you ill?"

"No, Your Grace. I'm only tired. It's been an eventful day."

"Do sleep well, then. My sisters were both serious in their plans for you this week. Agatha will carry Felicity around herself if she must, while I'm certain Isabelle will have you locked up and reading every verse she's ever written. You may have stumbled into a trap, Miss Winslow," he teased.

"I love to read young people's work, especially young women. Our world encourages them in such a narrow set of interests and discourages everything else. I think it's wonderful that Lady Isabelle wishes to be poet laureate. Even if her natural talent is rough, it's good to critique and encourage rather than denigrate."

The duke seemed pleased by this last remark. "You're a singular individual, Miss Winslow," he said. "I doubt I'll ever meet another person like you."

They'd stopped outside of the room she shared with Felicity.

His Grace was holding a candlestick to light their way along the stormy halls. Viola faced the massive gentleman, unsure who should say or do what first.

"Well. Good night, Your Grace. Thank you," she whispered.

Viola made a curtsy, keeping her eyes low. She stared at the tips of the duke's boots. They did not move.

"Thank *you*, Miss Winslow. This is the finest day I've had in many months." Huntington took her hand and pressed his lips to it.

The sensation was nothing untoward or disrespectful, but the touch of his mouth was still scintillating.

"I could say the same, sir."

Again, he lingered.

Should she perhaps pretend to swoon and have him catch her like a heroine in one of Felicity's ridiculous chilling tales?

He seemed intent on her, more serious than ever before. He seemed to hesitate on what to do. Perhaps he was debating whether to kiss her…

"Good night." The duke bowed his head and strode away.

Viola slumped against the door, relieved her knees hadn't given out on her in his presence. "You need to stop this," she whispered to herself as she pressed her forehead against the cool wood. "You can't embarrass yourself here."

She entered the room to find the place in shambles.

The window was open, rain spattering inside and dampening the carpet. Pillows had been flung all over the place, the bedclothes were in a tangle, and

Felicity was lying upon her back staring up at the ceiling with a frown.

The book had been thrown to the side of the room and lay with its spine broken and some pages bent. The dinner tray had been picked clean. She'd also torn pages from the sketchbook and had left charcoal pencils scattered on the floor.

Felicity had evidently tried to draw something over and over, crumpling her attempts into a ball and tossing them away.

"Felicity Berridge!"

The girl sat up and swore with creative vulgarity as Viola rushed over and shut the window. She closed the curtains and then stood over the bed.

"What on earth do you think you're doing?" Viola cried.

"You left me alone for *hours*! I was dreadful bored after I finished the book. Then I ate supper, and then the place was too stuffy and hot, so I had to open a window!"

"And fling the cushions all over the place?"

"It was something to do, wasn't it? Anyway, how was dinner? Did anyone comment on the ribbon I gave you?"

Felicity was less than pleased with the governess's replies: dinner was fine; the duke was fine company; the rest of his family was delightful; the food was excellent.

"I want details!" Felicity huffed in frustration. "I wish I could have been there. Trying to get the full tale out of you is bloody impossible."

"Don't use that word, young lady."

"Fine. It's bloody difficult."

"Well, I'm certain you'll have ample opportunity to judge for yourself. His Grace extended an invitation for us to stay at Moorcliff while you recover, and I've agreed."

Felicity let out the wildest cheer of triumph before collapsing back onto the cushions. It was absolutely mystifying.

"If I'd known you'd such a desire to see the castle, I'd have recommended you come along when the Duke of Ashworth visits! He would certainly prove easier company for the Duke of Huntington's family."

"I'm so glad we're staying." Felicity beamed, displaying all her teeth in a rather aggressive smile.

"This is still a sketching holiday, I'll remind you. Even if you're confined to the sofa, I'll expect you to work on your pencils."

"Oh, never fear. I practiced my sketching while you were at dinner. I thought you'd be pleased." Felicity snatched up a crumpled ball of paper from the floor and held it out as if providing Viola with a precious gift. She had drawn a woman fainting in a churchyard, a skull hovering over her in the air as it screamed and dripped blood. "From the *Bloody Skull of Urlich Castle*. You always say literature gives us the best subjects."

As she massaged her temples, Viola thought that at least life was normal whenever Felicity was about.

CHAPTER SEVEN

The duke lay atop her, pinning Viola to the bed with his muscled weight.

She could feel the pressure of his body between her legs, the burning ache she experienced as he lowered his head to kiss her. He murmured endearments, heated whispers of how gorgeous she looked. His lips caressed the soft flesh of her throat, and Viola realized that she was entirely without clothes now.

She'd never felt anyone's naked flesh against hers, and moaned in ecstasy as he moved against her, as the friction heated her whole body, as her mouth burned upon his and—

And then he kicked her in the hip. *Odd*.

Viola was punted out of the dream as she opened her eyes. *Oh dear*. She remembered where she was, in Moorcliff Castle.

She put a hand to her flushed face, embarrassed at how excited a dream had made her.

The kick had been administered to her by Felicity who was, thankfully, still dead asleep. The child's mouth hung open, a thin line of drool shimmering upon her chin.

One arm was flung over her eyes, and her wild black hair twisted along the pillows like a mass of snakes. Felicity gave one rattling snort, smacked her lips, and dreamed deeper. Her side of the bed was rumpled with her tossing. The girl slept more actively than most people did anything while they were awake.

Viola had been crowded to one far corner of the mattress during the night. Shaking her head, she got up and rubbed her eyes.

A bright line of light pierced through the heavy curtain, and when Viola shoved the curtains back, she could have cried out for joy.

The day ahead was a bright autumnal blue, not a cloud in sight. The rain had scrubbed the air thoroughly, so the hills around the castle rolled along the horizon with sharp visibility. Viola opened the window and poked out her head, shut her eyes, and inhaled.

She'd missed the Northumberland air. In the fall, you could drink it down as clear and cool as a glass of water. Everything had always seemed fresher in the north. There was also a more rugged beauty to the terrain.

She loved Somerset with its green fields and picturesque villages, but everything felt so safe and comfortable down there. Up here, you could feel the natural world bristling. Viola tilted her head, loving the whisper of the wind across the hills.

Then she heard the thump of hooves and looked down to watch the duke cantering by on a black horse. He'd dressed casually for a morning ride, the sunlight glinting on his golden hair. Viola's lips parted as she watched him ride away from Moorcliff, taking his stallion along a muddy but clear road into town.

She felt that pressure between her legs again, the same as she'd had in her dream. Quickly, she ducked inside and shut the window. She'd soon have to fix this infatuation. She wasn't about to humiliate herself by showing what she felt.

In her experience, the moment a man knew what

you wanted, he could easily control you. Your dignity rested in his hands. She liked the duke, but she
didn't trust anyone that much.

"Owww, put out the bloody light!" Felicity
yowled like a feral cat as she rolled onto her stomach and jammed the pillow over her head. She
whined and complained as Viola took the pillow
away.

"You'll be pleased to know that it's morning and
time to get up."

"I can't get up, remember? My ankle's twisted."
Felicity glared up with those feline eyes of hers and
stuck out her lower lip. She was an imp, an alley cat,
and a hurricane, all in one bony, adolescent package.

"A metaphorical getting up, then."

"A person can't perform metaphors." Felicity
yawned, showing her whole mouth of teeth in a
shocking display of roughness. "That stuff's just in
books."

"Fine." Viola went to pour a basin of water for
washing. "Then I suppose you'll have to sit here
alone the entire day while I spend time with all the
people in this castle."

"Oh, that's no fair!" Felicity tossed the pillow at
Viola, which missed her by a wide margin. "You
can't leave me chained up in this place all day! I
shall pull off the wallpaper."

"You will do no such thing." Viola made certain
not to smile; manipulating Felicity could be rather
fun. "If you promise to be very good, I might find
some people to carry you downstairs to the breakfast room. But only if you wash and dress with quiet
enthusiasm."

Felicity went about her morning rituals with
Viola's help as quietly as possible. Viola rang for a

servant, and soon a pair of footmen carried Felicity
between them as though she were a queen upon an
ambulatory throne. The girl adored the special treatment and went wild with excitement when she saw
what awaited them downstairs.

"A wheeled chair! Oh, this is bloody brilliant,"
Felicity said as the footmen deposited her in the
contraption.

The chair was made of wicker with a cushioned
seat and back along with a pair of handles on the
top, useful for anyone who wished to push the girl
about. Felicity began grabbing at the wheels to either side of her, huffing as she attempted to throw
herself this way or that.

"Felicity! Let one of us guide the chair, please,"
Viola said. "Thank you, Mrs. Moore."

The housekeeper beamed. "I'm only glad to give
it some use. We've had this since His Grace's father
first grew ill more than twelve years ago. He needed
a great deal of care and attention at the end, poor
man." She sighed. "I suppose we should've let this
go, but the children do like to keep every memento
of their parents that they can."

The children. Mrs. Moore had clearly served the
Montagu family a long while and seemed to dote on
Huntington and his sisters. It was easy to see why.
They were eccentric in their own ways, but also caring
and warm.

Except, of course, for the dowager. Viola knew
Her Grace did not like having a governess treated as
a guest in Moorcliff Castle. Politely avoiding conversation with the duchess this week would be wise.

Felicity twisted her head this way and that, gawking at the portraits and other treasures that lined the
corridors as she was wheeled along.

Finally, two footmen opened a pair of doors and ushered them into a lovely room papered in yellow silk, with the strong autumn sunlight glinting through the window. A buffet was laid to one end of the room with eggs, ham, tea and coffee and toast and every other delicious option.

The duke obviously was not there, and neither, thankfully, was the dowager.

Lady Agatha and Lady Isabelle were both seated at the table. The elder woman read a newspaper, while the younger slouched with her head in her hand and wrote another poem. Viola had to admire the young girl's industry, even if she believed the quality would be a bit dubious.

"Good morning, Miss Winslow!" Agatha folded her paper and smiled. "And hello, Miss Berridge. How is your ankle today?"

"Much better, my lady." The girl glanced about the room. "Is it just us for breakfast?"

Viola frowned. "Who on earth did you wish to see?"

"I was just hoping the duke would join us. I'd like to thank him for all his hospitality."

"That's very sweet, but unnecessary." Lady Agatha smiled. "My brother was only too happy to invite you to stay, as was I."

"So he's not going to be here soon?" Felicity pouted.

"He's out for his morning ride at the moment. He rarely breakfasts with us."

"Well. I suppose that's that, then."

Felicity's desire to see Huntington almost led Viola to the bemusing conclusion that the young girl had formed an infatuation. That was sweet, if foolish, and Viola hoped Felicity wouldn't prove a spectacle.

The last thing they wanted was to embarrass themselves.

"I'm sorry you won't be able to explore the castle as fully as you might like," Lady Agatha said. "A sprained ankle is a terrible impediment to a young lady with spirit."

"True. But it's all right; I've got my ways to get about. Look! This chair is bloody brilliant." Felicity gloated as the footman pushed her to the table.

"Felicity, do not use the word 'bloody' in conversation!" Viola whispered.

"It's more than fine." Lady Agatha laughed. "Cornelius says worse things every day."

"Who's Cornelius?" Felicity asked as Viola placed some toast and tea before her.

"A raven," Lady Agatha said. "He has the run of the house."

"Oh, brilliant! I've always wanted to see a raven up close." Felicity spread copious amounts of butter on her toast. "Genus corvus, largest being the corvus corax, or common raven, and the corvus crassirostris, the thick-billed raven." Felicity looked satisfied with herself, a common sight. "I'm right, aren't I, Miss Winslow?"

"Indeed." Viola began lightly tapping the shell of a soft-boiled egg with her spoon. "And what do we call a group of ravens?"

"A conspiracy! Or a treachery, or an unkindness. I rather like conspiracy myself. I should love to be part of a conspiracy one day." Felicity sighed in pleasure.

"My word." Lady Agatha appeared impressed. "How surprising to find a young girl with that type of knowledge."

"Felicity is a most precocious young lady," Viola

said. "Precocious" was a nice word for "irrepressible." "I doubt there's any girl in the *ton* who could
match her enthusiasm for the biological sciences,
engineering, or mathematics."

"I'm also partial to reading about arson," Felicity
said, piling raspberry jam onto her densely buttered
toast. "And haunted castles."

"My word." Agatha seemed to be too stunned for
any other words. "I'm sure you and Isabelle will
have much to talk about."

Lady Isabelle had quit her writing and now
stared across the table at Felicity.

The older girl appraised the younger as one wild
animal might another, sniffing about, trying to ascer-
tain the best way to approach. Felicity, meanwhile,
finally noticed the other young lady's presence.

"Oh! Hello." Felicity took an ungainly bite of her
toast. At least she chewed and swallowed before her
next words. "What are you writing?"

"Poetry," Isabelle said.

"What's it about?"

"The tragic ghost of a girl who drowned in a
well."

Felicity chewed another mouthful and nodded.
Isabelle had passed an important test. "I like ghosts.
Especially when they come back from the dead and
haunt the people who wronged them in life. Or
murder them. I do love a juicy murder."

Viola felt another headache coming on.

"Perhaps it would be thrilling if Giselle murdered
her treacherous half-brother," Isabelle mused.

"Always have a murder." Felicity crammed the
rest of the toast in her mouth and washed it down
with a gulp of tea. Viola and the Duchess of
Ashworth had struggled for years to improve

Felicity's table manners. The results were decidedly mixed. "Have you got any ghosts around here? I hear castles are lousy with them."

"Felicity," Viola warned, but Isabelle seemed only pleased.

"There's the one in the east wing! So many people around here don't believe in her, though." Isabelle turned reproachful eyes on her elder sister.

"Rubbish. I believe you."

"Did you sleep well, Miss Winslow?" Lady Agatha asked, obviously trying to steer the conversation away from the occult.

Viola thought again of that sinfully delicious dream of the duke lying atop her, kissing her and thrusting his body against hers. She cleared her throat.

"I did. I always seem to rest easier in the north." Viola added a sprinkle of salt and pepper to her egg. Though she searched for a different topic of conversation, all she could think about was Huntington. "I happened to see His Grace when he was riding out earlier this morning."

"Yes, that's always been Hunt's routine. Even when we were children, he was practically half a horse."

"Where does he go?" Viola remembered how informal she was being and winced. "Not that it's my business."

"Not at all. He never seems to set out with a destination in mind. I think it's his way of clearing his head before the day begins." Agatha chuckled as she turned a page of her paper. "Normally he keeps to such a schedule, it's good to see him add some unpredictability to his day. Well, he used to keep such a schedule. That debacle with Miss Fletcher shook him up quite badly."

Viola sipped her tea and thought again of how Huntington had spoken of Susannah last night. He'd realized his love for her had not lasted long once she had left him. Was he right? Was human affection that easy to shake? Was Viola's long and unceasing love of him only a sign of how malformed she truly was?

This was hardly the kind of cheerful thinking for breakfast. Viola needed action to get her mind outside herself again.

"May I borrow the carriage to go into town and collect our things?" she asked Agatha.

"Of course! Though you needn't go yourself, you know. The servants are more than capable of packing your belongings and returning them."

"Yes, it's too lovely a day to just rush about doing errands," Felicity said. "I want to see how well this chair rolls outside. Perhaps we could go sketching beside a mausoleum, or another decaying ruin!"

"We've got a few of those!" Isabelle said with evident delight.

"Well, perhaps that's a better use of my time, then." Viola smiled.

"Yes, absolutely. Who knows, maybe Hunt will be able to settle things for you at the inn himself," Lady Isabelle said.

"Why's that?" Felicity frowned.

"He's riding to Moorcliff Village to purchase more ink for me. I saw him as he was leaving and asked him. He'll be in town anyway."

"What a good brother," Viola said.

"He spoils Isabelle." Agatha chuckled.

"Miss Winslow?" Felicity shoved herself back from the table, almost rolling into a footman. "I just remembered. Would you go to the inn after all? I think I left my best set of drawing pencils behind, and I should hate for someone to overlook them while packing."

"Oh. Of course I will." Viola was puzzled. "But I thought you were keen to hunt for ancient ruins."

"Oh, they're ancient. If they've been around that long, they'll keep a while longer. Besides, I want to see about this haunted wing." She glanced at Isabelle. "You said there's a ghost?"

"Yes! She has a wonderfully tragic story." Lady Isabelle shot to her feet. "I do love tragedies."

"Let's go, then. I want to see where she lives." Felicity seemed quite comfortable giving the young lady orders in her own home, but Isabelle herself appeared only too delighted to oblige. The poetess gathered her pages and hurried to push Felicity in her chair.

"Remember, young lady, we are here on a sketching trip," Viola said as the girls began to run and roll out of the breakfast room. "We shall find a quiet spot sometime this afternoon and continue yesterday's exercise. And do not under any circumstances break anything or injure yourself more! Do you hear me?"

"Yes, Miss Winslow," Felicity called, sounding like a martyr as Isabelle pushed her out the door and down the hall. Lady Agatha laughed as she poured herself a cup of coffee.

"I do hope they'll be all right." Viola sighed. "My apologies, my lady. I must seem a terrible governess."

"Hardly. The girl has retained some grit and originality. I imagine that's owing to you."

"No, that's all Felicity. She was born knowing exactly who she is. I envy her that."

"You wouldn't be alone." Lady Agatha looked

sympathetic. "You're not really going to Moorcliff Village just for drawing pencils, are you?"

"I do like to keep busy. If Felicity and Lady Isabelle will be enjoying themselves the rest of the morning, I'll need an occupation. Besides, I think it's good for Felicity to spend time with girls her own age." Viola sighed. "I do wish she weren't so isolated."

"It's surprising how little we know about her, considering Hunt and the Duke of Ashworth are such friends."

Not that *surprising.* Felicity was the illegitimate daughter of an earl, and Ashworth had agreed to keep her parentage secret.

"I suppose everyone's entitled to their mysteries," Viola said.

"Too true."

When breakfast had concluded, Lady Agatha ordered the coach to take Viola to town. The duke still had not returned from his ride by the time she was setting off. Last night Viola had been terrified at the thought of spending time with Huntington, and today she couldn't help but yearn to see him again.

You mustn't be foolish.

But Viola remembered again and again how he'd kissed her hand, and how the duke had looked at her and spoken to her. He'd enjoyed her presence; of that she was certain. Then again, how eager could he be to see her if he rode off for hours in the morning and missed breakfast?

• • •

Villagers stared in mystification as the duke's carriage arrived before the Bull and Tartan Inn. Viola went upstairs with a footman and helped him sort everything into their cases quickly and easily. She located Felicity's pencil case beneath the bed and wondered how on earth it had gotten there. They hadn't brought a great deal of luggage, and the man loaded up the coach quickly while Viola settled things with the innkeeper.

First, there was the matter of two letters that had come yesterday while the women had been out.

One was from Lynton Park, probably the duchess writing to keep Felicity informed of all the little goings on. The other was a massive surprise, so much so that Viola nearly dropped the envelope.

It was from Betsy.

When they'd first stopped here at the inn, Viola had written a brief letter telling her sister that she was in the area. The family lived so close that it seemed only right to let her sister and the children know when she was nearby...even if it ran the risk of *him* finding out. Viola hadn't expected to hear anything back, though, and was shocked.

Why would Betsy reply? What happened? Had their father done something?

To think I told the duke that he was a dead solicitor. Viola always hated lying to people, but she'd been lying about her father for the past ten years. Viola made to open the letter but became sidetracked by the innkeeper.

"Your letter said you were stayin' for eight days." The man with the bristling mustache glowered at Viola. "Here you an' the young miss are clearin' out and it hasn't even been four."

"I'm afraid there was an accident. The young girl has injured herself, and we've had to make other arrangements." Viola wished she could speak more forcefully to this man, but, as always, she must be careful whom she antagonized. When you had little power in this world, it paid to be cautious. "We shall, of course, pay for half of our agreed-upon time. We didn't stay the night yesterday, so we will in fact be paying for more time than we spent in your lodgings."

"You think we got people bangin' down the door to stay here, missy?" The man scowled, the corners of his mouth becoming lost in his grizzled face. "I want the full eight days' payment."

"Or what?"

"Or I'll call the bloody constable and have you thrown in the clink."

Viola was all too accustomed to being called "missy" and "girl," to being threatened in some manner. As she grew older, she'd heard terms like "spinster" and "sour old maid" flung about when she was still within earshot. A woman in a governess's clothes received very little respect, and she'd learned to live with it.

But after last night, something within her had altered. For the first time outside of Lynton Park, Viola had felt seen. She'd liked it.

She wanted to tell the innkeeper that she was the Duke of Huntington's guest, but she didn't wish to hide behind another, more powerful person. She felt secure in herself; she wanted to show this fellow that he could not simply push her about.

"Did I sign any document that legally obligated me to pay for the full eight days?" Viola smiled, her ease seeming to disorient the rude man.

"Eh. Well. Not exactly."

"We stayed three nights in your inn, and I'm prepared to pay for the one additional night we did not stay, purely because you kept the room vacant for us. But now that we are leaving, I see no reason to pay for four additional nights, particularly when another person may take those rooms at any moment."

"Not a lot of visitors 'round these parts," the innkeeper grumbled. But as he said that, the bell over the door tinkled, and a bespectacled gentleman entered.

"Hallo! I wondered if you'd a room to let?" The man took off his hat and mopped his balding brow with a handkerchief.

The innkeeper shriveled further in on himself. He made some threatening, growling noise. "Fine." The man sneered at Viola. "That'll be two pound, fifteen shillings."

"As the full eight days would have been five pounds, I believe that is two pounds and *ten* shillings." Viola counted out the money with pleasant ease while the stodgy innkeeper continued muttering foul language to himself. That done, Viola closed the strings of her reticule and nodded. "Thank you very much."

"Never should've taught women to count," he snapped. Viola was headed for the door when the odious man let one more parting insult fly. "'Course, you know who needs their numbers? Plain-faced spinsters who can't catch a man."

Normally, she would pretend she had not heard and keep on walking, but today was rather special. Another visitor had just opened the door when the innkeeper spoke those last rude words. Upon hearing them, the gentleman stopped, blocking Viola's exit.

"You dare speak that way to a lady, sir?" the Duke of Huntington said.

CHAPTER EIGHT

Hunt had stopped to buy Isabelle that ink, and on his way out of the shop, he'd been surprised to find his own coach stationed at the inn across the street.

Surprised, that is, until he remembered promising to remove Miss Winslow's and Felicity's things from the inn. He'd gotten a certain lustful thrill at the idea that Viola might be there herself and so had gone to investigate.

He'd entered at the precise moment some odious man lobbed an insult at the departing governess. The woman had seemed so poised. Her coolness and reserve only stoked the fires of Hunt's admiration, but that git's cruel language had the duke ready to burn the place down.

"You dare speak that way to a lady, sir?" he snapped.

Everyone in Moorcliff Village knew the duke on sight, and the innkeeper's eyes bugged out in a most unappetizing manner. Miss Winslow halted before Hunt in shock. In the background, a maid dropped the bundle of pressed linen she'd been carrying. The only person who remained unfazed by Hunt's presence was the pleasant little balding man with the glasses, who smiled as he pressed on the bell in front of the innkeeper once or twice.

"Yes. Hallo! A room, please?" He cleared his throat, then waved his hand before the terrified man's face. "As for breakfast, do you do kippers? I am partial to a buttered kipper."

"Y-Yer Grace," the innkeeper squeaked.

Hunt stalked toward the desk, having half a mind to overturn the whole bloody thing. He must have looked as fearsome as he felt; he had ridden out before his valet had shaved him, and the stubble of yesterday had grown into a thin beard. He must look like one of Isabelle's characters, a man with a dead wife in a cursed attic.

"Answer me, sir." Hunt glared. "Why would you dare speak to a lady in such a hideous manner?"

"T-T'weren't my intention to disrespect her, Yer Grace!"

"Is 'plain-faced spinster' a term of endearment, then?" Perhaps if Viola dressed in the manner of a great lady, she'd receive the acclaim she deserved.

Greedily, Hunt envisioned her wearing a gown of emerald satin, rubies glistening in her ears. Then he imagined her wearing the rubies and nothing else. Then he had to get his mind out of debauchery and back to the task at hand.

"All's well, Your Grace," the governess said. "I've settled my business at this establishment." To the bespectacled man, she added, "They do make a fine buttered kipper."

"Oh, lovely!" The traveler looked blissful.

But Hunt was not disposed to grant bullies such as this innkeeper any kind of grace.

"I've not finished with this man," he growled. The fellow behind the desk paled and squeaked, a most unmasculine sound. "I insist that you apologize to this lady. I demand you make restitution to her for your offense."

"I, I'm sorry, Miss. Truly." The innkeeper hunched his shoulders about his ears. "Here. T-Take the money back!" He started shoving pound notes and coins toward Viola.

"No," she said. To Hunt's surprise, she seemed a bit annoyed. With the duke. "That's yours, sir. All I want now is to leave." She cleared her throat and curtsied at Hunt meaningfully. "Shall we, Your Grace?"

Hunt had never seen a woman yet who didn't wish to be rescued from someone as boorish as this man, but it seemed Viola was rescuing the lout instead.

Mystified, he glared one last time at the innkeeper for good measure. "I don't want to hear that sort of language out of your mouth again, sir."

"No, Yer Grace! I swear it!"

The duke left at Viola's side.

"I say, would it be too much trouble to butter some kippers now?" the newly arrived guest asked as the duke and the governess exited the inn.

To Hunt's surprise, Viola kept a brisk pace ahead of him all the way to the carriage. She would not meet the duke's eyes. Instead, Viola spoke with the footman, who of course bowed when he saw Hunt.

"What are you telling the lad?" Hunt asked Viola.

"I'm only making sure everything is packed, Your Grace, so we may return to Moorcliff." She spoke as normal in that soft, slightly husky voice, but Hunt perceived a touch of indignation about her now. The governess seemed full of fire today. Probably because of how that damned innkeeper had treated her.

"You needn't worry about that man back there, Miss Winslow. I handled the situation."

The governess's pale cheeks grew rosy. But he didn't think this was the sort of blush a woman gave when overwhelmed by awe at a man's chivalry; rather, she looked a bit tomato-ish with anger.

That Hunt should find her pique as erotic as her pleasure was another baffling revelation.

"Your Grace, I'd already settled the matter. I told you that when you happened upon us. You didn't need to concern yourself."

"I consider a man being rude to a lady my concern." Wonderful, now he was snapping at the poor woman. He didn't know why. Perhaps because he wanted little more than for Miss Winslow to view him as a hero. That was a rather adolescent wish.

"You all but pushed me aside so you could attend to the man yourself! Is that not rudeness of its own sort?" Viola appeared exasperated while the footman tried his best to ignore this small battle between them. "Do you think that's the first time in my life a man has been rude to me? That innkeeper wasn't even the worst offender. Yet you treated me as though I were a child in need of protection!"

Now Hunt was growing incensed. This woman was scolding him!

Hunt was unused to members of the fairer sex doing anything other than adoring every scrap of attention that he paid them. Women of substantial fortunes silenced any opinion in themselves they did not believe he would share. Meanwhile, Viola Winslow spoke with surprising force. He'd never known she could be as irritated as this.

Hunt had never known irritation could be such an erotic trait.

Every moment in Viola's presence revealed new and enticing details about her personality. He wanted to undress her very soul so he could admire the totality of her. He also wanted to undress *her*, wretched as that made him.

"You're certainly not a child," the duke said.

Indeed, she was every glorious inch a woman. "But I don't see how standing aside and allowing men to treat you poorly speaks well of me!"

"Because this is not about you, Your Grace! This is about my own dignity. I've managed it for years, and I'm rather prideful of it." Viola's blush only deepened with passion. She really did look gorgeous when she had this much color. "I appreciate your wanting to aid me, but I believe it's best to encourage people to fight their own battles, especially women."

"Interesting." Hunt appraised her, almost reveling in the challenge she now presented. "And if someone spoke that way to Miss Berridge or either of my sisters, would you feel the same way?"

"Well. That's different." She hesitated, but the fight in her remained. "There's a difference between ladies and governesses."

My grandmother would like very much to hear you say that, he thought grimly.

"For an admirer of Mr. Blake's radical poetry, you subscribe to many backward notions, Miss Winslow."

Now he was treading right up to the line of rudeness. In fact, he was stomping on that line and sticking his booted toes just over the edge.

"I understand the world in which I live, Your Grace. I want the world to be better, but I'm conscious of what it is right now. I don't wish to live in some fantasy; I'm not afraid of challenge."

"I daresay not." Hunt snorted. "In point of fact, I've learned that you are one of the most obstinate women of my acquaintance."

"Yes. As I've learned you are not nearly the even-tempered gentleman I'd believed you to be."

"That sounded remarkably close to an insult, Miss Winslow."

Here she hesitated, and Hunt watched a minor battle wage war in her expression. The governess knew she'd overstepped the line with him, and her natural shyness threatened to cause her to retreat. But Hunt had wounded her sense of independence and aroused her indignation, and as it turned out Viola Winslow did not suffer indignation from any quarter. She'd poked at his grandmother only last night, after all. She was an original, no doubt about it.

"I apologize if I've been rude, Your Grace. But I don't apologize for the essence of what I've said. All I've meant to say is that you needn't worry about me. Though it was good of you to do so." She sighed. "I don't expect the world to care about my feelings one way or the other."

That only made Hunt question how she'd grown up, and who her father might have been. Gentleman or not, was that man the reason Viola went through life eternally vigilant? Or had the world punished her after his death? Either way, it made Hunt feel sick.

"Unfortunately, your statement's had the opposite effect," he muttered. "I find I worry about you more than I did previously."

"Oh dear." Viola put her gloved hands to her cheeks. "This has all been much too informal. I don't know what's got into me."

"Not at all," Hunt said. "In fact, I'm rather pleased. This might be the first time I've ever seen you cross."

"How could that please you?"

"Because I like to think it's a sign that you've begun to trust me." *Forward? Undoubtedly. But true.*

"I trust you, Your Grace."

"Only up to a point." Hunt drew nearer to the small woman. "I'd like to think I could earn your trust fully, in time."

What time? The days they had before Viola left Moorcliff? But Hunt damned all common sense right now. He was too fascinated by this woman, too engrossed in her subtle charms.

"I'd like that too, Your Grace."

A bold admission from the woman, one that gave Hunt the most exquisite rush of pleasure.

"You really are surprising, Miss Winslow."

"In truth, Your Grace, I've surprised even myself today."

"You don't need to return to the castle straight-away, do you?" he asked.

"Well. I should oversee Felicity's sketch work, but she and Lady Isabelle are touring the supposed-ly haunted east wing."

Hunt laughed. "Then I think we should let them enjoy their time. Isabelle is in love with melancholic hauntings."

"Felicity adores tales of bloody specters, so I'm certain they'll become fast friends."

"Then why don't we have the luggage taken back to Moorcliff," Hunt said, "and instruct the coach to return for you in an hour? I haven't walked the streets of town for some time. My home always seems new through the eyes of a guest."

Viola looked down, shyness winning yet again. But she also smiled. "All right, Your Grace. As you wish."

Oh, he could tell that she wished for this stolen moment as well. How the devil had Hunt never no-ticed her in ten bloody years? Perhaps because she was not his to notice and could never be.

Hang it all, he wanted only an hour in her company and a walk, nothing indecent.

Hunt sent the carriage away with instructions to return, and then found himself walking the streets of town with Viola at his side.

The common sights, the narrow shopfronts with their peaked gable rooftops, the leaded glass windows, the villagers moving about their day all seemed to vanish. The only real thing in this place was Viola Winslow.

"People are staring, Your Grace," the governess murmured.

Indeed. As the duke passed by, people bowed or curtsied to him as per usual, but they also gaped in astonishment. "They haven't seen me for some time," Hunt said. "I've rarely left the castle these last fifteen months."

But he knew it was more than that.

The people were staring at Viola and him together. Some women stopped and began obviously whispering to one another, craning their necks in strained and silly ways to keep an eye on them.

"I'm afraid we're giving them something to gossip about," the governess said. "Even though there's nothing untoward happening, of course. I've never been so looked at in my life."

"How is that possible?" Hunt frowned. A woman as lovely as Viola should be noticed wherever she went. Again, Hunt thought of society's foolishness, the way it paid attention only to those who possessed wealth and status and flaunted both.

"It must be difficult for a duke to comprehend," Viola said in a lightly teasing manner. "You attract attention wherever you go."

"Indeed, Miss Winslow? How do you know

that?" He lifted an eyebrow. "Have you been spying on me?"

He loved the way she blushed.

"I tend to observe the people around me," she said.

But Hunt liked to think he held some special attraction for her.

"Speaking of observation," she said quickly, "I've been curious as to why the duchess calls you Hunt."

"An unusual nickname, yes. Short for Huntington, obviously. My Christian name is James, but for some reason my family never thought it really suited me. No one save Lady Agatha, that is, and she took to calling me Jamie." He shuddered in a dramatic fashion, which made Viola laugh. "Even when my father was still alive, everyone began to call me Hunt. They claimed it fit me better."

"I perhaps can see why," Viola said. "James feels soft and romantic. Hunt is vigorously masculine."

He loved that she appreciated his masculine vigor, but his apparent lack of romance frustrated him.

"But," she added, "I think that feels rather superficial, don't you agree? When one first looks at you, she sees someone powerful and domineering."

"And when she gets to know me better?" he murmured. "What are her impressions then?"

"Well…"

"Come, Miss Winslow. You've called yourself observant. So, observe me."

"You're very kind and good. The epitome of a gentleman," she said, eyes still cast to the ground. "James fits that part of you nicely."

He liked that she saw beyond the surface of his looks and his title, though Hunt did not like that she found him too much a gentleman. He couldn't resist the idea of tearing the clothes from her body and showing her in aching, sensuous detail how experienced he could be. How wonderfully good he was at being bad, if given the chance.

"Very nice. And as for yourself, why Viola?"

"Because of *Twelfth Night* by Mr. Shakespeare." Viola smiled. "While my mother was expecting, a troop of players arrived in town. My mother loved the play. When my twin brother and I were born, she named us Viola and Sebastian." Yes, after the heroine and her own twin brother.

"Wonderful," Hunt said. "Where is your twin now?"

"He didn't live three days." Viola became a bit removed. "My mother died a week after. Childbed fever, the doctors called it."

"I'm so sorry." Having lost his own mother as she gave birth to Isabelle, Hunt keenly knew the pain of such tragedy. He hated that sorrow had ever touched this woman, wished he could have protected her from it all.

"It was beyond anyone's control. That's what the doctor told my father. Sometimes babies are sickly, and sometimes women die of fever. There was no one to blame."

"Did your father blame someone for the misfortune?" Hunt asked.

"Indeed. He blamed me," she said in a soft voice.

So, Hunt had been right; before his death, Mr. Winslow must have been a bully and a brute indeed, gentleman solicitor or no.

"And you've no other family? Is that why you went to school after he'd passed?"

"I had no family who could properly look after me." That was an odd, slightly noncommittal answer.

Viola winced, and he felt she was growing ever more uncomfortable. Damn, how could he be so thoughtless? Of course she didn't want to discuss the most painful parts of her history.

"Forgive me for prying," he said. "I only find I'm interested in you."

"Then your society up here's been more limited than I thought, Your Grace." She relaxed a bit, even teased him. "We governesses all have a uniform story, more or less."

"I doubt anything about you is uniform, Miss Winslow."

He took such heated delight from making her blush at his compliments.

"I'm not sure how we got onto this conversation," she murmured. "Forgive me, Your Grace."

"Miss Winslow, I asked to walk with you. I asked about your name and family. If you don't wish to share something, I perfectly understand, but if you're worried about boring or angering me, then I should warn you, both are impossible."

"It's not impossible to become bored or angry," she said.

"Agreed. But I doubt it would be possible to be bored or angry with you."

She gasped in apparent surprise at his words. This time, she was not afraid to look him in the face. "Then thank you," she said.

Hunt noticed she had not addressed him as "Your Grace" and reveled in it.

"Come along. There's more to see, though I admit not much." Moorcliff was like many other villages in this country, but Viola took so much pleasure in her surroundings that Hunt changed his evaluation. Moorcliff Village became a grand place indeed, unique among other towns. Because it contained her.

By this time, they'd grown accustomed to people staring.

One young man ran over another with his wheelbarrow, and they argued between themselves as Hunt and Viola passed. The governess spoke a bit of her time at a charity school in Yorkshire, of the passion for education it instilled in her.

Hunt relished listening to her stories but noticed that Viola still grew stiff and distant when he touched too near her past. She did not trust him fully; she wanted to keep something close to her chest. If he tried to force her secrets, Hunt knew she would shut tight to him. He must be patient.

He wanted to see her in full bloom. He wanted to know every bit of her.

For a while, they wandered the streets and admired the shop windows.

Hunt always asked if Viola wanted to go inside, but she always refused. The one moment when her resolve weakened was as they passed a bookshop. She almost led them in but backed away at the last second.

"It's no trouble," Hunt said.

"But I can't waste any of our funds on needless purchases for myself." Viola seemed to light up as she gazed at the books through the window. "And books are my weakness. If I'd only enough money to buy a bun for supper, I think I should spend it on a book if I didn't restrain myself."

He wanted to offer to buy her any book she liked. Hell, he'd buy her the whole damn shop if she wanted it. No one had ever lavished extravagances on this woman, and Hunt wanted to be the first to do so. The only one, in fact.

He knew this was becoming dangerous, this thing between them, but he also knew he couldn't walk away. Not now.

"What is it you love so about them?" he asked as they walked away from the shop.

"I suppose they allow me to forget the outside world for a time. At least, that's one of their charms." She shook her head. "Listen to me. I make myself sound quite pathetic."

"Not at all." He hated how ready she was to lessen herself. "There's nothing pathetic about truth. I only hope one day your reality can be as thrilling as your life in books."

"That would be difficult, I'm afraid. I've got something of an overactive imagination."

A sublime feature in a woman, he thought.

"I believe life should be gratifying, don't you agree?"

"Well. Yes." She appeared shocked. "Though that seems quite the opposite of the dutiful life you've created for yourself." She clapped a gloved hand over her mouth. "How could I have spoken out of turn like that? Forgive me, Your Grace."

But he liked her speaking out of turn to him. And he found he had meant that. Living life with gusto was a virtue, wasn't it?

At least, it was a virtue for everyone but for men like him, custodians of a great legacy. If he could live a life for its own sake, there'd be nothing to prevent him from taking Viola into his arms this minute, from doing and saying every delicious and erotic thing he wanted to say and do to her. Sometimes, he bitterly regretted being the damned duke.

"For the last time, stop apologizing for having a

spirited opinion," Hunt said. They paused outside a jeweler's, a case of fine objects on display in the shop window. "I want you to feel free to be yourself around me, Miss Winslow." *Viola*.

"I shall do my best, Your Grace."

Something in the window caught her eye. She seemed to be looking at a cabochon emerald, polished and hung upon a chain of gold. Hunt realized how brilliantly the emerald would bring out the flecks of green in Viola's eyes.

"That's lovely," he said, though he looked at Viola as he spoke, not the necklace.

"A bit costly at my salary." She urged him away from the window.

"But you like it?"

"I suppose so, yes. Why ask, Your Grace?"

"Because I'm intrigued to see more of the woman behind the governess. You've always seemed so wise and removed whenever I've visited Ashworth. I confess, sometimes it felt like you were something other than human. I mean it as a compliment," he added, in case she should take offense. "I suppose I can't help but be curious, Miss Winslow. What is it you desire for yourself?"

"I..."

As they stopped upon a street corner while the coach rolled up, Viola's whole countenance changed as if a carefully painted mask had slipped away. He beheld her at her truest and most vulnerable. The pain and shyness mixed with a firm resolve, a secretly bold spirit, and desire. *Yes, desire*.

Viola looked at him with the most tender admiration and yearning.

She wanted him, he realized, as much as he wanted her. It was for only a second, but it lasted a proper lifetime. She hid herself away again, as she was so very good at doing, but Hunt had seen her. He knew her now.

He knew what he wanted.

His heart pounded, his arms itched to embrace her. He wanted to kiss her, kiss every soft and secret place on her body.

This must stop. You can't go any further.

"Thank you for the outing, Your Grace," Viola said as the footman opened the carriage door for her. "Are you coming?"

"My horse is tied up outside the printer's. I shall be along momentarily." He tipped his hat. "I'll see you at home, Miss Winslow."

The horses started and the coach rattled away, carrying the governess with it. Hunt watched until the carriage had passed out of the village, then went to get his horse. He reminded himself he had not said farewell to Viola. She would be waiting for him at home.

But she would not be able to stay, and it pained him.

CHAPTER NINE

"The aim should be to capture the subject's spirit," Viola said, walking slowly behind the two girls as they sketched. Diving into a drawing lesson helped to put the beauty and strangeness of her outing with the Duke of Huntington from Viola's mind. "A talented amateur may understand shading and proportion, but only an artist can find something's essential truth." She paused behind Felicity's chair and frowned. "Felicity, I believe you've made him too malevolent."

"But Cornelius practically drips with malevolence! Does he not?"

The raven did not, in fact, exude menace. He stared blankly at Viola and the girls, then ruffled his feathers.

"I was talking of Aristotle, dear. You've made him very cross indeed."

They were sketching in the old duke's study, a comfortable place that smelled of polish and the faint remnants of pipe smoke.

They'd chosen this room for the excellent way the light came in from the west, and because Cornelius had deigned to perch upon a marble bust of Aristotle. Felicity had drawn a curling sneer on the philosopher's face where a more neutral mouth should have been.

"It's artistic license." Felicity tossed her head with pride.

"We're sketching what we see, not what we wish to see. It's important to never lose sight of reality."

"Isn't reality terribly dull, Miss Winslow?" Lady Isabelle was hunched over, working on her sketch with quick, earnest strokes of her pencil. She'd allowed Viola to put up her golden hair in a proper style so it wouldn't get in her face as she drew. "I should like it ever so much more if life were like poetry."

"What, boring and hard to understand?" Felicity snorted; Viola withheld a sigh. "Now if life were like Mr. Winthrop's books, *that* would be something!"

"Who?" Isabelle looked puzzled.

"I'll read you his work later! I hope you like bloody skulls and castles in Prussia."

"Oh, I do! On both counts!"

Truly, this was a match made in heaven. Or perhaps its opposite.

Viola stopped behind Lady Isabelle and took in the image. She had a better sense of shading than Felicity, though her proportions weren't as strong. But she'd also eschewed Cornelius entirely and was sketching a crown of flowers upon the marble bust.

"You girls are impossible." Viola laughed despite herself.

"I should think we were irrepressible." Felicity grinned at Lady Isabelle. "What did you do?"

Isabelle showed off her sketch and the girls fell to whispering and giggling. Viola stepped back, allowing Felicity a moment to simply laugh with another young lady. The governess took up her own sketchbook from a nearby table.

"It would certainly help if we'd a subject who was neither stone nor a bird," Felicity said.

"Knickers." Sounding almost indignant, Cornelius soared from the room and croaked as he flapped along the hall.

"You should never insult your models." Viola laughed as she selected a pencil. "Besides, birds are tricky enough to understand. A human subject offers an especial challenge."

"Could I be of help in that department?" The duke entered the room, looking more orderly and clean-shaven than he had yesterday. Viola held her breath; this was the first she'd seen of him since her return to the castle. She'd convinced herself that there had been no moment between them earlier, but those feelings vanished with his presence. It seemed his eyes sought her out at once. "Forgive my interruption. I was coming in here for a book and overheard your bemoaned lack of a model."

"Oh, let Hunt sit for us! He's ever so much more interesting than Aristotle," Isabelle said.

"Probably handsomer too, I'd imagine." Felicity was cheekiness itself as she glanced at her governess. "Would you agree, Miss Winslow?"

"What *are* your manners, Felicity?" Viola hoped she wasn't blushing. "His Grace will be shocked. Besides, I'm certain he is too busy to act as our model."

"I offered my services, didn't I?" The duke pulled a chair over just before the desk and settled himself. "My book can wait. If it's agreeable to you ladies, of course?"

He spoke to the girls but looked at Viola. Her heartbeat quickened.

"Excellent. I've always said you'd a face for tragedy, Hunt." Lady Isabelle started a new sketch. "I shall draw you seated beside the grave of a lost sweetheart. Or perhaps a much beloved pet." Isabelle gasped. "No. That is too sad."

"I think Miss Winslow should show us how to

capture a person. She's a genius at drawing."

"Thank you, Felicity, but I'm no such thing."

"I should like very much if you'd sketch my portrait, Miss Winslow. I'm curious as to how you perceive me." The duke was all ease and good cheer, but she swore his gaze was heated.

Viola wished to protest, but the girls clamored loudly for her to draw Huntington. Why was Felicity so utterly willful? And why now, of all times?

Viola found herself seated before the Duke of Huntington, willing her hand not to tremble as she began to sketch faint lines upon the page.

"How does one draw, Miss Winslow? I've often wondered how you ladies can manage such likenesses."

"I begin with a few rough shapes. An oval for the head. It also matters what direction you're looking; I'll have to change how the features are aligned depending on your sightline."

"Mine should be easy to manage." He was looking straight at her, a smile gracing his lips.

Viola didn't think she'd be able to complete the picture without dropping something or fainting.

She sketched lines where the nose and eyes and mouth would go and then began to define his features. Every time she had to look up to take in the precise line of his nose (aquiline, exquisite), the shape of his eyes (large, deep-set), or the curve of his mouth (sensual, distractingly so), she became tangled in her thoughts.

Thoughts of putting a hand to his cheek, or placing her lips on his, of feeling his powerful arms wrap around her.

"Miss Winslow? Is something wrong?"

Drat! She'd been staring at the duke for nearly a

full minute! He gazed quizzically at her while the girls giggled.

"Ladies, it is important to take time with a subject." She tried to salvage this. "If you don't bother to understand the specific details of a face, it's easy to make it generic."

"Indeed? Pray tell, what are the specific details of my face?" The duke grinned. "Perhaps it's vain of me, but I'd love to know."

Somehow Viola had made the situation worse for herself. Why did she have to be so good at that?

"Well. That is." *Do not flirt, Viola. Under pain of death.* "Your eyes are spaced perhaps too far apart to be considered mathematically perfect." Her eyes widened.

The girls shrieked with laughter.

"That is a bold assessment." But the duke laughed, too. "An original one, I might add. I find that once a man achieves a certain rank, even his most uneven features are considered classically handsome."

"Yes. Flattery. As I was telling the young ladies, you must always look at the world as it is."

"Not a very romantic attitude."

"Romance isn't falling in love with a lie. It's seeing the truth of a person and loving them for it, not despite it."

The duke nodded. "Ladies, you're fortunate to have Miss Winslow as an example. Her honesty makes her one of the rarest creatures in England."

"Perhaps the rudest as well. Forgive me." Viola began to sketch, concentrating intently on defining the ridge of the duke's brow.

"Speaking of observation, that seems to be a characteristic of yours," the duke said. "When given a compliment, you apologize."

"She's always been like that," Felicity said. "She's too modest for her own good."

Viola turned in her chair, ready to stand up and wheel Felicity out of the room in a huff. The girl merely shrugged.

"Personally, I think Miss Winslow would make an extraordinary model," Felicity said. "She's got such a lovely face; the Duchess of Ashworth said she'd an impish quality once. I think so, too. Wouldn't you agree, Your Grace?"

"Felicity!" Viola hissed. What was the girl on about?

"I agree with the duchess. There is something almost faerie-like about Miss Winslow." The duke nodded. "You've an ethereal quality, I'd say."

"Such a good word, Your Grace. Ethereal." Felicity sighed, happily ignoring the warning looks her governess kept shooting her way. "I was thinking I ought to do a portrait of you someday, Miss Winslow. Perhaps I could even try an oil painting! Would you like such a painting, Your Grace?"

The duke chuckled while Viola felt her pulse in her very fingertips. "I believe I would, rather. I've no doubt you'd capture the rarer qualities of your subject, Felicity."

Viola was not going to be drawn further into this farce. "If you ladies would like me to demonstrate the finer points of drawing, you'll have to pay attention and cease talking nonsense."

"His Grace has commissioned a painting from me! That's hardly nonsense. Perhaps I might make a living as a portraitist. Wouldn't that be scandalous?" Felicity's delight bubbled forth.

"Oh, this is dull. Hunt, do choose a more dynamic pose." Lady Isabelle was thoroughly wrapped up in her work. "Perhaps a look of remorse, or terror. Or you might collapse as if the very soul has been crushed in your breast."

"Or you might try tilting your head, Your Grace." Viola struggled not to laugh at the duke's bafflement. "That should be easier." She heard the girls whispering behind her. "Ladies, what is it?"

"Perhaps Hunt might pose with something," Lady Isabelle said. "I'm looking about the room for the perfect object."

"Perhaps you might hand His Grace a book."

"Oh, books are dull," Felicity said. "Quite literally, I mean. What we need is something heroic! Something *sharp.*"

"Felicity." Viola hoped the warning in her voice came through.

"Have you any swords about the place?"

"Indeed! I have just the thing! Let me go and get it," Isabelle said.

"Take me along, I want to see if it's good enough," Felicity demanded.

"You do not order a young lady about in her own home!" Viola felt sure Huntington must be appalled by her young charge's lack of manners.

But Felicity appeared pleased as Lady Isabelle obeyed her with great cheer, nabbing the handles of her wheelchair.

"Just stay here with His Grace, Miss Winslow. We shall be back soon." Felicity waved her hand and Lady Isabelle rolled her away with alacrity.

"She is impossible." Viola huffed, but the duke seemed to struggle against laughter.

"She's spirited. Felicity's always had an animated way about her. I haven't seen my sister this lively in months."

"Then I suppose it's all right." They sat in companionable silence a moment; Viola began to wonder if Felicity had gone to another castle in search of the perfect sword.

As her hands sketched, Viola searched for a topic of conversation.

After all, she'd spoken so boldly with the duke this morning. She didn't think he wanted her to be meek and silent. Funnily enough, Viola didn't want that, either. "You said you came in here for a book?" she said at last.

"It was more of a journal, really. My father had a passion for antiquities. He took me to see the ruins of Hadrian's Wall growing up, and there's supposed to be the remnants of a Roman fort somewhere nearby. It's little more than a few strategic piles of stone at this point, but I've wanted to return. It's been so long I've rather forgot the way."

"You share a passion for antiquities, Your Grace?"

"Yes." He sounded quite thoughtful. "I confess I'm enthralled by the past. To my mind, you can build a better future for people only if you understand where you came from. The triumphs and mistakes alike can be instructive."

"Are you looking to build a second Roman fort?" Viola grinned.

"Perhaps not that, but the Romans left their mark all over this land. Frankly ingenious use of engineering, particularly when it comes to irrigation. Those sorts of things could benefit my tenants tremendously."

"You care for your tenants, then? Most landlords want only to receive their rent on time."

"Well, that's the thing. When I look at the

structures of the past, I see how the lives of men and women have played out over hundreds of years. All people want shelter and food, a safe place to raise a family. My land would be worthless without people to live off it, and it's in everyone's best interest if the farmers succeed at their task. If I help them to better irrigate their crops, if I ensure the soil is healthy, if I help to keep their lives and homes safe, then we all prosper. The money I make in rent should mostly go back into ensuring the health and stability of all of us. After all, history shows us what happens to greedy tyrants." The duke chuckled. "Their ends aren't usually kind."

Viola felt her heartbeat quicken. Huntington was noble, practical, fair-minded, and curious. The more she saw of him, the more she wanted to see. She cleared her throat, attempting to remain pleasant and neutral.

"Merely tilt your head, Your Grace, if you please. I need a better angle to sketch."

"Like this?" Huntington tilted his face slightly to the left.

Viola could tell where the light would strike his features to the most breathtaking degree. She would love to have a picture of him in that handsome state.

"May I?" she asked without thinking.

"Please. Show me how I can best serve." The duke's words made her quiver to the foundation of her soul. He seemed to mean more than what was said on the surface. Viola went to him and placed her hands on either side of his face.

"Just this way, please." Her voice hitched as she lowered his chin and then guided him into giving her more of his profile. Viola's throat was dry; she was touching Huntington's face, something she'd dreamed of doing for years. She almost regretted now that he had shaved his stubble. There'd been something so animalistic about him when he was disheveled. He looked perfect and godlike again in this manner. One couldn't really touch a god.

"Is that what you wanted, Miss Winslow?"

"I believe so, Your Grace."

"Good. I want you to be fully satisfied."

She was not imagining this, was she?

This tension between them that seemed almost to vibrate in the air, this suggestion that laced his voice? Afraid she would do something foolish, Viola released him and hurried back to her seat. Her hands trembled as she took up the sketchbook and pencil.

"I'm satisfied, sir. Thank you for taking direction so well."

"I tend not to enjoy yielding to others. I like having my own way too much. But it seems your lightest touch commands, and I don't mind at all."

"Perhaps it comes from being a governess. One needs gentleness as well as strength." She began to sketch again, defining his eyes. She realized she couldn't just do this from memory and looked up at him again for an instant. The instant lasted and lingered as he looked into her eyes in turn.

"Gentle strength is quite a contradiction," Huntington said. "But I expected nothing less. I doubt there is much about you that's ordinary, Miss Winslow."

The ground was shifting under Viola's feet, and she was emerging into a new world. She was modest but not ignorant; she knew the signs and knew he was flirting with her. Should she be frightened?

Angry with him for placing her reputation in jeopardy? Or could she allow herself to be as she naturally was, elated and scared. Mostly elated.

No. Mostly scared.

She was relieved when the girls returned, Isabelle wheeling Felicity who carried something on her lap.

"What the...?" Huntington rose to his feet. "Isabelle, tell me you didn't pull that off the wall."

"I knocked over nothing important!"

The girls had managed to lay hands on a claymore, a two-handed sword over three feet long. It was wrought all over with Celtic designs, and Felicity was holding it as affectionately as she might a child.

"It's made of Damascus steel. The very finest," Felicity said, proud of her knowledge. "Here, Your Grace. You ought to lean upon this and brood. Or you might wield it overhead in a two-handed swing! Though it might be a difficult pose to hold for long."

"I thought young ladies were supposed to abhor violence," Huntington grumbled.

Viola concealed a laugh. "One thing you should know about women, Your Grace. We often find the ordinary terribly stifling."

CHAPTER TEN

When Viola awoke the next morning, she thought she might be still in a dream.

She was in Moorcliff Castle, and the Duke of Huntington was paying her attention.

Last night Felicity had joined them at supper and insisted on playing cards and listening to music after dinner. The dowager had been irritated with the intruder girl's high spirits, but everyone else seemed delighted.

Viola and Lady Agatha had enjoyed a good conversation while Lady Isabelle played upon the pianoforte, but throughout the evening Viola had felt the duke's eyes on her. He had escorted Felicity and Viola back to their room, and once more he had lingered to have a chat.

This was so dangerous.

Nothing good could come of it.

A woman with Viola's past ought to be much smarter than to indulge in and encourage this behavior, but she knew by now that good things did not simply happen to people. Adventures did not sweep you away when you were not looking.

If you didn't seize moments of happiness, you would spend your life waiting for them to appear. While Viola was *reserved*, to put it politely, she had not yet quashed that part of her that yearned for the new and the exquisite. She was still young enough to dream.

So, at breakfast the next morning, when she found the duke seated at the table with his sisters,

Viola did not fade into the background as usual. She let herself be present. She smiled when the duke spoke to her. She answered him in turn.

"Now that you've lived in Somerset a number of years, how does it compare to the north?" he asked.

"I love it, but perhaps more because I love Lynton Park and my life in it. The south is heavenly, but it's too pretty and domestic."

"You prefer a bit of wildness, then?"

Her heart pounded at the suggestive note in his question.

"Miss Winslow adores nature. She's always teaching me about the different birds that live in the Park. She's read work by some Swiss fellow about taximony," Felicity said.

"Pardon?" the duke asked.

"Taxonomy," Viola corrected. "Monsieur de Candolle coined the word to describe the process of sorting things into types and groups. It helps to organize and understand the natural world."

"I see." The duke frowned. "That sounds rather rigid."

"Well. There are obvious differences between a lion and a field mouse, for example. Perhaps they are both mammals, but one would never make the mistake of placing them in the same group." Viola's throat felt a bit tight. "They don't belong together."

"I think lions and mice can do as they please," Felicity said. *Bold girl, as always.*

"But you asked about Somerset, Your Grace. I confess I still wish to make a trip to the Roman ruins at Bath. It's long been my ambition to go. Perhaps when Felicity debuts into society and goes to Bath for the winter Season I shall get an opportunity."

"You enjoy history?" The duke seemed pleased.

Indeed, it was a passion they shared. The only one they *could* share.

"She likes old things." Felicity certainly liked butting in this morning. "Your Grace, are there any ruins around here? Castles usually have plenty of ruins."

"In fact, there's the crumbling remains of an old chapel not two miles from here. It's long been one of my favorite places on the estate," he replied.

"Perhaps we might sketch there later this afternoon," Viola said.

"Oh, I can't wheel two whole miles! Besides, I don't like old things the way you do, Miss Winslow."

"Hunt, you ought to take Miss Winslow! Then she could sketch a bit and come back and show Miss Berridge." Lady Isabelle grinned. "I can take her around the east wing in the meantime."

An outing alone with the duke? Viola felt dizzy just contemplating it. She knew she ought to react, to reject the notion, but Huntington spoke first.

"Indeed. A fine idea." The duke seemed quite pleased. There was no mistaking this. He wanted to be alone with Viola.

While Viola believed in seizing opportunities for happiness, this might be too much even for her. She needed to keep a level head. "Felicity, I won't burden the servants with having to supervise you. We both know what mischief you get into."

"I should be happy to watch the girls." Lady Agatha was cheerfulness itself. "Take Miss Winslow, Hunt. Show her the chapel."

Somehow, Viola's greatest dreams and most horrifying nightmares came true simultaneously these days.

Half an hour later she found herself in a

two-person buggy seated beside His Grace. As they trotted along, she could barely recall a word he spoke to her or anything she said. She knew only it felt as though something were about to happen, as if the world was holding its breath and waiting.

Viola glanced at the duke.

The more time she spent with him, the harder she looked to see if she could pick out a flaw. Getting to know someone showed you their weaknesses as well as their strengths, yes? There should have been a mole, or a scar, or one eyelid that drooped lower than the other.

But there was nothing, and even if there had been she wouldn't have noticed.

The duke was everything and nothing like she'd believed him to be. He was handsome, yes, and charming and kind, but he could also be quick-tempered. Impatient. Even arrogant. The duke she'd wanted for so long had been as good as a character from a novel; this new version of him was so very physical, so real.

"Here we are," the duke said, pulling on the reins and bringing the buggy to a stop. As he helped Viola out, she swore he kept her hand in his longer than was necessary. "Well. What do you think?"

Most women, when being potentially courted by a duke, might prefer to be taken to a fashionable restaurant or the opera. They might hope to be brought to tea with royalty. To Viola, however, nothing could be more romantic than this crumbling chapel nestled at the foot of a hill.

It must have been abandoned at least two centuries earlier. The roof had caved in, allowing both sunlight and rain to fall on the floor below. The doors were gone, the windows long since broken, the stone steps carpeted in moss. Grasses and wildflowers swayed in the breeze at the base of the chapel or grew out of its crevices. This place was a fading memory of a lost world.

Viola adored it.

"Oh!" She forgot the duke for a moment and approached the chapel.

She poked her head inside and found more of those grasses and wildflowers sprouting from between the stones of the floor. One stained glass window hadn't been destroyed yet by time or weather, and autumn sunlight sparkled through the teardrop-shaped panes of red and blue and yellow glass. Their colored light shivered on the ground.

"Do you like it?" Huntington sounded pleased as he followed her inside the space.

"Of course I do!" She wandered toward the window, holding out her hand and watching red and blue waver on her skin. "I adore ruins."

"As I've said before, you're an original woman." The duke chuckled.

Viola felt no awkwardness now; she was too enthralled by the romance of the place. "When was this built?" she asked.

"Sixteen twenty-seven. It was intended to be added on to and eventually become the dower house, but the then-duke decided it was too far from both Moorcliff and the village to be practical." Hunt placed a hand upon one of the mossy walls. "They say my several times great grandfather had it built for his duchess. She was a very private woman and yearned for a place where she could collect her thoughts away from the demands of Moorcliff."

"He put a great deal of effort into it." Viola marveled at the little stone ornaments that had been carved into the cornices. A whole array of wildflowers had been etched painstakingly into these walls. "He must have known what she liked."

"They enjoyed quite a love match, the duke and duchess," Huntington said. Viola swore she could feel him staring at her. "Most of my family has enjoyed great luck in love."

"That's fortunate." She hoped he didn't notice her start to tremble, trying to contain the fireworks going off all through her body. As the duke came up behind her, slowly and steadily, Viola held her breath.

"My family keeps urging me to have the rest of it pulled down. There's nothing to be done with a ruin, and while it stands here the land's useless."

"Don't tear it down," Viola said at once. "I couldn't bear it."

"My thoughts exactly." Huntington stepped nearer until she felt him at her very back, until the warm scent of soap and good leather enveloped her. "Why do you like it so much?"

"I love ruined things, I suppose." She was not thinking as she spoke, and only the truest words came out. "It's so easy to love what's new, but to find the beauty in something that escapes most people's notice takes a special quality. Real love."

"You love what most people never see," he said, his voice both quiet and gruff.

"Perhaps it's why I've been homesick for Northumberland, though I left when I was only a child. Even if the landscape is desolate, it feels so true to itself. It hides nothing."

"You like Moorcliff, then?"

"It's the most beautiful place I've ever visited. Part of me wishes I could remain always."

The duke let out a soft, shuddering breath. She realized then how near he'd drawn to her during this conversation. She felt energy tingling all over her body, pulling her toward him as though she'd been magnetized. They were being drawn together by something purely natural.

"I know what you mean," the duke said. "I sometimes feel that if I never saw London again, I'd be only too happy."

"You don't seem to hate company," Viola said.

"I like people. Well, certain people. But the city's a hubbub of artifice; no one ever says what they really mean or gives voice to their truest desires. I've spent my life looking for something—and someone—purely honest. Entirely herself. I've often thought that once I found such a rare creature, I'd bring her to Moorcliff and live out our days in peace. I like to think of myself as a responsible man. There's no point to life without doing what's right, really. I'd live for two things, my duty to my tenants…and my wife. A man who lives for anything else is a fraud."

Viola had never felt such certainty of what she was feeling and what it meant. She felt both free and secure, excited and almost cozy with belonging. She shivered as he drew even closer. "If this particular woman were to ask you to leave this chapel untouched?"

"Not a stone would be altered. If she wanted the place restored to its former glory, it would be done." The air about them seemed to buzz with tension. "She only ever has to ask for a thing in order to have it."

"She must be very careful, then. A woman who receives that kind of power over a man has someone at her mercy. She must never abuse such a gift."

"What could have given you such a unique point of view?" he whispered.

"I suppose I know what it's like to be mishandled," Viola said.

"I hate that you know that."

"You do?" Her heartbeat was loud.

The duke towered above her, and she felt so small against him. There was security in this, a promise of safety that was also strangely exhilarating. In that moment, he was a buffer against everything bad in the world. Viola felt as if she had been searching for this moment her entire life and had stumbled upon it almost by pure chance.

"Of course I do." His arm circled her waist.

She was filling a place she'd dreamed of occupying for years. "Why?"

In answer, he leaned down to kiss her.

Be careful what you wish for; more tears are shed over answered prayers than unanswered ones; wanting something is often more exhilarating than getting it. Viola had believed that those sayings were true. That if she ever touched Huntington, or kissed him, it would never live up to what she had imagined.

As it turned out, all those terribly wise people had been wrong.

The brief instant his lips touched hers was more than she could have imagined, and she'd imagined a great deal.

This kiss was soft and quick and yet it was beyond anything she'd ever experienced. It was a chaste, exploratory kiss, gentle and yet promising all manner of wild, passionate experiences. She almost wept when the kiss ended, and the duke's lips hovered above her own. He groaned deep in his throat. She knew he was waiting for her to press forward and claim his kiss again. He had to know she wanted this, that she wanted him.

She wanted him badly. She wanted to capitulate into his arms and never leave. But Viola knew if she did that, she'd be swept away and never find her own two feet on the ground ever again. She'd only recently known how good it felt to stand firm and proud in herself; she knew she couldn't let that work be washed away.

And she knew to give in would be a mistake, a disaster for all involved. She had to be stronger.

"We mustn't," she whispered. "Please, Your Grace."

He released her at once and stepped back. His blue eyes burned into hers, and his broad chest rose and fell rapidly with his breathing.

"Forgive me," he rasped. "I don't know what came over me."

Apparently, a kiss could shake so many things loose. And speaking of loose, Viola was now ruined forever.

Then again, it's not as though she had any marital prospects to ruin. She was a thirty-year-old spinster governess, for goodness' sake. And she knew full well that the Duke and Duchess of Ashworth would never turn her out for kissing a man, even Huntington. Viola considered that this was the only time she'd ever have with the man she'd craved for years. Why not seize every opportunity? "Gather ye rosebuds while ye may" and all that. Poetry held the answer to every romantic question.

You're beginning to sound like the Duke of Ashworth!

"It was my fault, Your Grace."

"Absolutely not. It was mine entirely." He drew nearer. "I should never have taken advantage of you as I did."

That ruffled Viola a bit, the idea she was only a helpless thing to be toyed with, not a capable woman in her own right. "I believe I was glad to be taken advantage of, Your Grace."

"I wish we could stop with that bloody 'Your Grace' business." The duke winced. "Fuck, now I'm starting to swear." He scowled and shut his mouth.

Viola could not help it; she laughed. "My ears are hardly pristine, Your Grace."

"I'm a beast. You must think I've contrived to keep you at Moorcliff to seduce you."

Such a thought delighted her. It shouldn't have. "I think you kindly offered to let Felicity recuperate in your home. This just happened."

"No 'just' about it," he muttered.

"You've flattered me. But nothing good can come of this, and we both know it." She spoke gently, tried to conceal her own disappointment at her words. She hated being rational sometimes. "I know enough about life to understand that everyone has their place."

"That taximony nonsense again?" he muttered.

"Taxonomy." She chuckled. "Mine is a good place; I have no wish to put it in jeopardy."

The duke shut his eyes and sighed.

Viola wished she could be just a little more careless. But like Huntington, she knew she had responsibilities to people, to Felicity and the Ashworths. And whenever she imagined breaking every rule, Viola felt that line of fire at the base of her throat again and resolved herself to be calm.

She was marked by the reality of her past. There was no getting too far away from it. No forgetting what she was and was not, what she could and could never be.

"If you wish, I'll leave Moorcliff for the remainder of your stay. I'll claim business and ride off for a week or so. This won't happen again." The duke looked resolute as he offered the choice.

Occasionally, Viola became aware that the decision she was about to make, however minor it looked, would become a significant factor in her destiny.

She'd felt it when the vicar had offered to back her scholarship to the Wilkerson school when she was a child; she'd felt it when deciding between the Duke of Ashworth's offer and another posting; and she felt it now. Whatever path she decided on, there'd be no returning to this moment.

The wisest course of action would be to agree the duke should leave, or for Viola to volunteer to take Felicity and go. If Viola or the duke left now, that would be it. This one moment would be an embarrassing aberration in their lives.

But if she stayed, and if he stayed, then they put themselves at risk of something this delicious and dangerous happening again.

He couldn't marry her, for heaven's sake, and anything else was too scandalous to contemplate.

But if she left now, Viola was certain she'd regret it for the rest of her life.

"I don't want to drive you from your home," Viola said. "I think we're both capable of governing ourselves."

"Perhaps in your case." The duke looked at her with something akin to hunger. "Even at this moment, I find it hard." Hunt cleared his throat with vigor. "Hard to govern myself."

"This won't happen again," Viola said. "I can assure you."

From now on, they just wouldn't be alone together. Viola would be able to warm herself by the flame of his desire without being burned. She had that much self-control at least.

"How can you be sure?" he asked.

"Well. I'm a governess. Governing unruly charges is second nature to me." She smiled. "I doubt you're as much of a handful as Felicity."

The duke chuckled and gestured for her to leave the chapel ahead of him.

The sky above was still crisp and blue, though the wind had picked up. Viola wrapped her shawl tighter around her shoulders as the duke helped her back into the buggy.

"You may be mistaken in one thing, Miss Winslow." He gave a smile both wicked and wistful. "I think I can prove very troublesome indeed."

CHAPTER ELEVEN

What in hell was the matter with him?

As if Hunt hadn't made enough of a fool of himself with Susannah, now he had to compound his embarrassment with Miss Winslow?

They returned to the castle in silence, Hunt wondering how he could keep away from her the rest of her visit without drawing attention. More than that, he wondered how he could possibly stop himself from craving her.

A single brush of lips had kindled a fire in him, and the flames had fanned out of control. If she'd kissed him back, he might have become a rake and taken her in the middle of the ruined chapel. He might have hauled her over his shoulder and sped for the border and Gretna Green, forgetting his responsibilities to his family. Only Viola's good common sense had saved them both.

But damn it, he didn't want to be saved!

He'd never felt like this before, feverish and restrained. He could not stop thinking of her lips, of the lush curves of her body hidden beneath that gown, and he could not forget that she was forbidden fruit. She had told him no; she wanted to spare herself humiliation. Any other woman in England would have happily gone into his arms, but he had become besotted with the one woman who could easily reject his advances.

Twice now he'd offered himself to a woman and been turned down. Had he lost his touch? Was he a total incompetent when it came to love?

He meant that word, love. When she'd spoken dreamily of Northumberland and Moorcliff he had realized that here she was, the woman for whom he'd spent years searching. Someone intelligent and warm, someone who inspired passion in him the likes of which he'd never experienced, someone who loved what he loved and valued what he valued. He'd known her for ten bloody years and hadn't noticed! Until now.

And now she'd asked him to put all hope of her away forever.

There had to be some way forward. His mind was a churning maelstrom of pain and need as they drove into the castle courtyard. Hunt was determined to go inside and brood in his room until the solution to his problem presented itself.

But when they entered Moorcliff, a different sort of problem derailed his plans.

"Felicity!" Viola cried, aghast as her charge rocketed by in that blasted wheelchair, shrieking with glee as two footmen chased her, and that blasted raven winged overhead.

"Felicity!" Cornelius croaked.

"What are you doing?" Viola turned as the girl rattled past.

Felicity responded with a sort of whooping shriek, having the most delightful time.

"Oh dear! Oh dear!" Isabelle breathlessly hurried after the bizarre caravan.

Hunt stopped his sister in her tracks. "What the devil is the meaning of all this?" he boomed.

"Miss Berridge was curious to see how fast she could go if we first rolled her down an incline." Isabelle worried her lip. She did not usually see Hunt angry. "It's all right, I promise! She wanted us to push her down the top of the stairs, but I convinced her to go off one of the tables instead."

Down the hall came a crash that suggested the wheelchair had contacted a suit of armor. There was girlish squealing, manly shouts of horror, and a raven repeating the word "whiskey" over and over. Viola ran to get her charge while Hunt regarded his sister with bewilderment.

"This is unlike you, young lady. I thought you were going to show Miss Berridge the east wing."

"I did! I told her all about the Moorcliff haunt, and she claimed that her Mr. C.D. Winthrop wrote far scarier tales than any we could come up with. So that got me a bit piqued, and we had one of the servants retrieve that book from her room." Isabelle's eyes went wide as a pair of saucers. "That man is a genius! Truly, what is poetry compared to the tragic tale of a sailor long entombed beneath a castle's foundations whose bloody skull arises once a night to appear to the last heir of a dying aristocratic family and scream until morning?"

"What does a bloody skull have to do with Miss Berridge throwing herself down the stairs?" Hunt snapped.

"Off the table, as I said!" Isabelle was befuddled by Hunt's lack of understanding. "As for your question, well, I don't quite recall. We were having such a jolly time that when Miss Berridge asked to be thrown down the stairs it seemed a most natural progression."

Viola stormed back into the front hall, clearly struggling not to lose her temper as Felicity was wheeled about by one of the footmen. Cornelius rode on the back of the chair, his ravenly pride on display.

"Any bruises?" Hunt asked.

"I believe one of the footmen fell over the suit of

armor and banged his shin." The governess sighed. "But Felicity is unharmed. Somehow."

"I told you I've been studying how to take a fall! How else do you think I emerged from yesterday's tumble with only a sprain?" The girl looked pleased with herself. Felicity was so stubborn that Hunt sometimes wondered if she and Ashworth were not in fact related by blood.

"Forgive us, Your Grace. Perhaps a certain young lady should rest in bed for the remainder of the day." Viola let Felicity catch the threat.

"Oh, you wouldn't! And after the nice drawing I'd planned to make for you later." Felicity tsked with mock gravity.

"Would this drawing happen to involve the Bloody Skull of Whitewood Abbey?" Viola drawled.

"It's the skull of *Urlich Castle*, Miss Winslow! You really must know a little more about Mr. Winthrop's books before you mock them."

"They're so brilliant." Isabelle had never appeared more serious. "Perhaps the greatest art of this or any age."

Felicity wrenched control from the footman and scooted faster than Hunt believed the chair could move. Isabelle quickly took up her place at Felicity's side.

"We must continue reading," Felicity said, ignoring the adults. "Right now, Alonzo is about to enter the monk's secret chamber and uncover the *true* secret of the castle."

"Oh! I do love a good secret chamber." Isabelle gasped.

Viola stopped beside Hunt, allowing the girls to wander away. "I'm an utter disaster of a disciplinarian," she moaned.

"Well, no one died, and no bones were broken."

"Felicity has a way of making things energetic."

"All she needs is some fresh air and exercise." Hunt had an idea. "Perhaps it would do them both some good to get out. There's the pond not a quarter mile to the west, an excellent place for a picnic. This may prove to be one of the last sunny afternoons we'll have this year. If the girls agree to stop flinging themselves off tables and staircases, I think they'd enjoy such an outing. What do you think, Miss Winslow?"

"I think it's an excellent notion, Your Grace."

Greedily, he thought of the sun warming her fair skin, creating a more brilliant sparkle in her hazel eyes. He thought of being able to sit so near to her and it being nothing strange.

"Then let me arrange things. Collect Miss Berridge and we'll meet here in half an hour."

She curtsied and left, demure and contained as ever. Hunt gave orders and begrudgingly extended invitations to Agatha and his grandmother as well. It would look odd if they were not asked, and he needed to camouflage himself. If Miss Winslow— Viola—knew he had not put all hope of her away, she might feel obliged to leave. He must be stealthy, and above all he must be careful.

Twenty minutes later all was prepared. Hunt bumped into Isabelle on her way downstairs.

"Where's Miss Berridge?" he asked.

"She wanted to see if we'd any good Gothics in the library. I had to come up here to get my journal. One never knows when inspiration shall strike!"

Hunt was eager to head for the pond; he wanted his time with Viola to begin. Needing to hasten things, he decided to find Felicity in the library and wheel her out himself if he had to. He found the library door cracked slightly ajar and pushed in without knocking or announcing himself.

He froze when he found that the young girl's wheelchair was empty of its passenger. Hunt's mouth fell open when he saw Felicity Berridge, the so-called invalid, standing upon a ladder and stretching out her hand for a book.

"What the devil is this?" Hunt snapped.

With a squawk, the girl leaped down and landed upon the floor. There was nothing wrong with her ankle. She was perfectly fine.

"What kind of game are you playing, young lady?" Hunt adopted a stern tone that usually made Isabelle duck her head.

Felicity did not duck, nor did she wilt. She did not cower, or grovel, or simper. Indeed, she huffed and shrugged with insouciance.

"I suppose the charade is ended. Ah well. I knew I might have to explain myself sooner or later."

"Sooner. Now, as a matter of fact," he snapped. The girl stood before Hunt, hands on her hips. She was tall for her age, whippet-slender and gawky with adolescence, but there wasn't a trace of awkwardness about her demeanor. She looked him right in the eye. "What will Miss Winslow say when she learns of this?"

"She won't. Neither of us shall tell her, as it would derail my plans. I've worked far too hard to set all this into motion, I shan't have it spoiled now."

Hunt blinked. Was this child *instructing* him? "Explain. Now."

"We weren't supposed to come to Northumberland originally. I badgered Miss Winslow into bringing us, and I was the one who insisted on sketching Moorcliff Castle."

"For what reason?"

"The same reason I made sure to fall down the hill and pretended to sprain my ankle. I needed us to be taken in as your guests. It was the only way I could contrive for you and Miss Winslow to be alone together without loads of other people interfering."

Hunt's anger ebbed and his confusion flowed. "Why?"

Felicity shook her head. "Men really are slow. So that you'd fall in love and marry her, naturally."

A rational man would have been outraged by Felicity's admission, but Hunt had fallen deeply in love for the first and only time in his life and, as such, rationality was not high on his list of virtues at present.

He wanted to rejoice, pat Felicity's head, and buy her a parasol or a pony. Or a trebuchet. She might like that one best.

"So. This was all a plan of yours, then?" He needed to remain in control. He couldn't let this girl see how delighted she'd made him; it would murder his pride if nothing else.

"I've done everything short of yelling at you to get you to pay attention to her!" Felicity counted the details off on her fingers. "I tried to get her to spruce herself up with ribbons and such, I kept mentioning how pretty she is. You were so thick about it all that I wondered if you mightn't be too insipid to marry her. I should never let Miss Winslow saddle herself with someone like that. She's too fine for such things."

"My insipidness aside," he drawled, "I still can't see why you should want us to marry at all. I don't understand your reasoning."

"Be realistic, Your Grace. Governesses have

limited options for a happy retirement, don't they?"
The child plopped back into the wheelchair with the
ease of someone sitting down for a business meeting.
"Most end in miserable poverty. I shan't have that
happen to Miss Winslow. She's the most wonderful
person in the world, and I intend for her to live in
comfort and ease."

A surprisingly tender admission from one so
mercenary.

"First, I doubt the Duke of Ashworth would let
Miss Winslow go without a comfortable pension.
Second, isn't aiming to make your governess a duch-
ess shooting rather beyond the mark?"

Felicity snorted. "Perhaps we really *should* chop
rich people's heads off. France may have had the
right idea." Hunt resolved to never, ever let the
dowager and Felicity be alone together. "Frankly,
I'm uncertain as to whether you're good enough for
my governess, Your Grace. But I want her to be
happy, and you're the only option that will do, it
seems."

"Pardon?"

"I want Miss Winslow to have wealth, comfort,
and the man she loves. Why shouldn't she have everything she desires?"

Now Hunt himself had to sit down. His head was
spinning, a cry of exaltation lodged in his throat. He
couldn't stop himself from smiling. "She loves me?
How on earth do you know?"

Felicity perked up. Indeed, she bounced excitedly
in her seat. "Oh, I knew it! I knew you'd feel the
same if you only spent some time with her! I really
am too marvelously clever."

"Self-congratulation is a quality you and
Ashworth share," he muttered. "But you're certain

of her feelings?"

"She's loved you forever! Lord, why does no one pay attention?" She rolled her eyes, insolent chit. "I realized it when I was barely five. She always became so shy when you were about, it was obvious. When you almost married Miss Fletcher, it broke her heart."

Within the space of half an hour he'd left purgatory and entered paradise itself. Viola loved him, did she? She'd pined after him for years, had she? How could he have been so blind to how she felt, to who she was?

He was going to spoil her. He was going to lavish gifts and attention upon her, he was going to make her the happiest creature on earth.

He…had already been rejected. Firmly.

"Tell me, have you made any progress? Does she know how you feel?" Felicity asked.

"At the chapel, I kissed her." Hunt felt dizzy. "But she stopped it and asked me not to do so again."

Felicity spoke a word so vulgar he resolved to pretend he hadn't heard. "I feared that would happen. She's like a deer; one rustle in the underbrush and she takes off. Of course, you shouldn't have simply kissed her like that." She looked at him like he was a blundering novice. "You must have overwhelmed her, poor thing."

"Has anyone ever told you that you're rather insolent?"

"Yes, but I've chosen to take it as a compliment. Anyway, we must adopt a new strategy."

"Thank you, but I don't need to strategize with a child." He was feeling peevish. Viola had the patience of a saint; the girl was a nightmare. "Now that

I'm certain of her own feelings, I'm more than capable of handling matters."

"As you did with Miss Fletcher?" Felicity looked rather pitying.

Hunt had never wished to bury anyone alive before, least of all a girl, but he was warming to the idea. "Miss Fletcher did not love me. Miss Winslow, as you say, does."

"Yes, but she's wary. She'll give in to you only if you sweep her off her feet and make her so passionately in love, she can't resist you!"

"Well. Exactly. After our picnic, I intend to invite her to join me for a ride."

"She can't ride." Felicity frowned like she was doing a math problem.

"Fine. Then a walk."

"She'll know what you're doing. She's much too clever and will find a way out of it. We're going to have to trap her."

"This is love, not a hunt."

"Miss Winslow's instructed me in my Roman mythology. Cupid strikes with a bow and arrow, does he not?"

"Are you certain you and Ashworth aren't related by blood?"

"I'm trying to help you, Your Grace. Don't be stubborn." Felicity stroked her chin in deep thought. "The trouble is you're so old-fashioned. The intelligent, modern woman can't be stirred with picnics and the same old boring love sonnets over and over."

"No. Miss Winslow admires Mr. Blake's poetry," Hunt murmured.

"Precisely! She needs something grand and passionate. What she needs," Felicity said, leaping to her feet and scurrying back up the ladder, "is Gothic romance. It's all the rage these days." She snatched a book and pitched it at Hunt. *The Mysteries of Udolpho* by Mrs. Radcliffe. He paged through it as she continued. "What are flowers compared to meeting by the grave of a dead lover at the stroke of midnight? Who wants a man who simply says he loves you when you can have someone who looks at you like a ravenous wolf and growls? What's a better setting for a proposal, some boring old gazebo in the rose garden or the ruins of a haunted barricade?"

Hunt didn't know about the rest, but he knew Viola loved ruins.

Her admiration for Blake showed she was deeply passionate. He realized Felicity might know what she was on about, and that Hunt did not know how to overcome Viola's reservations. And he knew he must; if he wished to ever live happily, he must make her his.

But he had too much pride to simply beg an adolescent girl for advice.

"Young lady, I am a duke with over seventy thousand a year, a castle, and estates in most of the counties of England. I am a man of experience; you are a girl who's never left our shores once in your life. Yet you think you can instruct me in capturing a woman's heart?"

"Not just any woman. Miss Winslow." Felicity flopped back in her chair and glared. "I know her better than you. And while you may be a duke with a bloody fortune and a castle, you're still capable of bollocksing things up. If you don't wish to listen to my advice, we may as well tell her about my deception right now and leave Moorcliff. There's no way you'll ever win her hand without my help, and if you ruin all my carefully laid plans, I shall plot a suitable method of revenge. And as I've a long-held enthusiasm for catapults, rest assured it will be something unpleasant!"

"I am terrified for the man who eventually makes you his wife."

Felicity nodded. "As am I. So. Have we an agreement?"

If Hunt's first proposal of marriage had not ended in disaster, and if his recent attempt at a kiss had not been rejected, he would have ignored the girl and gone his own way.

But his proposal *had* been catastrophic; his kiss *had* been rejected; and he was certain that no one knew Viola Winslow as this girl did. Viola had as good as raised the child. So, if Felicity said that a new, modern way of romance was necessary, perhaps he needed to swallow his pride and listen. After all, love and happiness were at stake here. He must not lose.

"Should I choose to enlist your help," he said carefully, "what would you recommend?"

Felicity beamed in triumph.

"For starters, we're not having our picnic by the pond. I've thought of a much better location."

CHAPTER TWELVE

Viola thought a graveyard was as picturesque a spot for a picnic as any other, though it was perhaps less cheerful than most.

"This is a unique choice, Your Grace," she said to Huntington as the servants unpacked blankets and baskets. Two of them also carried Felicity about before resettling her in her chair, which she adored. "What made you favor this over the pond?"

"I thought the girls would enjoy a more unusual landscape to sketch."

"How thoughtful."

"Also," Huntington said, deepening his voice, "there's something about the atmosphere that quickens the blood. Don't you agree?"

"Er. Not really. The opposite, rather." What on earth was he on about?

"Right. That makes sense." The duke frowned as he surveyed the rows of marble plaques and stone angels. "Dead people and all that."

"Your Grace, would you come here a minute?" Felicity called. She leaned forward in her chair, looking cross about something. "I should like to be wheeled a bit uphill and I require assistance."

"The duke is not your servant, Felicity!"

But to Viola's surprise the man hastened to oblige the obstinate girl. He rolled Felicity this way and that, all while they engaged in a seemingly engrossing conversation.

Mystified, Viola went to sit upon the blanket alongside Isabelle and Agatha. The younger lady was absorbed in Felicity's Gothic pamphlet, and the elder read over a letter and grinned.

While her granddaughters read, the dowager sat and scowled at their gathering. She'd been placed in a chair, a footman shading her with a parasol.

Viola pretended she didn't feel the duchess glaring at her from time to time. She wished she could tell the old woman nothing had happened or ever would happen between the duke and her. Well, that was a lie. Something brief and wonderful *had* occurred, never to be repeated.

The memory of his kiss burned her cheeks. Meanwhile, the words Isabelle read aloud horrified her ears.

"Alonzo took up his sword as he lifted the torch higher. 'So, we meet again, Ransom! A coward always revisits the scene of his crime. I knew you would return to the spot where you murdered your own half brother, Rodrigo, whose bloody skull doth haunt the halls of my castle every night! Now, return to me my bride-to-be, or I shall disembowel you as I disemboweled your father's steward upon discovery of his nefarious plotting against the lover of my betrothed's long-lost sister!'" Isabelle pressed the booklet over her heart rapturously. "So many complications. Is it not grand? Agatha, doesn't it make you swoon?"

"For the wrong reasons, perhaps." Lady Agatha made a disgusted face.

"I should turn 'Giselle, the Tragic Ghost' into a novel worthy of Mr. Winthrop!" Isabelle pointed something out. "Look, just here? When the bloody skull shows up over the ramparts and sends Ransom to his death by falling into the moat? I had something like that in mind for Giselle's revenge against her half brother."

Viola needed to inspect Felicity's reading material more closely. Desperate for something less strange, she turned to Lady Agatha.

"May I ask if it's good news, my lady?" Viola nodded at the letter.

"Oh! Nothing too exciting." Lady Agatha's cheeks had turned a rather bright shade of pink. "My friend Esther Sims has written something very amusing. A story about her younger brother."

Lady Agatha tried to contain her burgeoning excitement, but it was too obvious. From the way she lovingly read the letter over again, it was clear she cherished its contents. This mysterious Mr. Sims and his amusing exploits, probably. Perhaps Lady Agatha was in love with the gentleman.

Of course, society would have nothing kind to say about a forty-year-old spinster who still harbored romantic notions. Even a duke's daughter with a substantial dowry would be considered unmarriageable at such an advanced age.

But so what? Viola thought with some indignation. Why shouldn't women hope for love and affection? Why should Lady Agatha be expected to let any dreams of happiness die because she was no longer three-and-twenty?

Why were women expected to take whatever they were given and be grateful?

Unable to stop herself, Viola watched Huntington as he wheeled Felicity about. He strode along, his steps large and powerful. He always seemed to be engaged in some new activity, which Viola found wonderfully energizing. The duke always looked ahead. He was strong in mind as well as body.

At the thought of his body, Viola ached inside.

She'd accepted long ago that she would never marry, or know physical love, and had made peace with that fact. But now she felt peevish at the thought that she would never know the sensation of his skin warming her own. The most unmaidenly thoughts darted through her mind, but she couldn't find the will to put them away.

"Miss Winslow? Agatha? Do listen to this." Isabelle read in a tremulous voice. "But lo! What should Esperanza see hanging above the ramparts like a ghoulish ornament but the same bloody skull that had screamed in her bedchamber only two nights before! And, with a hand laid upon her quivering bosom, the young girl recalled the mad monk's warning: that a new bride in Urlich Castle meant death to whosoever heard the skull scream three times!" She sighed. "Is it not the most astonishing prose?"

"Where precisely is this book set?" Lady Agatha appeared flabbergasted. "There are Spanish and Prussian names all over the place."

"Some border near where Spain and Prussia meet, I suppose." Isabelle returned to the book.

"They are in no way geographically connected! What on earth have your governesses been teaching you?"

"Miss Winslow!" Felicity arrived, wheeled by the duke. "His Grace says there's a mausoleum a short walk up the hill. I can't manage in my chair, but would you be sweet enough to go and make an etching of the plaque for me?"

"Really, Jamie. What a decidedly normal outing," Agatha said.

"Oh, you should go!" Isabelle brightened. "That's

the Lonely Duke's tomb. Hunt, you can tell Miss Winslow the tragic story on the way. It's *so* romantic and heartbreaking."

"You girls are making outrageous demands on Miss Winslow's time," the dowager snapped.

Viola wanted to refuse, but Felicity had turned those bright, pleading eyes on her and the governess could never resist such a spectacle.

Besides, they were in a family graveyard, the least likely spot for a romantic tryst. The duke would not try anything, surely.

"We shall return soon." Viola took up charcoal and paper.

She attempted to look unbothered as Huntington led her away from the party and along a narrow dirt path. They cut up and then along a hill.

In the distance, Viola admired Moorcliff's shimmer in the afternoon sun, the silver disk of the pond beside it. If only she could stay here forever. But for everyone's sake, not to mention her own, that could not be.

"So." She was too aware of the duke's sinfully delightful presence. Viola had to stop thinking about the kiss they'd shared, how she'd almost kissed him back. That would do nothing to strengthen her resolve. "The Lonely Duke. He sounds…lonely."

Huntington chuckled. "It was a bit more complicated than that. During the civil war, the then-Duke of Huntington supported the king's cause against the rebels. By all accounts, he was a man obsessed with honor and duty." *Rather like his descendent,* Viola thought. "He was betrothed to the daughter of a friend, a proper match."

"He sounds the opposite of lonely, then."

"Ah, but the poor old duke fell in love with a girl

who was entirely inappropriate. She was the daughter of a country squire with no dowry and no connections. My poor ancestor had to choose between duty and his heart. In the end, his heart won out. He married the squire's daughter in secret."

Viola found herself listening with the greatest care. "I take it things did not end happily?"

"To put it politely. The duke didn't realize it, but he'd married a rebel spy. The girl was a sworn enemy of the king and had been recruited to a simple mission. She was to marry the Duke of Huntington and assassinate him. The rebels hoped that with one of his most powerful supporters gone, the king would be easy to defeat."

Viola's throat felt dry. "So. She killed him?"

Huntington shook his head. "Fate would never be so simple. Apparently, the new duchess fell deeply in love with her husband. She was torn between her duty and her heart. Eventually, she decided to give them both up. This next bit's family legend, you understand, but it's said the duchess dressed herself in her bridal satin, went to her husband, and confessed her love and the whole plot to him. Then she stabbed herself in the breast and died in his arms."

"Good Lord!" They had arrived at a marble mausoleum, a rotunda of dark stone with weeping angels stationed along its roof. There was a brass plaque beside the iron gated door, reading *Henry Montagu, Duke of Huntington 1617-1692*. Remembering her promise to Felicity, Viola pressed the paper along the marker and ran her charcoal back and forth over the words. The name and date became imprinted on the page. "And then the Lonely Duke never remarried and pined away the rest of his days?"

"Er. Not exactly. His second duchess was the girl he'd been supposed to marry in the first place. They had five children."

Viola frowned at the mausoleum. "I think the Lonely Duke may have been misnamed, then. The truly sad story, to my mind, would be that of the rebel girl."

"Wasn't she a traitor?" Huntington seemed interested in Viola's reply.

Perhaps it was too bold, defending someone who'd conspired against his own family. But Viola's heart ached for this woman, and she refused to turn her back on the tragic duchess. Enough people had done that already.

"Only think about it. She was the one who remained true to her oaths. She knew she couldn't kill him and refused to live with that failure." Viola felt her spirits sink as she looked past the iron grate and into the dusky interior of the crypt. "He abandoned his duty to follow his heart, then forgot the woman he thought he'd loved easily enough. No, she is the nobler of the pair by far." Huntington didn't grow angry at Viola besmirching his ancestor's honor. Indeed, he seemed even more fascinated. "I'd like to see her grave, if I may."

"There isn't one. After the duchess's death, the duke took care of all the funeral arrangements by himself. He likely buried her in an unmarked grave somewhere on the estate, a way of hiding his shame."

"How awful." Viola wanted to kick the damned mausoleum, even though it would hurt her far more than it would the stone. "Perhaps I see now why Lady Isabelle is so taken with the tale. It's terribly sad."

"More than that. The old duchess's ghost is rumored to be the one haunting the east wing. According to Isabelle, that is. The woman apparently stalks the halls in her bloody wedding gown, crying out for her lost love." He shook his head and chuckled. "It's the most maudlin nonsense in the world."

But Viola didn't laugh. "I think it's lucky that there is no such thing as ghosts," she whispered. "I wouldn't wish such a dreadful fate on anyone."

"How do you mean?" the duke asked.

"It's sad because the lady would have to remain forever unnoticed, watching while the man she loved married another woman and raised a family with her." Viola refused to look at him as she spoke. "A ghost is never allowed to grow past her tragedy. She must mourn the same memory over and over, long after everyone else has ceased caring. I can think of nothing lonelier."

To her horror, Viola realized the duke had grown silent and grim. He walked away with his head bowed as if under some weight.

"Have I upset you? I didn't mean to," she said.

Huntington turned around, looking all amazement.

"Upset me? Perhaps you did, but not in the manner you think." Hope and despair intermingled in his blue eyes. "For hundreds of years, the Moorcliff haunt has been something of a family joke, and yet in one afternoon you've completely sympathized with the idea. When I consider it from your perspective, Miss Winslow, I see a kindness and depth of feeling I'd never thought possible. You're extraordinary. It wounds me," he murmured, "that I cannot possess...your qualities."

That I cannot possess you.

Was she imagining it, or were those the words he yearned to speak?

The world seemed to hold its breath as she considered him, the desire in his glance and the tension in his body. If he did not have a duty…if Viola was not who she was…

But she *was* who she was.

The duke thought her a typical governess, a woman of good breeding and no money who was making her way in the world. Under those circumstances the gap between their stations would be large enough, but the reality of her origins rendered that gap a veritable canyon.

The truth of her past and the pain she'd suffered would always be with her, and she did not want to share them with anyone else.

If that meant she had to live a life alone, so be it.

Viola wanted no one's judgment. Not even if judgment also meant she could press her lips to the duke's, lose herself in his arms. No matter how much she still yearned for that to be so, she must fight the impulse.

Felicity and I must go, she realized as she gazed upon the Duke of Huntington with unbearable wanting. *I was a fool to linger even a moment more. We must leave before tonight.*

As if in answer to her thought, a chill wind sliced past them and set the grass waving about wildly. The sky overhead had turned iron gray and was deepening to black. Thunder rumbled in the distance, and Viola saw rain begin to fall upon the far-off hills.

"We should return to the castle." The duke beckoned her. "Come, Miss Winslow."

The girls were sad to pack up the picnic lunch. On the rumbling trip back to Moorcliff Castle the heavens burst wide, and a freezing rain rippled across the road and the carriages. Viola had gotten a bit wet before she'd been able to climb inside, and now sat there shivering and watching lightning write itself upon the storm.

"Thank you for saving my etching," Felicity said beside her. The girl inspected the charcoal image with pride. "It's only a bit damaged at the corners. You're a genius, Miss Winslow."

"I hope this has proved to be a delightful outing, my dear. Apart from the rain, of course."

"Oh yes. I hope you've enjoyed it, too."

Viola could not recall a time she had been any happier. That was what made her so utterly wretched.

CHAPTER THIRTEEN

Viola brushed out Felicity's hair before putting it up, as the girl never kept herself tidy enough. Her young charge stared into the mirror, watching the governess at work.

"No one's hair needs to be brushed this much, you know."

"Perhaps if you did not fling yourself off so many tables, your hair would be less tangled." Viola smiled, unable to remain cross with Felicity. "Now you will be on your best behavior at dinner, yes?"

"I *can* behave perfectly." Felicity scrunched her nose. "Perfection is so often a bore, though, isn't it?"

"I can't disagree, though please do your best. The dowager duchess seems to derive pleasure from seeing us behave in an inferior manner."

"Yes, she's rather a snob." Felicity smirked. "Very well. I shall be on my best behavior at dinner. We'll see how the old lady reacts then!"

"I do wish you were less motivated by spite, but I shall take whatever I can get."

Viola was quick about her work. She'd always had deft hands, Betsy had said. Speaking of Betsy, she realized with a start she'd never opened the two letters from the inn yesterday. Too much had happened, including but not limited to a perfect kiss and impending heartache.

Viola wished she could show her emotions a bit more freely. She desperately needed someone to confide in just now, but Felicity was far too young, and it would be inappropriate to approach anyone else. She'd have to do as she'd done her whole life: swallow her feelings and get on with it.

"Here." She handed the Duchess of Ashworth's letter to Felicity. "What does Her Grace report?"

Felicity opened the letter and scanned its contents. "Violet is attempting to walk, and Arthur misses me." She seemed happy about that. The Ashworth children were as good as siblings to Felicity.

Viola appreciated how the duchess had made every effort to count Felicity as one of her children; she knew from experience how painful rejection could feel at such a young age.

Betsy's letter remained unopened. Viola had to remedy that and sighed as she sat down to read.

"Her Grace says they might get a new puppy! A spaniel." Felicity cheered. "I do hope it shall be a black and white one. I think them the most handsome kind. She also hopes I have not been too unruly. Wait until she hears how I sprained my ankle! I can't wait to write about the duke and Moorcliff. Won't everyone be jealous? Lovely."

Viola could not reply. Her sister's letter knocked every thought out of her head.

Vi,
Pleese com see us. We ned your help. It is verry impourtent.
Betsy

Nothing more than that, no hint as to what the problem might be.

But if Betsy was asking Viola to come see her, then something serious must have happened. Probably something to do with their father.

The thought made Viola sick.

Even after a full decade of sending what money she could to her sister, Betsy and the children hadn't been able to find a place of their own. Too many mouths to feed, too many bodies to clothe and shelter. Viola's earnings did not stretch far enough.

God, Viola's past was right on her doorstep now. Worse, it was on the duke's doorstep. Viola had worked hard to ensure that no one, neither the Duke of Ashworth, nor the duchess, nor Felicity, nor anyone else knew the truth of her past.

To make matters worse, Huntington might find out. He didn't know that Viola's family were tenants on his own land. Even if the wretchedness of Viola's birth didn't disgust him, he'd likely be insulted by her lies.

But she could not turn her back on her family, not for anything. Not even for the duke's good opinion of her.

If they were in trouble, then Viola had to help in any way she could. Her mind spun as she worked it all out. They lived five miles from the castle. There was no reason she couldn't pay a visit and then return to Moorcliff without anyone knowing the details.

But the journey to and from the farm would take up most of the day tomorrow, meaning Felicity and she would have to stay yet another night under the duke's roof. Another night spent close to him, the heat of his eyes and the nearness of his body. Viola felt dizzy.

Just once, she wished she could swoon as a gentlewoman might and lay her burden upon a man's shoulders. But that had never been the way for working women like her.

"Are you well?" Felicity folded up her letter.

"You're not sick, are you?" The girl became a bit panicky at the notion.

Viola smiled; wild as Miss Felicity Berridge might be, she was loyal to those she cared for. Putting away her letter, Viola went to put the finishing touches on Felicity's hair.

"Quite well. I need to make a brief trip tomorrow, that's all."

A knock sounded upon the door. Viola expected Mrs. Moore and was surprised when Lady Agatha poked her head inside.

"Oh! My lady, can I help with anything?"

"I believe the question's the other way around." The woman scanned Viola from head to toe. "Have you any other gowns, Miss Winslow?"

"No, my lady. This is the best I own." Viola had put on her dove gray dress with the lace collar. Perhaps it was plain to the eyes of the *ton*, but to her it constituted elegance itself.

"It's lovely," Lady Agatha said quickly, "but I was hoping you might indulge me. We're roughly the same size, and I've ever so many gowns that never get worn. Would you allow me to dress you for dinner?"

The offer was a surprise, but even more so was Lady Agatha's air of slight shyness. Normally, the woman was bold and direct. She seemed the type who liked to get things accomplished and people looked after. As Moorcliff was rather isolated, she probably did not get the chance to deal with new people often.

"Oh. Would that be appropriate, my lady?" Viola asked.

Felicity made a rude noise. "Hang propriety! You should have a new gown, Miss Winslow!"

"Felicity! This is not a place for you to have an opinion."

"As a personal favor to me, Miss Winslow, would you mind?" Lady Agatha remained friendly, but some of her firmness was back. There was no real way to retreat from this. Besides, Viola had always yearned for an opportunity to wear something fine. With Huntington about, it was a chance like no other.

Though an evening dress would have a lower neckline…

"Come along!" Lady Agatha pushed cheerily into the room. A lady's maid floated in behind her, carrying an armful of green satin. "I took the liberty of selecting something myself. I hope you don't mind."

Viola knew she couldn't object, even if she did mind. Lady Agatha reminded her of Felicity in many ways, irrepressible and yet charming. Felicity was delighted she'd be able to watch the transformation. When the lady's maid approached Viola, the governess stepped back instinctively.

"Miss Winslow?" Lady Agatha frowned. Viola's hand floated to the base of her throat.

"Um. The neck's a bit low, isn't it?"

"Well, it's an evening dress." The other woman looked baffled.

"There's just a bit of an unsightly mark. A birthmark," she added hastily. "It's right here. I prefer to keep it hidden."

Ever undaunted, Felicity plucked a green silk hair ribbon from the dresser and proffered it with a devilish grin.

"It will look splendid with the gown! It also reminds me of this one story where a woman wore a

ribbon around her throat. When her bridegroom removed it on their wedding night, her head fell off!"
Felicity sighed. "Now that's romantic."

"Let's aim to keep your head upon your shoulders," Lady Agatha said.

The maid was expert at her job, unsurprisingly.
Within moments, she had Viola out of her old gray
dress and into the emerald gown.

She'd never known anything so soft in her life;
the silk was like cool water on her skin. The elegant-
ly trimmed hem belled around her feet, and Viola
had to resist the impulse to swirl to watch her gown
float through the air.

They tied the green ribbon around Viola's
throat, though not before the maid caught a
glimpse of the "mark." She said and did nothing,
but Viola knew she recognized what it was and
could only hope the woman would keep quiet.
Viola liked privacy.

Then again, what *didn't* she like to keep private?
Sometimes Viola kept her own feelings so deeply
buried that she herself didn't know them. Perhaps it
was the reason she could feel so horribly lonely even
in a room filled with people.

If none of them knew how she truly felt, could
they really know her?

Viola thought of Huntington in the chapel this
morning, that one moment when they had kissed. It
was the first time in years, perhaps in her entire life,
when she'd done precisely what she wanted to. She'd
never felt so free.

The duke was the first person with whom she
could feel like herself. Ironic, wasn't it? The only
man who could be said to know her was the man she
could never have.

If Viola went on like this, she'd be as maudlin as Lady Isabelle in no time. After being dressed, she seated herself before the mirror while Felicity lounged upon the bed, surveying the maid's work on Viola's hair with glee.

"You have such a lovely face," the maid, Fincher, said, as she loosened Viola's hair and started weaving it into a more elegant—and complicated—style. "You shouldn't wear your hair in such a severe manner, Miss."

Viola could have argued that governesses didn't have time for doing their hair in elaborate fashions, but she was too stunned by the transformation currently taking place. Under Fincher's expert hands, Viola's hair was put up in a manner almost Grecian, with soft tendrils escaping to frame her face. Viola had always thought her features too rounded, but when her hair was like this, it made her look less like a full-cheeked young girl and more ethereal.

"You look like a faerie," Felicity said in approval, echoing Viola's thoughts.

"This is far too much," she stammered as Lady Agatha pulled her to her feet and faced Viola to look in the full-length mirror.

"I think you're our guest and should look the part." Lady Agatha beamed at the governess's now-unrecognizable reflection. "You've earned some luxury. I can tell."

"Indeed, she has," Felicity said. "I'm frequently exasperating."

No one argued with her on that point.

The gown was emerald silk trimmed in gold lace, the neckline a plunging V lower than any Viola had worn before. The green ribbon worked beautifully with the whole. Normally Viola dressed in blacks and grays; she'd never known how alive a person could look in a different shade. Her cheeks had rosy color to them and her skin seemed to glow.

"Fincher was right. It matches the green in your eyes." Lady Agatha appeared proud as the lady's maid neatened the last details, fluffing Viola's skirt.

"You're much too kind, my lady."

"Nonsense. I enjoy a little variety in my company. You and Miss Berridge are the most exciting thing to happen to Moorcliff since Hunt's return last year."

Hunt. The duke.

Viola would sit at his table dressed like this, and she couldn't imagine the tension growing between them would lessen. Disastrous though the impulse was, all Viola wanted in this world was for Huntington to see her dressed like this. She wanted him to like her more than ever.

You're going to regret it.

She shut out that sensible voice. It was as Lady Agatha had said. Viola was a guest, and she knew she could control herself. It was the one thing she always *could* control.

"You know, emerald is rather the Huntington color." Lady Agatha appeared almost sly as she spoke. "Our mother's engagement ring was an emerald."

"Oh?" Viola hoped she wasn't blushing too hard.

"It's been a family heirloom since the sixteenth century. The future duchess always receives it during her engagement."

"Ah. Yes." The duke had presented the emerald to Susannah the night she'd turned down his proposal. The thought made Viola's stomach cramp.

"Jamie's favorite color is green. He'll be pleased with the gown."

"Oh, I doubt the duke will notice." Viola's pulse was loud in her ears.

"Indeed?" Lady Agatha stole behind Viola to adjust some microscopic detail on the dress. "We'll see, won't we?"

The lady winked at Viola in the mirror and then departed with her maid.

Soon after, the footmen arrived to carry Felicity downstairs. Viola followed, trying to steady her thoughts. It wasn't so astonishing Lady Agatha had noticed something between her and the duke; she was an observant woman.

The shocking thing was that, unlike her grandmother, Lady Agatha seemed delighted by the prospect.

• • •

Hunt's valet left him impeccably groomed as ever.

The duke took a moment to fuss with every aspect of his appearance, wondering how it would please Viola. She was a sensitive woman of impeccable taste, and she must be charmed anew at their every meeting.

Their little outing in the graveyard had been unusual, to say the least, but he had to begrudgingly admit it had worked somewhat. The woman had revealed her true thoughts in such an artless way. Perhaps Felicity knew something of what she was about after all.

There was a knock and Isabelle pushed in.

"Oh dear." His sister clucked her tongue as she beheld him. "Miss Berridge was right. You look so much less interesting when you've been shaved."

"Excuse me?" A troubling thought suggested

itself. "Young lady, have you been conspiring with Felicity in these endeavors?"

"Getting you and Miss Winslow to marry? Of course I have." The girl circled Hunt, studying his appearance from every angle. "She mentioned it when Miss Winslow went to town to fetch the luggage. I think it's splendid! I should love it if your wife was a student of poetry. It would help me so very much!"

"You're not the one who needs to be pleased by my marriage," Hunt grumbled.

"Oh, you're already pleased with her. I can see how you look at her. So can Granny, which is why she keeps scowling. Oh, I have a thought!" She patted his shoulders. "Do sit down. I can help roughen your appearance a bit. Women do like a rough appearance."

"How on earth would you know?"

"Mr. Winthrop's writing, of course! He understands a woman's soul in a way no other male writer ever has." Isabelle jammed Hunt into a chair before the mirror and then began cheerily shoving her hands through his hair.

"The devil are you on about?" He waved her off.

"You must look disheveled! You must look as though you've been brooding alone here in your ancient tower, haunted by love for a woman you wish to possess as your own!"

"I will be more attractive to Miss Winslow if my hair is combed."

"If you say so." Isabelle sounded pitying as he made to neaten his hair. "But Miss Berridge says you've agreed to let her instruct you."

Hunt recalled the girl's threat of catapults. He remembered in Felicity's early childhood when she'd designed something called a Hedgehog Cannon. He wondered who was more of a tyrant, Napoleon

Bonaparte or Felicity Berridge.

More than that, he thought of Viola, and how her young charge could either be a help or hindrance in wooing her. With a sigh, Hunt allowed Isabelle to go about yanking his hair.

"There." She clapped her hands. "You look enigmatic."

"My head looks like a porcupine."

"It is the same thing."

Hunt patted down a few of the more vertical pieces of hair while Isabelle nabbed something from off his desk. It was a bottle of whiskey, of which he'd had only a sip today.

"What the devil?" Hunt spluttered as his sister poured a bit of the amber liquid into her hands and started flicking droplets at him.

"Think of it as a manlier sort of cologne. In Mr. Winthrop's stories, a gentleman is never more enticing than when he is disheveled and drunk. I assume I can't convince you to go to dinner without your coat?"

"You assume correctly." He brushed as much of the whiskey away as he could. "Has it occurred to you that Miss Winslow might not like me if I look like a madman and smell like a pub?"

"Hunt, please. Every woman yearns for a man who is just like that! If it weren't too late in your life for a change of career, I would suggest you become a highwayman. They're the most dashing of all!"

"I've decided I'm going to take your books away from you." He stood and neatened the front of his clothes. "I've also resolved to lock you away until you're thirty-five or I'm dead."

"Oh, you're silly." She stood on tiptoe and kissed his cheek. "Don't you know prison breaks are the most romantic thing in the world?"

CHAPTER FOURTEEN

When Viola entered the dining room dressed in that emerald gown, her eyes like jewels and her lips rosier than he'd ever seen them, Hunt was lost.

This transformation had to be down to Agatha's meddling, and while he usually found it tedious, right now he could have thrown her a parade.

Throughout dinner he ignored his grandmother, who made affronted noises and disguised them as throat clearings. Once, she pretended to choke on a bit of bread to wrest his attention from the governess, but all he did was pour her a glass of water. Hunt paid no attention to his sisters' playful bickering or Felicity's delight in trying to get Cornelius to say something rude.

No. All his true attention was reserved for Viola.

Even though she mostly kept her eyes on her plate, occasionally he would catch a glance of hers from across the table. He'd been surprised by her charms before, but seeing her dressed in a gown that complemented her beauty allowed him to realize she was the most ravishing creature he'd ever seen.

She was exactly like one of the faeries that the old pagans had believed flitted around the countryside. She was delicate, but also voluptuous. He couldn't help the way his gaze fell on the swell of her bosom, so daringly revealed in that cut of gown.

She wasn't only a fantasy, a nymph created out of thin air. She was a real woman with soft skin and kissable lips. He'd never known desire like this in his life. He hadn't believed a man could feel this way, not truly. Lust was common, but infatuation like this felt impossible. He wanted to spend hours worshipping her body. Merging with her, making them as one. He wanted to touch her, to be the only man who ever would.

His grandmother cleared her throat so hard, she almost gave herself a coughing fit. Hunt finally paid attention to her.

"Yes, Gran?"

"Ah, he speaks! Thank you for gracing us with your attention at last." Her lips were puckered in irritation. "If you hadn't noticed, the meal has concluded, and we ladies shall be adjourning to the parlor. You may join us once you have completed a cigar or a glass of port." She sniffed. "You may also find a moment to comb your hair, if you can manage."

"Hunt looks splendid this way!" Isabelle cried.

"Cigar, port, comb. Yes, I've my assignment well in hand," he drawled.

"Why don't we have some music tonight?" Agatha smiled. "We could even dance! It's been ages since we had any dancing."

"With an invalid girl, a governess, an old woman, and his two sisters, Hunt will have quite a selection of partners." The dowager rose with frosty dignity.

"Dancing sounds wonderful." Then, feeling bold, Hunt said, "Wouldn't you agree, Miss Winslow?"

"I…" Some of his boldness appeared to have infected her as well. "Yes, Your Grace. I believe I would."

"Excellent!" Felicity pushed back from the table, her chair rolling into a footman. The poor man caught her, eyes bulging as the chair got him in a, er, personal place. "This will be such fun." The girl nodded quickly at Hunt as if she were tipping him. She approved of his plans. Threat of being catapulted to death receded before him.

Hunt allowed the ladies their privacy for the briefest possible time. After a rushed glass of port, he joined them in the music room. Felicity was already at the pianoforte picking out melodies, Viola seated on the bench beside her.

"Like this, dear. Remember how we practiced? The thumb in *this* position." Viola played with elegant confidence.

Everything this woman did was elegant. He was feverish for the merest touch of her hand; he needed to dance with her.

"Miss Winslow, you play so well," the dowager said, glaring at her grandson as she spoke. "Why don't you play the first few numbers?"

"Don't order her about, Gran." Hunt stared the old woman down, but Viola obliged the duchess and started playing.

Isabelle and Felicity "danced," by which Isabelle pushed Felicity's chair off in one direction and then hurried to catch it. In keeping with much of Hunt's life over the past year, this would probably end in disaster.

But maybe Isabelle needed a little disaster.

She'd been so animated all day, not once moping around the library or wandering the garden listlessly studying flowers. Giselle, the tragic ghost, had taken a holiday.

It hadn't occurred to Hunt how deeply his own isolation had affected his family. It seemed all Isabelle required to grow lively was real companionship. And Felicity certainly kept things engaging, if also a little perilous.

"She looks happy," Agatha said, tugging at

Hunt's sleeve. He obliged her with a dance, keeping time with the music while avoiding being trampled by the girls. "I haven't seen her like this in ages."

"Perhaps Ashworth might have her at Lynton Park for a time. She and Felicity seem to do well together."

"Perhaps you might join Isabelle there." Agatha was as subtle as a brick with the word "subtle" painted across it.

"Dare I ask what your plan for me is?"

"You're always so suspicious. I only think it would be nice for you to spend time with Ashworth and his family!" Agatha grinned. "Who knows what might come of it?"

Was she talking of Viola? God, she had to be.

Agatha had dressed the governess for dinner, done her hair, fixed every detail to make her more ravishing than ever. Hunt grew stern; Agatha didn't know what kind of incendiary material she was playing with.

"Chaffin Manor is a mere five miles from the Park," he said, speaking of their estate in Somerset. "Why should I need to stay with Ashworth?"

"You shouldn't keep isolating yourself, Jamie. There's so much you'll miss out on if you do."

Hunt wondered if she spoke from experience; he wondered if she regretted never marrying. He suddenly asked how his older sister had come to be a spinster in the first place.

Agatha was a handsome woman with an enormous dowry and connections to the Huntington line. As a young debutante, any man in London would have taken her if given half a chance. Neither Hunt nor his father had ever pressed Aggie to marry, both consumed with running the estate and maintaining the legacy. Love came easily to the Montagus, after all. Everything would turn out well. It always did for their family.

Horrified, Hunt wondered if he'd done his sister a great disservice.

"Don't look so serious," she said as the music stopped. Agatha lifted a brow. She never looked more elder-sister-ish than when she did that. "Try to enjoy the moment."

I can't do that, can I? A man with my responsibilities must always have one eye on the future. I promised Father, after all.

"Miss Winslow, might I have a go?" Agatha hurried over to the pianoforte and replaced the governess. Viola stood by the side of the room, smiling at Felicity and Isabelle.

"Play a waltz next, my lady!" Felicity looked a bit red-cheeked and wild-eyed as she craned her neck and instructed Isabelle. "This time, let go in the middle of a spin and we'll see how far I roll."

"I say, this is rather a lot of work." Hunt's sister huffed more than a lady in fine evening dress should. The dowager appeared livid at all the wildness on display.

"I'll control Felicity," Viola said, heading for the girls.

"No." Hunt put out an arm and stopped her. He would not let her go; he would keep her here, wearing that delectable gown, looking at him with those exquisite eyes. Agatha began a waltz. "They're enjoying themselves, and I believe Isabelle is tired out." In truth, if the girls had been attempting to leap off the chandelier he wouldn't have minded. All Hunt wanted was this moment of privacy with the governess. "Miss Winslow? Would you do me the honor of a dance?"

He waited for her to stammer, to try to beg off. Instead, she looked at him with those extraordinary eyes, and he understood she was appraising him. Judging whether she wished to take another risk. Viola chose not to please him, but to please herself.

It was wildly erotic. Especially when she smiled and said, "Yes, Your Grace. I would like that. Thank you."

Apparently, the spirit of rebellion was catching tonight. Her hand was in his, and his other hand fell to her delicate waist. He could feel the ample curve of her through the silk of her gown and had to concentrate on not becoming too bloody excited.

"Though…" Viola worried her lip. "I've never waltzed, I'm afraid. At least, not with a man. I know the steps. I've practiced with Felicity, but I've never…"

She'd never had a debut, had never been presented anywhere. It was a staggering injustice, though Hunt was secretly pleased to have her first real waltz.

"That's no trouble," he murmured.

The music room vanished; Agatha's playing became silent; the girls were no longer squealing and racing about. Hunt's sole attention fell upon this woman in his arms. He focused on her sweet, kissable mouth; on the rise and fall of her generous breasts; on the tendrils of dark hair framing her face; on those half-lidded, languorous hazel eyes.

I want you. The words burned inside him.

"You'll show me how to properly dance, Your Grace?" She beamed.

I'll teach you more than that. I'll teach you

pleasure like you've never known; I'll show you ec-
stasy. Just bloody kiss me again.

Somehow, he swallowed those words.

"There's no real trick to it. Simply follow my lead, and I'll take you in the right direction."

"Will you, really? I'm not so sure." She'd meant to lightly tease him. The playful side of Miss Winslow was emerging, a flower budding after a long winter.

"I'll show you the steps." He moved, his body guiding hers across the floor. She was so damn small in his arms, yet she did not feel fragile now. She felt warm and radiant, more alive than anyone he'd known before. "There's no dance you can't master. I'm certain of it."

"With you as a teacher, Your Grace, I'm positive I could learn anything."

He imagined her naked and lying on a rug before the fire, the brown of her hair highlighted in the glow. He imagined moving above her, inside her, the way she shivered as he made her climax. He thought of kissing her lips for hours on end, teaching her how good it could feel to be loved by a man.

They did not speak as he helped guide her faltering steps. Hunt didn't trust himself to say anything. After a few minutes, Viola began to pick up the idea. She had a good understanding of rhythm, as evidenced by her playing earlier. Hunt sped the dance up a bit, but not too much. He wanted Viola to remain in control, and more than that, he wanted to luxuriate in this experience.

"Come. We ought to talk about something, don't you think?" he said. "I'd suggest discussing the weather, but as it's been abysmal the last two days, I don't know there's much to discuss." As if in agreement, thunder rolled outside the window.

"It's really a most dramatic setting," she replied with a laugh. "No wonder your castle's haunted."

"You mustn't pay tales of the bloody duchess any mind. Nothing's ever happened here more terrifying than my grandmother's occasional battle with gout. Though that in itself is rather frightening."

"I haven't seen Felicity look this well in some time. Despite the sprained ankle."

Yes. Hopefully the girl would continue playing the invalid to perfection.

"I could say the same for my sister. Agatha suggested letting the two spend time together down at Lynton Park. If it would be agreeable, that is."

"I'm sure Their Graces would like nothing better."

"No, I meant agreeable to you. You've enough to occupy yourself with Miss Berridge, I've no doubt."

"Oh." She blushed. "You don't need to consult me on such things, Your Grace."

"I think we both know that isn't true."

That electric charge between them returned, stronger than before.

"Agatha also suggested I accompany Isabelle to Somerset. Now I would very much like to consult with you about that," he murmured.

"So. The choice is to be mine, then?"

It felt as if the world held its breath about them.

"I would have it no other way. So. What do you choose, Miss Winslow?"

The music stopped at that crucial moment, and he was forced to release Viola. She hesitated, as if on the threshold of giving her answer. But then the noise of the outside world seemed to rush back in on them, and she shook her head, returning to her senses.

"Thank you for the waltz, Your Grace." She curtsied. Then Viola was gone, back to the instrument.

Hunt's temples throbbed. Whenever he felt himself making progress, shyness snatched her away.

"Hunt! Come dance with us." Isabelle was slumped against the back of Felicity's chair, her hair tumbling out of its updo. It was clear his two coconspirators wanted a word. Hunt took Isabelle's place at the helm of the chair.

"Why don't we have a walk about the room instead?" As Viola played, he pushed his guest at a leisurely pace. "Is there something you wish to say?" he muttered.

"The dancing was good, but you're being much too polite with her." Felicity sounded exasperated.

"I am a gentleman, not a pirate or a highwayman or a lunatic. I must always be polite with a lady."

"Oh Hunt." His sister sounded plainly sorry for him. "I pray you don't die alone."

"Politeness is old-fashioned." Felicity got him to stop walking and kneel beside her chair, acting as if a bit of her skirt had become caught in the wheel. This low, with his back to the dowager, they could have a more animated chat. "The modern woman yearns to be challenged. You need to pick a fight with her. Tell her she's wrong about something. Say you're disappointed in her. Then, when she gets angry, you must get closer and closer until you are just within kissing distance and then…!"

"And then we kiss?" Hunt glared at the girl.

"Either that or one of you stabs the other. I suggest kissing."

"Indeed. I don't think stabbing will do much to help you just now," Isabelle added.

"Miss Winslow is a shy, tender woman. Why

would she ever wish me to berate her?"

"She's also a woman of vast intelligence. Trust me." Felicity narrowed her eyes. "Challenge her."

"Wouldn't you know it?" Hunt shoved the chair forward at a healthy clip. "Time for you ladies to be in bed."

"Good." Felicity looked pleased. "Then you accompany her to our room alone. Be sure to keep her up late; she'll be easier to kiss if she's tired."

The child was a monster.

After another two hours, the adult party broke up. As the girls had hoped, Hunt walked Viola back to her room. He kept their pace slow, trying to think of something clever or romantic to say. Unfortunately, his heart was pounding like some bloody schoolboy's and all his words had dried up.

"I'm afraid I need to ask a favor, Your Grace," Viola said.

"What is it?" His throat tightened; he waited for her to ask him to send her and Felicity away.

"I heard in town of a nearby farm. Not five miles from the castle, in fact. I should like to go there tomorrow and see if they've any apples to sell. Felicity has a great taste for them, and I'd like to give her a treat while she recovers. Would it be possible to borrow a cart after breakfast?"

"Of course." He could have asked why she needed to go five miles for fruit when he could provide Felicity with a damn pineapple if she required, but he was so relieved Viola needed only to make a day trip that he'd grant her any absurd request. "I'll lend you the coach."

"Thank you so much." She looked soft with relief as they approached her bedchamber. His time was running down. Should he say she was beautiful? Recite a sonnet? Kiss her hand with delicacy and tenderness? "Well. I shall say good night, then."

They'd come to her room, and he hadn't done a damned thing.

He could practically hear Felicity behind the door gritting her teeth and drawing up plans for a man-sized catapult. Hunt was angry with himself for being so ineffective.

"Good night?" he muttered. *Oh, why not? I can't make things any more stalled than they are now.* "Is that all you can say to me?"

"Your Grace?" She was stunned by his harsh tone.

The old Hunt would have apologized, but the new, more Gothic duke needed to prowl and snarl and challenge the governess. So he prowled. Or at least he paced.

"I get little glimpses of the woman I believe you to be, but then you hide her away under insipid politeness. It's infuriating."

"I beg pardon?" Her eyes widened.

"How can you think and feel so radically and then live so quietly?"

"What right do you have to speak this way to me?" Viola pulled back her shoulders and mentally advanced upon him. It was sheer heaven. "I thought you were a gentleman."

"And I thought you unlike any other lady I had ever met, but we've both been disappointed."

Viola's cheeks flamed. "It's easy for a man like you to fling insults about. Why did I expect any different?"

"I see you wish to know me only as the mask I present to the world. How utterly ordinary."

She bristled. He'd made her bristle! Astounding!

"Don't speak to me of wearing masks! Have you any idea how much a governess must conceal of herself in daily life? All my choices must be geared toward self-preservation. Meanwhile, men like you issue commands without a moment's thought! Your arrogance is terrifying."

Arrogant. Yes, he liked that she found him arrogant. Hunt approached her, worshipping the fire he saw being stoked within her.

"I believe, madam, that it is you who are arrogant." He tried to pitch his voice lower to a growl, but attained only a rumble. Better than nothing. "You clearly regard me as inferior in intellect and sensibility. How like any other governess."

"Yet I thought I was unique among those in my profession." Viola crossed her own mental blade with his. Felicity had been right; the woman had hidden passions that required so little to inflame. "I see you've trapped yourself in a lie, Your Grace."

"At least I'm finally getting close to your own truth."

"My truth?" Her face paled. "What do you mean?"

"Your passion. Your intensity. Your strength." He meant it, too. She could be so gentle and refined, but a spark of wildfire dwelt within her breast. The power that simmered inside her made Hunt need her only more. "To think you were content to hide all those from me for so long. How was I expected to notice you if you hid your light away?"

"I didn't want you to notice me." Her voice grew tremulous. Both were pulled together, helpless against the physical law of attraction.

"Why? Have you any idea how much of my time

you've wasted?" That finally *was* a proper growl. She placed a hand to his chest as he came nearer, but not to push him off. He could feel her trembling; he himself was primed with desire. "So many hours spent searching for a kindred spirit, for something rare, and you selfishly hoarded your true self. I don't think there's anything worse than cowardice."

"Cowardice? How dare you speak like this?" Her words came out breathy. She did not sound furious. Rather, her lips parted. Her eyes searched his, hungry for his gaze.

"How dare you," he replied, "live like this. How dare you lie?" Hunt was burning now, desperate to touch her. Desperate for more.

The magnetized pull of attraction drew them closer together and before either could lob another challenge or insult at the other, they were kissing.

This time, the kiss was fierce and exquisitely mutual. Their mouths opened, he devoured her lips and folded her into his arms. Her kiss burned him, fulfilled him.

Hunt gave little grunts as he gripped the back of her hair, pressing her harder against him. They stumbled against the wall and began to oh so slowly slide to the floor. Viola was both assertive and wonderfully yielding; her lips demanded more from him repeatedly, yet she also submitted herself to his embraces.

Hunt wanted to carry her back to his room. His cock throbbed, straining at the front of his breeches. He could only imagine how soft and slick she would be if he made love to her. Their kissing continued, heightened, became almost bruising in its intensity. Finally, she pulled away and gasped for breath. Hunt held her close, refusing to set her free. Wanting to keep her in a luxurious cage, a spoil of conquest.

He would take her up against the wall if she gave him a chance.

"Oh God," Viola whispered, almost swooning in his grasp. Her lips brushed against his again and again, her hunger for him apparent and growing wilder. "Your Grace."

"Call me James." He kept his mouth hovering over hers, ready for another soul-melting kiss. "Speak my name."

"James." No one ever called him that, and he only ever wanted to hear her say his name like that again. She was breathy with desire, almost feverish in his arms. "James, I want…"

"What do you want?" he growled. "What can I give you? Name it."

"Felicity!" He hoped she meant the emotion and not the girl. Viola broke their embrace. "She might hear us through the door! What have we done?"

If Felicity *was* listening, she'd likely be silently cheering by now.

When Hunt tried to return the governess to his arms, Viola broke away and rushed to her chamber door. She slipped her messy hair back into place and ensured her clothing was not too disheveled.

"This did not happen," she whispered. "No one must know! Do you hear me?"

With that horrified pronouncement, Viola slipped into the chamber and shut the door.

Head spinning, Hunt began to wander the hall back toward his own rooms. For thirty seconds, she had been his with no masks and no distance. She'd been fire in his arms.

She'd been honey and heat, and he did not ever want to lose the taste of her.

Viola reopened the door. "Your Grace?" she whispered.

"Hmm?" He forced himself not to sprint back; that would not look disheveled or dangerous.

"Um. Pray don't forget about the coach tomorrow."

"Ah. I won't." He stared at her. She stared back. "Good night, then."

"Yes. Very good. Good night." Viola started to close the door. "That is…yes. Goodbye. Good night. Good."

With that, the woman vanished yet again.

Hunt staggered back to his own rooms, and on the way happened to chance a look at himself in a hallway mirror and notice something unusual. Something he hadn't seen in months, over a year.

Hunt was grinning.

CHAPTER FIFTEEN

Viola had slept fitfully.

She awoke from another heated and vague dream of the duke and lay in bed while Felicity snored beside her. She lingered over every detail from the night before.

The way Huntington had looked at her, the way he'd danced with her, and then the sudden passion of their moment outside her room. He'd made her angry, and anger apparently loosed all her inhibitions. Viola had never known she could yell at someone before, least of all a man. Even more astonishing, she was rather good at it.

Most astonishing of all, she'd liked it. And the kissing that had followed, the ecstatic embrace, the heated press of his lips, she'd more than liked that.

We must get out of here, she thought. *Before I lose my mind entirely.*

But first she must help her sister. To do that, Viola needed to get up.

"Go away!" Felicity growled when Viola opened the curtains. The girl jammed a pillow over her face and uttered some words Viola hoped she hadn't heard correctly.

"Young lady, a girl of breeding does not snarl in the morning." Viola took the pillow from her charge. "Nor at luncheon, nor at any other time of the day."

"But men can snarl all they like, can't they?" Indignant, Felicity sat up, her black curls now resembling a head of Medusa's snakes. Brushing those out would be a chore.

"Gentlemen don't snarl." Viola poured water into the washbasin.

"They do in Mr. Winthrop's books! Men in those books snarl, grunt, growl, purr, hiss, and do all other sorts of catlike things. I say, do you think when men fall in love, they become cats? That would be jolly amusing."

The duke had certainly growled and hissed his words of desire last night. Viola's heart sped at the memory.

"I think that this is a lot of nonsense for the morning."

Felicity got out of bed and hopped her way to the basin with Viola's help. The girl seemed to be doing better on that ankle. Hopefully they would be ready to go tomorrow morning. Viola smiled as her charge finished splashing water on her face and sat down, allowing the governess to disentangle her hair.

"I looked over your sketches yesterday," Viola said. "Your sense of proportion really has improved."

Felicity beamed. "Well, I still get tripped up by proper shading."

"I can help with that. After breakfast, we'll sit down for a bit and work together."

"This has been the most wonderful holiday. Thank you." Felicity did not smile sweetly often, but when she did, it had a way of parting the clouds around Viola's heart. Maybe Viola couldn't have Huntington, but she did have someone in this world who she loved very much.

"We'll work a bit, then I must go on an errand. I want to look at your progress when I return later this afternoon."

"May I sketch Cornelius again? He's an excellent model."

"If you can get him to stand still long enough, you may."

The footmen helped Felicity back down the stairs and escorted the two ladies to the breakfast room. To Viola's chagrin, the dowager duchess was the only family member present. She was already made up for the morning with icy perfection.

"Good day, Your Grace." Viola passed Felicity some toast and poured tea for herself. "I trust you had a pleasant night."

"Presumably not so pleasant as your own." The old woman exhibited thin-lipped disdain. Could she possibly know what had happened between Viola and her grandson? "I imagine this way of living makes a nice change for you, Miss Winslow. Not many governesses can boast dining with a duke on multiple occasions."

Felicity glowered at the duchess, her cheeks bulging with toast.

"The Duke and Duchess of Ashworth are liberal employers, Your Grace. They have always made me feel a member of the family."

"Indeed. It would explain a great deal." The dowager cut into a piece of ham. "You seem comfortable taking hospitality."

Viola needed all her poise just now. She pretended she was sitting inside a crystal box, watching the world around her, knowing nothing could hurt her. Unlike the freedom of last night, now she must be aware of her station.

"His Grace is a generous host. I can never repay him for his kindness."

"Though I'm certain you'd like to try." The woman sipped coffee. Viola didn't like what those words implied.

"I assure you, ma'am, we've no wish to strain your hospitality much longer. I've an errand this afternoon, and my intention is to leave for Somerset tomorrow morning. If His Grace will extend his largesse one last time and help us with a coach, that is."

The dowager seemed mildly pleased with this news. "I'm sure Hunt will be happy to help. The coach should be free tomorrow; if you'd been leaving today, it would have been hard to arrange."

"Your Grace?"

"I mean only that I've business in town today and require the carriage myself. I'm leaving just after breakfast, hence my early rising."

"Will you be gone long, Your Grace?" Viola's heart thudded.

"Why on earth should that matter?"

"Only that His Grace said I might use the coach myself this afternoon. For that errand."

"My word. You certainly don't mind taking whatever you can get."

"See here—" Felicity began, looking ready to throw teacups in her wrath.

"Yes, I see, Felicity." Viola shook her head, warning the girl. "It's all right, spills happen. I'm sure we can get you another cup."

The last thing Viola wanted was to show this old woman that her charge had the manners of a convict.

"I'm afraid I shall be rather late out. Hunt might have remembered that." The dowager tsked. "I'm certain he can have the cart prepared for you. If you don't mind such a low form of transportation, that is."

Felicity shoveled more toast into her mouth so

she did not curse.

"Thank you, Your Grace. You've been most kind." Odd, wasn't it, to say people were kind when the opposite was true?

For much of her life Viola had told flattering lies to keep herself in school, or in a job, or even alive. She was tired of it. She wanted to be able to look the duchess in the eye and say what she thought. What she felt. What she wanted.

Whom she wanted.

"I am not the generous one in the family, Miss Winslow. My grandson holds that title. Hunt is a good man, but he is still a man. He loves to help wayward ladies; he might even allow certain passions to be roused within him by those ladies in their predicament." Viola recalled his furious words last night, his powerful kisses. She felt ill. "But I should mention he is likely to be soon engaged to the Viscount Crawford's eldest girl. Her mother and I have written to each other. It is a sensible match. I say this in the spirit of friendship, you understand. I want to help you avoid any…embarrassment."

All Viola's feverish, half-hopeful fantasies crumbled to dust.

The duke hadn't kissed her out of burning love, but because she had roused his animal desires. He was without female companionship up here, and Viola happened to come along at a low moment. He would never think of marrying her. She already knew all that, yet she'd thrown herself into his arms anyway.

She was determined not to regret any of it, but she was just as determined to protect herself. She would not become his plaything, and she was appalled he could have viewed her only thus.

Viola wished to complete her visit to Betsy as soon as possible. She wanted to leave Moorcliff by tonight.

"Her Grace is generous, but I'm uncertain what she means."

"No disrespect intended, dear girl. Richer, more powerful women than you have had their heads turned by my grandson. He's a prize many have coveted. Only look after your own interests; that is all I mean."

"Indeed. Thank you for the advice, Your Grace. It is very good, especially as you are so uninterested yourself in the outcome." The words and tone were polite, but the dowager duchess caught the true meaning and appeared peevish. Viola gave a bloodless smile, rose, and took control of Felicity's chair. "I should see about arranging that cart. Good morning."

"Odious harridan." Felicity seethed as they wheeled down the hall. "I should like to stick her with a hatpin in the worst possible location!"

"Ladies do not say such things," Viola said. "They may, however, think them as much as they like."

"I liked how you got a jab in at the end there." Felicity chortled. "That 'uninterested' business. Very good! You can run rings about any old duchess, Miss Winslow."

"I have no intention of gaining that habit," Viola replied evenly.

Viola set Felicity up in the sunroom with her sketch pad and a sleeping Cornelius nestled on his perch.

For a while, the governess closely observed the girl's sketching, suggesting improvements and complimenting what was good. While they worked, Lady

Isabelle found them and helped pass the time by reading "Giselle" aloud. The poem was…long.

At half past eleven, Viola rose to head for the farm, leaving Lady Agatha in charge of the young ladies. Viola put on her gloves and bonnet and cloak, then hurried to the front yard to take the cart. She was no great driver but felt much surer of herself than she would on horseback.

As she cut across the courtyard, Viola saw the cart had not been readied. The two-person gig had, rather. Her heart stopped when she saw the duke standing by the vehicle, tugging on his own gloves.

"Your Grace?" She came to a halt beside him.

"I hoped you wouldn't mind if I escorted you, Miss Winslow. The terrain can be rough."

With anger, Viola realized his promise of the coach had been false from the start. He had not forgotten the duchess's plans; rather, he'd arranged everything to his liking. He'd contrived a way to spend more time alone with her, and Viola doubted he'd anything chivalrous in mind.

He was treating her as his diversion, which was insulting enough. Worse, though, was that if he accompanied her to the farm, he'd learn her great secret. Then he'd likely scorn her as well.

If Viola hadn't needed to see Betsy, she'd have gone back inside.

"I should like a little privacy," she said stiffly. Huntington's triumphant expression vanished. "Thank you for the kind offer, Your Grace."

"This isn't kindness," he said.

"Then perhaps it shouldn't be offered at all. Good day." It was rude, but Viola's nerves had split with the strain. She curtsied, then walked through Moorcliff's gates by herself.

The road to the farm took her off into the more desolate part of the countryside, and Viola shivered as she got a few hundred yards from the castle; the wind was particularly icy today.

Bollocks. She wasn't going to be able to walk ten miles round trip, not in dropping temperatures such as these. She stopped on the road, struggling to control her frustration as she heard the gig approach from behind.

"Whoa." The duke stopped his horse. "Have I offended you?"

"No, Your Grace." Viola shut her eyes, trying to sort out which would be the worse course of action. Giving in to the duke? Abandoning Betsy and the children? Viola sighed. One of those was much, much worse than the other. "I don't like being manipulated."

"Forgive me, then. I wanted to spend time with you. I meant nothing untoward." Huntington swore a bit as the wind picked up. "Perhaps we should turn back. This errand of yours can likely wait."

No. If she didn't go to Betsy today, right now, Viola wouldn't get another chance. She had no intention of remaining in Moorcliff Castle for longer than another night.

"Actually, I'd like to continue on, Your Grace." Viola climbed into the gig alongside Huntington. Hopefully, her rigid body language would discourage him from becoming too familiar. "Might we continue together?"

Huntington seemed confused by her ever-shifting mood, but he acquiesced.

"On we go." He cracked the reins and the gig trundled along. They were seated near enough together that Viola could feel the outline of his leg against her own.

She needed to think of how to handle this situation without shouting.

"You seem moody, Miss Winslow," he said. Viola was indeed struggling with her temper. A real gentleman would never have worked to get her alone like this, not after last night! "Is something wrong?"

"Whatever could be wrong?" she muttered.

"Come now. I thought we were friends." Huntington sounded cross.

"Friends don't manipulate their friends, do they?"

"True." He cracked the reins and urged the horse to a canter. "Friends don't kiss each other, either."

"Yes, but that was a moment of madness." Viola watched him from the corner of her eye. "We agreed last night wasn't to be repeated."

"Forgive me, but we agreed to no such thing."

"It was implied in how we parted!"

"You really ought to say what you mean, Miss Winslow." He adopted a sinful, almost wicked grin that sent a bolt of slick heat straight to her core.

"And if I said I wanted there to be absolutely no kissing ever again? What would you say to that?"

"Then I would respect your wishes utterly." He was once more the perfect gentleman, his words laden with sincerity. "So. Is there something you wished to say to me?"

This would be the perfect moment to state in plain language that she wanted nothing to do with this temptation.

"What I want," Viola said, "is to perform my errand and then return to the castle in peace." She paused, letting a look of smug triumph appear on his face. "And I do not wish to ever kiss you again, Your

Grace. Kindly see that it's done."

Take it back! It's not fair. The thoughts came and went, but even if Viola felt a bit morose at the notion she would not kiss Huntington again, it did please her to watch him scowl with indignation. He hunched his shoulders and cracked the reins.

"Then I have my instructions," the duke muttered. Why did she take so much pleasure in seeing him disgruntled? "Well. Service deserves service in return. Might I ask a favor of you?"

"It depends on what you wish, Your Grace." She could feel her pulse in her fingertips.

"That right there. 'Your Grace.' For our little trip this morning, I'd like us to be on a rather more informal basis."

"I shudder to think of the devilry you're suggesting. *Your Grace.*" But she grinned in delight as he made a rather snarling sort of noise. Perhaps Mr. Winthrop knew about men after all.

"I'd rather you called me Hunt for today. Or even James." He leaned in a bit nearer and spoke low. "Depending on which aspect of me you feel is closer to the surface?"

"The rugged or romantic, you mean? And if neither is forthcoming? Wouldn't 'Your Grace' be more proper?"

"Call me whatever you like, so long as it isn't Duke or Your Grace. And only if I may call you Viola in turn."

"This seems like a rather dangerous game."

"I've never lived dangerously before," he replied.

"Oh? Says the man who's called others to a duel on more than one occasion?" Viola felt herself becoming that forthright woman from last night, the woman who returned a man's challenging words.

"I've taken risks. I've had my share of adventures and affairs." The word "affairs" made Viola blush. "I've risked money on a game of cards, or my good name in pursuit of pleasure. I've risked my pride when I asked a woman to marry me. But I never knew danger to myself until recently."

"And what could have placed you in such danger?" Viola wished her voice didn't sound so faint.

"It's a 'who' rather than a 'what.'" He glanced meaningfully at her.

"If there's danger, perhaps it should be avoided at all costs."

"I daresay. But here's the rub; I find myself rather addicted to it."

Viola felt the same. She knew that she could be sensible for only so much longer. It would be wise to put all these feelings away and live out the rest of her life in quiet dignity. Taxonomy again. She was a field mouse, not a lion. If she remained in the lion's den, she'd be devoured soon enough.

"Well. I do not appreciate danger. Your Grace."

The duke muttered something and drove on in brooding silence.

As they traveled, Viola tried to plan.

Whatever would Betsy say when her sister turned up in a gig driven by the bloody Duke of Huntington?

Viola wondered what Betsy would look like now, how changed she would be. Ten years was a long time to go between visits. Betsy's life, like Viola's, had been laden with its share of difficulties.

Widowed for almost twelve years, she'd raised four children on her own. Geoffrey was the eldest at sixteen, Clara was fourteen, Nan thirteen, and Jacob the youngest at nearly twelve. Betsy had only just become pregnant with the boy when her husband, Francis, died of a fever. With nowhere to go, she'd returned home to her father with the children, to what they'd hoped would be a temporary solution. Unfortunately, with no husband and four small children to feed, leaving the farm hadn't been easy.

Viola thought of her mother's and Sebastian's graves on that hill near the house. She thought of the tree that shaded them, where Viola had gone to practice her letters and be peaceful when a very young child.

She tried not to think of her father. At least he would be working the fields today, or in town for market. She hoped she wouldn't see him. If her father became involved in all this, concealing the truth from Hunt, from James, from *the duke,* would become impossible.

• • •

A short while later they crested a shallow slope and caught sight of the farm in the distance. Viola heard the pigs grunting in their pen from here, the lowing of a cow in the barn. A young girl was standing outside the front door of the squat stone cottage, feeding a gaggle of white, fluffy chickens that pecked at her feet.

It must be Nan. The child had grown so. Viola recalled vividly when Nan had given her that poppet, told Viola that the doll would keep her safe on her journey down to "sunset." Even though Viola had to remain careful just now, she found herself grinning with eagerness to see the child.

"Whoa." The duke brought the horse to a stop and Viola got out.

Nan looked up, and her shock was so great, she dropped her apron and the rest of the chicken feed scattered on the ground. The birds scratched and pecked in clucking joy.

"Mam! We got visitors!" The girl bounded over to Viola and the duke, giving the best curtsy she could muster. "H'lo. How do you do?" she asked them.

Viola's niece did not recognize her. When last they'd met, Nan would have been only three years old. Viola had to suppress the overwhelming urge to grab the girl and hug her tight. Lord, if she started crying, everything would be over. All her secrets would come tumbling out.

"Hello," Viola said quietly. She inspected the girl. Nan was already half a head taller than her aunt and had Betsy's and Viola's hazel eyes. She'd also inherited a mop of carroty red hair. All Betsy's children had taken that brilliant shade from their father. Viola cleared her throat; she had to play along with her own game. "We were wondering if you'd any fruit to sell. Apples especially."

"Apples?" Nan's eyes nearly popped out of her sockets at the sight of the duke's fine gig and his finer clothes. "Hard to believe folks like you need to stop off at our little place for apples!"

The duke chuckled, obviously charmed as he made a respectful bow to the young girl. Viola's heart had been in danger of stopping earlier; now it was in danger of melting. Even if Nan hadn't been her niece, she loved that he was courtesy itself to a farm girl.

"James Montagu, Duke of Huntington. At your service, Miss," he said.

"The...the duke?" Nan's mouth fell open and she

put her hands to her cheeks. The comedy of the scene was heightened by the chickens pecking about her feet. "Oh! Oh, Mam will faint. Sorry for not recognizing you, Yer Grace!"

"Nan?" A woman emerged from the cottage and out into the sunlight.

Viola's heart beat slower as she recognized Betsy straightaway. There was ten years in age between them, though with farm life and raising four children single-handedly, the difference seemed more like twenty.

Betsy had been the nearest thing to a mother Viola had ever known. Her spirits lifted at the sight of her.

She saw her sister smile, then noticed Betsy's concern as she took in Huntington and his gig.

"Your Grace?" Betsy hurried over and dropped into a curtsy, nabbing Nan by the wrist and pulling her down to do the same. "Forgive us, we didn't realize you…" Betsy looked from the duke to her sister, clearly flabbergasted.

As much as Viola hated to do it, she had to pretend this was their first meeting. They'd gone too far to call off the charade now, especially in front of the duke.

"Ma'am, I was hoping to purchase some apples, if you have them." Viola widened her eyes, nodding a little. *Play along* she practically screamed in silence.

Betsy had always been quick to catch on. She looked from the duke to Viola and nodded in understanding. "Of course, Miss. Why don't you follow me? Nan, don't stand about gawking at His Grace all day long. Would you care for a cup of tea, Your Grace?"

"Thank you, Mrs…" he said.

"Lumley, sir."

"That would be very nice, Mrs. Lumley."

Viola tried to think how they'd conspire to have a moment alone together, she and Betsy. God, this had all gotten so bloody complicated. No; she'd allowed it to become so complicated.

But then Nan swooped in to save the day.

"Would you like to see the pigs, Yer Grace?" Nan asked breathlessly. "My next job's to feed them."

"The duke doesn't want to pay a visit on our pigs, Nan!" Betsy hissed, but Huntington seemed to be enjoying himself.

"Please, I'd be delighted. Would you do me the honor, Miss?" Huntington extended his arm, and Nan looked ready to swoon as she took it.

"Have you ever slopped a pig before, Yer Grace?" she asked as she led him away.

"Nan!" Betsy sounded exasperated. Viola struggled not to laugh.

"I've always longed to," the duke told Nan in perfect seriousness. "Thank you for the opportunity."

Poor Betsy seemed liable to faint. Once out of sight of the duke, the sisters hugged each other tightly. Tears stung Viola's eyes. Her older sister kissed Viola's cheek, then cupped her face in her hands. The two laughed a moment, unable to believe the sudden, happy reunion. Soon, though, they needed to get to business.

"What the devil is this all about?" Betsy whispered.

"It's complicated. I'm the Duke of Huntington's guest along with my charge, Miss Berridge," Viola replied. "My employer, the Duke of Ashworth, and His Grace are close friends. I've known the man for years."

"He don't know the truth about us, eh?" There was no judgment in her sister's voice, only understanding. She let Viola into the cottage. "Can't say I blame you, keeping it a secret. Do none of them know where you come from?"

"I may have stretched the truth," Viola said softly. A polite way of saying she'd lied for years. "But not because I'm ashamed, Bets. Not of you or the children."

"Believe me, I understand." Betsy huffed and hugged Viola again, smelling of lye and strong soap. It was the scent of the rare happy bits of Viola's childhood. "Fancy folk like the Duke of Huntington would gawk if they knew you come from a place like this. Why'd you bring him here, anyway?"

"He brought me. It was the only way I could contrive a visit," Viola whispered.

"Contrive. Dukes, and such. Good Lord. And Pa always said your education were a waste." Betsy whistled as she put an arm around Viola and guided her to the table.

"Where *is* Pa?" Viola felt wary as she looked about the cottage.

Much was as she'd left it ten years ago. The same long wooden table and stools settled around it, the same small stone hearth blackened with soot and cooking grease. An iron kettle hung over the flames, steam already issuing from the spout. None of the children were around besides Nan.

"Pa and the boys are workin' the fields," Betsy said as the kettle began to sing. She took it up with a cloth and poured the water into a white teapot. "Clara's gone into service down in Cheshire at one of them big houses. We don't see her often." Betsy puffed out her cheeks as she replaced the kettle and sat down, gesturing for Viola to do the same. "She sends money home when she can."

"About that." Viola frowned. "I know what I send isn't much, but if the children are old enough to work now, shouldn't you be able to get a place of your own?" An idea struck her. "If Geoffrey's sixteen, he might be old enough to take over a lease on a farm. I'm sure His Grace would be happy to help!"

"Still can't get over how you drove up in a smart gig with a duke, easy as you please." Betsy chuckled as she poured the tea into chipped cups. Her cheeks and nose had gone perpetually red from standing before a fire or over a steaming pot for years on end.

"I mean it. If you still need to get away from Pa—"

"It ain't like that." Betsy took up a knife and cut into a rather small loaf of bread. She sliced it as she continued. "Might as well tell you, Vi. Every penny you send us goes into his pocket."

She couldn't have heard that right. "Excuse me?"

"Pa takes the money soon as it comes every month. Says it's to pay for our keep here, me an' the children."

"The children are all old enough to work now," Viola snapped. Normally, when she thought of her father, panic stuck her through the belly, froze her muscles. This, however, made her so angry, she forgot that fear.

"He also says...that it's your way of repaying him for, well..."

"For what I took from him, you mean?" Viola felt hollowed out yet again. Her mother and her twin brother, both gone within a week of her birth. Silas Winslow would believe until his dying breath, it seemed, that his youngest daughter had been responsible. Viola shut her eyes; getting angry would solve nothing. "What can I do for you, Bets? You said in that letter that it was important."

"It's Nan." Betsy watched out the window as her youngest girl merrily showed Huntington the pigs. "She's old enough to go into service, but she ain't strong like Clara. She'd get too homesick after a day, I know it."

Viola watched her niece. She giggled with the duke, who looked delighted by the creatures, leaning his arms on the fence and speaking with Nan as she slopped them. He truly was a natural with children. Her heart ached.

"Yes. She's a tender little thing," Viola said. "I can tell."

"I wondered if you'd try to get her a post at the Duke of Ashworth's house. If she had family near, I think she'd settle in and work well." Betsy looked pained as she brought out a few thin scrapings of butter. "Course, if you've got to keep up appearances, you can't go about revealing the truth to His Grace."

"Never mind about that. If I must confess my 'fabrications' to help you and Nan, of course I will." Even if it cost Viola the Ashworths' favor, she'd do it. "That's not what concerns me, though. Does Nan truly need to leave the farm? Things aren't as bad as all that, are they?"

"It ain't just about needing more money." Betsy worried her chapped and worn hands. "Pa's hard on the kids, Nan especially. Says she's too much like—" Betsy stopped her mouth, but Viola understood. Nan was too much like her Aunt Viola. "I want her to have a better chance at life. She's grown up so nervous 'cause of, well…"

Because of Silas's temper. Viola knew firsthand how devastating that could be.

"Of course I'll ask the duke," Viola said. Perhaps she could even ask Huntington. Moorcliff was close enough that Nan could see her family on the regular. Perhaps she could ask this favor of him on the drive back, though that would mean confessing the truth of today to him. All the truth.

He may be disgusted with all my lies Viola thought. *Though perhaps he won't be. Perhaps he'll understand.*

Perhaps, Viola realized, the time had come for the truth. Here and now, over tea, with Viola's sister and niece about them. Huntington could look around this farm, this tiny cottage, and know every one of her secrets. He could be the first person outside of her family to ever know Viola truly.

In fact, she wanted him to be the first.

"Thank you, Vi." Betsy looked relieved. "Now then. Let me go call His Grace and Nan in for tea."

But the door flung open as she spoke, and it was not Huntington who entered the room. The man who sauntered inside fixed Viola with a look of deepest loathing.

"Viola," her father growled. "So. You're back."

CHAPTER SIXTEEN

Silas Winslow was the sort of man you could easily lose in a crowd.

He was neither tall nor short, with a grizzled, receding chin, hooded eyes, and a surprisingly small, sharp nose for a face as large as his. Perhaps Viola was being unflattering, but a lifetime of experience had taught her to view Silas without charity.

"Hello, Pa." Viola needed to mention the duke, and quickly. Silas might behave if he knew Huntington was about.

"What're you doin' here, then?" he muttered.

"Why are you home so soon?" Betsy winced when their father cast a harsh eye upon her.

Viola hated that her sister still walked in fear of the man. Indignant, she wanted to stand up and tell her so-called father what she'd thought of him all these years, every vengeful thing she'd ever wished to say.

Being with Huntington these past days had started warping her into someone unrecognizable. Someone stubborn, someone who talked back. Someone who refused to be made to feel lesser.

Someone her father would hate even more than he already hated her. For Betsy's sake, she must regain her wits quickly.

"The boys are still in the field. We need another sickle. When I come back for it, I saw some fancy cart out front." He glared at Viola. "Payin' us a call all the way from Somerset, eh? That Duke of Ashworth must be treatin' you right if you've got a smart little cart like that all your own."

Viola didn't like what his tone implied. "The duke's a gracious employer, but I'm only visiting. I've been on a sketching trip with my pupil, Miss Berridge."

"Sketching trips. Sounds like real hard labor, that." Silas kept scowling as he poured water and splashed some on his face. He dripped on the floor as he toweled off. "Seems you're makin' the most of that fancy education you squeezed outta the vicar."

"Betsy says you've received my monthly payments." Viola could not take such easy bait; he wanted her to fight back. "You could thank my education for that money, you know."

"What the bleedin' hell are you doin' back here, girl?" he snapped.

Over the years, Viola had imagined she'd been unfair to her father while growing up. Perhaps he was rough and coarse…and yes, occasionally violent. But he couldn't hate her. She must have been an overly sensitive child.

Yet one look at Silas and the years vanished between Viola now and the frightened young girl she'd been.

Betsy once told Viola, soon after "the incident" as they called it (the mere idea of which made the mark on Viola's throat burn anew), that Pa had been a loving father and husband long ago. He'd been a good man, but when his wife and son died, they took the best part of him and left the dregs for his daughters.

"I wanted to look in." She wouldn't tell Silas that Betsy had written to her out of fear. "It's been a long while."

"Hmmph. Betsy, call the girl in here and tell her

to fetch more water." He slammed the now-empty jug onto the table.

Tell him about Huntington. Tell him!

"I should mention that I haven't come alone," Viola said.

"What, you got that brat of a pupil along with you? Where's she, then?"

"Felicity is not a brat, and she is not here!" Viola's restraint was cracking.

"Maybe this whole 'sketching tour' story's just that. A story." Silas glowered at her, narrowing his eyes. "You drive here in a posh cart like that with a piece of horseflesh that fine and expect us to believe you're nothin' but a governess?"

"What are you suggesting?"

"You a kept woman for some rich man?" Silas smirked, wiped his lips. "Aye. The fellow must have no taste or breeding if he'd settle for some farm girl as a mistress."

He was alternately so near the truth and yet so far.

Silas seemed to have grown worse in the past ten years, difficult as it was to believe. He was now awful to her immediately, rather than passive and mean-spirited for the first hour or two.

"I'm no one's kept anything. I'm a governess, as I was educated to be. Now, I think perhaps it's best I should go." She'd seen to Betsy and promised help with Nan; Viola couldn't see how any good would come from bringing Huntington into this. Viola got the feeling that if this little debate with Silas continued, the duke might very well put her father through the window.

"Oh, Vi. Must you run off?" Betsy looked so sad, and Viola hugged her sister.

"I'll take care of Nan. Don't worry. And I'll see about getting you the money from now on instead of him," she whispered. Viola headed for the door. She'd urge Huntington to come away quickly.

Viola's father grabbed her by the sleeve and whirled her about. Her back struck the wall, and she cried out at the short, sharp rap her skull made against the wood. Tears of pain blurred her vision.

"Yer sister went to all this trouble to make tea for you, and yer too good to sit with her? Gotta get back to yer damn watercolors and perfumed dukes, eh?" Once again, Viola had made him furious in mere seconds, and she hadn't even tried. "You come and go as you please in this house, wreck everything, and then fly away! You good for nothin' little trollop!"

Viola could feel it again, the line of pain across her throat. She was eight years old, huddled in a corner waiting to die. She'd smelled the ale on his breath from the pub, shut her eyes, and thought *This is the end*. She hadn't even been afraid. She'd been too numb to feel.

"Let me go!" Viola snapped. "You don't know what you're doing."

"Oh, I shouldn't be handlin' such a fancy bit of fluff this way, that's what you mean?" he snarled.

Viola knew she ought to scream as he brought back his hand to slap her, but she was dunked into that horrible night in her childhood all over again. He'd pressed her against the wall, then got the knife, and then—

And then Silas let her go.

Huntington wrested the man off Viola before throwing him against the opposite wall. Silas's feeble attempts at fighting back were nothing; he might as well have been a housecat pawing at a lion. The duke loomed over her father, keeping the man from coming at Viola again. Huntington's eyes were on fire, his luscious mouth frozen in a murderous sneer.

"The hell do you think you're doing?" the duke snarled.

Viola almost sank to the floor; this was so much worse than anything she'd imagined.

At the sight of the duke, Silas's hateful looks fell away.

"Yer Grace?" How different he was when facing an angry man. When his opponent wasn't a woman or a child, he became positively lamblike. Viola had never known him with her mother; Betsy said he'd been different with her. But Viola couldn't see how a woman as apparently wonderful as her mother could love such a man.

"What gives you the right to strike a lady?" Huntington snapped. Silas's face turned a bright crimson with fear. "Speak, sir! Unless you wish me to horsewhip you myself?"

"Your Grace, no!" Viola had to stop this now. She grabbed Huntington's arm, forcing him to relax. Betsy, meanwhile, had rushed outside to tend to Nan.

"Listen to Vi, she knows I didn't mean nothin' by it," Silas whimpered. He hunched his shoulders, making himself as small as possible.

"Vi?" Huntington's scowl deepened with growing confusion. "How the devil do you know the young woman's name?"

Viola shut her eyes.

"He's my father, Your Grace," she said.

She felt Huntington stiffen beneath her hands.

"Your father." He sounded numb with disbelief.

Huntington visibly appraised the man trembling before him. "Your father was a solicitor," he said softly.

Viola could only imagine what Huntington must be thinking. She knew that blushing and stammering and bowing her head in shame would make this picture only more pathetic.

"I know," she murmured. "That wasn't true." *I lied.*

Huntington stared as though she'd sprouted another head. As though he didn't know her...and he did not. Now he could look at this cottage, at the pigs outside, at the violent little man trembling before him, and see what Viola truly was. Not only a tenant farmer's daughter—*his* tenant, as a matter of fact—she was also a liar.

"But I thought that woman's name was Lumley," he muttered.

"Mrs. Lumley is my widowed sister," Viola replied. While this went on, Silas began to straighten up, though he continued to cower against the wall. "We came here today because she wrote to me at the Bull and Tartan and asked me to visit. I came because she indicated she was in trouble; I've been sending money to her and my nieces and nephews since I took my post at Lynton Park. I've been trying to help them lead an independent life." *Away from him.*

She looked at Silas and saw in the gleam of his watery eyes that he was not in any way sorry. That this little interlude with the duke had made him only more bitter and resentful of her.

He might take this out on Betsy and the children, on Nan in particular. The thought made Viola wretched. She hated herself for shattering Huntington's illusion of her, but much more than that, she hated that she'd made life exponentially worse for her family.

"I see. Mrs. Lumley?" Huntington called, never looking away from Viola. "Come in here, please."

"Yer Grace, I want to apologize again." Silas shut up at once when the duke gave him a mere look. When Betsy entered, Nan trailing behind her, Huntington spoke.

"Ma'am, how old are your sons? Miss Winslow mentioned she had nephews."

"Er, sixteen and eleven, Yer Grace."

"Sixteen is just old enough to sign a tenancy agreement," the duke said. "A farm has become available nearer to the village. I'd be happy to offer the tenancy to your elder son, and the rest of your family. Save this man."

"What?" Silas looked sweaty with fear. Viola's mouth fell open.

"Really, Yer Grace?" Betsy became wide-eyed with shock.

"Indeed. A condition of the tenancy will be that this man," the duke said, regarding Silas as though he were an insect, "is not to be allowed on the property. As for you, sir. You may stay on at this farm until your lease is up, at which time you will vacate the premises. I shall not renew our agreement." The duke was normally warmth and even fire, but now he was ice. Viola had never known anyone could look so cold.

"B-But I can't maintain one farm all by meself, Yer Grace!" Silas cried.

"You can hire laborers, I'm sure. But one thing you will not do is abuse your daughter or grandchildren again. Or Miss Winslow." *Especially Miss Winslow* was what she heard. "If you don't like these terms, you are free to leave now."

"This is a misunderstandin', Yer Grace."

"It is not. Now I think it best we return to Moorcliff, Miss Winslow." Huntington offered her his arm. "It looks like rain."

He was more than handsome or rich or titled or charming; he was the best man she'd ever known, and she'd lied to him repeatedly and without hesitation. Being a man of honor, he'd looked after her family, but he must despise her now. Perhaps that was for the best.

Viola gave Betsy what money she had on her, and Betsy agreed to take the children to a neighbor for a few nights until they could move to the new place. Viola had never seen her sister look so light and giddy.

In one hour, it was all over. They'd never have to rely on Silas again.

At least I helped set something right.

Viola hugged her sister and Nan. When the girl found out the identity of their mysterious visitor, she was ecstatic. Soon, Viola climbed into the gig and rolled away from the farm, Nan chasing after and waving. Silas didn't come out to watch his daughter drive away, unsurprisingly.

Soon after, it was Huntington and she alone together again beneath the ever-darkening sky.

The wind sliced past the gig, causing Viola to tug her shawl tighter about her body. She didn't speak, and neither did the duke. For about a mile, they continued in icy silence.

"Are you well?" the duke finally asked.

"Yes, thank you." Thank you was far too small for what she wanted to say to him. *You've changed my life; you've saved my family; I know you despise me now.*

"Is that all you can say?" he snapped.

Viola stiffened; she was sorry for lying, but she wasn't going to be yelled at by any man ever again. Today had made that plain to her.

"What would you like me to say?" Tears threatened, but she beat them back. "That I appreciate what you've done for us?"

"Damn everything, Viola!" He was fury itself in that moment, a regal, utterly masculine pillar of anger. "Why did you lie to me? To everyone?"

"I know that my birth was far less delicate than you believed. I'm certain that you think I've perpetrated a terrible fraud against the Duke of Ashworth. I certainly wouldn't blame you for despising me."

"Despise you?" That seemed to anger him most of all. "You think I could ever despise you? And despise you for being some farmer's daughter? Is that the kind of man you believe me to be?"

Viola's heart threatened to stop. "What?" she whispered.

"I don't care where you come from, damn it! I care that you didn't trust me with the truth about that man. Was he always that vicious?"

"Yes."

Huntington snarled and snapped the reins, driving the horse faster. "If I'd known the way he treated you, I'd have—"

"Done what? What more could you have possibly done? Don't you understand that you've already saved my family?" Ah, there were the tears bubbling up again. "By giving Geoffrey tenancy of his own farm, you've rescued them. For years, they've done everything they could to get away from Silas. Now, in one fell swoop, you've given them freedom. My niece, Clara, can return home from service, and Nan needn't leave home at all. They can all work the farm together."

"Nan was going into service?" Huntington frowned.

"Betsy wanted me to find her employment at Lynton Park, since she'd have some family around then. I was going to tell you the whole truth later just so I could ask if you'd have her at Moorcliff Castle. That way she could be nearer to home."

"You wanted me to take your niece into my home as a servant." His brow creased.

"Does that offend you?"

"Hang it, Viola. My offense doesn't come into this at all!"

"I'm afraid it does." She still couldn't quite believe that he'd moved on from her deception this quickly.

"Why, because I'm some fool duke with a blasted title?"

"No. Because I care about what offends you!" She swallowed a lump in her throat. "I care about you."

The duke yanked upon the reins, stopping the horse on the road.

"You do, then?" He looked rather wild, almost frightening in his intensity. He did not seem to despise her; in fact, he had never looked more hopeful.

"Yes, James." She had not meant to say his Christian name, but it slipped out. He looked half-wild with frustrated ecstasy as he faced her.

"And I care for you. Which is why the mere thought of treating your family as my servants, or *you* as my servant, wounds me terribly. If your sister and her children need my help, I'll do more than give them the bloody farm. I'll send the boys to school if they like; I'll give your sister money to open a shop, to do whatever she pleases. You have only to ask me."

He was offering to change her family's lives in every conceivable way, and all for her. He knew her secrets now, and he still sought to help her. Viola knew one thing for bloody certain.

She was going to kiss this man, and damned be the consequences.

At that instant, the sky lit with a blinding flash of lightning, and the thunder crackled simultaneously. The horse screamed. The poor beast reared on its hind legs, pawing at the air.

"Whoa!" The duke called, but the creature was too spooked. As Huntington yanked futilely on the reins, they were dragged off the road and across the field. Viola clung to her rattling seat, gripping the sleeve of the duke's coat.

Then they must have struck a hole or a stone because she heard the hearty snap of wood. The world tilted sideways, and Viola was flung out of the carriage.

CHAPTER SEVENTEEN

The wheel axle had snapped, and Hunt knew immediately that this gig would be going nowhere. But he couldn't think about the gig or the frantic horse when he saw Viola go tumbling into space to land hard upon the ground and roll.

It was as if he himself had landed in such a rough way; if she were hurt, he'd be in agony. If it were anything serious, he'd lose his bloody mind.

Hunt shouted her name as he leaped from the gig and rushed to her side. She lay in a crumpled ball on the ground, but she was awake and breathing.

Hunt gathered her into his arms, lifted her, and bade her put her arm around his neck. He'd never held her before, and she was as light and pleasing as he'd imagined she would be.

"Are you well?"

"Yes, James. I'm fine."

Then he was fine, too. He could've had a broken leg and felt no pain right now. If she was unhurt, anything could be managed. He yearned to hear her say his name once more.

"Bollocks!"

Well. Not quite what he'd had in mind.

"The horse!" Viola pointed over his shoulder. "The gig!"

Damn. The frantic horse galloped across the field, dragging the broken gig after it. The vehicle created furrows in the earth, but even with reduced speed, the horse would be impossible to catch. If Hunt tried following the beast, he'd be taken in the direction of moorland and nothing else.

They needed to walk back to the castle, then. It was only another three miles or so.

"Are you able to walk, or shall I carry you?" he asked.

Viola eased out of his arms, took a few experimental steps, and sighed in relief. "I should be fine. I'll be bruised something horrible tomorrow, but nothing is broken or sprained."

Then that was good, though he wished he could have carried her. He liked carrying her, feeling the warmth of her, the soft and womanly curves. Fuck, he was going to become aroused just thinking about this. Walking three miles with a turgid erection would be no fun at all.

They stepped back onto the road and walked quickly; the lightning flashed again, and he imagined at any moment the floodgates would open and rain would drench them. They needed to hurry home, and then he'd have the servants draw Viola a hot bath. She'd be provided with soaps and lotions, everything to ease her comfort. He'd probably need a bath as well, but the thought of her soaking in a tub, her rosy skin warmed by the water, made him feel quite hot enough.

"Oh dear," Viola said when the deluge started. The rain turned the road ahead into a muddy soup.

"This is fine," he said, placing a hand upon her back to help guide her forward.

The rain increased in its fury and volume.

"This is fine," he repeated.

"What?" Viola cried. "I can't hear you."

Then it began to hail. Little balls of ice pelted them both.

"Is this fine?" she cried.

"This is less than ideal." He scooped her back into his arms, to which the governess made a noise of protest. "We'll move faster this way."

"Indeed?" She didn't sound as though she believed him. *Wise girl.*

Hunt rushed along. Despite the barrage of ice, he felt warm and delightful with her in his arms. He hurried them down the road, certain they'd find shelter soon. After all, how isolated could the Northumberland countryside be?

Fairly isolated, now he thought of it.

After a quarter of a mile, it was clear they needed help.

Viola was shivering in his arms, and he was having a damn hard time seeing anything. A cottage appeared out of the dark of the storm, materializing so suddenly that he almost thought it Isabelle's terrifying Moorcliff haunt.

"I think it's the groundkeeper's cottage," he shouted, setting Viola on her feet. However, there were no lights in the windows. Was anyone home at all? Cursing, Hunt raced to the door and banged upon it with his fist. "Borman, are you there?"

"I doubt anyone's home." Viola arrived at his side. "What shall we do?"

"Apologize later and buy the man another door." Hunt slammed his shoulder against the door twice, and the lock broke on the third attempt. His shoulder was damned sore, but at least they were safe.

The cottage was snug, a parlor with a stone hearth, a stove beyond it, and a bedroom beyond that. Hunt went straight to the bedroom, apologizing in silence to Borman and his wife, both of whom, he finally remembered, were on holiday.

He didn't think it right for anyone to go

through a man's private drawers, not even a duke, but Viola and he could not sit in these wet clothes for hours. The only other option would be nudity, and while his cock became a staunch supporter of the idea, he doubted the young woman would agree.

He found a lady's cotton night rail that would fit Viola well, though Borman was a smaller man than Hunt. As such, spare clothing would be difficult to come by. He'd figure that out later.

"Here." He brought the nightgown to Viola, who'd begun struggling to light a fire in the hearth. "Change into this. Once the fire is lit, we'll boil water for washing."

"Th-Thank you." She snatched the gown and rushed into the bedroom to change. Hunt busied himself with the fireplace and regretted she'd shut the door for privacy. God, he was a bastard.

She emerged soon, a sheepish vision in white with damp tendrils of hair curling about her shoulders. She'd located some towels and handed one to him while she rubbed her own hair dry.

"You ought to change as well," she said to him as Hunt took the towel.

"Erm. About that. I don't believe Borman has anything that will fit."

"Oh dear." Her eyes widened.

"It's fine. I'll sit before the fire and be warmed in no time. The clothes will dry." He was going to die of pneumonia, but it was a small price to pay for her comfort.

"Don't be so foolish," she said. What a cross, animated thing to say. He loved it when she became informal with him. "You need to change out of those clothes. I'm certain the, er, towel will suffice. You can't catch your death; I won't allow it."

"Yes, ma'am." Hunt grinned as she remembered herself.

"Forgive my rudeness."

"Unforgiven. Your rudeness rather delights me."

He left her with a smile on her face.

Hunt lit candles back in the bedroom, then stripped the wet clothes and laid them out to dry, cursing fate as he wrapped the towel about his waist. He was going to be nearly naked in front of the woman he adored.

Under normal circumstances it would be cause for celebration, but this was different. Viola was different.

Today he'd learned just how cruel her life had been. She'd worked far too hard to escape from poverty and misery only to have him toy with her.

He needed to protect her, even from himself. Hunt sighed, weariness already settling upon his shoulders.

When he returned, she was seated before the fire with her knees hugged to her chest. Upon seeing him, her mouth fell open.

"Oh my," she whispered. "I've never seen a man so…bare before."

• • •

Would the towel hold well enough? Yes, but barely. And in truth, Viola hoped it would fall.

She'd known the duke was a strong man, but there was knowing a thing and then there was seeing it. The firelight painted his sculpted form in golden tones and velvet shadows worthy of a Renaissance master. She could imagine Michelangelo would have been thrilled to acquire such a perfect model.

Huntington's chest was broad and exquisitely defined, the slope of his shoulders perfection. His long arms were sculpted with muscle.

Viola imagined those bare arms wrapping around her while her shift conveniently dropped to the floor. His stomach was flat, the ridges of his abdominal muscles carved in precise detail. This was to say nothing of the light trace of hair on his chest, or the cunning line of dark hair that began at his navel and slipped beneath the towel.

Viola forced herself to look no further; that was forbidden territory. *I'm becoming debauched. The worst part is I like it.*

"You must keep quite active," Viola said, praying she did not faint. "Most dukes would let themselves go a bit doughy."

"Doughy?" Huntington tilted his head to the side, appraising her. "I take it that is the clinical term for dukely dissolution?"

Viola clasped her knees tighter. She had never been so flustered before. "I suppose I'm no expert on dukes, Your Grace."

"Please, it's James. Or Hunt. Or whatever you'd like. I think I'd answer to anything you called me."

Viola couldn't resist. "Such as Jamie?"

He groaned. "That would make me think of Agatha, but I'd survive."

She grinned. "Jimmy?"

"That makes me sound like a poor London chimney sweep, but all right. I'd accept it stoically, as a man must."

"What about Fluffy?"

"Fluffy?" He looked aghast.

"I doubt any woman in England has ever called a

duke by the name Fluffy before. I should be most original."

"You'd be surprised. There are many twisted deviants among the English upper classes."

"Don't I know it? I've served the Duke of Ashworth for years, after all." Viola tapped a finger to her chin. "I'm sure he's been called even worse than Fluffy."

"You may be right. Pooky, for example, would be so much worse."

"Should I adopt Pooky as your sobriquet instead?"

"If you did, I would bear it with manly honor." Every line of the duke's body screamed of power, even if he was wearing only a blasted towel. It sent a prickle along Viola's nape, and her nipples stood at attention. Hopefully he wouldn't notice.

"I shan't burden you with Pooky. It's too much. Fluffy it is."

"You are a most outrageous woman." He didn't sound put out, though. In fact, his voice lowered so every word he spoke was redolent with sinful delight. This man's voice was the equivalent of melted chocolate, or aged whiskey. "Fine. I am the Duke of Fluffy whenever you wish."

"I was rather thinking Fluffy, Duke of Huntington."

"You can get away with this outrageous behavior only by giving me something in return, you know."

"Oh?" Her skin tingled. "What is that?"

"You must allow me to call you by the name that I find most suits you."

Her heart thumped harder. This could go very wrong. "Very well. A name like what?"

"Like Viola." He smiled in a rather wicked fashion. "You should ever be known to me only as Viola.

Or 'the lovely Viola' or 'the brilliant Viola' if you require greater detail."

She bit her lower lip to contain the cry of pleasure. Viola knew she couldn't hide her blush, which had to be scarlet at this point. The duke seemed to notice, and it pleased him. "That sounds nice, then."

"Anyway. This towel won't do the trick. I saw extra linens in the bedroom wardrobe."

When he returned, the duke had wrapped the winding sheet around his body and draped a section over his shoulder. It made him look even more muscled and masculine, really. He resembled ancient sculptures of gods or heroes.

"A very Grecian look," Viola said. "You might be on your way to Athens for a debate."

"How serious you make me sound." Huntington sat before the fire and faced her.

"I suppose I like that seriousness. Most members of the *ton* turn everything into a game, including other people's lives."

"Indeed. We're exceptionally good at that," he muttered. Hunt brooded into the fire a bit, allowing the light of the flames to dance across his cheekbones and define his sculpted jaw.

Viola, meanwhile, knew she was growing distracted.

She couldn't help thinking how beneath that sheet, all his tawny skin and steely muscles and… other things…were waiting to be touched. All it would take was the whisper of cloth falling away, and he'd be naked before her. Viola had never seen a naked man, had not much wanted to before. But now she wanted it; she needed it.

She hugged her knees tighter still.

"Are you warm enough?" he asked, and Viola

thought she'd be warmest of all in his arms. She bit her tongue.

"Quite. I'd worry for yourself, if I were you. You're the one with barely anything on."

"I've done worrying over myself. I've been too preoccupied with myself for far too long." His eyes seemed to hold hers captive. "I'd rather look after others now."

Her cheeks heated.

"It's what I've always liked about you." It was a soft admission, but this little moment was a stolen dream inserted into reality. The hail continued to pound the roof, and outside the roads were all darkness. In here, they were the only two people on earth. "You're a decent man. That, and you mostly display good sense."

"Mostly?" He quirked a brow.

"Well. You *did* almost throw my father into a wall today. But then you showed remarkable restraint."

"I wanted to beat him senseless," Hunt growled, his gaze burning along her face, her clasped arms over her knees. "That makes me a brute, but I could never stand to let anyone harm you."

"Thank you," she whispered.

Her body ached and throbbed at his words. What would it be like to be cherished by this man? She hoped this Miss Crawford knew her own luck.

Miss Crawford is not here. Tonight, it is only you.

She had this one afternoon, it seemed, one evening's storm to be as open with him as she wished. After a lifetime of caution, Viola was sick of it. Just once, she wanted to *feel* alive, not merely *be* alive.

"So. Ashworth doesn't know the truth?" he asked.

"No. I never offered up the lie unbidden." Viola sighed. "But I always hinted at the same story I told you when asked. I was an orphaned solicitor's daughter from Hexham, sent away to school because my father left no money behind to provide for me."

"Why did you feel the need to tell such a story?" He was not accusing, merely curious.

"A governess must do more than educate. Reading, writing, and French are not enough. A governess is supposed to instruct girls in how to be a lady. How to enter a room, how to converse, how to hold themselves. Not many would think a tenant farmer's daughter naturally capable of such an education." The duke did not speak; he knew she was right. "I acquired all my 'tricks' only because of a teacher at the Wilkerson school, Lady Sophie Wilson. She was the Earl of Brideshead's daughter but had no desire to marry. I was supposed to learn only enough to work in a schoolhouse, but she encouraged me to excel. She gave me advanced instruction in French, taught me much of literature and geography, even helped perfect my needlework. She transformed me into something like a lady because she said she could tell I was made for finer things. She said that all women deserved a chance to become the truest versions of themselves."

"She sounds like a remarkable woman," Huntington said.

"Oh, she was. She did her best for me, even helped secure my position at Lynton Park." Viola's gut ached at her next thought. "Though sometimes, I wonder if it wasn't all a serious mistake. Sometimes I wonder if I haven't doomed Felicity with my self-ishness." It was a raw admission; one she'd scarce even made to herself before. "Perhaps she's as wild as she is because my own coarse breeding came through, despite my best efforts."

"I saw Miss Berridge at dinner last night. She behaved with perfect grace and poise. She simply has too much spirit to be overcome by anybody. Even the Duchess of Ashworth can't control her. But I know all of Felicity's best qualities and accomplishments are down to you." He regarded her with hunger, but also with the most respectful tenderness. "You're a true lady, Viola. Never let anyone tell you otherwise."

She had to avoid speaking, lest her quavering voice show him how happy he'd made her. Absently, her hand moved to massage her throat; thankfully, the nightdress's collar was high.

"Is something wrong?" He was too damned observant.

"No." She snatched her hand away.

"I realized I've never seen your neck before."

"An odd admission, that."

"It's true, though. You only ever wear high-necked gowns."

"I'm a governess. Modesty is expected."

"Even at dinner last night, you tied a ribbon 'round your throat."

"The color suited me." Viola could feel something emerging in her, rather like bending over the river and seeing her reflection in the water. The nearer she drew to the surface, the more detail she noticed. The harder it was to ignore what was before her.

"Did something happen to you?"

For over twenty years Viola felt like she'd carried a giant sign about wherever she went: Something Happened to Me.

She felt certain others could see it, notice how shy she was, how she moved at the edge of rooms, afraid to draw attention to herself.

This man had asked the question she didn't know she'd always wanted to hear.

"Perhaps."

"Tell me, if you please." He bowed his head. "But only if you would like me to know. I won't press you."

It was everything she'd wanted: the fact that he'd noticed, the fact that he'd asked, and the fact that he would not force it from her.

All he offered right now was strength and support. So, Viola did what she had never thought she would, especially in his presence, and unbuttoned her collar.

The scar cut just above her collarbone in a thin, ropey line. It stretched perilously close to her jugular. Already, her hands were shaking as he drew nearer, his brows furrowing in horror.

"Who did that to you?"

"You already know, don't you?"

"*Him.*" That cold venom was the only way to speak of Silas, she realized. Huntington put his fingers to her throat and skated his fingertips along the length of the scar.

Sometimes she could still feel it burning, even after all these years, burning in a flash of pain as her blood started to run and she thought *I'm dying.*

But Hunt's touch was like balm or cool water.

Normally his hands made her feel hot, but this was pure comfort. She was soothed as she'd never been before.

"When did this happen?"

"When I was eight. He came home one night

especially drunk." Viola paused, almost dizzy. She'd never told anyone this before, and naturally hesitated. But she wanted him to see her. Know all of her. "I remember the exact date, December twelfth. A week after my birthday. The anniversary of the day my mother died."

Most children looked forward to birthdays, but Viola had always feared hers with a sickness. During her birthday week, her father drank more heavily than usual and was quicker to say cruel things. And then that night, he'd stayed at the pub far longer than was his custom. Even Betsy had worried. She'd been putting dinner on the table, unable to wait for him any longer, when Silas had pushed into the cottage absolutely stinking of ale.

Betsy put down the big knife she was using to slice the bread and went to speak to him, but he shoved her aside and turned the full hatred of his gaze onto Viola.

"Should've been you," he'd slurred. She'd never seen him like this before; he looked like he truly wished she were dead. "Why them gone? Why not you, damn your blasted hide?"

Yes, his wife and his only son, both dead. He'd been left with another useless daughter, another mouth to feed.

Viola tried to make herself small as she always did, retreat into her mind where she'd constructed a fantasy home filled with friends. She could sit at the kitchen table, share tea and biscuits, and watch through the windows as Silas berated her. But that night, that wasn't all he'd done.

He'd grabbed the knife and slammed Viola to the wall, laying the blade across her throat while Betsy screamed. Viola had gone quite still, a numb sort of understanding stealing over her: she could die right now.

"He tried to cut your throat?" Hunt sounded horrified.

"He didn't try anything." Viola watched the flames so she would not burst into tears. "I remember it felt like a line of fire, and then there was blood all over my dress. I fell while Betsy wrestled the knife from him."

"Why the hell didn't the magistrate get involved?"

"Because we were too afraid." *Pathetic, but the truth.* "Afraid of him and of what life would be without him. We couldn't keep the farm going just ourselves. We had no money. Betsy brought me to the vicar. He told her she ought to report him, but she pleaded with him to find another way. So, he wrote to the Wilkerson school and found me a place. I left home one week later, and over the past twenty-two years I've seen my father exactly twice, including today. I could've done without both those visits."

She knew the duke would pity her, be angry on her behalf, but now he'd see where she truly came from. She was nothing, came from nothing, and was unworthy of words like "lovely" and "brilliant." She was pathetic.

He glowered, cracking his knuckles absently as he thought.

"I know you're angry with him," she said.

"I'm furious with him. I could kill him right now." Hunt made his hands into fists, the power in them undeniable. "But more than that, I'm furious with myself."

"What? Why should you be?"

"This all happened on my family's land, and nothing was ever done."

Her heart warmed. He was always ready to take responsibility, even when it was not his fault. He cared about her, took his family's duty to her seriously. It was one of the things she frankly adored about him.

"A duke can't possibly know every single detail of his tenants' lives! And you would have been only a boy then, away at school." Viola wanted to soothe him, but he only shook his head. His self-disgust seemed to deepen.

"If your father had been carted away, you and your sister wouldn't have been able to keep the tenancy, it's true. You'd have been paupers, and my father would have simply given the farm to a man who could make full use of it. Bring in a profit." James was a sculpture of quiet rage. "My father was a good man; maybe he would have offered you and your sister positions as servants at Moorcliff, but what then? You'd have both spent your lives scrubbing out chamber pots and lighting fires, grateful to be 'useful' at all."

"You can't blame yourself or your father," she said. After all, it wasn't the dukes' fault that their world was balanced in such a precarious, unfair way.

"I became a subject of gossip in the *ton* and have spent more than a year sulking over my bruised pride. Your own father cut your throat when you were just a child, and you never complained. You faced a cold world all on your own and endured it at eight years old." He shook his head. "You are the finest person I've ever known, Viola."

Tears flooded her eyes. Viola wiped them away. "That's kind of you to say."

"It's not kind. Nothing about me is remotely kind," he growled. "If I were kind, I'd have left Moorcliff Castle yesterday, or sent you and Miss Berridge home to Somerset. I would not have kissed you, or danced with you, and I certainly wouldn't be sitting here now thinking only of the taste of your lips. No, not only that. Thinking of what a rare creature you are, how bright and beautiful, a woman of infinite compassion. The world doesn't deserve you, and I sure as hell don't, either."

"You're wrong." She had left the earth now, was spinning somewhere up toward the stars. This moment had been worth a lifetime of waiting. "I always felt that I didn't deserve you. That I never could."

"I hope now you've seen how foolish that was," he murmured. A tear slipped down her cheek. It was like standing at the edge of a lake on an early summer morning, preparing to dive in and feel the instant of shock at the cold. But she knew that once she adjusted, it would feel like heaven. The plunge was the hardest step.

"I think perhaps we've both been foolish." She smiled. "In fact, I believe we're about to be very foolish indeed."

"How so?"

It was like gravity. One body collided with another because it was the will of nature. Viola moved toward him and, without hesitation or thought, wrapped her arms around his neck and kissed him.

CHAPTER EIGHTEEN

Her whole life, Viola had felt as though she never belonged anywhere.

She had people she loved, like Betsy and Felicity and the Ashworths, and that love kept her tethered to something, but she'd always felt as though she were stopping in for a visit. She had never found a place that had made her think *This is where I'm meant to be.*

Until now.

Huntington responded to her kiss at once, sliding a hand into her damp hair. Viola murmured in pleasure as he guided her forward, allowing her to straddle herself upon his lap.

"Oh." There was only a thin layer of cloth between her and his body, and Viola felt the throbbing length of him against her thigh. She shut her eyes, pleasure shivering through her.

"Do you want to stop this?" he breathed, kissing her throat. His lips fell to the scar above her collarbone, and Viola moaned as he trailed kisses across it. The scar was a part of her, a part of her past, and he didn't want her to hide it away to complete a perfect fantasy; he wanted it. He wanted all of her.

This would never end in marriage. Anyone would tell her this was a mistake. But no one else had lived Viola's life and felt what she had felt. This was her chance at something she'd never believed she could have. She would not waste it.

"Viola? Should we stop?"

She kissed him again, opening her mouth to

allow the kiss to deepen. She moved on instinct, rubbing her body along the length of his ever-hardening member. James moaned, and his tongue stroked hers. Viola wove her hands through his hair, devoured his mouth. She pressed against him, felt the strong beat of his heart. She wanted the sensation of his naked flesh against hers. She wanted all of him.

Tonight, she would deny herself nothing.

Scarcely breathing, Viola unbuttoned the rest of the cotton shift and slipped the sleeves from her shoulders. The garment pooled at her waist, and she felt the chill of the night air upon her breasts and stomach. She looked into James's eyes, willing herself to be brave. The duke looked down, and she could tell he liked her: she felt that new, wondrous part of him jump in enthusiasm.

"You're the most beautiful woman I've ever seen." He passed a warm, rough hand along the column of her throat before cupping her left breast. He squeezed, and a tongue of fire flickered through her. Viola was wet, that tender opening between her legs throbbing with need.

"Then you must not have seen many," she teased. Self-effacement came as naturally to her as breathing.

"No, Viola." He made her look at him, her face cradled in his hands, his blue eyes searching hers. "You must know how beautiful you are. You must know how I've dreamed of these lush curves." He cupped her breasts again, rolling her nipples with his thumbs. She cried out as he pinched them; she felt a budding sense of excitement in her body the likes of which she'd never known before. "How I've wanted to hear those cries of excitement." He breathed these words into her ear before laying a kiss upon her neck and enfolding her into his arms. Viola's eyes fluttered closed as the upper part of his drapery fell away and there was nothing between them.

She could no longer hear the pounding hail or worry about the way the wind creaked against the door or whistled through the cottage's cracks. She was here in his, in James's arms, and he was whispering the most wonderful things to her.

"I want you," she said after another breathless moment of kissing. "I want all of you."

"Oh God." He groaned as his lips found her tight, beaded right nipple. His tongue flickered across its tender expanse over and over until Viola could feel that rising excitement in her body nearing a pinnacle. "I must protect you. I'm such a rotten bastard."

"You *do* protect me, James." She kissed his lips, his forehead, reveled in the sensation of every bit of his face beneath her lips. "I understand everything, and I'm not a child. I've wanted this—wanted you—for years. And if I had one wish before I died, this would be it."

"Viola." He breathed her name over and over as he kissed her breasts, her neck. He lifted her then, his hands cupping her bottom. Viola gave a small shriek as she wrapped her legs around his waist on instinct, but he would not let her fall. "I still don't think you understand how beautiful you are."

She'd never felt as beautiful as this. He carried her across the parlor and into the bedroom. She realized he'd lit candles around the bed earlier, to help him see better. That was good; she wanted to see him. She wanted to see every inch of him.

James laid her upon the bed. She sank down on the blanket, the mattress beneath her comfortable as sin. He stood at the foot of the bed and watched her, hunger in his gaze, his entire body on display for her approval.

As a student of the natural world, Viola understood how mating occurred. To her, it had always been a clinical understanding, as easy to comprehend as the mechanics of a bird in flight. She'd understood in a technical manner what a man would look like laid bare and aroused...but she hadn't known how it would feel to see him.

Powerful was a word she could use. Enormous was another. That part of his body was long and obviously hard. It curved slightly toward the tip, and she wondered if she could manage to fit her whole hand around its girth. While her hands were small, it was still a daunting prospect.

And a delicious one.

James tugged at the bottom of her night rail and slid it from her body with ease. Then Viola was entirely naked before him, too. For a moment she wanted to hide away; no man had ever seen her undraped before, and she almost crossed her arms over her chest. But the way he was looking at her made her feel more than beautiful. She felt worshipped. At once, Viola felt her whole body relax. Being unclothed before him suddenly became the most natural state in the world. The duke put a knee onto the mattress, shifting the bed with his weight. Viola would soon have that weight atop her, pinning her down. The thought made her breath come faster.

"Please," she whispered.

"Let me explain your beauty in detail." The duke leaned over her and kissed her deeply. "These lips," he said, "are soft as sin and ripe as berries."

She had no words; all ability to talk fled as he kissed her throat, as he trailed the tip of his tongue along her scar. Viola's thighs clenched, the sensation unexpectedly arousing.

"Your body is so lush, so beautifully rounded. Touching you is the most blissful experience I've ever known." He kissed her breasts once more, laid burning trails of kisses between them, along her stomach. He parted her legs—Viola was too drunk on pleasure to ask what he was doing. "These legs," he whispered, kissing along her inner thigh, "I can't tell you how I've imagined them wrapping around my body as I sank into you. Claiming you."

She wanted that more than anything. She was sick of being lost, yearned to be found.

Then she gasped at the feel of his breath upon her sex, already so tender and engorged by her arousal.

"More than anything, I've wanted to taste you." Then he kissed her there, on her opening. Viola cried out; every inch of her skin was now so sensitive to his touch. She was burning, but it did not hurt.

"James."

"Keep saying my name. Don't stop," he said, and then she felt him part her slick folds, felt his tongue lap once against some secret little bud she'd been too afraid ever to touch. Ever to even hunt for, though she knew it existed, knew it would give her pleasure.

He traced the tip of his tongue around that cunning little spot only twice before Viola's whole body exploded in ecstasy. She wailed as she lifted off the mattress, her back arching with the overpowering sensation. It had all happened so quickly, as though she'd been burning for release for heaven knew how long. The pleasure kept coursing through her, wave upon wave of it. She gasped, reveling in how the first time she'd known real ecstasy was with him. With James.

"More?" he asked.

Viola looked down at the duke nestled between her parted legs. The shine of her body was on his lips, and she wanted more. She needed it.

"Yes," she said. "More." Giving orders to a duke in bed would have seemed impossible yesterday, but now it felt only too natural.

She watched him as he kissed her, licked her, as he blew upon her most sensitive spot and then sucked that little bud into his mouth. Another rush of euphoria sent Viola to paradise, and she screamed his name over and over.

She reached down and ran her fingers through his hair, watching him work her with his mouth. He gave her another surge of pleasure, and another, until she was spent and flushed, scarce able to open her eyes.

"Please," she whispered. "I want you, James."

He moved forward, aligning his core with her own so that Viola could feel the hot, steady throb of his member against her opening. His weight pinned her to the mattress. She'd never expected a man could be so heavy on top of her, yet she did not feel crushed or pinned down. She felt secure beneath him, secure as he kissed her and she tasted the tang of her own body on his lips.

"You're sensational," he breathed. He looked into her eyes as he reached down and adjusted himself, the tip of his erection prodding her opening. "God, you're so wet."

"I need this. I need you."

She kissed him now, kissed him hard as he groaned deep in his chest. Viola gasped as she felt him begin to fill her, to stretch her beyond what she'd thought she could handle.

"I'll go slow. I'll be gentle with you," he whispered. He rubbed the tip of his cock along her seam, stopping at that little point of delight between her thighs. Viola's breath quickened as she felt him press against her. Her body could not seem to wring enough delight out of his, out of this moment. Already she was throbbing, desperate for another burst of ecstasy. He stroked himself up and down the seam of her, up and down, all while Viola clung to him. When he gave her another release, she buried her scream against his neck. Tentatively, she did what she'd only dreamed of before and wrapped her legs around his waist.

"Not too gentle." It was a murmured order.

"God, Viola," he growled. She felt him trembling on the precipice of animal abandonment. Then he began to rock his hips back and forth slowly.

Viola winced when at last the tip of his erection slid inside her; her body, despite its arousal, was too small and his too large for this to be without pain. But she'd always known that there could be no victory without sacrifice. And pain such as this was hardly a sacrifice when the prize was him. The Duke of Huntington. James.

It was James she loved, she realized, more than the duke.

The man who grew cross, who could be arrogant, who could be tender and vulnerable, funny and foolish, the man who cared for his tenants and believed in defending those who couldn't defend themselves, he was better than the perfect god she'd fantasized about for years.

"Please," she whispered. "Take me. Do it now."

"Are you sure?"

She urged her hips forward, feeling him slide in a fraction of an inch more. With a groan, James obliged her, and, with a single thrust, sheathed himself fully within her body.

Viola gasped as he stretched and filled her, the sudden, sheer intimacy of it overwhelming. James was wonderful, refusing to move until she asked him. Viola breathed heavily, allowing herself time to adjust.

"Are you all right?" he asked.

"I'm more than that." She kissed him, the strangeness of having him within already subsiding. "This is wonderful."

Scarcely breathing, Viola felt him begin to move inside her. His strokes were deep and fluid; he would pull out of her to the very tip, then glide back to fill the space within her utterly. His hips pumped as he rode her, and Viola's legs wrapped tighter around his waist as she felt her body adjusting to the rhythms of his.

She looked at his face, his eyes half-lidded with his focus on pleasure. She jerked her hips against his as he moved, wringing an enthusiastic response from his lips. Viola looked up at the ceiling, unbelieving. She'd given up her virtue, and not to just any man.

She couldn't imagine ever taking any other lover.

As her climax began to hasten again, it was more than physical pleasure that filled her. The tightness between her hips was wonderful as she was wound up, but the fire in her body and soul made all of it sweeter. If this was the only time in her life Viola ever knew love, she could still die happy.

Better to wait for what you truly wanted than to settle for anything else.

"God, Viola." He rode her harder, and Viola felt the motion of his back muscles beneath her hands. James's voice tightened. "This is astonishing."

"It is." She thrust her hips against his vigorously now, meeting him stroke for stroke. James gave a sharp cry at the sensation.

"I'm going to spend," he hissed.

His cock slid in and out of her, in and out, until it rubbed one final time against that perfect spot and Viola screamed as loud as she liked, shuddering all over with the force of the orgasm. The duke gave three more intense thrusts, and then his body left hers in a hurry. He turned on his side, groaning as he spent upon the bedclothes.

And that was that.

Viola was no longer intact, and she was now happier than she'd ever thought she could be. She lay on her back, relishing the slick soreness between her legs. She closed her eyes and laughed softly.

"You know, laughter immediately following such a performance is not the most comforting sound a gentleman may hear," James teased.

"I assure you, it's not mockery. Only bliss." She melted a little more as he kissed her cheek and neck.

"You're sensational," he murmured.

"For a beginner, I hope it was adequate."

"You don't understand." He made her look at him. There was only rough tenderness in his eyes. "It was the greatest experience I've ever known."

Viola wanted to hide; how was that possible? She could not be the most beautiful woman he'd had, and certainly not the youngest.

"You must say that to all the spinsters, Your Grace." She meant to tease, but James seemed stricken by her words.

"It's you, Viola. Everything about you is the best I've ever known. Your mind." He kissed her lips. "Your body." Her neck. "Your soul."

She bit her lip; she was afraid she'd start weeping with joy otherwise.

"Then you may as well know. This has been the most exhilarating moment of my life," she whispered.

As the storm continued to rage overhead, James pulled the blankets over them and held her close in the candlelight.

His skin warmed her own; she hadn't realized how much being naked in another's arms could relax a person. She pressed her head to his chest and listened to the wind, feeling cozy and safe in this bed. In his arms.

"Do you think you're spent of exhilarating moments this evening?" He nibbled her earlobe. "Or might there be more in our future?"

"A good governess believes in practicing technique until all is done perfectly." She smiled, basking in the warmth of her own happiness.

"Then we'd better get to work."

He slid atop her, and for hours they applied themselves most vigorously to their studies.

• • •

When he awoke, he found sunlight streaming through the windows and Viola still in his arms.

Hunt had been afraid this would be a dream, but he found the small, delicate woman curled up in his embrace. He was wrapped around her from behind, his cock starting to twitch in an enthusiastic "good morning" against her plump backside. Viola shifted in her dream, moaning a little in pleasure. Fuck, he needed to wake her.

As he kissed the nape of her neck, he thought of all the ways in which he was a bastard. He'd seduced this vulnerable young woman…though she had been happy to seduce him back. In fact, he'd been shocked last night at how insatiable Viola had proved to be. She loved the feel of him inside her; she'd told him that breathlessly as they moved in perfect tandem, speeding to their next mutual climax.

It should have shocked and horrified him. By societal standards, even married women should not say such lewd things to their husbands. Anyone would tell Hunt that the governess was a loose woman, damaged goods before he'd even taken her to bed.

Hunt would kindly tell those naysayers to stuff their wrong opinions up their puckered sphincters.

Viola was the most exquisite creature he'd ever known.

With her, sex had gone beyond mere bed sport and into something almost sacred. He trailed kisses along her back, across her shoulder, relishing the taste of fresh air and heather. Had that come from being thrown about in the storm yesterday, or was that taste simply her own? She was a force of nature, unspoiled by the world of man.

His cock stiffened as he thought of taking her again. If only they could stay in this cottage forever, shut from the world and languishing in the bliss of each other's bodies. No clothes allowed. Just freedom.

"Good morning." She turned to face him, her hair rumpled upon the pillow. She smiled with kiss-swollen lips, making Hunt hungry for more. Her smile lessened as she studied him with those quizzical hazel eyes. "How do you feel?"

"Reborn," he growled, gathering her close and kissing her.

"Should we discuss all this?" She sounded delirious as he kissed her neck.

"Discuss how ecstatic I am?" He nibbled her collarbone. "How utterly gorgeous you look in the morning light?" His lips brushed her nipple as he spoke next. "How hard you've made me?"

Vulgar words that he should use only on jaded, married women. Yet when Viola sighed with delight, he felt cleansed, not dirty at all.

"Your Grace—"

"James. Please." He lay atop her and hoisted himself onto his elbows, looking deep into her eyes. She gazed up at him without fear, this small, naked woman with so much less authority in this world than he had. She was the most courageous person he'd ever known, and that aroused him only further. "When we're alone, it's James."

"Or Fluffy?"

He grinned. "Or Fluffy."

"I confess I'm afraid of what comes next." Viola wrapped her arms around his neck, pulled him close. "I know I ought to claim I regretted last night."

"But you don't?"

"Not for a moment. Not ever." She was so serious about that, about him. Hunt kissed her once more.

"Are you too sore, my dear?" he whispered, sliding one finger tentatively inside her body. Already, she was silken and wet as could be.

"Not terribly." She kissed along his jaw. "You do realize we'll need to eventually eat something." True, they'd missed two meals yesterday. Funny how Hunt couldn't care less about all that.

"Excellent idea." He kissed her breasts and began to slide down her body again, ready to take his place between her thighs. "I'm famished."

"Oh, what am I doing?" Viola sighed as Hunt spread her legs, kissed the inside of her thigh.

"Hallo? Is anyone there?" A man's voice boomed out rather close by. The voice grew louder, and the sound of horses' hooves and carriage wheels thumped and rumbled along respectively.

Hunt froze like a boy caught sneaking a midnight treat from the biscuit tin. Viola sat up, bundling the blankets to cover her nakedness.

"Your Grace?" the voice called. "Is anyone there?"

"I believe a rescue party has arrived," she whispered.

"Damn them," Hunt growled. "Why couldn't they have the decency to leave us to die?"

CHAPTER NINETEEN

An hour later Viola walked into Moorcliff Castle's receiving hall, wrestling with a whole snarl of conflicting emotions.

There was joy, obviously, as well as deep, deep satisfaction that came from more than just the physical act of love. Her contentment lay in how tender they had been with each other. Her whole life, Viola had never expected such tenderness, and it was better than she could have imagined.

She was also bracing herself for the blow of their inevitable parting, for she still had not deluded herself that this would lead to marriage. She had ruined herself for the chance at one moment of pure bliss, and she refused to regret it.

But as she entered Moorcliff, all Viola's many emotions changed to surprise as Felicity wheeled herself over to her governess in a panic.

"There you are! We thought something horrible had occurred!" The girl flung herself out of the chair and hopped the last steps to Viola. Felicity wrapped her in a tight hug, and…was she sniffling? Viola could count on one hand the times she'd seen Felicity cry over the past ten years.

"Dearest, it's all right. We're fine."

"The horse dragged the broken gig all the way back here in the middle of the night." Felicity was now struggling not to weep, in the process turning her face the purple of an aubergine. "We feared the worst! Perhaps you'd died in a ditch, or been abducted by highwaymen, or murdered by some demonic fellow with a knife!"

"Perhaps you ought to read something other than Mr. Winthrop, dear." Felicity would not have been frightened by so many lurid possibilities if she were enjoying *Patience and Grace*. "Anyway, we were perfectly safe. We took shelter at the groundskeeper's cottage."

"Oh? You and the duke?" Felicity perked up a bit. "I trust nothing untoward occurred."

"Felicity Alice Berridge! What a shocking suggestion!"

How could you possibly know? Viola hoped a blush would not give her away.

"So His Grace was a perfect gentleman the entire time?" Felicity looked bewildered.

"He is a duke, young lady. He is a gentleman through and through." Except for the moments when he was less than a gentleman. Those had been so delicious, Viola grew almost dizzy recalling them.

"Unbelievable." Felicity shook her head in consternation.

"I beg pardon?"

"Erm, I mean it's so unbelievable…that such good men exist in this world." Felicity collapsed back into her chair and hunched up. She looked as if she were sulking. "Our society would collapse without honorable men being all very, you know… honorable."

It was almost like Felicity wished her governess had been debauched by a duke. Viola decided that once back at Lynton Park they would have to spend ample time with Reverend Fordyce's Sermons. Even if it was the dullest book in the world, Felicity's character needed adjustment. Or at least she needed to get better at hiding her true thoughts. And speaking of Lynton Park, it was time to return home.

It pained Viola to consider, but after last night she and Huntington would not be able to go too long without slipping up and revealing something. Viola had no wish to cause scandal or bring embarrassment on the duke, on James, not for the whole world.

"Well. You ought to spend some time with Lady Isabelle," she said at last. "I aim for us to leave the castle by no later than two in the afternoon."

"No, we can't!" Felicity cried. She made an outraged face.

"Why on earth not? We must return home!"

"Because…because Lady Isabelle and I are adapting "Giselle, the Tragic Ghost" into a novel! I'm doing the illustrations. We can't just leave now!"

"I'm certain the duke will be happy to send Lady Isabelle to Somerset for a long visit. You can continue to work on the novel then."

But Felicity grew only more incensed. She wheeled herself backward, her face turning crimson with outrage.

"You just don't want me to have any friends." The child's eyes glittered with rage and perhaps even the faintest trace of tears. "I'm supposed to hide myself away at Lynton Park like a mistake. Well, I refuse!"

"Young lady, you do not speak to people in that tone." But Viola's heart broke a bit. Was that how Felicity felt? A stain to be covered up? Viola knew that feeling all too well.

"It's true, isn't it? I'm a bastard. I don't have any parents. Everyone just wants me to grow up, find a husband, and pretend to be invisible my entire life. I should be grateful the Duke of Ashworth bothered to look after me at all."

"Where's all this coming from?" Viola felt like she'd been struck.

"I don't want to leave Moorcliff Castle! I can't believe you want to ruin all my plans!"

"Felicity!"

But the willful girl spun herself about and wheeled off so quickly that Viola couldn't catch up with her.

Over the past few days Felicity had become a very demon with that wheelchair. She could probably race a horse at this point, she was so adept at speed and maneuvering herself.

Viola stopped and, alone in the hallway, put her face in her hands. She was weak with love and happiness, she was aching with the threat of departure, and now she worried that she'd wounded Felicity without meaning to after all these years.

She must be the most incompetent woman on the planet.

• • •

Felicity Berridge was not the type to let anyone foil her plans. Once she wanted a thing, she pursued it until she had what she craved. As a little girl it had been easy to demand sweets or toys until the adults in her life gave in. The only adult who'd ever stood a chance against her was Miss Winslow. Felicity revered her governess, thinking her the cleverest woman in England. If their world wasn't ruled by thick-headed, imbecilic men, Miss Winslow might have become Prime Minister. Felicity thought such level of power a better retirement package than being a duchess, in truth, but given the narrow constraints of their society a duchess would have to do.

"I can't believe it," Felicity muttered. She was seated beside Isabelle in the library, paper and ink scattered haphazardly around them. To take her mind off the Miss Winslow situation Felicity had tried to work on the novelization of "Giselle," but she could never focus on one task for very long. Isabelle scribbled away while Felicity shredded a sheet of paper into little bits for something to do. "They were in the most Gothic situation possible! I could never have arranged anything so perfect. Caught in the middle of a storm, stranded in an abandoned cottage, isolated for miles, and what happens? Nothing! Your brother is a perfect gentleman. He makes me sick."

"Hunt has many fine qualities, but badness has never been one of them." Isabelle sighed. "He didn't compromise her in even the slightest way?"

"No he didn't, the scoundrel." Felicity wished she could stop all this invalid nonsense. Right now, if she didn't have to pretend a sprained ankle, she would have kicked Huntington right in his tall, muscular backside. "And now we're supposed to leave."

"You can't!" Isabelle's eyes widened. "There's so much of "Giselle" left to do! Besides, I don't want to go back to being alone with Granny and Hunt always sniping at each other. Life would be so much more pleasant if Miss Winslow lived here."

"Yes, you'd like having her. She's good with poetry and lots else besides." Truly, the prospect of losing her governess was the only thing that saddened Felicity. But she had always been known as a tough little thing, and she didn't believe in being miserable.

"More than that, if she were to become the duchess then you could come and stay whenever you like. I didn't realize having a best friend could be so jolly."

No one had ever called Felicity their best friend before. The village children had played games with her when they were small, but Felicity always remained something of a secret. She didn't have many friends her age, and certainly none who enjoyed vampires and murder as much as she.

"Really? You think I'm jolly?" Felicity had been called irascible, devious, maniacal, wild, a strong contender for the Antichrist, and all when people were in a good mood! No one had ever called her jolly before.

"If not for you, I would never have learned of Mr. Winthrop. You're the only person who truly understands me." Isabelle clutched Felicity's arm. "I don't want to go back to being alone."

Neither did Felicity. She felt a bit better at the prospect of losing Miss Winslow to the duke if it meant gaining a best friend and access to a haunted castle whenever she wished. If only that duke would debauch her governess like a true nobleman!

"We're going to pull this off," Felicity said. "Somehow."

Ugh, but how? As always, she turned to the classics for inspiration. Felicity took up a copy of Matthew Lewis's *The Monk* and started leafing about looking for when the Devil turned up. The Devil always had good ideas.

"It's a shame we have no ancestral curse to break," Isabelle mused, chewing on the tip of her pen. "If only something supernatural would occur to tell Hunt that Miss Winslow is his ideal match."

"If we could only get the bloody Moorcliff Haunt

to appear," Felicity grumbled. "People always listen to ghosts. Like in *Hamlet*!"

"Yes! Though we should take care not to have everyone die at the end." Isabelle squeaked with a sudden burst of inspiration. "Oh! I may have come up with the most brilliant idea."

"The most brilliant?" Felicity narrowed her eyes. Competitive by nature, she was certain she could come up with something even brilliant-er given the opportunity.

"If the Moorcliff Haunt won't reveal herself, we can contrive to have her speak to us anyway!"

"But how?" Procuring a spirit on demand was challenging.

"Leave that to me. All my dramatic skills are about to be tested, but I'm certain I'll triumph!" Isabelle appeared giddy. "Oh. But we must also find a way to have you stay another night!"

"You take care of the ghost business; I'll make sure we stay on." Felicity looked around the library. "Now. What here is breakable but replaceable?"

"I don't think that vase is *too* ancient." Isabelle pointed out something that looked Chinese in provenance.

"Excellent." Felicity prepared to take a wheeling leap at the antique. "Time for a falsified concussion."

CHAPTER TWENTY

Felicity had smashed her head on a priceless Ming vase, but Hunt couldn't be too angry with the girl.

The accident meant that Miss Winslow and her charge had to remain in his castle at least one more night. What's more, though, there was no time or opportunity to confer with his fellow conspirators.

Hunt had the idea that Felicity and Isabelle were planning something. They kept shooting him meaningful looks during the day (though Felicity also seemed rather annoyed with him) and then announced at dinner that they wished to hold a séance that evening, intent on summoning the Moorcliff Haunt to speak to them.

"Oh no," the dowager said at once, downing half a glass of wine in one gulp. "The last attempted séance ruined the bathroom. Absolutely not."

"We're not going to use water as a divination tool again, Granny." Isabelle was all wide-eyed earnestness. "I'd like to try a planchette this time. Miss Berridge is open to the possibility of ghosts as strongly as I, and that means I finally have someone who can help!"

"What is a planchette?" Miss Winslow looked apprehensive. Hunt had to agree with that sentiment.

"The Chinese had an ancient technique for communing with the spirit world. You take a board with a lot of letters and numbers upon it, then two people place their hands on the planchette, which is a panel that can move about easily. They ask questions and the spirits guide their hands to give the answer!"

"Is there any long-lost family treasure you've spent decades looking for?" Felicity asked. "We can ask the Haunt if she knows where it is."

"Wonderful. Now we are in league with the Devil Himself! I shall faint." Hunt's grandmother looked less inclined to collapse than she did to spit in the Prince of Darkness's face.

"It's not anything to do with demons, Granny. The English really are very backward when it comes to family ghosts. The Chinese are far more sophisticated."

"My dear girl, I take the summoning of ancestral spirits to be the height of rudeness! One ought always to be able to decline an invitation."

"I appreciate how thoroughly mad everyone is being just now," Agatha said, massaging her temples. "But I'm afraid I shall have to give the séance a miss. The weather is wreaking havoc on my head again."

Indeed, there was an evening thunderstorm for the fourth night in a row. The wind bellowed and rain lashed the castle walls. Intermittent thunder and lightning announced themselves, setting the whole party on edge.

Even Cornelius was flustered, circling the dining room several times with throaty cries of "whiskey" and "knickers" and even "bollocks."

At least it wasn't another limerick. Cornelius's repertoire was salty, to be polite about it.

"Your Grace, you needn't allow the young ladies to summon the dead if you don't wish it," Viola said.

What a sentence. But Hunt smiled, because anything she said at this point was the most heavenly sound. He'd let Isabelle and Felicity invoke doomsday itself if only he could sit with Viola Winslow for another hour.

Besides, from the way Felicity kept glaring mean-ingfully at him, Hunt had the idea he stood to profit from this ghostly misadventure.

"I've always wanted to observe a séance, Miss Winslow. I trust you'll join us?"

"How could I refuse such an unusual request, Your Grace?" She smiled.

He wanted her there. He wanted her with him tonight and tomorrow night and every night thereaf-ter. Right now, Hunt was trying not to fixate on the promise to his father, a "true lady" for Moorcliff's mistress.

He would figure this out later; for now, for to-night, he wanted only to be near her.

After supper Agatha retired to her room and the girls began to organize the séance. The dowager groaned endlessly but did not leave.

Hunt tried to approach Viola with confidence, even though he felt as elated and out of his depth as a boy with his first infatuation. He seated himself next to the woman as the servants obeyed Isabelle's instructions, moving tables and finding enough can-dles.

"Are you afraid they'll contact the ghost after all?" he whispered.

"Of course not. Ghosts don't exist." She smiled, looked at him with those bewitching hazel eyes, and then returned her attentions to her pupil.

Hunt's gut ached to think that she was now try-ing to put distance between them. Perhaps she thought him a cad for not immediately proposing marriage after the ecstasy of last night. Perhaps she believed him to be a coward and a libertine. Perhaps his inaction had killed all her feeling for him!

Perhaps Hunt ought to take out the gift he had hidden in his pocket now, and, in plain view of the room, offer it to Viola. The little box felt as if it were burning a hole in the fabric of his breeches. Hunt began to rise as Viola turned from him.

"Miss Winslow," he said.

"All right, everyone, sit down! Lady Isabelle and I must concentrate!" Felicity scooted herself to the table, nearly knocking into the furniture in her excitement.

All talk had to cease while the adults settled in and watched the girls at their supernatural experiment. But Hunt could barely restrain himself; he appreciated the young ladies' help, but now they were getting in the way of his conquest!

Isabelle had laden the table with candles of varying heights and stages of melting. The candles' glow suffused the girls' faces while lightning flashed through the room. The storm cascaded against the windowpanes.

"I fear a bloody skull will rise from the floor and begin screaming at any moment," Viola whispered. Hunt chuckled.

"O former Duchess of Huntington! We invoke you to come to us tonight and speak, o spirit! Give us a sign that you are with us now." Isabelle took up a handbell and rang it several times. "Come and ring the bell to show us you are close!"

They all waited a moment. Then another moment.

Felicity began to look antsy in her chair, and finally nabbed the bell and rang it herself.

"Oh! My hand! Something grabbed my hand and made me ring!" she called out, not exactly selling the performance. "What's with the bell nonsense?"

Felicity hissed.

"The artistic temperament moved me!" Isabelle hissed back.

"Perhaps Agatha had the right idea." Hunt's grandmother looked as if she had a tremendous headache.

"O Bloody Duchess, lay your hand upon this planchette and speak to us! Answer our questions if you will. Do you consent?"

The girls waited with their hands on the planchette, and then, with a gasp, they watched as it slid across the board and landed upon a YES painted in black lacquer in the corner. Hunt wondered if he ought to pretend to be astonished.

"You must have moved it!" Felicity cried, acting rather badly.

"I swear I did not! I can feel the icy chill of a spectral presence upon my neck!" Isabelle replied, her delivery stilted and overwrought simultaneously.

I wish they were slightly better actresses. Hunt frowned; whatever they had in mind for him wouldn't work if they were this easy to read.

"O Bloody Duchess, tell us your name," Felicity said, yelling over the sudden clap of thunder.

The adults watched with bemusement as the planchette moved to the M, then the A, then the R and the Y.

"Mary! Was Mary the name?" Felicity asked.

"Why, how astonishing! Mary, former Duchess of Huntington, have you a message to impart to any of us here in the room?"

Instantly, the planchette slid to YES.

"To which of us would you speak?" Isabelle shut her eyes, really getting into the spirit of communion.

"Erm, why don't you keep your eyes open?"

Felicity grumbled. "The duchess probably doesn't have an easy time seeing the board what with being dead and all."

"Felicity is unusually bizarre this evening." Viola sounded dizzy. "And the threshold is quite high."

"Pardon, Duchess. To whom would you speak?"

Hunt was not alarmed when the planchette spelled out the word J-A-M-E-S with the help of the girls.

"Whatever could the poor old duchess want to say to me?" He attempted to look as serious as possible. His grandmother, meanwhile, asked for a second glass of brandy from a footman. She'd swallowed the first in one go.

"O Mary, Duchess of Huntington, what wouldst thou say unto mine elder brother, James?" Isabelle cried.

"Why are you talking like that?" Felicity looked bewildered.

"Speak! Speak!"

The planchette began to slide about the board once again, interrupting its journey to land on different letters. Isabelle carefully spelled the letters and then announced the words they formed.

"Take," she said. "A. True. Lady. As…"

Good God. Hunt's heart pounded, his throat tightened, he wanted to hug Isabelle and to shake her and ask what the bloody hell she thought she was doing.

Take a true lady as Moorcliff's mistress, their father's final request to Hunt.

The dowager looked baffled now, and perhaps a little alarmed. He saw where this was going. The ghost would pass along Hunt's father's words, and then spell out the name of his "true lady." It would begin with V, and then I, and then oh, he did not know how he would react when the moment came.

But first, the "ghost" needed to finish spelling out the sentence.

"Moorcliff's." Isabelle leaned forward as the final word was spelled. "M. I. S. T. E." She frowned, and the planchette stopped in its journey. It looked as if a tug of war was ongoing between at least two of the three parties involved. "Um. Would you care to try that again, O Duchess? I believe there was a mis-spelling."

"No, the ghost knows how to spell." Felicity narrowed her eyes. "Let the duchess continue."

"If she's saying "mistress" then there should be no E there," Isabelle hissed.

"We don't know it's mistress! And it *would* have an E there, as the ghost clearly understands!"

"O Duchess, does Miss Berridge know how to spell properly?" Isabelle winced as she tried to drag the planchette toward NO.

"Stop mucking this up!" Felicity gritted her teeth and tried to wrestle the planchette to YES.

"Another brandy." The dowager held out her crystal glass. "My headache is becoming severe."

Hunt decided never to rely on ghosts or adolescents ever again.

"What are you ladies trying to spell?" Viola asked, sounding tired.

"Mistress, obviously!" Felicity snapped. "I mean, that's what the ghost wants to spell!"

"I thought as much. There is no E there, Felicity."

"I told you!" Isabelle took her hands off the planchette in triumph, and it went flying off the table to land on the carpet. "Mister-ess? Of course it's wrong!"

"Maybe that's how they spelled it two hundred years ago! Or maybe her spelling is not top-notch! The duchess has been dead rather a long time, you know!"

"Both of you stop it now," Hunt grumbled. The girls appeared sheepish, aware how colossally they'd fouled things. "I think this little game's gone on long enough."

"What were the two of you attempting anyway?" Viola asked.

Oh, bollocks. Hunt winced, hoping that their confession would not incriminate him. The last thing he wanted now was to appear a perfect fool to Viola.

"Er. It was the ghost, not us," Felicity muttered.

"See here, young lady—"

The whole party flinched as the dowager duchess let out a long, shrill scream. Hunt's grandmother clapped a hand to her mouth and pointed with the other.

"What is it?" he cried, looking to where she pointed.

The parlor door had been opened, and in another gargantuan flash of lightning he saw a woman standing there. The woman, no, the apparition was dressed in bridal satin. He glimpsed the dress for only the briefest moment, but it was clearly centuries out of style. A veil shrouded the creature's face, and a garish bloodstain decorated its bodice. Hunt was shocked. It couldn't be…could it?

"Oh! The ghost!" Isabelle leaped to her feet in triumph. "*It's the ghost! We did it!*"

"*Bloody hell!*" Felicity jumped out of her wheelchair and charged headlong at the apparition. "*We're geniuses!*"

Isabelle chased after the other girl, leaving the

adults with an overturned planchette game, a spilled glass of brandy on the carpet, and a fainting dowager. Hunt immediately called for more brandy and tended to his grandmother.

"Go chase the young ladies, they can't have got far," he said to a footman.

"I don't believe it," Viola said.

"A ghost! An actual ghost," the duchess moaned. Hunt coaxed her to take some brandy.

"No." Viola pointed at the vacant wheelchair. "Felicity's ankle is quite unhurt!" She paused then turned to Hunt. "And Your Grace doesn't seem bothered by that in the least."

Oh, damn everything.

"It's a rather unusual night," he said as one of the footmen came racing back into the room.

"Your Graces! The garden door's open, the young ladies must have gone outside!"

Isabelle! He was going to lock her away until she was forty.

With a cry of frustration, Viola rushed out of the room. Hunt chased after her, ignoring his grandmother as she yelled for someone to explain what on earth was happening.

Though the servants begged him not to go, Hunt barreled out into the rain. He was drenched to the skin within moments, wiping streaming rainwater out of his eyes as he squinted into the dark night.

A burst of lightning illuminated the landscape, and he saw Viola diminishing as she ventured forth into the storm. Hunt called her name and chased after her, staggering ahead blindly until he almost stumbled upon the woman.

"James!" Viola clung to him in gratitude. It was so wet out here, it was almost like they were drowning at sea. "I can't find them!"

"We shall do this together. Come." He sheltered his arm about her shoulders and trudged forth into the rain, both shouting the girls' names against the wind.

Even though he feared for his sister, with Viola here and close he could not be fully upset. Nothing in the world could be completely wrong when he was touching her. She was the anchor he'd been searching for his whole life. She was fast becoming the calm center of his world.

If they weren't searching for children in a rain-storm, he'd have liked to kiss her now. Kiss her until they were both breathless, until he could get them out of this bloody weather and into a private bath. His loins ached at the mere thought. But until his sister was recovered, his loins must do nothing at all.

Viola shrieked when lightning split the sky once again and outlined the skeleton of a gazebo up ahead. Hunt ushered the governess up the steps and stood alongside her, both dripping wet but at least now out of the storm. Rain pattered on the gazebo's roof as Hunt peered into the darkness and shouted the girls' names again.

"Felicity must have been tricking us this entire time," Viola murmured. She seemed stunned; even for a girl like Felicity, this level of deception was obviously abnormal. "Why on earth would she do such a thing?"

"Um. To spend more time with Isabelle, proba-bly." Hunt was not about to grow nervous. Viola was not *his* governess, after all!

"James?" She moved to his side. "Please answer my next question honestly. Did you know Felicity was lying about her injury before tonight?"

He might have used the darkness as a cloak, but unfortunately another inopportune bolt of lightning revealed the duke to the governess. Hunt could tell by the widening of her beautiful eyes that the guilt was apparent in his own expression.

"I see. How long have you known?"

"Since before our trip to the graveyard." *Oh, why not?* He might as well top off the madness on display tonight. Why would any woman choose to marry into such an insane family, even if they *did* live in a castle? "Truthfully, I enlisted Miss Berridge's help."

"Her help? In what?"

"Her help in wooing you, of course! It's why she contrived to come here in the first place, why she pretended to be injured. She confessed the whole thing to me. She wanted us to spend time together and fall in love."

"She did what?" Viola sounded horrified. "But why?"

"She wanted you to have an ample retirement package."

"She *what*?"

"But her plan worked rather too well, I'm afraid. You see, before I knew anything about her schemes, I'd fallen in love with you." There. The words were out. She could now see the totality of his humiliation. "I *am* in love with you. Hopelessly. Completely. Devotedly." He was growing cross with how much of a fool he must now look to her. Love made men like Ashworth more dashing, while it reduced him to a shambles of his former competent self. "Perhaps it seems ridiculous, recruiting the help of a bizarre adolescent in matters of the heart, but I no longer trusted my own intuition. After the way I bungled things with Miss Fletcher, I couldn't be certain I knew anything about women at all. So yes, in the plainest terms, I've been attempting to win your heart. And as is now obvious, I've collapsed well before the finish line."

He was flustered, an un-erotic emotion if one ever existed. Hunt waited for the lightning to reveal Viola's irritation, her disdain, her pity.

Instead, when the sky lit up once more, he saw she was laughing. Laughing quite strenuously. In fact, she was a bit bent over.

Somehow that hurt his pride worse than pity would have.

"I'm glad I've provided some amusement," he grumbled.

"Oh James."

Then he felt her hands upon his chest, her arms around his neck.

He lifted her in his embrace, relishing the curving, womanly weight of her. Their lips met, and she kissed him with such sweetness and assurance that all the wretchedness of this night, all the wretchedness of this year, all the wretchedness of his whole arrogant, misspent lifetime vanished like raindrops on the earth.

Viola kissed him again and again, renewing his soul more with every touch of her lips.

"You are not at all the man I thought you were." She laughed breathlessly. "For years I thought you the most regal, most stoic, most perfect specimen of manhood to ever exist."

"Well. How glad I am to have disabused you of those notions."

"And you are indeed perfect. You *are* regal and stoic, and you are so wonderfully a man. It's just that you're so entirely human as well. You're human, and you're kind, and you give of yourself so fully and freely. That's what I love about you most of all."

"Viola?" He felt dizzy, wanted to hear those words again. That one word in particular, the one that started with *L*. She obliged him.

"I love you, James Montagu. Duke of Huntington." She kissed him for a long, perfect instant. "The title is incidental, of course."

She was the rarest creature in the world, a woman who loved him despite his dukedom, not for it. A woman who liked as well as loved him.

Moorcliff Castle housed countless exquisite treasures, fantastic pieces the likes of which few could dream. But Hunt knew as he kissed Viola while the storm raged all around them that she was the true incomparable jewel, the one treasure he could never afford to buy but must still possess.

"Oh, we did it!" Isabelle squealed.

"Bloody hell, I'm a genius."

The duke and the governess found they had an appreciative audience huddled on the other side of the gazebo. Isabelle and Felicity had wisely sheltered here to wait out the storm. Felicity looked especially pleased with herself.

"Young lady, you are to return to the castle this instant!" Viola managed to sound stern even while wrapped in his arms. What an extraordinary woman.

"But look how well things have turned out! You're not cross, are you, Miss Winslow?"

"Oh, Felicity." Viola smiled with great sweetness. "I am absolutely furious."

CHAPTER TWENTY-ONE

Viola did not think she would ever get out of this bath again.

Even though her fingers had shriveled, and the water was now tepid, she wanted only to luxuriate in the lingering steam and reimagine every moment of the last two hours.

Well. Apart from the bloody apparition and Felicity wailing about how unfair the governess was being in punishing her.

Though Viola would be grateful to the girl until the end of her days, Felicity still had to be sent to bed right away for her week-long deception. Viola and James had tempered the punishment a bit, allowing Felicity to stay the night in Lady Isabelle's room. Right now, the girls were probably revising "Giselle, the Tragic Ghost" and gossiping about their shared victory.

Viola didn't know how the girls had contrived that grisly visitation from the Bloody Duchess, but she had to admire the showmanship. Felicity would deny it forever, but she must have been responsible for the haunting.

I will make it up to Felicity, Viola thought. *None of this would have happened without her.*

Viola hadn't realized a person could become physically weak with happiness. Thinking about James now made her giddy rather than wistful, and she could not stop herself from smiling. It was instinctive in her to be afraid of such an overabundance of joy, but Viola was trying to change her ways. She wanted to experience ecstasy now, not just humility.

When she finally got out of the bath and put on her night rail, Viola returned to her chamber and sat upon the bed, wondering how she'd ever fall asleep tonight.

James had said that he loved her, and she had told him that she loved him. Knowing that she had his love, something she'd wanted for over ten years, felt like being given a key to every locked room in a palace. Viola couldn't wait to spend hours and days and weeks exploring every little alcove in such a breathtaking abode.

A knock came at the door.

"Yes?" She crept over to it, hoping to hear the duke's voice.

"May I come in?" It was indeed James. Viola didn't temper her enthusiasm; she swung open the door and greeted him with her eager embrace. Their lips met, and as they kissed over and over, he pushed the door shut with his boot. "Forgive the late hour. I wanted to ensure no one would see me come here."

Yes, it was past midnight. But Viola hadn't been tired in the slightest.

"Now that you're here, Your Grace, how may I help you?"

"As I've already told you. Start by never calling me 'Your Grace' again. It's James. Or Hunt. Whichever you prefer."

"Or Fluffy," she teased.

"Yes. Even that."

"I think I like James. No one else calls you that," she whispered.

"Indeed. I would like for you to be special." He kissed her neck, his mouth doing the most decadent, wondrous things. "You can't help being special, of course. You're the most invigorating creature I've ever known."

"Are you certain your company up here in the north hasn't been too restricted?" She meant to tease, but James cradled her face in his hands.

"If I had one request, Viola, it would be for you to never speak so ill of yourself again." He sounded truly pained.

Though modesty was Viola's natural state, she resolved to change it. At least a little. Since meeting her father again, something had begun to shift inside Viola.

She'd allowed him to make her feel small once more, allowed herself to cower before him. She'd always seen herself as he saw her, even after she went to school. Viola had seen herself as lesser, less valuable than her twin brother, less lovable than her mother. She'd seen herself as a weed taking up space in the garden, choking the life out of two brilliant blooms.

But the duke—James—had shown her how she'd undervalued herself. He looked at her now as though she were something miraculous. She saw what a good, noble person he was, and that someone like that could find her extraordinary… Viola's eyes filled with tears; she didn't know if she could convey to him fully the depths of her love, how astonishing he was to her in every sense. Perhaps she could try.

Perhaps she could spend her life trying.

As if reading her thoughts, James released her.

"I haven't come merely to see you, though that was worth the trip on its own." The tall, regal duke appeared almost uncertain as he stepped back and reached into the pocket of his trousers. "I had one of

the footmen run into Moorcliff Village this afternoon and retrieve something for me. I had to give it
to you."

He produced a small box. Viola accepted it with
trembling hands and slowly lifted the top.

"Oh!" She gasped. On a bed of white satin lay a
necklace, the cabochon emerald she'd admired in the
shop window days earlier. She lifted the jewel, almost dropping it in her delight and nervousness.
"Your Gr—James, I can't possibly accept something
like this. It's too costly a gift."

"It's not simply a gift. The emerald I wanted to
present to you is currently in London, safe at my
bank. I needed a quick substitute."

"For what?" But her knees had already grown
weak, and she sat down upon the foot of the bed.
She recalled Lady Agatha's words at dinner a few
nights ago: *the Huntington emerald…engagement
ring…presented to every future duchess…*

Even after the declarations of love she hadn't
fully allowed herself to dream of this possibility.

"From your expression, something tells me you
know already what this signifies. But in case there's
any confusion, let me make things plainer."

Viola felt weak with joy and fear as the Duke of
Huntington slowly knelt on the carpet at her feet. To
see such a masculine, powerful man in such a position, and to see him this way before her, was almost
too much to be believed.

"The Duke of Huntington always presents his
future bride with the Huntington emerald ring. It's
an heirloom that's been passed down the line for
centuries. A year ago, I used the right emerald to
propose to the wrong woman. Now, I'm asking the
right woman with the wrong stone." He shook his

head, bemused. "All things considered, I prefer this way of doing things."

"You're asking me to…" She couldn't finish. She was about to cry.

"Viola Winslow, I'm asking you to marry me. I want you as my wife, as the Duchess of Huntington."

If she woke from a dream right now, she'd never recover. But it was, thankfully, no dream.

"Even knowing what I am and where I come from?" she whispered. Viola recalled the sentence the girls had fumbled at the séance tonight. "What did that mean, a true lady as Moorcliff's mistress?"

"My final promise to my late father. He knew how important it is to find a true partner in marriage."

"But I'm no lady."

"You are," he said, wonderfully stubborn, "and I now have no doubt my father would have agreed. The Huntington estate is my entire life, and I need the perfect woman at my side. It's why I avoided marriage for so long. I need someone who understands her duty to my servants and tenants as I do, who wants to preserve Moorcliff and its histories. I need her to be elegant, sensitive, intelligent, courageous, and for my own sake, I would like her to be beautiful and passionately in love with me, as much as I am with her. Do any of those words fail to describe you, Viola?"

She wasn't going to diminish herself any longer. A mere day ago, she would have disagreed with beautiful immediately, and possibly courageous as well. She'd never felt elegant before.

But Viola felt elegant now, and courageous, and yes, even beautiful. Perhaps that was the great secret to love; you love not only the other person, but the person you become when you are with them. Viola didn't care about becoming a duchess; she wanted only to be herself as she was right now. With James.

He watched her with hunger and disbelief as she undid the clasp and wound the emerald about her neck. Viola smiled at him, positively giddy.

"You should know something. Green is my favorite color, too."

"I take it this is a yes, then?" he growled. The duke moved upon her at once, and Viola lay on the bed with his body hovering above her own.

She kissed him, and they both knew that was all the answer he required.

• • •

As a boy, Hunt had believed he'd always know what was right, both for others and for himself. Himself especially; he had been certain that when he found the perfect woman to be his duchess, he would know her at once.

Then the years had continued apace, and he'd started to realize that there was no "right" woman. He would have to pick one and improve upon her, start with a solid foundation and build from there. Only children believed there was one absolute correct match in the world. Hunt had given up fantasy a long time ago.

But he'd been a fool.

The perfect woman had been hiding in plain sight from him for over a decade, and he could only be endlessly grateful that he'd realized it before making an enormous mistake. Now that he had Viola, he planned to keep her. They would marry, she would be the perfect duchess, the most exquisite wife, and if any of those gossiping fools had something to say about it, they were free to fling themselves into the sun. Hunt no longer worried about anyone else's opinion except his own.

And Viola's. He cared for hers, too.

She was warm and soft, and he thrilled to listen to the noises she made as he stroked her curves through the thin cloth of her nightgown.

"I can't believe this is truly happening," she whispered.

"Neither can I. This is wonderful. Perfect, even. You have made it so." He began to unbutton her collar, and she looked up at him with languid eyes. He could never get enough of those eyes staring up at him in bed. "You're the rarest creature alive. Some kind of woodland nymph, or demi-goddess." He kissed her throat.

"I'm just a woman," she replied, passing her fingers through his hair. She spoke shyly.

"No 'just' about it." Yet it was true; she was a woman. What an exciting, indescribably wonderful thing to be. As Hunt removed her gown, he kissed every exposed inch of her flesh. Viola moaned as he cupped her breasts in his hands, as he trailed kisses along the soft expanse of her stomach.

"Oh James," she breathed, making him so hard, he thought he'd pass out. When he began to part her legs, she stopped him. "Wait. I want to undress you first."

He was only too happy to oblige.

She undid his cravat, unbuttoned his shirt, unbuckled his trousers. When he was undraped, he lay upon the bed. She kissed every newly exposed inch of his skin, as he'd done for her. He hissed out a breath when she flicked the tip of her tongue across his nipple again and again.

"You're a bloody seductress," he rasped. Viola slid down his trousers, blushing when his erection sprang free. The sight of it made him bold. "Viola. Put your mouth on me. Taste me."

"Yes." She kissed the swollen crown of his erection, and he fisted the blankets underneath him to stop from spending too soon.

Hunt lay back upon the bed, watching Viola with her dark brown hair tumbling all about her shoulders. She fitted her lips around the tip of his cock, and he felt her tongue swirl around that most sensitive part of him again and again. He groaned in his throat as her head began to bob, taking a bit more of him deeper into her mouth with every pass. When he felt that pressure building at the base of his spine, he stopped her. Viola brought her lips to his, eagerly straddling him. With the candlelight limning her from behind, she looked like some ghostly apparition.

But when she took hold of his cock and pumped him, she was deliciously earthy.

"You'll make me spend too soon," he whispered. Then, too overcome with lust to think of respecting her delicacy, he growled, "I want to watch you ride me."

"How?"

She gasped as he helped her, showed her how to adjust herself and then slide inch by inch around his cock. Hunt growled with the pleasure as she shuddered around him, her silken walls fluttering. Viola adjusted herself, eyes closed as she moaned with the strange pleasure of the new sensation. He wrapped his hands around her delicate waist and showed her how to move, up and down, the way to swirl her hips.

She was an adept student, and soon Viola was riding him well. He thrust up into her, delighted at the coos of surprise and erotic ecstasy she made.

Slowly, she took his hands and guided them to her breasts. Opening her eyes, she locked her gaze with his as she rode him. The movements of her body were sweet and sensual, and the depth of feeling in her gaze conveyed something indescribable. He felt the coming orgasm spark in the tip of every nerve in his body.

"How are you doing this to me?" he murmured as she sped up, their bodies making obscene noises as she went.

"It's no more than you're doing to me." She gasped, and he squeezed her nipples as she fucked harder than ever. He looked at the creamy mounds of her breasts, the soft width of her hips, the triangle of hair adorning her sex. There was no timidity about her now, no wilting, fallen woman who gave herself helplessly to a man of his stature.

It was, Hunt realized, making love with an equal. It was joining the missing part of his soul with a fitting piece.

"I'm going to spend. Viola. Fuck," he groaned as she rode faster.

"James. Yes, James." She gasped and cried out as her body stiffened, as he felt the orgasm overwhelm her. Hunt groaned his triumph as he spilled his seed deep within her body.

After a seeming lifetime of decadent pleasure, she collapsed against his chest. He kissed her shoulder, lifted her hair, and kissed the nape of her neck. She was dewy with sweat, as was he. For moments, he only held her, relishing the feel of her body.

"I love you." He would never get tired of saying those words. "God help me, I love you to distraction."

She propped herself onto an elbow and gazed down upon him, her hair curtaining him from the rest of the world. He liked this, just the two of them in this moment. No secrets or clothes between them.

"Please say that again." Her voice was tremulous.

"I love you, Viola Winslow." He kissed her, would never stop kissing her. "I love you."

She kissed his cheek, and he felt the faint dampness of her tears against his skin. He also heard such light, tinkling laughter in his ear.

"Well. I'm glad you got there in the end, Your Grace." She beamed, teasing him even as tears slid down her face. "Heaven knows I've had to wait for you to catch up."

CHAPTER TWENTY-TWO

Hunt awoke while it was still dark. Viola was asleep in bed beside him.

He wanted to kiss her and awaken her, but he knew she must be tired. They had passed a wonderfully athletic few hours last night. A future duchess needed her rest, and he couldn't be found here by the servants. Not until after the wedding, of course.

He hurried back to his chambers, where he undressed again and tried for a bit more sleep, but Hunt could not manage it. He only lay there grinning like a fool as the sun slowly rose behind the gray hills. When the clock struck an acceptable hour, he rang for Smollett. The valet appeared rather relieved.

"Your Grace! I wasn't sure where you'd gone off to last night. Glad to see you're safe. After that sighting of the Moorcliff Haunt, the maids have been all on edge." Given how green the man's complexion looked, Hunt thought it likely Smollett feared the ghost as much as the women did, if not more.

"After I'm dressed, I want you to have a letter taken to my London solicitor. There's something I need arranged at once." He needed that emerald ring. Hunt believed in doing things properly, and until his family ring was on Viola's finger, he would not feel their engagement was official.

"Of course, Your Grace."

"Also, take a message to the dowager's lady's maid. I'd like to speak with her before breakfast." Explaining all this to his grandmother was the one duty Hunt didn't relish, but it needed to be done.

The valet went about his work, helping Hunt with his toilette and dressing. Soon after Hunt finished writing his letter to the solicitor, Smollett came to take it and to announce that the duchess would receive Hunt in her chambers. She was breakfasting alone today, still shaken by "the visitation" of last night.

Hunt decided not to argue about the ghost; he wanted his grandmother as uncombative as possible before he delivered the news.

Not that it would do much good either way.

The dowager might quite literally explode when he told her that the future Duchess of Huntington would be Miss Viola Winslow. He anticipated something of a scene, but nothing could change his mind. He finally knew what and who was right for him, and that made everything easier.

Hunt couldn't recall when he'd last felt this good. This was ecstasy; the whole future looked so damn enticing now that he could picture it with Viola at his side.

Hunt found his grandmother seated before the fire, sipping tea. She beamed as Hunt took his seat across the table from her. She was in far too good a mood.

"I'm so pleased, Hunt."

"Are you?" Suspicious, Hunt asked, "Why?"

"I know you've written to Murray. I saw the letter before Smollett took it downstairs."

Hunt stifled a groan. "A man's correspondence is private, Gran."

"Not from his grandmother, naturally. You're retrieving the Huntington emerald, then? Such perfect timing. I wrote to Lady Crawford only yesterday trying to arrange a date for Miss Catherine and her brother to visit with us. I've no doubt they'll be happy to oblige."

Hunt calculated the best way to handle this situation. Perhaps he might send his grandmother on an impromptu trip to Japan and leave her there for a decade or so.

"Before you begin planning the wedding," he said.

"Begin? Hunt, please. I've been planning this for the last ten years! I've already compiled a list of invitations for the ceremony. I should think two hundred guests. No more. We don't wish it to be vulgar, after all." It broke Hunt's heart a bit to see her so giddy, almost like a young girl. "Miss Crawford will have to tell me her colors so I can arrange to have them displayed. Oh, and the florist! I should think a Christmas wedding in London will be just the thing. Montagu House at Christmas will be at its best. I'm so very happy, my dear."

He couldn't let her float around in misguided enthusiasm much longer. It would be cruel. "I'm glad, Gran, but—"

"Then of course there's the discussion of a dowry. Leave that to me. Lady Crawford and I can settle that between ourselves. I simply can't wait!"

"I'm afraid you'll have to wait. There's no reason to write to Lady Crawford or to invite Miss Crawford and her brother to visit us."

"No reason? Whyever not?"

"Because I do not intend to marry Miss Crawford."

"But...but you're arranging the Huntington emerald!"

"Yes. But not for Miss Crawford."

He watched her face change by degrees as the realization took hold. There would be no dowry, no Crawford colors, no modest two-hundred-person reception. Two rather puce-colored spots appeared in the withered apples of her cheeks.

"For whom, then?" she snapped, but it was clear she knew.

"Don't make this difficult, Gran. There's no point to arguing. You know very well who's to be my wife."

The duke and duchess regarded each other with brittle understanding.

"Enlighten me. Precisely whom are you planning to ask to marry you?" The duchess clutched a butter knife with impressive strength. Hunt wondered if she'd attempt to butter him to death.

"Miss Winslow. And I'm not planning anything. I've asked, and she's accepted me."

"Is there a reason why you've chosen a mere governess as your prospective bride?" The dowager's eyes flashed fire.

"Viola is no mere anything. She's an incredible woman, and I've fallen in love with her. I'm sorry, Grandmother, that you're disappointed in my selection. But honor won't allow me to turn away from her, and neither will my heart."

"Your heart." The woman scoffed. "Men often confuse the heart with another, baser part of their anatomy."

"I never knew you to be vulgar before."

"My dear boy, I am possessed of as much potential vulgarity as a merchant seaman! I choose not to deploy it out of good manners, but right now, you've brought me to the absolute limit of my endurance."

"Get all that vulgarity out before you meet with

Viola to offer your congratulations. She's the woman who'll be replacing you in the household, after all. You'll want to make a good impression." While the dowager began to smear marmalade on her toast with lethal intent, he got up to head for the door.

"You are a fool, Hunt. I never thought such a thing before, but I've clearly had too much respect for the male sex. I'll give Miss Winslow this, she's cunning enough to be a duchess. She went and ruined herself knowing she'd back an idiotic, honorable man like you into a corner." Hunt reared up, his jaw clenched. He didn't take kindly to being called foolish, and he liked any insult to Viola even less.

"That's the opposite of what happened. You don't know her at all."

"Oh, so something *did* happen, then? I should have guessed as much. A cheap, crafty girl ensnared you with clandestine humping. How you disappoint me, Hunt!"

"Clandestine humping?" He snorted. "Are you certain *you* haven't been reading C.D. Winthrop's stories?"

"Wealthy men know so little of the world. Working women possess an animal intelligence no Oxford don can hope to match. This Viola is a clever little minx, I'll give her that."

"I won't let you insult her." Hunt lost his last bout with patience. Viola was going to be the next Duchess of Huntington, and she deserved every respect that afforded.

"James, don't do this." The duchess rose to her feet. "I'm not asking this for myself or your sisters, though Lord knows they'd share in your disgrace. Your father begged you to take only a true lady for

Moorcliff and the Huntington line. Forget any thought of gentility for the moment. This Miss Winslow must be nearly thirty! She might not be able to provide you with a male heir."

"Women older than her have become mothers several times over." But he knew, deep down, that this was the first somewhat sensible thing his grandmother had said, and it shamed him. Yes, he was putting the Huntington line at risk. He was being, in this way, very selfish indeed. But he needed Viola. Surely if he needed her, it was understandable.

"It's a risk, and an unnecessary one. Not to mention the ridicule this marriage will heap upon the family. The Huntington estate is the most respected in the whole of England. In many ways, it's more respected than the crown itself! You'll be the duke to throw all of that away simply to marry a woman who seduced you?"

Now he felt cut to the quick. His father had been all about duty to the title, the estate, the family. Hunt was, in fact, putting all that at terrible risk.

"Are you suggesting I abandon my duty to her?" he muttered.

"Of course not. I'm asking you only to be sensible. Is marriage the only thing you could offer this woman that would allow you to keep your honor? Or do you plan to marry her purely for selfish reasons and destroy what your ancestors took centuries to build?" Hunt was baffled. And wary.

"I'm afraid to ask what else you think I might offer her."

"You wouldn't be the first man of the *ton* to take a mistress, Hunt! You could provide her with a house, with ample money, with a barouche, with clothes and jewels, with everything she could ever wish! Marry Miss Crawford and keep Miss Winslow as your paramour. It's the proper order of things!"

Hunt was well accustomed to the spectacle of men being beastly to women, but he had not contemplated just how cruel one woman could be to another.

His grandmother was blithely suggesting he hurt and humiliate two innocent ladies, all to keep himself secure. Many would have agreed with her, too. They would have called Hunt reckless and selfish, even though this was the least reckless action he'd ever taken. With Viola, somehow everything felt simultaneously secure and exhilarating.

"I love you, Gran. Because I love you, I'm going to pretend not to have heard any of that. But understand that if you ever make such a suggestion again, we'll have a falling out from which we may never be able to recover."

And before the duchess could argue further, he left.

. . .

When Viola awoke, James was gone.

She wasn't surprised, given how appallingly late it was. She couldn't remember the last time she'd slept until well after the sun had risen. Yawning, she sat up and blushed to find herself naked between the sheets. That only reminded her of every delicious thing they'd done last night. She and the duke.

She and her future husband.

It was really happening, wasn't it?

Viola touched the cabochon emerald dangling about her neck and tried to think of how she would explain this to the Ashworths. Susannah had known of Viola's feelings for James a while now and would likely be only too delighted by these developments. She'd nothing to fear from the Duke and Duchess of Ashworth, but she was still nervous. They might think her a wanton, shiftless woman who'd been careless of Felicity in order to ensnare Huntington.

But those thoughts quickly vanished. Felicity was the most wonderful and diabolical child in England. Ashworth would probably commend her for orchestrating all this. After dressing, Viola went downstairs to look in on her guilty young charge. Felicity and Lady Isabelle had apparently enjoyed an eventful night themselves.

"We got another fifteen pages finished." Felicity yawned, her eyes swollen, clearly from lack of sleep, when she greeted Viola at breakfast. The governess and the girl were the only ones downstairs at present; everyone else must have finished a while earlier. Felicity dug into her eggs with relish. "I believe 'Giselle, the Tragic Ghost' shall be the greatest novel in the English language."

"I do love your confidence." Viola had often thought that young girls would do well to have the same overweening confidence in their abilities as boys.

"Can women be knighted for service to the arts? Isabelle and I should be allowed to at least split a knighthood for distinguishing ourselves." Felicity gazed at Viola rather directly. "Miss Winslow? What are you wearing?"

"Hmm?" Viola startled when she realized she was still wearing the cabochon emerald. She swiftly tucked it into the collar of her gown while Felicity beamed.

"Was that a gift from the duke?"

"You are far too inquisitive, young lady."

"You've always said young ladies should be inquisitive."

"I believe there are limits."

"Not for me. Limits are so utterly dull." Felicity mused over her teacup. "So. Has he asked you to marry him yet?"

"Felicity!"

"I think a man ought to propose after kissing you in the gazebo. It's one of the most scandalous places to kiss a woman."

There were other, far more scandalous places, but Felicity should not know about them for several years yet.

"Believe me, we're not finished discussing your little charade," Viola said.

"And the duke's. He helped me, you know." Felicity grew indignant, obviously wanting only to be petted and praised for her cleverness.

"Still. What you did was not acceptable."

"But you love him, and he loves you. If I hadn't acted, you'd have been miserable and apart from each other!"

Viola hesitated because that was exactly true.

"But the way you went about it was unladylike."

"So I should have told you to go marry the duke? Or I should have told him to come to Somerset and spend time getting to know you? Would either of you have listened to me?" Felicity was the most headstrong girl in the world, and for the first time Viola found she had no good reply.

"Yes. But…" Viola searched for words. "It might have all worked out very badly."

"So can a lot of things in life." Felicity shrugged

and buttered herself some toast. "If you don't try, you get nowhere."

She was willful, obstinate, and completely right. Viola would never have orchestrated such a situation. She would never have attempted to win the duke's love. A product of her father's abuse, she would never have believed herself worthy of being a duchess. But Felicity had believed for her, and more than that, Felicity had tried to help her. Not many people in this world would do so much for someone else.

"Shall I tell you something, Felicity? You might be the most generous person I have ever met." Viola stroked the girl's mop of wild, black hair. "I'm very proud to have had a hand in raising you."

"Well. You'd better let me come to Moorcliff often." Felicity speared a sausage. "I don't think I'll do that well with a new governess." The girl wasn't the type to show her feelings, but Viola could sense the plaintive note beneath her rather flippant words. Felicity would miss her, as she would miss Felicity.

The breakfast room door opened, halting their conversation. A maid hurried over to them.

"Beg pardon, Miss. Would you be so kind as to come with me? There's a man in the drawing room who insists on seeing His Grace."

"Oh. But why should the man want to see me, then?"

Viola's blood chilled at the maid's next words.

"Well, the man says he's your father. Mr. Silas Winslow. He says he needs to speak to His Grace about what happened yesterday at the farm."

CHAPTER TWENTY-THREE

When Viola entered the drawing room, she reminded herself that she was no longer the scared little girl she'd been more than twenty years prior.

She had an education, she had a home, she had friendship and love, she had everything he had said she did not deserve. But when Viola saw the diminutive shape of her father near the window, shoulders hunched and hat in hand, a queasiness settled upon her.

"Yer Grace!" Silas whirled about, but his nervous expression disappeared when he beheld his daughter. "Oh. You, is it?"

"Yes, it's I." Viola held herself with more poise than she naturally felt. "Have you been causing a scene in His Grace's home?"

"Hoity toity, eh? Has he given you the run of the place, then? I expect you're dabblin' in more than watercolors with his dukeship." Her father's eyes narrowed, malice etched in every line of his face.

"The servants asked me to come in. I take it you've made them nervous."

"I want only to speak with His Grace about the tenancy. He don't understand; I got nowhere to go if I lose the farm."

The fear was real, and even though Viola should have had no compassion left, she could not help some of the pity she felt. She knew how inhospitable the world was to people like her father and herself, how frightening it was to lose the little niche you'd carved out.

She wanted Betsy and the children safe, but she didn't relish to think of Silas wandering the world on his own. He was not a lovable man, and his end would probably be ugly if he'd nowhere to go, no one to help him.

"If you promise to leave now, I'll speak to His Grace," she replied. "You won't lose the tenancy. I can guarantee that."

"Got real pull with the duke, have you?" Silas could not resist the ugliness bubbling inside his soul, not even when he stood to lose so much. "Makes sense. He probably gives you plenty to pull at night."

How a man could speak to his daughter in such a filthy manner Viola would never understand.

"You're only humiliating yourself, Pa." She wished she could yank out that emerald necklace and show it off, tell him that she was soon to be Duchess of Moorcliff Castle. But Viola was wise enough to know it would only inflame the situation, and she wanted Silas out of here fast, both for his sake and her own. "I'm going to do you a kindness and leave now. Plead your case to the duke and I shall pretend we never saw each other."

"You take my wife. You take my son. You turn your sister and her children against me, and after you've poisoned their hearts, you help them leave me. Betsy won't even see me no more."

"That is not my fault. You're the one who killed their love." Viola began to shake with rage now, not with fear. Not so long ago she would have borne those accusations and berated herself for being so inadequate as a daughter and person. But she had James's love, and Felicity's loyalty. To be so loved by good people meant that Viola herself had worthiness in her. "You blamed me for Ma's death and

Sebastian's even after the doctor told you no one was to blame."

"I lost everything 'cause of you!" Silas balled his felt hat into his hand, looking ready to attack. Viola's natural urge was to flee or to bow her head, but if she was to be a duchess then she could not cower. She had to be brave.

"You didn't lose everything. You still had Betsy and me, but we weren't good enough for you!" Viola's voice rose. She could not recall the last time she'd truly yelled, and Silas appeared surprised by her temper. "You didn't want two little girls, and you made it so that we didn't want you, either. Ma and Sebastian were a tragic accident, but the rest of your life's been your own fault. Now I'm leaving. I hope you and James can sort this out between yourselves."

"What?" Silas's eyebrows lifted. "James, is it? You've got a nerve, girl, callin' a duke by his Christian name."

Oh, damn. She hadn't been careful enough, and her hesitation was all that Silas needed. He stormed toward her and grabbed Viola by the collar of her gown.

She plunged back into that horrifying moment in her childhood when he'd grabbed her and put the knife to her throat. She was frozen in her own body as he shook her by the collar, as she heard the cloth give a little tear.

When Viola yanked herself away, his fingers grasped for her again and snagged on the gold chain of her necklace. She gasped when she felt the chain break, and Silas held the jewel in his hand. Her father blinked at it, trying to work out how such a costly treasure had found itself around a governess's neck.

"You gonna tell me where this came from, then?"

He sneered. "Either you're a thief or a whore, Viola. Shouldn't have expected anything else from a strumpet like you."

There was a moment of the most blistering clarity as Viola beheld the odious man holding James's gift to her.

Silas was the reason she wore high collars, the reason she feared to let anyone see her neck. He'd left her with a scar she could never erase, only hide. Despite being guilty of such a foul deed, her father showed no remorse. But now he was holding an object given to Viola in love, and he scorned her for it.

There was no helping this man. He'd allowed himself to become rotten through and through. He'd taken so much from Viola, but he wasn't going to take this. Not the best part of her. In that moment, she felt all her fear and shame die.

"*Whiskey.*"

Silas cried out as a great black bird swooped in upon him. Cornelius uttered the battle cry of "whiskey" over and over as he swiped at the offending man with his raven's talons. When Silas shielded himself with his arms, he dropped the emerald necklace. Forgetting vengeance as soon as he noticed a shiny object, Cornelius nabbed the emerald and flapped around the room, cawing in triumph.

"What the devil?" Viola breathed.

If Cornelius had been a threatening surprise, Hunt appeared alongside the two Winslows like a vengeful apparition. His blue eyes blazed with fury.

"You," the duke said with icy precision, "utter. Absolute. *Bastard.*"

• • •

Hunt had no idea why the butler had let the putrid man in here.

Probably because Winslow had explained his connection to Huntington's guest. The instant he'd been informed of the farmer's presence, Hunt had rushed to see the man. Not only because he wanted Silas Winslow dealt with swiftly so he could force him out of Moorcliff, but because Hunt feared Viola might end up becoming involved. When he'd entered the drawing room only to find the hateful man yanking Viola's necklace away, Hunt had felt the chilliest calm wash over him. And when the man called Viola a thief and a whore, the calm had melted under the flame of the purest rage the duke had ever known.

Now Winslow cringed and cowered before him like a mangy dog. Hunt wanted the man angry; he wanted Winslow to attack so that Hunt would be justified in brawling with the fellow, in throwing him out the window. Hunt was not beyond killing the man, not now.

If he'd known how the fiend had scarred Viola when last they met, he wouldn't have let Viola stay his hand.

"Yer Grace! Please!" The farmer practically scuttled across the rug, insect-like as he attempted to get away. "I-I can explain!"

"I've no doubt you'd love to try, Mr. Winslow. But I have no interest in listening to any explanation."

"Oh! What on earth is happening?" his grandmother cried as she sped into the room after him. She'd followed Hunt down so she could harangue him about Viola, but now she got to watch as Hunt eviscerated his future father-in-law.

"You were a fool to come here, Winslow. Do you

have any idea what's going to happen now?" Hunt snapped.

Before the duke could make a single move, Viola charged past him.

When he reached for her, she held up a hand to him. She was the epitome of firmness in that moment, a governess made of pure steel. Both men stopped short in the face of such boldness.

"James, no. I must handle this." Viola shook her head.

"He doesn't deserve your mercy."

"He won't receive it, but this is my responsibility. Please. Do not interfere."

Hunt knew Viola to be the gentlest soul in the world, but he also knew her to have an iron will. She could also be bloody terrifying when she wished it; he felt a bit proud at that realization. Whatever was about to befall Silas Winslow could be nothing good.

"All right." He took a step backward and crossed his arms. "But I shan't leave you with him," he growled. "If you need me, I'm here."

"I know." For an instant, gentleness shone in her eyes once more. She looked to him with gratitude; she knew he would never leave her to face anything alone ever again. Overhead, Cornelius called the tenant farmer some of the ugliest names in the English language. The dowager moaned in horror, but Hunt had never been fonder of the bird.

Viola turned to her father as he cowered.

"I want you to listen to me and understand everything I'm telling you, Pa. You are to walk out of Moorcliff Castle without a backward glance. From this day forward, I will behave as though you are already dead. If you come near me, Betsy, or the children ever again I will send the Duke of

Huntington after you to make good on his desire to kill you. I am in deadly earnest."

"You ruined things again," he muttered.

Oh, Hunt was going to kill this bastard, but Viola pressed forward.

"No. *You've* ruined things over and over, and now you've ruined them for the last time." Viola had never sounded so self-assured, so much a great lady. She was every inch a duchess, and Hunt was proud that she was his. "Get out. This family has had its fill of you."

Hunt saw the man tremble with rage. It was unlikely Silas had ever heard a woman speak to him in such a way before. He began to advance on Viola.

Immediately, Hunt started to charge forward, but he needn't have bothered. Unperturbed, the governess slapped her father across the face. The sound echoed in the room. Silas touched his cheek in a daze. Likely he'd never been struck before, least of all by a woman.

"Get out. Now." Viola was all steel.

To think that someone so soft and tender also possessed the resolve of a damned general. Hunt fell in love with her all over again, even deeper than before.

Silas didn't take his leave of the duke or duchess. He merely hurried out and slammed the door behind him, rude to the last.

"See that he leaves," Hunt told the butler, who'd watched the whole transaction with bugged eyes. "And make certain he never is let in again."

"Yes, Your Grace."

Then Hunt went to Viola. He turned her around and put his arms about her. She went to him gladly, pressed her cheek to his chest and allowed herself to be enveloped by him. He was never going to let her go from this moment onward.

"Did he hurt you?" the duke whispered.

"He tore my collar. Oh, and Cornelius has my necklace."

Indeed. The raven was perched atop the doorway, the emerald dangling in his ebony beak. Hunt wasn't certain they could retrieve it before he either carried it off to his nest or swallowed the damn thing.

"I'll get you another." He chuckled, squeezing her tighter. "In fact, I sent off to London for the emerald ring just this morning."

"Hunt, I would like to speak with you alone." His grandmother inserted herself into their conversation. "Miss Winslow, would you be so kind as to allow us some privacy?"

"Gran," Hunt warned.

"Yes, Your Grace. Of course." Viola curtsied and quickly left the drawing room.

"Whatever you're about to say, it will have no effect on me." Hunt was already planning how to give the news of his upcoming union to the Ashworths, trying to work out if he should try to arrange a special license to marry in haste. But the dowager would not be put off.

"Who on earth was that person? Miss Winslow called him Pa! But I thought her father was a dead solicitor from Hexham."

"Yes. Well. She had to keep her family background a secret to help with her job prospects." Hunt wished his grandmother could just let this whole embarrassing spectacle go and move on to more important things. But the dowager had never moved on from anything in her life.

"She lied, Hunt. She's the daughter of a drunken

farmer and she lied to you."

"She told me the truth already. Days ago," he snapped.

"And does the Duke of Ashworth know? Has she lied only to you?"

No. In truth, Viola had *not* been honest with the Ashworths. Admitting that would make his position look only weaker, and that made Hunt angry.

"Stop saying lied. Do you have any idea what that woman has had to overcome in her life? She transformed herself from a farm girl into a lady through sheer force of will. She's more accomplished than most women of the *ton*. She's struggled against obstacles that could have easily destroyed her, and she's managed to come through. She is intelligent, courageous, and wise. Viola is the ideal woman to become my duchess, and I don't give a damn about who her father is!"

"Your father always said to take a true lady—"

Hunt felt himself ready to explode.

"Haven't you been listening? Viola *is* a true lady! Father would have agreed with me. He was your own son; how could you know him so little?"

That seemed to hurt the duchess a bit, and Hunt felt a cad. But there was no backing down in this fight. He wanted Viola, he needed Viola, and he would have her. The dowager could not prevent this.

"Hunt, listen to me. This isn't about Miss Winslow. It's about our family."

"What? You don't wish for our ancient bloodline to be polluted with a farmer's daughter?" he snapped.

"This isn't about blood, it's about reputation. You have already damaged this family with your first attempt at an engagement. I'm not blaming you! But it is the truth; we've all become so isolated since that unfortunate incident with Miss Fletcher. The one way back to the *ton*'s acceptance is through your marriage to a suitable girl like Miss Crawford." If Hunt never heard the name Miss Crawford again in his life, he'd be only too glad.

"We're one of the richest families in England. If you put all our land together, we'd have a fair portion of Derbyshire for ourselves. I don't think we need to rely on those fools in the *ton* for survival."

"Not economic survival, no, but what about social? Isabelle hasn't even debuted into society yet. Do you want her future chances of a good marriage crushed before she's even had an opportunity?"

"I think Isabelle prefers bloody ghosts to men."

"At present, yes. But she's still only a child." Damn it all. Hunt wanted to ignore this, but he couldn't. Isabelle deserved every opportunity in the world; if he robbed her of that, he'd be doing a disservice even greater than tarnishing the Huntington name. "She doesn't even know what she wants yet. If you marry some farm girl governess, the gossip will never die down. Many of the best families won't give Isabelle a second look, not even with her dowry and bloodlines. Your father let down Agatha, and now she'll be a spinster forever. Will you do the same to Isabelle?"

"Father didn't let Aggie down. She never wanted to marry."

"Maybe. But it's a terrible risk, don't you think?"

Enough. His temples throbbed. He wanted an end to discussion, to debate. He wanted Viola. Even if he risked everything, he couldn't live without her.

"You've always seen catastrophe lurking around every corner, Gran. I know the Revolution frightened you, but you must stop anticipating constant danger. This family and the estate are more than sturdy enough to withstand a bit of idle gossip."

"That's what they all thought before the Revolution began." His grandmother never let up, Hunt would give her that. She held her suspicions by the throat and throttled them. "No one is too big to be destroyed, Hunt. We certainly aren't. If not your family, could you at least think of the Duke of Ashworth?"

"What's he got to do with any of this?"

"He's already taken in a bastard girl as his ward." The dowager was blunt as ever. "She's a wild little thing to boot. That's already created gossip, and then there's the matter of Miss Fletcher and that club owner she married." His grandmother shuddered. "The Ashworths have plenty of speculation to deal with already. If you marry their governess? You'll all be cemented in the *ton*'s eyes as incurable eccentrics. Miss Berridge already has a great deal of struggle ahead of her, poor thing. She has nothing to inherit, and it's unlikely many families will welcome a match with an irascible bastard girl. If you and Miss Winslow marry, the girl will be even more notorious. Do you want her life to become harder than it already is?"

No, he didn't want that. Hunt, as a man of duty, needed to remember his responsibilities to his family, to his friends, to his employees, to his tenants, to his legacy.

But the problem was that he'd finally fallen in love, and now he could not let her go. It didn't matter if the world itself would be doomed if he wed Viola, he was prepared to make that sacrifice. Even if it made him the worst man alive, he would not budge from her side.

"I believe we shall all weather the storm and come out fine the other side," he said. "The Ashworths and Felicity and Isabelle and all the rest of us will not pay a great price for my simply falling in love with a woman."

"Oh, you fool. You sweet, careless fool!" she snapped. "Don't you care about Moorcliff Castle?"

"I do. But I care about Viola more. I care for her more than my title or wealth or the estate. I'm of no use to Moorcliff Castle without her; that ought to count for something."

His grandmother slowly sank into a chair. She refused to look at him now. "Then you're truly prepared to put your own desires over your duty. I never thought you, of all men, would do such a thing."

There was no point arguing further. Hunt left the drawing room, stopping outside the door. He put a hand to the wall, rubbed his face. His father, duty, Isabelle, the estate, Viola, they all tumbled about in his mind like a kaleidoscope of hopes and fears. He needed solace, something to calm the turbulence in his soul. And he found it when Hunt turned about and nearly collapsed into Viola. She'd been hovering by the door for the whole conversation, it seemed.

"Poor thing. I nearly knocked you down." He held her close, leaned down and kissed her. "Were you spying on me, my dear?"

He meant it to be playful, but she stiffened in his embrace. Her kiss, though she gave it gladly, felt somehow mournful. When Viola cradled his face in her hands, when her lips lingered upon his, Hunt had an immediate sensation of panic. Something was wrong. Terribly wrong.

"Viola?"

"Yes?" She had her arms around his neck, her kiss on his cheek. He held her tightly against him, prepared to keep her locked in his embrace if need be. If she tried to leave him. But why would she do that?

"You listened, didn't you?"

"I'm sorry. I couldn't help myself."

"It's all right. Everything will be quite all right."

"Yes." She sighed. "It will."

But then she broke out of his arms and moved away. When he tried to reclaim her, she skirted his grasp. Hunt wanted to grab her by the arms; he was like a man snatching at a fading dream, trying to remain in bliss even as he begins to wake up.

"What are you doing?" he asked.

"I'm doing what's right for all of us, Your Grace. I'm leaving Moorcliff. And you."

CHAPTER TWENTY-FOUR

Viola knew it had been wrong to listen to the duke and duchess's conversation, but she'd still hovered near the door and strained to catch every word.

She'd been prepared for the dowager's attack upon her character, her low birth, the fact that she'd lied to everyone for more than a decade. Viola had been ready to accept all those charges against her with stoicism.

But she hadn't imagined what her marriage would do to James.

How selfish, to not spare a moment's thought for the duke or his family. Or for Felicity! Every word the dowager had said was true: Felicity had a hard road ahead due to her birth, and the only way to secure her future was to have her marry well.

If Viola indulged her own happiness, she'd be letting down the little girl she'd raised and loved.

And then there was James. No; the duke.

She must think of him only as the duke from now on, there could be no informality between them. He'd suffered enough ridicule already after his disastrous relationship with Susannah. Viola was the only thing in the world that could make all this worse for him.

If he wanted a future for Isabelle and respectability for the rest of his family, then the duke could not marry her. It was impossible. The most painful thing of all was that he clearly did not believe that. He looked at her with possessive hunger, with a desire that warmed every part of her body and soul. He wanted her at any cost.

She had to be the stronger one now. She couldn't give in.

"What do you mean you're leaving me?" he rasped.

"We both know the answer to that."

"If this is to do with my grandmother—"

"It's to do with your family and the Ashworths. I can't sacrifice everyone else's happiness for my own sake."

"Viola." He approached her, but still she kept out of his reach. If she folded into his arms, she might not be strong enough to see this through. "You're letting fear control you. We don't know that our marriage would lead to ruin and mockery."

"We know there's a chance that it would. A decent chance, too."

Now he seemed to grow agitated, starting to pace in front of her. If he was getting upset, he likely knew she spoke the truth.

"Even if there is trouble, it will pass. Isabelle's chances in society won't be destroyed, I swear it."

"What of Felicity? Her future is already uncertain, and I can't be the one who places her in greater danger. I love her too much for that."

As I love you too much to ever bring disgrace upon you. The thought sat heavy in her heart.

"This is madness!" The duke was sliding from fear into anger, a rather short journey. He swiped a hand through his hair repeatedly as he moved back and forth. He was like a very wealthy, powerful lion trapped in an ornate cage. "You can't be this cowardly. I refuse to let you do this to us!"

Viola bristled a bit. She could be called many things, but not a coward. Not now.

"If I were cowardly, I'd have married you despite my better judgment. This is likely the bravest and hardest thing I've ever done."

"Then don't do it." He didn't try to touch her this time, but still Viola felt herself being pulled toward him. Her body naturally urged toward his wherever he went.

She'd taught Felicity a bit of the physical sciences, how gravity was a mutual attraction that drew objects together with inescapable force. It was the sort of thing that governed planets and the stars themselves. It was irresistible.

But she had to resist.

"Viola." The duke would not relent. It was as wonderful as it was horrible. "For the first time in my life, I know precisely what I'm meant to do. I'm supposed to marry you. You're supposed to live here as the Duchess of Huntington. It's as if the whole thing had been preordained from the start!"

"But that's impossible," she said softly. "That's against the laws of nature. One random event leads to the next."

"I'm talking about love, not nature. I love you, for God's sake. I don't care if it happened at random, it happened. What could be more natural, indeed, than to marry you?"

She weakened and finally let him hold her again. His lips sought hers, and the fever in her body was the hottest and sweetest sensation she'd ever known.

She memorized the feeling of his kiss, the warmth and strength of his body against hers. Viola wished she could let herself be just a tiny bit more optimistic, but life wouldn't allow for that. She couldn't trust complete happiness. Anything so potent and perfect was always a trick.

She should have known it would not end happily. She'd been frustratingly naïve.

For several breathless minutes on end, she kissed the duke. But when he tried to hold her even tighter, when his breathing grew heavier and she could feel his desire rigid against her body, she had to release herself. He let her go with a noise of sheer frustration.

"We need to think about this calmly. We need to talk," he said.

"There isn't anything to say." Viola knew the words she had to speak in order to break the spell. "James, I love you. But I no longer want to marry you."

"Because you're afraid."

"No. Because I know what I want for myself and for you and for Felicity. And I don't want this." Even as it snapped her heart in two clean pieces, she looked him in the eyes and said, "I don't want you. Not now. I can't. I don't."

That was the only thing she could have said to make him stop fighting.

If he thought she wanted him, he'd fight against any obstacle, travel to the far reaches of the world. But when he realized that she meant it, that she no longer wanted to be his wife, then he had nothing left to overcome. There was no point in struggling for what didn't exist.

"You can't make this decision in haste," he murmured.

"I'll stay another week if you like. It won't change my opinion." Viola fought back her tears. "I'd rather not, though. It would be too painful."

"Viola…"

"Please, James. If you truly love me, please let me go."

She was going to spend the rest of her life weeping over this, but it was a sacrifice she was more than willing to make. The Duke of Ashworth and Felicity had given her a home and a reason to live. She would not repay them with shame. Not even if she broke her own heart in the process.

The duke looked as if he might not let her walk away. He strode toward her, held her by the arms.

"Viola. You are the most exhausting, wonderful woman alive." He claimed her mouth in a kiss, one that was as decadent and greedy as sin itself, yet also heartbreakingly tender. She kissed him and held on to that kiss as long as they were both able.

Then it ended, and his mouth hovered just above hers. God, she wanted to kiss him again. She wanted to kiss him forever.

Instead, she let him go.

"Do you love me, then?" she whispered.

"You know I do." He sighed. "Shall I arrange a coach to take you and Miss Berridge now?"

"That would be most kind, Your Grace. Thank you."

He took her hand before she could walk away.

"I'm not letting go of you. Ever." He seemed haunted. "I will never marry anyone else."

Men really were the true romantics. Women had to be endlessly practical, yet another injustice foisted upon her sex.

"I think you should give that ring to Miss Crawford. Excuse me, I must pack."

She pulled from him and rushed away before another oath could be pronounced, before another bit of her heart could break.

Viola returned to her bedroom alone and began assembling the bags with a maximum of haste.

Absently, she reached up to touch the cabochon emerald, the little bit of him she could cherish forever. But it was gone; Cornelius had snatched it. Her father had ripped it away from her.

That was the thought that broke Viola. She sat down on the bed and wept. She gave herself only five minutes to grieve, of course; there was too much work to be done.

• • •

For the next several days, Hunt became the damned Moorcliff Haunt himself.

The servants whispered about him in corridors and hurried out of his way when he approached. His family barely spoke at dinner, and even Cornelius had low spirits. The raven had stolen away Viola's emerald, and it was probably snug in some fool nest by now. Hunt wondered if he might have the bird plucked and served at Christmas dinner.

Even his grandmother had stopped haranguing him about Miss Crawford. She allowed him his space and privacy now. When he'd informed her of Miss Winslow's intentions to leave him for the sake of the Ashworths and his own family, the old woman had been quite speechless for the first time. The dowager had rallied her acerbic spirits, saying that Viola was doing this only to inflame his love and make him reckless.

But she'd seen Hunt make one last appeal to the governess to remain. She'd seen Viola's restraint and sorrow as she took her leave of Moorcliff, and she'd seen Felicity's own furious bewilderment at watching all her plans go to pot.

"So. She means it, then?" his grandmother had

said quietly as she watched the coach drive out of the castle courtyard. "I must confess, I'm stunned. That shows a greater strength of character than I could have anticipated."

"More than you expected of a farm girl, you mean?" he'd snapped, and then gone back inside.

Hunt's days were routine now.

He woke, took a morning ride, breakfasted, worked, lunched, worked, dined in silence with the family, and worked until he sometimes fell asleep at his desk.

His life was accounts, tenancy agreements, letters to and from London, and nothing more. He'd resolved himself to a life of perpetual bachelorhood and passing on the title to Cousin Stephen when the time came. And he planned to be bloody miserable in the meantime.

He had once been the type to bounce back from any adversity with good cheer. Even after the humiliation with Susannah, he'd been mostly amiable up at Moorcliff for the family's sake. But now he decided to descend into the full-blown Gothic.

He would snarl at anyone who disturbed his work, he intended to grow a beard, and he planned to eventually wall himself off in his tower bedroom, pulling down the bricks on occasion so as to be seen at Christmas and Isabelle's future wedding.

It had been, put mildly, tense.

And then, one week after Viola's departure, Hunt received a parcel from Murray. He stared at the emerald engagement ring, noting the ripple of purest blue that shone in the green expanse when put to the light.

It was a treasure. One Viola deserved to wear.

Hunt needed some exercise before he started

bellowing and smashing furniture and otherwise being rather disagreeable.

He stalked out the castle walls and headed into the wilderness beyond. It was almost November now, and the brightness of October was deepening to the more somber hues of late autumn. Then he had winter to look forward to.

Hunt didn't know what guided his steps. Perhaps he wanted to explore new territory. Perhaps he wasn't paying attention and became lost. Either way, he soon looked up and realized he didn't recognize this stretch of wood, and the dark was coming on swiftly.

"Well. I'll either die of exposure or be eaten by a passing nocturnal animal." He looked up at the sky peering through the bare branches. "Finally, something to look forward to."

He heard the faint murmur of the brook ahead and headed in that direction. If he followed the stream, it should lead him out of the forest before too long.

Hunt soon found the water and began to pace alongside it. The bank sloped down to the brook, and he thought about playing here with Aggie when he'd been a child.

His mind wandered, and perhaps that's why he noticed something he'd never seen before.

It looked rather like a cave carved into the rock and earth of the bank. A naturally occurring phenomenon, surely, but most caves do not naturally come with iron-latticed gates occluding their mouths.

Mystified, Hunt picked his way carefully down the bank and sloshed through the cold water to reach the other side. His ankles and feet were soaked, but what of it?

Hunt peered through the now-rusted iron gate and glimpsed what appeared to be a marble statue. It had been carved to display a woman seated upon a bench, her eyes cast down, a rose of stone in her lap.

To Hunt's surprise, he found a bronze plaque had been placed on the door.

> *Mary, Duchess of Huntington 1619-1643*
> *Love is too young to know what conscience is*
> *Yet who knows not conscience is born of love?*

His mouth fell open at the realization that he had stumbled upon the grave, or at least, a shrine to the Lonely Duke's own first duchess. The woman who'd plotted to betray her husband had, it seemed, been immortalized in a work of art, and then secreted away.

"Was he ashamed of her?" Hunt muttered.

"I don't think so," Agatha replied. She came into view on the bank overhead looking as practical and pleasant as ever in her fur-trimmed pelisse and bonnet. Hunt swore vehemently at the shock of her sudden appearance. At least he didn't fall into the brook, though he came close. "Sorry, Jamie. I saw you trudging out onto the moors and decided to follow to make certain you were all right."

"You might have caught up with me!" he snapped.

"You looked like you wanted to be alone with your thoughts." She slid down the bank and hurried across the water to join him. "So. We found it at last. The resting place of the 'Bloody Duchess' herself."

"You didn't find anything. I did," he said, peevish as humanly possible.

"You're in a foul temper, I see. Not unusual these days." Agatha looked at him with sympathy. "I understand. It's hard to be away from the person you love."

How in the bloody hell could Agatha possibly understand such things? She was a spinster. She'd never been in love. Hunt had the restraint not to say such things, of course.

He stared at the iron gate and the statue instead. So much care had been taken with this place, and it had been hidden away so neatly.

"Why would he lavish so much attention on something no one would see?" he murmured.

"I think someone did see. The duke." Agatha touched the brass plaque. "Look. It's faint, but you can still see how the letters of her name are a bit smoothed over. The rest of it isn't. That's what happens when people touch a spot over and over again."

"So the Lonely Duke came out here to spend time with her." Hunt frowned. "Why not bury her in the family graveyard, then? She was a duchess, after all."

"I'm sure it would have been frowned upon. It's likely that after the Lonely Duke died, his heir might have knocked down her monument or even had her dug up and placed elsewhere. The duke wanted her to rest in peace. He wanted to shield her from those who'd say ugly things about her."

"So he spent the rest of his life mourning her." Hunt felt a bit dizzy as he looked at the statue. Perhaps the Lonely Duke had earned his title, then. Hunt imagined living a life, marrying and raising a family, and all the while yearning for something that could never come back again. That was a true haunting, nothing like Isabelle's stories of screaming phantoms and bloody skulls. "But no one ever knew."

"It's a lonely prospect." Agatha tugged his sleeve. "We must start walking back. My shoes are soaked now, and I want to be home before dark."

Hunt helped her across the stream and then walked alongside her, leaving the shrine behind them.

His mind was preoccupied with the Lonely Duke, with his first duchess, and with Viola. He had his own stable filled with ghosts, it seemed. Speaking of which...

"Aggie?"

"Yes?"

"It was you, wasn't it? You were the bloody specter who appeared during the séance that night." The solution had announced itself to him soon after the Bloody Duchess's appearance, of course. But he hadn't found an opportunity to discuss it with his sister until now. Too much brooding to do.

She chuckled. "Who else could it have been?"

"You scared Gran half to death."

"Yes, but only halfway."

He snorted. "Were you in on the plot, then?"

"Oh no. The girls had no idea what I was about. Miss Berridge revealed her ruse to the party, after all. She wouldn't have done that if she'd known I was coming."

He stopped walking. "You knew it was a ruse?"

Agatha became slightly coy, studying the tips of her gloves.

"I suspected. I checked her ankle, remember? She thought she could fool me, but I could tell it wasn't sprained at all."

"And yet you kept silent?" He was befuddled. "Why?"

"Because I wanted Miss Winslow to stay with us." Agatha grinned. "I thought new people in the castle might be good for you. Then when I watched you both over dinner and saw how taken with her you'd become, I knew she had to stay."

That touched him deeply, that his sister had looked out for him in such a way. She'd always been the type to take care, to nurture and support where she could. Hunt blustered, trying to find his words.

"Yes. But. You knew it couldn't lead anywhere, though."

"No. I didn't know that." She shrugged. "You're the bloody Duke of Huntington, James. You've your responsibilities, yes, but you also have vast benefits to go with the job. One of those benefits is you can help sway society any direction you wish. Granny is always ready for the guillotine to fall, but she's too cautious. If you want to marry a governess, you're in the position to make such a thing perfectly respectable."

"I agree with you," he snapped. Why was he angry with her now? Because it all sounded too good to be true? Because it gave him hope? "But Viola didn't agree, and I can't force her."

"Miss Winslow cares about her charge and her employers. And you, James. She'd never do anything to harm you." Agatha took his hand. "She's willing to hurt herself for your sake. You can't just allow her to do that!"

She was right, damn it. Hunt's heart began to beat faster.

"But Felicity. Viola would never do anything to jeopardize her future." He was giving her reasons to argue with him now. He wanted someone to tell him that it was possible. It wasn't too late.

"Surely this is a conversation you can have with Miss Winslow and Ashworth! There must be some path forward for you both. I refuse to let another Duke of Huntington live a false life while grieving a true one. It's unfair to you and to Miss Winslow."

Hunt didn't know why he was being stubborn. Perhaps because he wanted so badly for Agatha to be right; the idea that he would fight for Viola and lose her all over again terrified him.

"Thank you for caring, Agatha, but I don't need you to fret over my life. You've your own to worry about."

"Only that's not true, is it?" For the first time she sounded angry. "I can't live my own life, Jamie. Not while yours remains unsettled."

"What are you saying?"

"I've had to put my own life and my own heart away for years so that I could help raise Isabelle." Agatha sounded raw with frustration now, as if something secret had been building pressure inside her and was now liable to explode. "I knew she needed something like a mother, and Granny is ill-suited to such a task. While you remained unmarried, there was no duchess, so I had to stay. I had to be there for her, for both of you."

"Agatha." He was stunned. "Are you saying there was someone you wished to marry?"

"There *is* someone I have always loved," she said quietly. His sister stared at the ground and worried her gloved hands. "Perhaps not in a way you might understand, Jamie. But our friendship has grown only closer over the years, and the bond between us strengthened into, well. Something." She was actually blushing now; he'd never seen her blush before. "Miss Esther Sims and I have wanted to set up together as spinster companions for some time now. But I couldn't leave. Not while you still needed me."

Hunt was quite speechless. Not because of Agatha's revelation, but because of her sacrifice. Montagus were frequently lucky in love. She must have known where her heart lay for years but had been unable to claim it because of *him*.

Hunt imagined sacrificing Viola to give Isabelle and Agatha what they needed. Such a burden was too great to imagine.

But Agatha had done all that for her family without complaint. She hadn't sworn and brooded and bemoaned her lot in life. She'd done what was right, and she'd done it gladly. Hunt had wasted time and waited for love to deliver itself in a neat package, and she'd broken her own heart and let him.

"Forgive me." He took Agatha by the arms. "I've been a wretch."

"Well. Finally, you admit it." She hugged him, laughing a bit. "Ever since we were in the nursery, I've waited for this day."

"You don't have to wait any longer. I promise."

She gazed up at him with hope. "Do you mean it, Jamie?"

He thought about the Lonely Duke visiting that isolated shrine for decades on end, his pain never acknowledged. He thought about Agatha wasting years yearning for someone without any hope of happiness.

He thought about Viola driving away in that coach, and he thought of the Huntington emerald that was even now sitting on his desk.

Hunt had always liked knowing exactly what he had to do, and now the path ahead of him was clear. For the first time in a week, he smiled.

"We need to return to the castle. I have a letter to write and a coach to arrange. I leave for Somerset at once."

Agatha beamed.

"And, of course, you'll change your shoes before you go?" She was an elder sister through and through. "They *are* soaked, after all."

"If I need to waste time changing my shoes, then we'll really have to hurry."

He'd meant it as a joke, but Hunt found he could not get home fast enough. That is, he needed to get to the castle. That was only the first stop on his journey. Home was waiting for him all the way in Somerset.

CHAPTER TWENTY-FIVE

Felicity had a talent for surprises, but normally they were of the rambunctious, slightly horrifying type.

When she'd brought in a garden snake and had taken to wearing it as a necklace, that had been a bad surprise. When she'd faked an injury and contrived to make a duke fall in love with Viola, that had been both a wonderful and terrible surprise. Today, however, Felicity's surprise was very pleasant indeed.

Viola had never seen the girl sketch anything so well as the lilies growing in Lynton Park's westernmost garden.

"This is superb." Viola couldn't hide her amazement.

"*Lilium longiflorum*." Felicity was proud to show off her botanical knowledge. She was sitting alongside her governess upon a stone bench, taking in the sun as they worked. It was an unusually warm day for late October, and they were determined to savor it.

"You could almost pick this off the page." Viola couldn't get over how well Felicity had shaded the petals of the flower or defined the stamen growing from its center. "I'm only surprised you didn't draw the roses instead. They're your favorite flower, aren't they?"

"Yes, but lilies are yours." Felicity beamed. "I thought you'd like it."

Viola was not one for huge displays of affection, but she gave the girl an impulsive hug. "It's beautiful."

"Besides, it's like that William Blake poem, isn't it?" Felicity shut her eyes and recited, "*The modest rose puts forth a thorn/The humble sheep a threatening horn/While the lily white shall in love delight/Nor a thorn nor a threat stain her beauty bright.*"

"I see." Viola pretended to be stern. "You're a faerie changeling. What have you done with Miss Berridge?"

Felicity cackled, delighted as ever to be thought something wicked.

"If you must know, I suppose I've taken to poetry. At least, Mr. Blake's works." Felicity nodded to herself. "He doesn't get too carried away by his own fanciness. It's easy to understand him, so it's easy to think about what he's trying to get at."

"I said something quite similar myself once."

Yes, to Huntington. It had been less than two weeks since that night in the duke's library, and Viola still couldn't help the almost breathless pain she felt whenever she thought of him. She'd lie in bed and stare at the ceiling and feel the weight and warmth of him upon her. She could still hear those words whispered in the dark, that he loved her.

Night was the only time she allowed herself to cry about it.

At the very least, nothing truly disastrous had occurred. Her courses had started today, so she was not pregnant by him. If she had been, Viola might have felt compelled to accept his offer of becoming his wife to avoid even greater notoriety and heartbreak for all involved. Perhaps in some dark, sad part of her soul she almost wished she *had* been expecting so she could have accepted him.

She missed him. His voice, his body, his stubbornness and wit and the scorching heat of his kisses.

Viola knew that one day she'd feel grateful just to have had the time with him. One day those memories would be like jewels she could take out of a case and look upon with fondness. It just wouldn't be today, or tomorrow.

"Miss Winslow? Are you all right?" Felicity asked in an unusually gentle manner. The two of them had agreed not to mention to the Duke and Duchess of Ashworth what had transpired up north. Viola didn't want to add pressure to a situation that should simply be allowed to fade away. While she felt a bit wretched keeping such a weighty secret from her employers, she wanted everyone to be as secure and comfortable as possible.

Also, if they found out how Felicity had meddled the girl would be in for a scolding the likes of which hadn't been seen since the bloody struggle between Lancaster and Plantagenet.

"I'm well, Felicity. All is well."

"I don't believe you." Some of that stubborn resolve poked through. "I don't care about your reasons; it was wrong to leave Moorcliff Castle!"

"Some things simply can't be. It's our duty in this world to understand the difference between what we can change and what we can't." Viola adopted a stern expression, one even Felicity had been known to fear.

"That French Revolution had the right idea," Felicity muttered, kicking at the ground.

"There will be no more talk of cutting rich people's heads off. I had my fill of the subject on the trip home."

"Do you think the Duke of Huntington will bring Lady Isabelle for a visit soon?" Felicity tilted her head, observing Viola in a rather keen manner.

"I'm sure he will send her down. I'd imagine he'll write to the Duke of Ashworth and arrange it."

"But what if the duke came with her?"

"That's up to him. It has nothing to do with me."

"But you want him to come, don't you?"

"Felicity. The Duke and Duchess of Ashworth will provide for my retirement, I assure you. The Duke of Huntington is not my only path out of financial ruin."

"I'm not talking about money now. You love him, don't you?" Felicity put the sketch pad aside and took Viola's hands. "I want you to be happy! I want you to have everything you want."

Felicity was the strangest girl; you couldn't invent her. She was as wild and chaotic as a summer storm, but there was a kindness in her no one could match. If she loved a person, she loved them fiercely. Viola smiled as she put a hand to the girl's cheek.

"When I see you growing into a most remarkable young woman, I *am* happy. You've given me a life I can be proud of." Even if Viola's perfect dream of happiness hadn't come true, she did have someone she loved and looked after. And when the day came that Felicity married a respectable gentleman and went on to live a secure, comfortable life, Viola's sacrifice would have been worth it. That was some comfort.

"My word. Felicity is sitting still," the Duchess of Ashworth said, coming down the path toward them with Susannah in tow. The two women were a study in contrasts. Julia was tall and blond, the epitome of statuesque elegance. Susannah, meanwhile, was short, red-haired, and quite slender. That is, apart from her rather advanced pregnancy bump, which she patted. Julia gave a warm, slightly mischievous smile. "I don't know how you've succeeded in taming such a wild ruffian, Miss Winslow, but well done."

"I'm hardly tame, Your Grace." Cheekily, Felicity put down her sketch pad and leaped to her feet. "Now I've completed my sketch, I might resort to all types of devilries."

"Is that a challenge?" The duchess pretended to be quite mortified. "I must warn you, Felicity, I absolutely forbid you to race to the edge of the pond and back."

"It'd be beneath my dignity, Your Grace?" Felicity grinned, showing most of her teeth.

"Oh Lord, no. Racing is a dignified pastime. But as all good society knows, one must *never* race faster than a duchess. It's a matter of precedence."

"Here we go again," Susannah muttered. Viola struggled not to laugh.

"Well in *that* case." Felicity turned and bolted down the path. "Better run fast, Your Grace!"

"Duchesses do not run, they *glide*." With that difference noted, Julia rushed down the path to overtake Felicity.

"I do adore my stepsister," Susannah said, her breath leaving in a rush as she sat alongside Viola and rubbed her ever-expanding pregnancy bump. "But she's the most competitive person I've ever known. Well, I suppose it's a tie between her and Ashworth."

"I'm certain if the duke and duchess heard that, they'd start a competition to determine once and for all who is most competitive." Viola laughed, as did Susannah.

"Ugh, even laughing makes this one kick." Susannah patted the bump again. "And I'm only six months along! Every day Rafe looks at me swelling and swelling and goes a little more cross-eyed."

"Mr. Winters must be excited."

"Oh, he is." Susannah glowed whenever she spoke of her husband. The love between them was hopelessly plain. "We're lucky he's not following me everywhere I go, carrying blankets and umbrellas and anything I might need. He started doing that back in London, and I had to lock him in his study and shout through the keyhole that he was allowed out only if he agreed to stop asking how I was feeling. By that point, we were up to three times per minute at least."

How wonderful to be loved so by the person you yourself adored. After having received a taste of such affection, Viola could only imagine how glorious a whole lifetime would be.

"You're both very lucky," she said.

"We are." Susannah cleared her throat. "How was Huntington, by the way?"

"He seemed well. When we left, I believe he was considering a proposal of marriage to a Miss Catherine Crawford." Viola wondered how she'd react when the announcement of such an engagement appeared in the paper. She hoped she'd be strong.

"I suppose that's good. I'd like to think of him happy with somebody." Susannah's questing gaze felt like it would strip Viola down to her foundations. She wondered if she might excuse herself to go collect Felicity.

"His Grace was very amiable."

"Miss Winslow, do you ever get tired of saying only what you believe other people wish to hear?" Susannah appeared almost cross.

"Whatever do you mean?"

"Last summer when the duke and I didn't marry, you were clearly relieved. You spent several days as a guest in his home, and you're speaking as though nothing happened!"

"Nothing did happen." Viola was so accustomed to denying her own feelings about anything and everything, that the lie came out smoothly. Normally that would be enough, so why did she feel her throat starting to swell shut? Why did she have to grip the bench beneath her, so her hands didn't obviously tremble? "Why should anything have happened?"

"Look at you, you're shaking." Susannah took Viola's hand, and the governess required all her self-control not to snatch it away. The other woman spoke tenderly, which made the feelings only worse. "Why can't you say what's bothering you?"

"Because I'm not like you and Her Grace." In all her years, Viola had never snapped at any of the members of Ashworth's family, not even Felicity at her most frenetic. But the ceaseless, pounding ache in her heart had worn her down at last. The sheer injustice at the way she'd been born and the way it would always divide her from these women broke something within her. "You came from good stock, with dowries and expectations. You're family, and I'm staff. And it doesn't matter how kind anyone is to me, that's what I'll always be!" Viola turned away, grabbing her handkerchief to dry her eyes. No sooner had the angry words passed her lips than she felt mortified. "Please excuse me, ma'am. I'm tired."

"Stop this ma'am business." Susannah took Viola by the arms and gently forced her to turn around. Though she had every right to be furious, Susannah spoke with softness. "We know you very well, Miss Winslow. The whole family knows you. You're not simply staff."

"You're wrong. No one knows anything about me." Viola couldn't remember the last time she'd been on the verge of blubbering uncontrollably. This was horrifying.

But Susannah wouldn't let her leave, only gently prodded until the truth came slipping out. Viola finally confessed the lies she'd told about her family for years; she told about the farm where she'd grown up, the reason she'd left, and she confessed that she and Huntington had grown close during her time at Moorcliff Castle.

The more she spoke, the more Viola anticipated seeing disgust in Susannah's face, but there was nothing of the sort. There was only a deep sympathy.

Viola did not expose Felicity's role in all of this; she had no doubt the girl would lay claim to it sooner or later. Viola told about Huntington's proposal and her ultimate reasons for rejecting him.

Susannah held Viola's hand tight while the governess finished her story.

"I'm sorry for all of it. The lies and…and the duke." Viola stared at the ground. "You can't want me to instruct Miss Berridge any longer now that you know."

"I have no right on earth to judge you for any of this. If anything, I judge myself." Susannah looked pained. "I knew I'd made things difficult for poor Huntington, but I'd no idea the amount of ridicule he's endured. No wonder he hasn't shown his face in town. To think you've both had to shoulder the burden for my own foolishness makes me feel wicked."

"Please don't blame yourself, Mrs. Winters. The whole thing was madness. It wouldn't have worked even without you. I can't place Their Graces in the path of ridicule, and I can't damage Felicity's chances in society."

"The *ton* is filled with shallow, preening fools," Susannah said. "That's true. It's also true they have the collective memory of a very stupid goldfish. The scandal shall pass, I'm certain. And you'd be twice the duchess I ever would have been. You're designed for it, whether you were born in a cottage or a palace."

"But…" Viola couldn't entertain this much hope. It hurt too dreadfully.

"No. I won't hear any argument. If you love him and if he loves you, there's no reason on earth for you not to marry. The Ashworths don't care a fig about what the fools in London say."

"But Felicity—"

"Is Felicity. She was never going to be anything other than herself. She'd never marry the sort of person who'd care about gossip, anyway. I have no doubt if England disappointed her, she'd set sail for the far corners of the world and build her own fortune."

"She's always wanted to be a pirate." Viola felt tired just thinking it, but she also knew Susannah was right. Felicity was a force of nature; she would never let a roomful of pampered men decide her destiny. No. No, Viola couldn't look for an excuse. She must do the right thing for all of them. "But I'm only staff, as I've said. I don't belong in your world."

"I can speak for Julia and Ashworth when I say that you're part of the family here, Miss Winslow. Viola." The woman's warm amber eyes crinkled at the corners with a smile. "You raised Felicity and held the house together long before my stepsister arrived. Felicity adores you, and I know the duke and duchess feel the same. You're not beneath any of us. I promise that you're not."

Viola felt almost dazed. She'd never really known what she had with her situation. She'd never understood until just now how radically different this family was from the so-called fashionable ones. She'd spent much of her life believing she needed to be perfect, to fulfill a function to be valued at all.

But Susannah was right; the Ashworths and Felicity had never demanded such a thing from her.

Neither had Huntington. He'd been the first to learn all her secrets and shame, and he'd never once blamed her for any of it. He'd never accused her of deceit or been disgusted by her lack of pedigree. And Viola had felt so free with him, utterly assured of his care. Before she'd ever trusted another living soul, she'd trusted him.

The ache without him was so terrible that it almost overwhelmed the quiet, surprised happiness of this moment with Susannah.

"You beat me only because I tripped," Felicity grumbled as she followed a triumphant Duchess of Ashworth back along the path. Despite being a duchess and mother of two, Julia took a jaunty delight in her victory. Susannah murmured something about her stepsister being incorrigible.

"In time, you'll build up your strength, my dear." Julia sat beside Susannah and fanned herself, a bit breathless. "I think Felicity and I have earned a spot of tea after such exercise. Shall we retire inside? I need to speak with Mrs. Sheffield about looking out the guest linen, anyway."

"Who's coming to visit?" Susannah asked.

"I received a letter from Huntington. He's coming to Chaffin Manor and has asked to bring his sister round to visit with Felicity. I've said yes, of course. They should be in Somerset the day after to-morrow."

"Oh, that's brilliant!" Felicity crowed. "The duke's coming too?"

"Erm. Yes, though I thought you'd be more excited to see Lady Isabelle," Julia said.

"Oh, I am. The duke's dull and old." Felicity jumped up and down. "I'm *so* glad he's coming!"

"I must say, I'm a bit confused by your reaction."

Viola was too numb with shock to say anything.

"The duke is coming?" she asked, her voice faint.

"Why, yes." Julia frowned. "Susannah, both you and Miss Winslow look awfully stunned. What on earth is going on?"

"Now can I tell her? Please?" Felicity begged Viola.

"Oh no." Julia looked resigned. "What did you do, Felicity?"

"I fell down a hill." The girl bristled with pride.

"I take it that is not the end of the story?"

"We may need that tea," Viola said. "This will take a while."

• • •

Upon arriving at Lynton Park, Hunt was wary when Ashworth asked to see him in the game room. It was where the family kept all their hunting trophies of years past, with the heads of mounted deer looking rather plaintive. *Don't anger them; you could end up where I am* seemed to be the message.

When Hunt entered to find the Duke of Ashworth waiting alongside Rafe Winters, the Wolf of Mayfair himself, he became even more suspicious. Rafe might be one of the richest men in London, but he'd also been a notorious criminal in years past. Between Rafe and all the stuffed deer, Hunt got the impression he'd be nursing a bloody nose at some point. Or be dead. Or both.

"Well. I hope the trip down wasn't too…uncomfortable." Ashworth stood before his desk and glowered from beneath a curl of dark hair. Rafe was seated with an ankle crossed over his knee, that silver-headed cane of his resting comfortably upon his lap. Hunt imagined the cane knocking a few of his teeth loose.

"Yeah," Rafe said. "We've been waiting for you." He smirked and reached into his coat pocket.

Good Lord, what did he have? A gun? A knife? Hunt tensed as Rafe pulled out…

A bag of sweets. While Hunt stared, nonplussed, the Wolf of Mayfair popped a boiled peppermint drop into his mouth and chewed it with relish.

"Sorry," he muttered. "I always enjoy a snack when I watch a really good scene."

"Winters, this is not a theatrical event. It is a family matter," Ashworth snapped as Rafe fished another sweet from his bag. Hunt didn't want to dance around this any longer.

"If you'd like to pummel me, I'd be only too happy to allow it," he said.

"You allowing it takes half the fun away," Rafe said.

"I'm not pummeling you." Ashworth continued to glare, though.

"I'm assuming there'll be no challenge to a duel either?"

"No, no duel. I'm not after your blood, and besides, my wife tells me I'm not allowed to die just yet and she'll bloody kill me if I disobey her."

"In lieu of violence, then, perhaps I might offer an explanation?" Hunt asked.

"We could have a bit of violence first and *then* the explanation," Rafe said.

"Why are you here, exactly?" Hunt snapped.

"The autumn chill's bad for my busted knee. Going up the stairs right now would be killer." Rafe grinned as he ate another peppermint drop.

"Both of you shut up. Rafe, no one is busting anything belonging to anyone. Make peace with it." Ashworth strode over to Hunt, jaw and shoulders squared. "As for you, we need to talk."

"I take it you know everything that transpired at Moorcliff Castle?"

"More or less. I don't care to hear details, you understand. I want to discuss results."

A sudden thought set Hunt on alert.

"You haven't done anything to Viola, have you?"

"Why would I? She's not the guilty party here."

"Guilty?" Now he was offended. "Guilty of what?"

"I appreciate you offered to do the decent thing and marry her." Ashworth scowled. "But seducing the girl? I was a damned fine rake before my marriage, but even I could never think of debauching a poor innocent like you've done."

"You've every right to judge me harshly." Now it was Hunt's turn to feel angry. "But don't ever make Viola out to be weak and pathetic. She's the strongest person I've ever known."

"*Miss Winslow* isn't pathetic, you're right. But the way you allowed her to simply leave after everything that had transpired was an insult. Now that I think of it, perhaps you *could* do with a few blows about the head."

"Couldn't agree more," Rafe said, rummaging through his bag.

"Before we start the killing-me portion of the evening, I need you to look at this." Hunt snatched the leather box from his pocket, undid the gold clasp, and opened it. He proffered the emerald engagement ring to Ashworth.

The other duke's mouth fell open, and the righteous anger fled his eyes. "Oh. I see."

"I assume that's for Miss Winslow." Rafe sucked a peppermint drop in thoughtful contemplation. "If not, this just took a very interesting turn."

"Shut up," both dukes said.

Ashworth studied the ring with narrowed eyes. "Well. What of your Miss Crawford?"

"That never existed. I made a mistake when I let Miss Winslow walk away. The greatest mistake of my life, and I aim to tie up all loose ends."

"I don't think Miss Winslow will be thrilled to learn she's becoming a duchess for the sake of tying anything up," Ashworth said. "As I consider her part of my family, I won't stand to have her insulted."

"If loving her more than my own life is an insult, I suppose she'll have to be," Hunt snarled. "I don't think any man in this room can claim they never made grievous missteps while courting their own wives."

Ashworth appeared humbled. Even Rafe put the damn bag of sweets away.

"Suppose that's true," he muttered.

"I don't want to marry her to cover up my own indiscretions," Hunt said. "Nor do I wish to marry her because I simply need a duchess for Moorcliff Castle. I want to marry her because she's the only woman I want to marry, if that makes sense. I need her. I can't bloody breathe right without her. I'll spend the rest of my damned life working to deserve her so long as she marries me. This has nothing to do with pride or duty; it's everything to do with love."

Hunt meant it. His entire life, he'd fulfilled every vow he'd ever made because it was expected of him. He'd been proud of himself for being so dutiful, always in control. He'd seen love as an extension of his duty. He'd proposed to Susannah as a duke, but for Viola he wanted only to be a man. The duke bit was incidental.

"Impressive." Ashworth cleared his throat. "Well. You certainly bested my own marriage proposal. Then again, Julia's the one who proposed, but you beat hers as well. Never tell her I said that, of course."

"Hope you memorized all that," Rafe said. "Those were pretty words, but we're not the ones you need to convince."

"Indeed. Obviously, I need to speak to Viola," Hunt said. "Where is she?"

CHAPTER TWENTY-SIX

The duchess had insisted that Viola be relieved from her duties while the duke spoke with Huntington.

Viola walked down to the edge of the lake as the sun began to lower on the horizon. She wrapped her shawl tighter about her shoulders as the wind sighed past her. The half mile trek back to the house would be rather chilly, but she'd needed the space. At least Felicity and Lady Isabelle had been reunited. They'd be with the duchess and Susannah right now, probably recounting with breathless glee the tragic fate of Giselle the ghost.

How easy it was to find pleasure in sad stories when you were very young. To most fourteen-year-old girls, heartbreak seemed like some faraway faerieland, the same as romance or old age. To the innocent, disasters always happen to somebody else. A tragic eternity lasts only as long as it takes to turn the page. Perhaps that was why the older one got, the more one enjoyed a tale with a happy ending.

Even if happiness was the most fanciful notion of all.

Viola froze when she heard footsteps on the path behind her. They were the heavy, booted footsteps of a rather large man.

"Miss Winslow," Huntington said.

"Your Grace." Her heart hammered when she beheld him, saw how changed he looked from when she'd seen him at Moorcliff. The disheveled hair and stubble had been groomed out of existence, and his clothes were once again impeccable and orderly. He looked just like the man she'd fallen in love with on the road to Lynton Park all those years ago. He was a young god again.

But he was also so different.

When they'd first met, he'd appeared all certainty and ease, a person who had never known want in his life. Now, he looked at her with quiet strength and dignity, yes, but also an unabashed need. He looked as though he were starving, and the sight of her was sustenance.

"I spent hundreds of miles preparing what I'd say to you," the duke murmured. "I even jotted down notes on some of Isabelle's extra paper. I arrived at what I thought was an excellent statement filled with sober good sense and even some verbal flair."

"I see." She did not.

"But now I've found you, all the words can go hang," he growled.

To Viola's immense shock, the Duke of Huntington knelt on the ground before her and took out a small leather box.

When he opened it, she found herself staring at an emerald ring. *The* emerald ring. The one he'd used to propose to Susannah over a year ago; the one he'd wished to give Viola when he proposed the first time.

"Oh dear," she whispered.

"Viola Winslow, would you do me the honor of becoming my wife?"

She hadn't known what to expect, but she hadn't expected this. In truth, Viola had expected that Ashworth and Huntington would start dueling with swords or brawling with fists before the duke would simply pick up and propose to her again.

Now here he was. He did not seem to care that he

was forsaking his duty to his family and his father's legacy.

He'd had more than a week to think all that through, but he had chosen her regardless. Viola felt a fierce surge of love for that.

He was prepared to take the risk, and the Duke and Duchess of Ashworth had assured Viola that they did not fear the *ton*'s gossip. All those barriers between James and herself had fallen away. Yet the fear took hold of her, deeper even than it had been before. Now that she had no more noble excuses, Viola found she'd never been more terrified of anything.

"I...I don't think that's wise, Your Grace."

"What?" Huntington shook his head. "No, hang on. I had a wonderful few lines back in the game room. Winters told me to write them down."

"The proposal was lovely," Viola said. "But I can't ask such a sacrifice from you, and I don't think I'm strong enough to face the world as a duchess."

"What do you mean?" He seemed bewildered. "As a duchess, you'd be one of the most secure women in England."

"But I'd be open to endless scrutiny. It wouldn't be hard for society to learn about my past. It could be used to hurt me, and even worse, to hurt you. I'd rather have self-respect and be alone than be wealthy and titled and worried every single day that I'm a disappointment, or that I've ruined your life."

It was almost a relief to say it all out loud. When Viola had dreamed of Huntington all these years, she'd often fantasized he lost his dukedom somehow. That they were two ordinary people going about their own private lives, paying no mind to what fashionable people dictated.

"I understand." James spoke gently as he rose. "I do. I know how selfish I'm being."

"Selfish? You?" She shook her head. "You've come here to offer me love and security. That's hardly selfish."

"You don't understand," Huntington said. "I didn't come here with any intention of saving you; rather, I selfishly hoped you might save me."

"What?"

"Viola."

She'd always liked her name, but on his lips no word sounded more poetic. The duke—James—approached her with seeming caution, as if afraid she might run away.

"I whispered your name to myself on the journey down here. I thought of you over and over, every detail of you. Your eyes. Your lips." He was near now, and his hand touched her cheek. "I've been in agony for days, wanting to touch you. But wanting to speak your name and have you hear it, that was the worst. Because your body and your kiss intoxicate me," he growled, leaning nearer. "But your mind and your heart are what I yearn for more than anything."

It wasn't right that a man could be this handsome, this powerful, and this seductive. What woman could stand a chance against him?

Viola could feel all that terror of the unknown dying away as he put his arm around her.

"I want to whisper your name in the morning. Speak it to anyone who'll listen throughout the day." The duke kissed the corner of her mouth, and Viola shuddered with pleasure. "At night, I want you to hear me murmur it in your ear. The last thing you hear before you sleep. Viola, I love you. Viola, I want you. Viola." He captured her face in his hands and lifted her gaze to his. "I need you. And I've needed nothing. Nothing until you."

"I see." She felt dizzy with happiness, radiant with bliss. "Perhaps that's worth a little social discomfort."

"I should hope so." He chuckled. "Viola Winslow, I want you to be my wife because I love you. Because I had never known love until I'd known you."

This time, she didn't wait for him to kiss her. Viola pressed her lips to his and wasn't shy. She let him know with every kiss she gave just how much she wanted him. How much she expected. How much she deserved, and he deserved, and all the ways in which they would spend their lives making the other exquisitely happy.

"I do like to clarify things," he murmured against her lips. "I'm counting this a yes."

"Yes." She laughed even as her vision blurred with tears.

Viola tried to keep her hand from shaking as he took the emerald ring from the box and slid it onto her finger. Viola stared at the jewel, trying to understand all the steps that had led her from her father's farm to this moment. All the different twists in the road she'd had to go down to reach this point.

In some ways, this seemed like a miraculous end to the journey. But Viola also knew that this was only the beginning.

"Yes, you'll marry me." He kissed her lips, held her close. Viola groaned deep in her throat as she felt the throbbing excitement of him against her thigh.

"Yes. I will."

She was more than hungry for him, more than

ready to satiate every greedy urge she felt. Viola
pulled him so close that they tumbled onto the grass
beside the lake. She welcomed his touch, murmured
endearments and encouragements when James ran
his hand along her stockinged leg.

Even though she was engaged now, propriety
demanded she go no further until after the wedding.
But Viola had long since abandoned propriety.

She sighed in pleasure when James slid his hand
between her thighs and touched her slick, intimate
core. She gazed up at him as he worked her with his
fingers.

"Look at you," he breathed, practically glowing
with pleasure as he wrung ecstatic moans from her
lips. "You're a bloody miracle."

She could have teased him, said she didn't allow
Felicity to use such language, but the sheer overpow-
ering bliss took her over and she called his name as
she climaxed. He slipped one finger inside her body.
She rode him until she was properly spent. While
James kissed her again, she fumbled with his belt.

"I want all of you inside me," she whispered
against his jaw.

"Then I won't deny you," he growled.

Within moments, the hot length of him sprang
free, and Viola traced her fingertips along the steel
and velvet of his cock once before allowing him to
position it between her spread legs.

When she felt him push inside her, she shook
with the already burgeoning climax.

"I love how easy it is to make you come." He
raised himself on his elbows over her and luxuriated
in their coupling. His cock slid in and out of her
sleek wetness, and Viola gazed up at him in adora-
tion. "I want to hear you call my name in the heat of

ecstasy again and again."

"James." She shut her eyes as the hot bloom of pleasure ignited between her legs again. "Oh, James."

"Viola. Come for me."

She did as he asked. She came with him inside her, holding him as close as she could. She'd hold him this way for the rest of her life, the same way he'd hold her. It would never be enough, a lifetime of this, but it would be far, far better than anything else.

She held him close to her, relishing the soft, undone way he groaned as he achieved his own pleasure. She felt his hips thrust, felt him surge inside her body, and then lay beneath him as he stilled. He smelled of musk and cologne, of nature and sin and every good thing. She kissed every inch of his face.

"I'm afraid we'll need to clean up," she whispered in his ear, loving the way laughter rumbled in his chest. James helped her to her feet, helped her adjust her gown and brush bits of grass from her back and hair.

So.

She'd been tumbled in a field, like the farmer's daughter she'd always been. And he knew that about her, her past and her hopes and her dreams. He knew all of her and loved every bit. Just as she loved him.

"I'm afraid we'll need to change into something finer as well." He kissed her neck, his hands on her shoulders. "Last I saw, Julia was looking out some champagne and ordering an especially fine supper."

"What?" Pretending to be shocked, Viola wrapped her arms around him. "That's good of Her

Grace, but they didn't know I'd accept your proposal!"

"Well." He shrugged. "I *am* a duke, after all."

"And no one could believe I'd resist such an offer?" She laughed at his expression of pretend irritation. "I believe you're more than your title, Your Grace." Viola smiled as he kissed her. "Or should I say, James?"

"As you are more than anyone or anything I've ever known, Viola." His grin was sweet and wicked at once. "Or should I say, Your Grace?"

CHAPTER TWENTY-SEVEN

The next month both slipped away and dragged on endlessly.

Viola was grateful they weren't having an enormous wedding before the whole of the *ton*. She knew how resentful the society mothers were of the seemingly inexplicable match between the nation's most eligible bachelor and a mere governess. She wanted to put off the aristocracy's scrutiny for as long as she could. James agreed, though he detested the idea that anyone would be rude to his wife.

The Duke and Duchess of Ashworth were too delighted for words, and Susannah burst into floods of happy tears when she heard the news. The Ashworths had insisted on having the ceremony at the chapel in Lynton Park.

The guest list was small but very fine and included Betsy and the children. When Viola had informed her sister via letter that she and the children were to be family to the Duke of Huntington, and that from this point on their lives would be fantastically different, she received the most astonished and misspelled reply in history.

Silas, on the other hand, did not receive a letter or an invitation. By all accounts, he'd abandoned the farm before the lease was up. No one knew where he had gone. No one cared to know.

Viola received letters of congratulation in the weeks following the formal announcement. One came from Lady Agatha, who had set up companionable housekeeping with Miss Esther Sims in

Mayfair and was delighted. Agatha thanked Viola for giving her the opportunity to begin a new life. She and Miss Sims, it seemed, were now the *two* merriest spinsters of the *ton*.

Julia and Susannah worked alongside Viola to choose the perfect winter flowers, the perfect wedding gown, all of which Viola loved, but none of which, to her, mattered as much as having the perfect bridegroom. It was fortunate that she had exactly that.

In the weeks leading up to the wedding, Viola's days were filled with everything from planning the ceremony to "duchess lessons" as Julia put it. Viola had always been a quick study, but there was so much to learn about being a leader of society that she almost felt faint.

"It's one thing to know different types of spoons or what direction the gravy is passed," she told James as they walked in the gardens around Chaffin Manor, his home "in the neighborhood" and where they would spend their first weeks of married life. "But I'm still afraid I'll be hopeless at entertaining and setting fashion trends and, oh, everything else to do with the public side of things."

"First, I know you'll master every task. You always do. And second, none of that's the most important of a duchess's duties." He stopped her beneath a tree on fire with red and golden leaves and kissed her. Whenever he kissed her, Viola felt as though everything was miraculously right. "I don't need you to be a fashion plate or to give the most lavish parties. I need a partner, a friend, and a lover." He lifted one brow, mischief in his eyes. "I trust I've found all three."

"I shall have to think on it."

When he kissed her, it became difficult to think at all. But she tried.

Once she became engaged, Viola's duties as Felicity's governess took an understandable sidelining, and she helped Julia find a proper replacement. At first, all the excitement around the upcoming wedding and the new life that awaited Viola distracted her from more subtle concerns. But when Felicity's new governess, a Miss Harper, proceeded to walk out of Lynton Park after finding a dozen frogs in her bed, Viola knew something was amiss. Felicity had always been wild, but never antisocial. When Julia wanted to discipline the girl, Viola opted to visit Felicity in her room instead to have a chat.

"What do you want?" Felicity muttered by way of greeting when Viola came in. The girl was seated before her window, hugging a cushion to her chest.

"That's hardly the polite way to greet a friend." Viola sat in the window seat alongside Felicity. The girl stared at the dying autumn trees and wouldn't look at her former governess.

"We're not friends," Felicity snapped. "You've barely talked to me in a week. How could we be friends?"

Mystified, Viola said, "I'm sorry. There's much to do before the wedding. But you can always come and talk to me, you know."

"Sure. It's the only way you'll be able to remember I exist." Felicity tossed the cushion aside, grabbed at a sketch pad, and started scribbling on the paper. Viola saw once again the adorable, irascible little four-year-old girl she'd met ten years before. Felicity had rarely cried, even as a small child, and right now she was making a concentrated effort not to let fall any tears.

"Lissie, what is it?" Viola took Felicity's hand, stopping the girl's sketching.

"You haven't called me that in a long time." Felicity wrenched her hand away.

"Not since you were a little girl, no. But then again, the way you acted toward Miss Harper was exactly the way a little girl behaves."

"Why should you care?" Felicity snapped. "I'm not your responsibility anymore."

"How can you say such a thing?"

"It's true, though. Now you're getting married, and Isabelle shall get to spend more time with you than I do. I'm sure you'll write to me from time to time, and I'll write back, and then you'll write back again telling me all the grammatical errors I've made in my letter."

Viola was shocked. "My dear, I thought this was what you wanted."

"Yes, but maybe I didn't think you'd be so happy to leave me." Felicity crossed her arms. "Fine. It's not as though you really cared about me. You were only ever paid to."

Viola's chest ached because she understood this kind of pain only too well, the feeling that you can be so easily discarded or overlooked when someone new and "better" comes along. After all, Felicity's father had cast her off the minute she was born. Only Ashworth's charity had saved her from a dire fate. Viola wrapped her arms around the resistant, slightly squirming girl.

"The only thing that grieves me about this marriage is that I have to stop being your governess." Viola petted the girl's hair as Felicity finally loosed a few of those pent-up tears. "That's why I've spoken with Her Grace, and she and the Duke of Ashworth would be more than happy if you split your time between Lynton Park and Moorcliff Castle."

"R-Really?" Felicity pulled away, her green eyes widening in hope. Viola stroked her cheek.

"Really. You and Isabelle can spend much more time together. And so long as you don't abuse your new governess, you can stay as long as you like." Viola sniffed, a bit emotional as well. "You're one of the great loves of my life, Felicity. Wherever I am, you have a place to call home."

For the first time in the ten years Viola had known the girl, Felicity started blubbering. After a good ten minutes of getting it all out, of course, the young lady was back to her irrepressible self. She even volunteered to write an apology to Miss Harper, though she would never deny how funny the trick had been.

Ah, well. Small steps.

"I'm glad you're apologizing. It's the right thing to do. Besides." Viola winked. "I need my maid of honor to have only the most unimpeachable character."

"Me? Your maid of honor?" The girl's face lit up. "Oh, Miss Winslow. That's a terrible idea, but I'm ever so glad you asked!"

Viola laughed. "So long as you don't include a catapult in the wedding, I'll be quite satisfied."

Felicity sulked a bit. "Oh, fine. Since you asked, I won't."

Viola hoped that was a joke. Even though it probably wasn't.

• • •

Hunt looked into the mirror, allowing Smollett to adjust his cravat and the sleeves of his morning coat. A man usually married only once, and Hunt intended to look flawless to match his bride. He doubted he'd get there; Viola seemed devoid of flaws, particularly today. But he could try.

"I think you should at least take a sip." Ashworth was doing his best-man duties, namely, drinking from a discreet flask and trying to get Hunt to have a taste as well. Ashworth was sprawled out upon a chaise, smiling up at the ceiling as he sloshed his whiskey back and forth. "I remember the day I married Julia. I toasted her beauty with Percy and the other groomsmen. Then I toasted her beauty with my valet. Then I toasted her beauty with my own reflection, the best drinking partner imaginable."

"I worry about you sometimes, Ashworth." Hunt shook his head as Smollett finished brushing off his jacket. They were mere moments from the ceremony, and this was the kind of outrageous behavior his best man exhibited? Granted, being Ashworth, it wasn't in the least surprising.

A knock came upon the door, and Hunt was surprised to see two women enter. Normally, the groom's quarters were not a place for ladies, not even ladies he knew very well.

"Agatha!" Hunt turned, pleased to see his sister. "And...good Lord."

"Hardly," his grandmother drawled.

"That's my cue to leave, I take it." Ashworth bowed to the ladies and swept out the door. It was likely he didn't want to be within range of the dowager's temper; she'd weaponized it well over the years. Hunt had, of course, sent her an invitation but had not anticipated she'd accept. He hadn't heard from her since he'd left Moorcliff with Isabelle, letting his grandmother know he'd every intention of proposing to Viola.

"I hope you've come in the spirit of peace," he said, polite yet cautious.

"Oh Hunt." The old woman settled herself upon the chaise that Ashworth had recently vacated. "My entire life I've held fast to the belief that duty matters above all else."

"Yes. I know the feeling." He frowned. Where was she going with this?

"I maintain that. But…" She sighed. "When you reach my rather outrageous age, you'd rather have family about you than your own pride."

Hunt smiled and kissed the old woman on her cheek. He squeezed her shoulder, gently of course.

"I'm very glad you've come," he said.

"Well. Your Miss Winslow has the firm backing of the Duke of Ashworth; it's *almost* a patronage. That helps a great deal to sell this union to the rest of the *ton*. Besides, the woman herself is rather impressive." It sounded as if it pained her to admit. "I must acknowledge her as an intelligent and elegant female. Especially considering her rather *agrarian* antecedents." His grandmother's gaze hardened. "And then, of course, one must be prepared for revolution."

"Sorry?" Hunt said.

"Don't ask questions, just keep smiling," Agatha muttered out the side of her mouth.

"It's obvious! When the guillotines begin rattling, having a granddaughter-in-law from the lower classes will be a great boon. They say such a bloody revolt can't happen in England, but one should always prepare for every eventuality." His grandmother finally smiled, looking downright comforted. "Yes. Viola will be the thing that keeps our heads firmly attached to our necks."

"Keep. Smiling." Agatha was wearing an impossibly wide grin, her teeth on gleaming display. "Pretend this never happened."

Well, if fears of revolution got the dowager to accept the new Duchess of Huntington, then he could deal with a few eccentricities.

"I'm delighted to hear your, er, strategy, Gran."

The dowager left to find her seat, and Agatha gave Hunt a sisterly squeeze before retiring as well.

"How's Miss Sims?" he asked. Teasingly, he added, "Did you really have to entrap me into marriage so you could finally run away together?"

"It wasn't a trap! It was a plot." She gave him a friendly jab in the shoulder. "And a good one, I'd say, if it brought you Viola. I could tell the moment I met her in the library, Jamie. She's perfect for you." Agatha's eyes seemed to twinkle. "Papa would be so pleased. I'm certain the Lonely Duke would have been happy as well."

Hunt thought again of that quiet monument to lost love hidden away in the woods. He wondered if all those from the past could see those alive now, still fumbling and still learning from the previous world's mistakes.

But Hunt forgot about ghosts and mistakes as he turned at the altar to find Viola beside him, dressed in a gown of cream silk with winter flowers in her hair. He forgot the world as they spoke vows before the congregation and he slipped a gold band upon her finger.

When he was allowed to kiss his bride, he smiled to find his reflection in her tear-limned eyes. And when he touched his lips to hers, binding them together forever, his thoughts were not on his dukedom, his estate, his family, or even himself.

His thoughts were filled with Viola, and utterly blissful.

He couldn't tear his eyes from her during the wedding breakfast, and he was greedy for the moment when it would finally be them alone together in his carriage. Finally, Viola changed into her going-away frock. Isabelle had composed a poem on the occasion with Felicity's help. The poem was titled "Wedding Bells" and employed the questionable device of having the last word of every line rhyme with "bell."

"'Up high above, the wedding bell/shall chime and chime and wish you well/upon your honeymoon, where you'll dwell/in bliss forever, much like a spell/cast by a witch standing over a well.'"

"I told her to add the witch bit," Felicity said to the crowd of baffled adults. "It's sort of a metaphor."

"Isn't it beautiful?" Isabelle dabbed her eyes, taken with her own genius.

"Lovely." Ashworth beamed at the girls, then whispered to Hunt, "I don't suppose you'd take them with you? Please?"

"Surely you can handle them for a fortnight."

"Perhaps. If I lock them in the attic. Who knows, they might actually like it."

Hunt was glad when the coach arrived and he could help his new duchess inside. She kissed Felicity, embraced Julia and Susannah, and Hunt shook hands with Ashworth. He even got a surly nod from Rafe Winters. Then the new Duke and Duchess of Huntington waved from the window as they headed onto the road, bound for a new life together.

Finally, Hunt had his bride all to himself. Viola yielded to him beautifully, entering his arms with a sigh as he kissed her. They rumbled along the north-ern road. At first, Viola thought they were headed for Chaffin Manor, but noticed when the carriage went east instead of west.

"Are we going to London, then?" She seemed baffled.

"No. We'll head for Chaffin Manor soon enough." He kissed the tips of her fingers, relishing the little gasps of ecstasy she made. "But I thought we might make a brief detour."

"To where, exactly?"

"Bath, of course."

"Oh." Viola blushed. "Yes, of course. This would be the perfect time to visit, after all." The Bath "Season" began in November and ran through to spring. It was the most fashionable spot in the south-west of England, a destination for the gentry and gossiping aristocrats. There was a constant rotation of balls and parties, all of which were designed to let the cream of society be seen. "I suppose you must introduce me at some point."

"I think you misunderstand me." He cupped her cheek in his hand. "I have no intention of sharing you with anyone."

"Oh?" Her eyes widened with hope.

"Rather, I thought of something you might en-joy."

They could have stopped at the town house that Huntington owned in the city, but that would have made them too conspicuous. They lodged for the night at a comfortable inn on the outskirts of town, certainly a far cry from the grandeur normally ex-pected of a duke and duchess. But, as Hunt had imagined, Viola adored it.

But that was nothing compared to her reaction

when he drove them down in a gig as the sun began to lower behind the ruins of the Roman baths.

"Oh!" Viola clapped her hands together, fingers pressed against her lips. "You remembered!"

"Of course." He smiled as he stopped the gig, and Viola climbed out. Together, they approached the crumbling statuary and columns. The water of the baths was quite murky, but it still steamed; the Romans had chosen the natural hot springs well, after all. Viola wandered along a line of arches, gazing about her in wonder.

"Do you know something? When we first met on the road to Lynton Park, you asked if I liked Somerset." She traced her gloved fingertips along a column as she wended her way about it slowly. "I wanted to say that I'd always dreamed of seeing the Roman baths. That I wanted to visit at sunset, and perhaps find the ghost of a lost legionary." She looked radiant when she was happy. Viola lifted onto her toes and kissed him. "I was too afraid to be forward, so I didn't mention any of it. And now here we are."

"I would have known to bring you here even if you hadn't already mentioned it." He slid a lock of hair from her eyes.

"Because you know me?" she whispered.

"To know you is to love you." He kissed his wife, his duchess. "And I know you so very, very well, Viola."

EPILOGUE

SEVERAL YEARS LATER

Viola shut the door on the quiet nursery.

Lord Sebastian Montagu, Marquess of Roark, was enjoying his first Christmas, it seemed, and was tucked up in his crib sound asleep. His elder sister, little Sophie, doted on her baby brother and had tried to climb into the crib alongside him. Getting the girl back into her own bed had required a little persuasion, but eventually it had succeeded.

Viola walked downstairs, enjoying the peaceful quiet of Moorcliff Castle at night. Peace and quiet were rare during the Christmas season, especially this one. They'd rather a full house, er, castle. There was the dowager, Betsy, and the children, of course. Agatha and Miss Sims were also in residence, along with Felicity and Isabelle.

Not that Viola minded. She'd craved a place to call her own and people to call her family for as long as she could remember. She had all of that now. But most of all, she had James and the children.

Speaking of, she'd seen the children to bed. Now for her husband.

Viola knew where he'd be.

She found him in the supposedly haunted east wing, wandering the portrait gallery. Normally he would stop before his father's, but tonight he looked upon the Lonely Duke instead.

There was no portrait of the man's first duchess, but Hunt had undertaken a slightly macabre yet romantic project years earlier, bringing the woman out of the woods and laying her to rest at long last beside her love. Perhaps it was a mere gesture, but it had seemed right to do.

"Are any ghosts prowling tonight?" Viola smiled when he jolted in surprise.

"For a duchess, you walk around rather like a cat." He took her in his arms and kissed her, the kind of kiss that lasted and warmed every inch of her body.

Viola wanted to take him upstairs and warm all his body in return.

The snow fell in large, soft flakes outside the window, and she thought how nice and snug it was in their bed.

"And no," he whispered in her ear. "The castle is decidedly ghost-free."

"Isabelle will be disappointed. Though at least she and Felicity have outgrown ghosts somewhat."

"Yes. Felicity's moved on to fencing." He chuckled, catching her lips with his.

"Odd, isn't it? The girls are no longer as obsessed by the spirits haunting this castle as you are," she said.

"I wouldn't call myself obsessed. Only watchful."

"Of what?"

"Well. It's nice, I suppose, to be visited by the past. That is, the pleasant parts of it."

Viola knew what it was like to be haunted by the past herself; she knew that part only too well.

"That's why I think you're wasting your time, Your Grace." She kissed him, teased him as he gazed at her quizzically. "There are no ghosts in Moorcliff Castle."

"Come now. Every castle needs at least one good haunt."

"I think that ghosts are sad memories persisting," she said quietly, tracing her fingertips along the chiseled slope of his jaw. "There are no sad memories in Moorcliff any longer. At least, none that persist."

He smiled fully.

"No, you're quite right. You've driven away all the bad memories, my love," he murmured.

"Then I've only returned the favor." Viola kissed her husband and laughed breathlessly when he caught her up in his arms and carried her down the long, carpeted corridor toward the staircase.

"I'd prefer you repay me in another manner." His hungry gaze hinted at every exquisite, sensual thing he wished to do to her tonight.

"As long as you're prepared to reciprocate." She laughed as he set her on her feet at the top of the stairs.

"It seems we'll never be done paying the other back." He kissed her deeply. "I must always be in your debt."

"I'd have it no other way."

He carried her to their bedchamber, kicking the door shut behind him.

Viola sighed her pleasure as he lay her upon their bed, a fire crackling merrily in the hearth. She moaned when James kissed her, and she pulled him down to lie atop her. When she found herself in his arms at the end of a long day, every irritation evaporated.

"My duchess," he whispered, kissing her deeply. Viola groaned as he began to slide her gown up the length of her thigh.

"My husband," she murmured.

Then she gasped as something fell out of the very air itself and landed on the pillow. It was a broken chain of gold with a green stone dangling from it.

"Oh my goodness." Viola sat up and laughed. "The cabochon emerald! It looks as though Cornelius has finally returned it."

In response to the duchess's words, they heard the rustle of wings somewhere on top of the canopy. The raven croaked, obviously pleased with himself.

"I'm grateful," the duke muttered. "Though I'd appreciate it if he'd give us the room while we were intimate."

"As long as he's quiet," Viola said. She kissed her husband, relishing the contented noise that rumbled in his chest. "Where's the harm?"

"I suppose you're right." He pulled her back into his embrace.

"There was a young Marquess of Blunt
Who spent half his life in a punt
In the river one day
A mermaid came to play
So he stuck his pole right up her—"

"Darling?" Viola said. "Please evict the family raven."

"With pleasure, my love," James replied, and kissed her.

ACKNOWLEDGEMENTS

Thank you to the ever-wonderful Jen Bouvier for all your help in shaping my book and ushering it along its journey. Thank you, Rebecca Friedman, the greatest agent of all time. Thank you, Lydia Sharp and Liz Pelletier. Thank you to the amazing team at Entangled, Bree Archer, Jessica Turner, Curtis Svehlak, Elizabeth Turner Stokes, Heather Riccio, Riki Cleveland, Nola Carmouche, and Nancy Cantor. Thank you to Brandie Coonis for being something of the Isabelle to my Felicity, God help us all. Thank you to my family and friends, I'm blessed to have you all in my life.

She's found the perfect plan to avoid marriage...

A LADY'S RULES FOR RUIN

USA TODAY BESTSELLING AUTHOR
JENNIFER HAYMORE

Miss Frances Cherrington has long been criticized as independent and prickly. And she's fine with it. Truth be told, she'd *prefer* to be a spinster—damn her family's desires. But it's a conversation with the devilishly handsome yet highly infuriating Earl of Winthrop that inspires the perfect escape from her nuptial troubles. Frances could ensure that *no one* will marry her—by happily ruining her own reputation...

The Earl of Winthrop knows more about ruin than anyone suspects. He's just uncovered a secret that would tear his name—and everything he's worked for—to the ground. Certainly, marriage is out of the question...to say nothing of his growing attraction to the forthright and delectable Miss Cherrington.

Though all of London is abuzz with Frances's "disgrace," she's determined to use her freedom however she sees fit. Even if it means spending more time with a man who sets her body on fire. But when Frances's misdeeds catch up to her, the ruinous disaster she finds herself in blazes out of control, taking all of her options with it.

Overboard *meets* The Duchess—*with a twist—in this sweeping romance.*

AN

EARL

TO

Remember

USA TODAY BESTSELLING AUTHOR

STACY REID

Miss Georgianna Eleanor Heyford may be naught but a gentleman's daughter, but even she's heard the rumors about the Earl of Stannis's exceptional charm and good looks. Surely she can cater his luxurious yacht party without getting swept away. But a terrible misunderstanding leaves Georgianna fired, furious, and with little recompense. Which is precisely when her opportunity for vengeance washes ashore…

Daniel Rutherford, the Earl of Stannis, has absolutely no memory of who he is. They tell him he must have fallen overboard, and the only person he seems to recognize is the lovely Georgianna—who strikes a chord of familiarity…and the faintest memory of heating his blood. Only now this inelegant, poorly dressed woman claims to be his *wife*!

But the truth is, Georgianna is finally getting her revenge. The dashing earl will work off the money he owes her and no one will be the wiser. Except the longer he stays with her and her younger sisters, the more it feels like he belongs there. And that perhaps he'd find a forever place in Georgianna's heart…at least, until his memory returns…

*Don't miss the exciting new books
Entangled has to offer.*

Follow us!

 @EntangledPublishing

 @Entangled_Publishing

 @EntangledPub

 @EntangledPub

The Governess and the Duke is a funny, steamy Regency Romance with a happy ending. However, the story includes elements that might not be suitable for all readers. Parental abuse, depression, trauma, and hangovers are shown in the novel. Readers who may be sensitive to these elements, please take note.